AFTER THE
DOWNFALL

Other Books by Harry Turtledove

HARRY TURTLEDOVE

AFTER THE
DOWNFALL

NIGHT SHADE BOOKS
SAN FRANCISCO

First Edition

ISBN 978-1-59780-130-0

Night Shade Books
Please visit us on the web at
http://www.nightshadebooks.com

Dedication

In grateful remembrance of Dr. Jorge Petronius (1963-2005).

I

Berlin was falling, falling in ruin, falling in fire, falling in blood. Back when the war was new, Göring said you could call him Meyer if a single bomb ever fell on the capital of the *Reich*. Had anyone held the *Reichsmarschall* to his promise, he would have changed his name a million times by now.

Göring never said a word about shells or machine-gun bullets. Back in those triumphant days, who could have imagined Germany would go to war with Russia? *Not* needing to worry about Russia helped make the destruction of France as easy as it was.

And who could have imagined that, if Germany *did* go to war with Russia, she wouldn't knock down the Slavic *Untermenschen* in six weeks or so? Who could have imagined that those Red subhumans would fight their way back from the gates of Moscow, back across their own country, across Poland, across eastern Germany, and into Berlin? Who could have imagined the war was over except for the last orgy of killing, and all the *Führer*'s promised secret weapons hadn't done a thing to hold off Germany's inevitable and total defeat?

Captain Hasso Pemsel and what was left of his company crouched in the ruins of the Old Museum. The space between the Spree and the Kupfergraben was Berlin's museum district. These days, the finest antiquities were in G Tower, next to the Tiergarten. People said the massive reinforced-concrete antiaircraft tower could hold out for a year after the rest of Berlin was lost. Maybe soon they would get the chance to find out if they were right.

A Russian submachine gun burped bullets. Behind Hasso, something shattered with a crash. It might have come through two or three thousand years, but a curator had decided it wasn't worth taking to G Tower. Nobody would study it any more—that was for sure.

Where was the Ivan with the burp gun? Pemsel spotted motion behind a pile of rubble. He squeezed off a short burst with his Schmeisser, then ducked away to find fresh cover. A wild scream came from the direction of the heap of bricks and paving stones. It didn't lure him into looking. The Russians were past masters at making you pay if you fell for one of their games.

Like it matters, Hasso thought. *You're going to die here any which way. Sooner or later? What difference does it make?* But discipline held. So did a perverse pride.

1

He refused to do less than his best, even now—maybe especially now. If the Russians wanted his carcass, they'd have to pay the butcher's bill for it.

A few meters away, his top sergeant was rolling a cigarette with weeds that might have been tobacco and a strip of paper torn from *Der Panzerbär*. The *Armored Bear* was the last German newspaper going in Berlin; even the Nazi Party's *Völkischer Beobachter* had shut down.

Karl Edelsheim was good at making do. Like Hasso, he'd been in the *Wehrmacht* since before the war, and he was still here after almost four years on the Eastern Front. How much longer he or any of the German defenders would be here was a question Hasso declined to dwell on.

Instead, he said, "Got any more fixings? I'm out." If you paid attention to what was right in front of you, you could forget about the bigger stuff... till you couldn't any more.

"Sure, Captain." Edelsheim passed him the tobacco pouch and another strip of newspaper. Hasso rolled his own, then leaned close to the *Feldwebel* for a light. Edelsheim blew out smoke and said, "We're fucked, aren't we?" He might have been talking about the weather for all the excitement or worry he showed.

"Well, now that you mention it, yes." Hasso didn't wail and beat his breast, either. What was the point? What was the use? "Where are we going to go? You want to throw down your Mauser and surrender to the Ivans?"

"I'd sooner make 'em kill me clean," Edelsheim said at once. The Russians were not in a forgiving mood. After some of the things Hasso had seen and done in the east, he knew they had their reasons. Edelsheim had fought there longer. Chances were he knew more.

Another burst of submachine-gun fire made them both flatten out. They might have been ready to die, but neither one was eager. Hasso had seen a few *Waffen*-SS officers, realizing Germany could not prevail, go out against the Russians looking for death, almost like Japanese suicide pilots. He didn't feel that way. He wanted to live. He just thought his chances were lousy.

Most of the bullets thudded into the wall in back of him. One spanged off something instead. The sound made Hasso turn around.

The *Wehrmacht* captain saw... a stone. It was perhaps a meter across, of brownish-gray granite, and looked as if it were dumped there at random. But, like the other exhibits in the museum, it had a sign above it explaining what it was. *OMPHALOS*, it said, and then, in Greek letters, what was presumably the same thing: ΟΜΦΑΛΟΣ.

"What the devil's an omphalos?" he asked Edelsheim. A couple of Russians scrambled out to drag off a wounded man. He didn't fire. A minute's worth of truce wouldn't matter.

"Beats me," the sergeant answered. "Animal, vegetable, or mineral?"

"Mineral." Hasso jerked a thumb over his shoulder.

Edelsheim looked, then shrugged. "I'd say that honking big rock is. What the hell is it?"

"It's Greek to me," Hasso said. But he was curious enough to crawl over to read the smaller print under the heading. When the world was falling to pieces around you, why not indulge yourself in small ways if you could? He wouldn't get the chance for anything bigger—that seemed much too clear.

"Well?" the *Feldwebel* asked.

"'The Omphalos Stone, from Zeus' temple at Delphi, was reputed to be the navel of the world,'" Hasso read. "'It was the center and the beginning, according to the ancient Greeks, and also a joining place between this world and others. Brought to Berlin in 1893 by *Herr Doktor Professor* Maximilian Eugen von Heydekampf, it has rested here ever since. Professor von Heydekampf's unfortunate disappearance during an imperial reception here two years later has never been completely explained.'"

"Ha!" Edelsheim said. "What do you want to bet some pretty girl disappeared about the same time?"

"Wouldn't be surprised." But Hasso's eyes went back to the card. "'And also a joining place between this world and others.' I'll tell you, Karl, this world doesn't look so good right now."

"So plunk your ass down on the rock and see what happens," the sergeant advised. "How could you be worse off, no matter where you end up?"

The shooting picked up again. Someone not far away started screaming on a high, shrill note, like a saw biting into a nail. The shriek went on and on. That was no sham. That was a desperately hurt man, one who would die soon—but not soon enough to suit him.

"Good question," Hasso said. "Another world or this same old fucked-up place? Here goes nothing." The patched seat of his field-gray pants came down on the navelstone.

***

Sergeant Edelsheim turned his head to jeer at the captain while he was on the rock. The whole goddamn country was on the rocks now. That was pretty funny, when you—

"What the—?"

One instant, Captain Pemsel was there. The next, he was gone, as if by trick photography in the movies. He might never have been in the museum with Edelsheim.

"*Der Herr Gott im Himmel!*" Sudden mad hope surged through the sergeant. If there was a way out, any way out … What he'd told Pemsel was true for himself, too. Wherever he went, how could he be worse off?

He turned and, half upright, scrambled toward the Omphalos. Half upright turned out to be a little too high. A burst from a Soviet submachine gun slammed home between his shoulder blades. He went down with a groan, blood filling his mouth.

One hand reached for the navelstone: reached, scrabbled, and, just short of its goal, fell quiet forever. And none of the tough Russian troopers who overran the museum cared a kopek for an ugly lump of rock they could neither sell nor screw nor even have any fun breaking.

***

When the Omphalos seemed to stir beneath him, Hasso Pemsel wondered for a heartbeat if he was losing his mind. He hadn't really expected anything to happen. He hadn't really believed anything *could* happen. But what he believed didn't matter, not any more. He'd mounted the stone with hope in his heart. That was enough—far more than enough.

He hung suspended for a timeless moment. What did Hamlet say? *O God! I could be bounded in a nutshell and count myself a king of infinite space, were it not that I have bad dreams.* That came to Hasso only later. At the time—if *time* was the word for this flash of existence apart from everything—he knew only that, whatever else it was, it was no dream.

And then he was back in the world again—back in *a* world, anyhow—and he was falling. He dropped straight down, maybe a meter, maybe two: surely no more than that, or he would have hurt himself when he landed. Or maybe not. He came down in a bog that put him in mind of the Pripet Marshes on the Russo-Polish border.

Training told. As soon as he knew he was hitting water and mud, his hands went up to keep his weapon dry. A Schmeisser was a splendid piece when it was clean, but it couldn't take as much crud in the works as a Soviet PPSh or a British Sten.

He floundered toward the higher ground ahead. The setting sun—or was it rising?—flooded the unprepossessing landscape with blood-red light. And that was one more impossibility, because it had been the middle of the day in Berlin.

Hasso shrugged and squelched on. Maybe he'd got shot the moment he plopped his can down on the Omphalos. Maybe this was nothing but a mad hallucination before the lights went out for good. But he had to act as if it was real. He'd spent too many years fighting to quit now. He'd been wounded three times. He was damned if he'd throw in the sponge for no good reason.

"Maybe I'm damned anyway," he muttered. He shrugged again. If he was, he couldn't do anything about that, either.

He hauled himself up onto dry land. As he did, he realized it was artificial, not a natural feature of the swamp at all. It was a causeway, long and straight and not very wide, with a well-kept dirt road atop it. Somebody needed to go from Here to There in a hurry, and the swamp happened to lie athwart the shortest way.

Somebody *badly* needed to get from Here to There in a hurry. This causeway would have taken a devil of a lot of work to build.

He stooped to examine the road. The long shadows the sun cast (it was setting, definitely setting) showed no trace of tire tracks or tread marks from panzers or assault guns. They did show footprints and hoofprints, some shod, others not. And there were unmistakable lumps of horse dung.

Hand tools, then, almost certainly. Which meant…

Hasso Pemsel shrugged one more time. He had no idea what the hell it meant. It meant he wasn't in Kansas any more. He'd seen *The Wizard of Oz* when it got to Germany, just before the war started.

A flash of motion on the road, off to the east. Before Hasso consciously realized he needed to do it, he slid into cover, sprawling on the steeply sloping side of the causeway. All the time he'd spent fighting the Ivans had driven one lesson home, down at a level far below thought: unexpected motion spelled trouble, big trouble.

Ever so cautiously, Schmeisser at the ready, he raised his head for a better look. As he did, he wondered how many magazines for the machine pistol he had left. Four or five, he thought. And what would he do once he used them up? He grunted out a syllable's worth of mirthless laughter. He'd damn well do *without*, that was what.

Somebody was running up the road toward him. No, not somebody. Several somebodies, one in the lead, the rest between fifty and a hundred meters behind. The leader ran with an athlete's long, loping strides. The others pounded along, showing not much form but great determination. The dying sun flashed off sharpened metal in their hands. They were armed, then. The man in the lead didn't seem to be.

A few seconds later, as the leader drew closer, Hasso sucked in a short, sharp, startled breath. That was no man running for his life. It was a woman, running for hers! She was tall and blond and slim, and the rags she wore covered enough of her to keep her technically decent, but no more.

If she hadn't been very weary, weary unto death, she would have left her pursuers in the dust. Her build and her gait said she was used to running in a way they weren't and never would. But her sides heaved; sweat plastered her fair hair to her face. Plainly, she was at the end of her tether. How many kilometers had she run already, knowing it would be the end if she faltered even once?

Hasso's hackles rose when he got a good look at the men who thudded after her. They were short and squat and dark, with curly black hair and the shadows of stubble on their cheeks and chins. One of them carried a hatchet, one a pitchfork, and the third what Hasso at first took to be a sword but then realized was a stout kitchen carving knife.

The woman glided past him. Her head didn't turn his way; she must not have seen him dive for cover. Not surprising, not with the sun in her face the way it was. She didn't look back to see how close her enemies were. All her attention was on the way ahead. He admired that even more than he admired her elegantly chiseled features. She would go on as long as she could—so she proclaimed with every line of her body. But her harsh panting said she couldn't go on much longer.

Her pursuers were worn, too, but not so worn as she. They could still talk to one another as they ran. Their harsh, guttural language meant nothing to Hasso. He didn't think it was Russian … but then, he hadn't really believed these were the Pripet Marshes, either.

Deciding what to do and doing it were quick, easy, almost automatic. Just before the three shambling men came abreast of him, he rose up a little and gave the leader—the one with the pitchfork—a short burst in the chest. As the fellow crumpled, Hasso shot the man with the carving knife.

The swarthy man with the hatchet showed admirable presence of mind. He flung the weapon at Hasso just before one more burst from the Schmeisser caught him in the midsection. The *Wehrmacht* captain ducked. The hatchet spun past, less than half a meter above his head. It splashed into the swamp.

He scrambled to his feet, ready to finish off any of the three who still showed fight. But they were all dead or dying fast. He looked down the road in the direction from which they'd come. Were more like them trotting along in their wake? He didn't see anybody else, not for a couple of kilometers.

Slowly, he turned toward the woman. She'd stopped when she heard the gunfire. Now she was trying to catch her breath, her head down, her hands on her knees. After most of a minute, she straightened, looking at him with as much curiosity as he felt about her.

Curiosity wasn't the only thing he felt. She'd seemed striking as she ran past. Now he saw that striking was much too mild a word. She was improbably, outrageously, beautiful. If she was only a product of his wild imaginings in the split second before the pain of a mortal wound seized him, he had more imagination than he'd ever imagined.

She said something. Whatever tongue it was, he didn't understand a word of it. He didn't care. He could have listened to her forever, no matter what she said. Her voice was a honeyed caress.

But she stopped and waited expectantly. He realized he needed to answer. "I'm sorry—I don't understand," he said in German. A tiny frown creased the perfect skin between her eyebrows—she didn't follow him, either. He said the same thing in French, remembered from school, and then in bad Russian acquired at the front. She shook her head each time.

She slowly walked toward him. Little by little, he realized what a mess he was: filthy, unshaven, in a wet, muddy, shabby uniform. He would have apologized if only he knew how.

She pointed to the dead men, then to his machine pistol, and said something that had to be a question. *You killed them? With that?* What else could she be asking?

He nodded. "*Ja.* I did for 'em, all right." He stuck to German from then on. Why not? At least he'd be sure of what he was saying. He jabbed a thumb at his own chest and told her what his name was.

"Pemsel. Hasso Pemsel," she repeated thoughtfully. His name had never sounded so good as it did in her mouth. She laid an index finger between her small, upstanding breasts. "Velona," she said.

He touched the brim of his coal-scuttle helmet, echoing, "Velona." He couldn't make her name seem nearly so wonderful as she did his.

"Pemsel. Hasso Pemsel," she said again, and then something else that had his name in it. When he just stood there, she laughed at herself. She must have forgotten he couldn't follow what she was saying.

What she did next didn't need any words. She pulled off the torn and tattered shift—Hasso couldn't come up with a better name for it—she was wearing, spread it out in the middle of the road, and, naked, lay down on it. She beckoned to him to join her.

His jaw fell. He almost dropped the Schmeisser. What went through his mind was, *You're a hero, pal. Here's your reward. Beats the hell out of the Knight's Cross, doesn't it? Even with Swords and Oak Leaves.*

No, his imagination definitely didn't work this well. He'd saved a couple of German women from death or a fate worse than or both together. They didn't want to screw him afterwards to say thank-you. They wanted to go off somewhere and have hysterics. That seemed reasonable enough to him.

But Velona was plainly different all kinds of ways. She played by way different rules. When she spoke again, it was with a touch of impatience. *What are you waiting for, big boy? Come and get it.* In case he was a congenital idiot, she twitched her hips and opened her legs a little.

He looked up the road again. Nobody. He looked down the road. Also still nobody. The two of them were the only live people for quite a ways. It was lay her or jump in the swamp.

"If you're sure…" He stopped, feeling dumb. If she wasn't sure, she was auditioning for a stag film. She'd get the part, too.

Awkwardly, still wary, he got down beside her. She nodded, as if to say, *It's about time.* When he took off his clothes, he was careful to keep himself between her and them—and between her and the Schmeisser. But she wasn't interested in the uniform or the weapon, not then.

Her hands roamed him, soft and knowing at the same time. He stroked her, too. This all felt more surreal than a Max Ernst painting, but he didn't care. If it was a figment of his dying imagination, his brains were working overtime. He was less and less inclined to believe that, though. Everything was too vividly detailed, from the grittiness of the hard-packed dirt to the sweaty heat of Velona's flesh to the way her breath stirred the hair above his left ear.

He rapidly discovered that under her curves she had muscles to rival an Olympic athlete's. Well, the way she ran had already told him that much. He was broader through the shoulders, and probably outweighed her by twenty kilos, but he wasn't sure which of them was the stronger.

Then she kissed him, and he stopped caring. Had he run all that way, he thought his mouth would have been dry as dust. Hers was warm and moist and sweet. His hand slid between her legs. She was warm and moist there, too. She made a small sound of pleasure, down deep in her throat. Her hand closed on him. He made the same sound, only an octave deeper.

He was disappointed when she broke off the kiss, but only for a moment. Limber as an eel, she bent to take him in her mouth. He wasn't sure he'd ever had a woman do that before without being asked. He also wasn't sure how much he could stand without exploding.

The thought had hardly crossed his mind before she pushed him down and over onto his back and impaled herself on him. She rode him like a racehorse. She made that pleased noise again when his hands closed on her breasts. She teased his nipples, too. He hadn't thought they were especially sensitive, but they were, they were.

As his pleasure rose toward the crest that said he would have to come soon, he decided he would rather drive things himself. When he rolled the two of them over, Velona let out a startled yip and then laughed. So did he. He poised himself above her and thrust home again and again.

Her breath came faster than it had when she was running. Her face went slack with pleasure. She gasped. "Pemsel! Hasso Pemsel!" she cried in a high, shrill voice. Her nails scored his back. A wordless groan escaped him at the same time. He drove deep one last time, and tried to stay at the peak forever.

Whether he wanted it to or not, the world returned, the way it always does. Velona said something to him. He couldn't understand it, of course. But he understood when she mimed pushing him off her. He had to be squashing her, and that ragged shift wasn't much to protect her from the ground. He went back onto his knees.

She got to her feet and brushed as much of the dirt off her behind as she could before she put the shift back on. Hasso also stood, and did the same thing. His clothes were more complicated than hers; he took a little longer to dress. By the time he finished, she was walking back toward the men he'd killed.

She didn't let lovemaking distract her long. Her gesture could mean only one thing: *pitch them in the swamp*. Two of them wore rawhide boots. He pointed to those, and then to her feet. Did she want them if they fit?

Velona shook her head and looked revolted. "Grenye," she aid, pointing to the corpses. "Grenye." To her, the word must have explained everything.

It didn't explain one damn thing to Hasso, but he wasn't inclined to be critical. And Velona wasn't fussy about grabbing Grenye boots, whatever those were, only about wearing them. Into the water and muck went the bodies and the knife and pitchfork. The bodies would come back up soon enough; Hasso knew that all too well. If Velona also did, she didn't care. She nodded, as at a job well done.

"Where now?" Hasso asked her, as if she understood.

And maybe she did, for she linked arms with him and started west down the road—the same direction she'd been going before, but not the same killed pace. As the sun kissed the western horizon, Hasso slipped his arm around her waist. She smiled and swayed close and rested her head on his shoulder for a moment. He had no idea what he'd just volunteered for, but she made one hell of a recruiter.

***

Castle Svarag struck Hasso as … well, medieval. What else would a castle be? It had no running water, though there was a well. It was a long drop from the seat in the garderobe to where the stuff landed, but that was as close as the place came to sophisticated plumbing. Fires and torches and candles and oil lamps gave light after sundown. Food was either very fresh or else smoked or salted or dried; none of Velona's people knew anything about canning or refrigeration.

Had Hasso fallen into this world in 1938, he would have thought it too primitive to bear. Coming here in 1945, he'd done without running water and flush toilets and electricity and refrigeration for five and a half years of war. He missed them much less than he would have back in the days when he took them for granted.

And there were compensations he'd never had in Poland or France or North Africa or on the Eastern Front. Velona kept coming to his bed. She started teaching him the local language. And she vouched for him with the castle's commander, a dour noble—Hasso thought—named Mertois. Hasso wouldn't have wanted Mertois angry at him, as the commandant was close to a head taller than he was and proportionally broad through the shoulders.

Average men among the Lenelli—Velona's people—stood close to two meters tall, and some, like Mertois, were considerably bigger than that. They had yellow hair, blue or green or gray eyes, granite cheekbones, and chins like cliffs. Back in the *Reich*, Hasso had been a big man. Here, he was decidedly short. The Lenelli had never heard the name of Aryan, but they exemplified the ideal. To all of them but Velona, the first impression seemed to be that he barely measured up.

Then one—a bruiser called Sholseth, who was almost Mertois' size—picked a fight with him. Hasso got the idea it was as much to see what he would do as for any real reason except maybe boredom. Out of what passed for fair play with the Lenelli, Sholseth made sure Hasso understood they *were* fighting before he uncorked a haymaker that would have knocked Max Schmeling's head off.

It would have, had it landed. But it didn't. Unlike Max Schmeling, Hasso wasn't in the ring. He didn't have to box with Sholseth. *Wehrmacht* combat instructors taught all sorts of dirty but highly effective techniques. Action on the Russian front was a whole separate education.

Hasso grabbed Sholseth's arm just behind the wrist. Half a second later, Sholseth flew through the air with the greatest of ease. The big Lenello had time to begin a startled grunt, but it cut off abruptly when he slammed down on the rammed-earth floor of Castle Svarag's great hall.

Hasso had hoped that would put him out of action, but he started to get up. The *Wehrmacht* officer kicked him in the ribs—and had to skip back in a hurry, for a long arm snaked out and almost tripped him up. He didn't want to get locked in a grapple with Sholseth, not even a little bit.

The boot to the ribcage made the Lenello flatten out again. Hasso darted in and kicked him once more, this time in the side of the head, not *too* hard. Hard enough, though. Sholseth groaned and went limp.

A pitcher sat on a table a few meters away. Hasso walked past half a dozen staring Lenello warriors, picked it up, and poured two liters of not very good beer over Sholseth's head. The big man groaned and spluttered. His eyes opened. He made a horrible face and clutched at his temples. The *Wehrmacht* officer nodded to himself. Concussion, sure as hell. Sholseth wouldn't be worth the paper he was printed on for the next few days.

Another Lenello said something to Hasso. It was probably, *How the devil did you do that, you shrimp?* With an inward sigh, Hasso made a gesture inviting him to find out for himself. Beyond a shadow of a doubt, one of these big apes would cream him. But how many he smashed up first would go a long way toward showing where he fit in the pecking order.

He flattened four and had a fifth on the ropes before the fellow landed a blow to his solar plexus that folded him up like an accordion. He couldn't do a thing about it, either. The Lenello was groggy, but not too groggy to fall on him like a landslide and thump him while he couldn't fight back. Hasso got paid back for some of what he did to the soldier's friends. He'd known that would happen, too, which didn't make it any more enjoyable while it was going on.

When he could, he got up and washed the dirt and blood off his face. The Lenelli pounded his back, which hurt almost as much as getting beaten up had. They pressed mug after mug of that indifferent beer into his hand. He drank everything they gave him. Maybe it would numb him a little. Any which way, it was less likely to give him the runs than the local water.

Sholseth asked him something. The battered would-be tough guy was drinking beer, too. His head had to be killing him. Hasso didn't understand the question, but it was bound to be something like, *Where did you learn all that stuff?*

Another Lenello made cut-and-thrust motions and shook his head as he asked his own question. That had to be, *So how come you can't use a sword worth a damn?* Hasso shrugged. Nobody'd ever bothered teaching him a weapon like that. He had no trouble with a spear. If you could fight with a bayoneted rifle and an entrenching tool, spear drill was a piece of cake.

He could use a crossbow, too, once he figured out how to crank it up to reload. Its bolts flew flat and straight, like bullets. The Lenelli even had sights to aim along. A hunting bow, on the other hand … To call him hopeless gave him the benefit of the doubt.

Someone in the watchtower winded a horn. One long, flat note—the warriors relaxed. That meant more Lenelli on the road approaching Castle Svarag. A series of shorter blasts would have been trouble: the Grenye sneaking around again.

Hasso wasn't sure how things worked around here. He hadn't seen enough of this world yet. He hadn't seen any of it, in fact, except for the swamp and the stretch of road between where he'd rescued Velona and this castle. But the Lenelli seemed to have *Untermenschen* problems like the *Reich's* in Russia.

Here on the frontier—and this was the frontier, plainly—the big blond warriors controlled towns, castles, and, when they traveled in force, the roads between them. The countryside belonged to the local barbarians.

Shouts came from outside the castle. Who was who around here was pretty obvious. Even so, the newcomers and guards went through the rigmarole of sign and countersign. That made Hasso chuckle, which hurt his sore stomach and bruised ribs. He might be in another world, but a lot of army rituals stayed the same. What worked one place worked in another. People remained people.

Chains rattled and clanked as Grenye servants—or maybe they were slaves—

lowered the drawbridge. Horses' hooves thudded on the thick oak timbers—faced with iron on the outside, to ward against fire—as the new arrivals rode in.

As one man, the Lenelli in the great hall went out to see what was what. They were as eager for news and gossip as any garrison at an isolated post—and they didn't have radios.

Everybody turned out to see what was what, in fact: everybody who was tall and fair, anyhow. Mertois tramped out half a minute or so behind the warriors in the great hall. More soldiers came out of the stables. Velona and other women took places between and in front of the men.

Velona started to smile at Hasso, but the expression froze when she saw he'd been knocked around. He nodded, as if to tell her it was all right. *You should see the other bums*, he thought.

Half a dozen men had come in. Five were knights in slightly rusty chainmail. They were all stamped from the same mold as the soldiers in the garrison. The sixth was ... something else.

He rode a unicorn. Hasso blinked and rubbed his eyes. Unicorns were the stuff of myth and legend—except this one wasn't. Its horn was silvered. So were its hooves. They all shone even brighter in the sun than the unicorn's pure white coat and mane and tale. Its lines made the big, heavy horses around it look as if they were carved by a sculptor who was earnest, well-intentioned, and more than a bit of a blockhead.

The rider made the knights seem the same way. He wore polished jackboots that would have gladdened the heart of an SS man on parade, tight suede breeches, and a clinging shirt of shimmering bright green silk that should have looked effeminate but somehow didn't. Like the unicorn's horns and hooves, his conical helm was silvered, and flashed in the sunlight. Only his sword, a businesslike cross-hilted weapon in a battered leather sheath, said he wasn't a refugee from the set of a bad movie.

Graceful as a cat, he slid down from the unicorn. Hasso expected him to march up to Mertois and start giving orders; his harsh, handsome features were those of a man used to being obeyed, and at once. But the stranger strode over to Hasso himself. He didn't hold out both hands to clasp, as the Lenelli usually did in greeting. Instead, he sketched a star in the air between them. It glowed with gold fire for a moment before fading.

Hasso's eyes widened, even more than they had when he saw the unicorn. Unicorns were merely legendary. This was flat-out impossible—but it happened anyway.

"You saw?" the stranger demanded ... in Lenello. Yes, he spoke his own language, but Hasso understood as readily as if it were German. That was impossible, too, but as true as the glowing golden star, as true as the unicorn's switching tail.

"I saw, all right. How the devil did you do that?" Hasso Pemsel answered in German, and the man in boots and breeches and silk also understood him.

"Magic," the fellow said matter-of-factly. Hasso started to get angry before realizing the newcomer wasn't kidding. "I'm Aderno, third-rank wizard in King Bottero's service. You will be the outlander Velona spoke of when she summoned me."

"Velona... summoned you? Not Mertois?" Hasso wondered whether he'd figured out anything at all about what was going on here. He didn't even understand the chain of command.

"Yes, Velona, of course." Aderno took it for granted, whether Hasso did or not. "Now tell me—what color did the star seem to you?"

"Gold," Hasso answered automatically.

"*Gold?* Something, yes, but *gold?*" That was enough to shake Aderno out of his air of snooty superiority. He stared down his long, straight nose at the German. "Are you certain?"

"Why would I lie? And what difference does it make, anyhow?" At last, somebody who could understand Hasso when he said something—and the cocksure son of a bitch didn't want to believe him. Hasso wondered if he could do unto Aderno as he'd done unto Sholseth. Maybe he could knock sense into that long, arrogant head if he couldn't insert it any other way.

"You don't even know." That wasn't a question. Aderno turned away and spoke to Velona. When he did, his words were only gibberish to Hasso. His magic seemed as sensitive, and as adjustable, as a radio tuner. Hasso couldn't follow Velona's reply, either. He sighed and shrugged. She was the one he really wanted to be able to talk to, and he still couldn't. Life seemed to work that way. Aderno gave his attention back to him. "Tell me how you came here." That seemed clear enough.

Hasso did. He couldn't see any reason why he shouldn't. And talking about it—at last being able to talk about it—was a release, and a relief.

When he finished, Aderno sketched another sign in the air. This one glowed the color of the wizard's shirt. "The truth," he said, sounding faintly surprised.

"Why would I lie?" Hasso asked again.

For the first time, Aderno looked at him as if he'd said something stupid. "Outlander, man from another world, there are as many reasons as there are fish in the sea, as many reasons as there are leaves on the trees. You could have been part of some new wicked plot the Grenye have hatched—"

"No!" Velona broke in: one word of Lenello Hasso could follow.

"No," the wizard agreed. "But it could have been so, which is why I applied the truth test. Or you could have been one of our evildoers on the run, looking to cover your tracks with a tale too wild to be disbelieved. Or you could have been a disgraced man looking to start over somewhere far from where you were born, and using a strange story likewise. Not too hard to pretend not to understand or speak. But no. You are not pretending. And if you saw gold in the air..."

"You still haven't said what that means," Hasso reminded him.

"It means your life, and mine, and everyone else's, get more complicated than any of us might wish," Aderno said. Hasso wanted to hit him for talking in circles. Decking a genuine wizard, though, didn't strike him as smart. Aderno went on, "And it means you can't stay in this miserable backwater post." Mertois grunted at that. Aderno ignored him. "I shall take you to Drammen." Seeing Hasso look blank, he condescended to explain: "To the capital."

II

Once the Lenelli made up their minds, they didn't screw around. Inside of an hour, Hasso was on a horse riding west. He wore his own short boots, trousers, and helmet. Grumbling still, Mertois doled out a padded shirt, a mailshirt to go over it, and a thin surcoat to go over that. The castle commander also gave Hasso a sword. He said something as he did. *For decoration only*, Hasso guessed. *Don't try to use it, not if you want to go on breathing.*

He still had his Schmeisser. As long as his ammunition lasted, he was the toughest guy in town, even if only Velona knew it. Enough rounds for a few hours against the Russians—or a few minutes if things got hot. How long would it last here? Longer, anyhow, because none of these bastards had a weapon to match it.

Not only Aderno and his escort accompanied Hasso. At the wizard's urging—or, more likely, command—Mertois sent along half a dozen of his men. And Velona rode out of Castle Svarag, too, which pleased Hasso for all kinds of reasons. It wasn't just that they were lovers, though that sure didn't hurt. But she was his sheet anchor here. Everything that had happened to him since happened because she ran by right after he squelched up onto the causeway.

The machine pistol and the extra magazines fascinated Aderno. Hasso made sure he unloaded the Schmeisser before he let the wizard handle it. Otherwise, Aderno might have killed half the people near him just by clicking the safety off, squeezing the trigger, and spraying the weapon around.

The Schmeisser's cartridges interested Aderno even more than the piece itself did. He held them up close to his face to examine them—much closer than Hasso would have been comfortable eyeing them himself. He hefted first one, then another, then another. At last, reluctantly, he nodded and handed them back to Hasso.

"Your wizards understand the Two Laws well," he said.

"Which Two Laws?" Hasso asked. He would rather have told Velona what beautiful eyes she had, but he didn't know nearly enough Lenello for that. Talking to a wizard about sorcery wasn't the same thing—not even close.

He did succeed in surprising Aderno, anyhow. Aderno's eyes were almost as blue as Velona's, but Hasso wouldn't have called them beautiful. *Haughty* struck him as a much better word. "Do the wizards in your world guard their secrets so closely, then?" Aderno asked, sounding … jealous? "You don't even know what the Laws are?"

"You don't get it," Hasso said. "We haven't got any wizards. Till I sat down on the Omphalos, I didn't believe in magic. We've got scientists. We've got factories." He wondered how the translation spell would handle those two words.

"If that were so, I would call you as mindblind as the Grenye," Aderno said. "But you saw gold, so I know this cannot be true." He frowned, studying Hasso like an entomologist looking at a new species of flea through a magnifying glass. "Maybe the very laws of your world are different, forbidding magic or making it difficult."

"Maybe." Hasso shrugged. He neither knew nor cared—and he didn't want to go back and experiment. An Ivan with an evil temper would plug him if he did. He glanced over at Velona. No, he didn't have the words yet … but one of these days he would. In the meantime, he was stuck with the wizard. "Tell me about these Laws, then."

"You truly do not know of the Laws?" Aderno asked, and Hasso shook his head. They happened to be riding past a Grenye farm. The Lenello wizard waved towards it. "Without them, without being able to use them, we would live like that."

The farm put Hasso in mind of what he'd seen in Russia. If anything, it was even more backward, even more disorderly. The man of the family was chopping wood. Every few strokes, he would swig from a jug. Hasso wouldn't have wanted to get lit up while swinging an axe, but the peasant didn't seem to care. He paused to bow as the Lenelli went by, then attacked the wood with fresh ferocity.

His wife was weeding in the vegetable plot by the shabby, thatch-roofed farmhouse. Her butt stuck up in the air. Aderno mimed swatting it. Hasso chuckled. He and his men had played those games with peasant women. Some of the gals liked it. Others … Well, too bad for them.

A swarm of children, from almost grown to barely past toddling, worked around the farm. A boy with a beard just starting to sprout tended a handful of pigs in a stinking muddy wallow. He also bowed to his overlords. Hasso didn't like the look in his eye when he straightened.

A girl a year or two younger tossed grain to some chickens. She might have been pretty if you fattened her up and scrubbed off a lifetime's worth of dirt. Would anyone ever bother? Would it ever occur to anyone that he ought to bother? Hasso didn't think so.

"You think these are bad, you should see the wild ones," Aderno said. "These are partway civilized, or at least tamed. They know better than to yap at their betters, anyhow."

Hasso wasn't so sure of that. He cared for the way the peasant swung the axe no more than he liked the smoldering fury in the youth's eyes. They might be cowed, but they seemed a long way from tame. And … "Those bastards who were chasing Velona—they were wild?"

"Wild, yes," Aderno answered. "Without magic. Without hope of magic. Too stupid, too mindblind, to harness the Laws of Similarity and Contagion."

There. Hasso finally had names for the Two Laws. Names alone didn't help much, though. "What do they mean?" he asked.

Aderno clucked like a mother hen. He really couldn't believe Hasso didn't know. Plainly giving him the benefit of the doubt, the wizard said, "Well, you're still a stranger here." He might have been reminding himself. "The Law of Similarity says that an image is similar to its model, and if you do something to the image, the same thing will happen to the model. Actually connecting them in a magical way is more complicated, but that's the idea. Do you understand?"

"I think so," Hasso said. Gypsies and other frauds used the same notions in the world he knew, but they didn't really work there. Here... Well, who could say? What was he doing here if magic was nothing but a load of crap? "And the Law of, uh, Contagion?"

"An obvious truth: that things once in contact remain in contact—in a mystical sense, of course," Aderno replied.

"*Aber natürlich*," Hasso said dryly. And if that wasn't real, pure, one hundred percent bullshit ... then maybe it was something else.

"Little by little, we use our magic—and our strong right arms—to teach the Grenye that even dreaming of standing against us is far beyond their feeble abilities," Aderno said. "Sooner or later, they will learn."

"That would probably be good," Hasso said. All the same, he wished he had eyes in the back of his head, a wish he'd also had many times in Russia. The squat, dark men who'd been chasing Velona hadn't learned their lesson yet—he was sure of that. And, thanks to his Schmeisser, they never would now.

***

Later that afternoon, they stopped in a peasant village. It reminded Hasso too much of the hamlets he'd gone through in the Soviet Union. Oh, the details were different. And it wasn't just that modern things were missing: no phone poles, no electric wires, no radios, no tractors or beat-up cars. The huts, of wattle and daub or of stones chinked with mud, didn't look much like their Russian counterparts. And the Grenye looked more like gypsies or Jews than Slavic peasants.

But the air of rundown despair pervading the place could have come straight from the USSR. Much the biggest and finest building in the village was the tavern. Four or five men sprawled in drunken stupor near the entrance. A tipsy man staggered out singing something Hasso couldn't understand. It sounded like a dirge, though. Another man with a pinched, worried face scuttled in. If he wasn't on his way to drown his sorrows, Hasso had never seen anybody who was.

All the Grenye who could stay on their feet bowed to the Lenelli. Across the road from the tavern stood a smithy. The front was open to the air, the better to let smoke and heat escape. The smith wasn't very tall, but Hasso wouldn't have wanted to tangle with him—he was a mass of muscle. Heavy hammer in his right hand, leather apron and gauntlets warding him from sparks, he too bent double as his overlords rode past. What he thought while he did it ... was perhaps better not contemplated.

"What would happen if we went into the tavern?" Hasso asked Aderno.

"The tapman would serve us," the wizard answered. "If he thought we weren't looking, he might spit in the beer. If he *really* thought we weren't looking, he might piss in it. But he would serve us."

"Is there any way you could make the Grenye like you?" the German asked, recalling Russia again.

Now Aderno laughed in his face. "Certainly, outlander. We could fall over dead right here. We could come down with a plague that makes the flesh drip off our bones. We could burst into flames. An earthquake could make the ground open up and swallow every last one of us. The Grenye would like us fine ... after that."

"Why do they feel that way about you?" Hasso knew why the Russians felt that way about his own folk. The Germans in the USSR had earned such feelings, since they felt the same way about Slavs—and acted like it. And now Stalin's hordes were avenging themselves inside the *Reich*, something Hitler surely never imagined when he hurled the *Wehrmacht* and *Waffen*-SS at the Soviet Union in 1941.

"They're only Grenye," Aderno said. "Who cares why they feel the way they do? It doesn't matter, not even a counterfeit copper's worth."

Plainly, he thought Hasso was wasting his time with such questions. The *Wehrmacht* officer tried one more: "How long have you ruled them here?"

"A couple of hundred years—something like that," Aderno answered. "Velona would know better than I do. Long enough to teach them they can't beat us. That matters. Who's strong and who isn't: once you know that, you know everything you need to know. I dare you to tell me it's any different in your world."

"Well ... no," Hasso said. "The answers aren't always what you want, though."

"They have been for us," Aderno said. Remembering the grinding German retreat across Eastern Europe, remembering the doomed last stand in Berlin, Hasso envied the Lenello his certainty.

Instead of stopping in the Grenye village, the travelers rode on till they came to another Lenello garrison. Castle Kalmar was as close to identical to Castle Svarag as made no difference. Even the commandant might have been Mertois' first cousin. He was deferential to Aderno and even more so to Velona. Because they vouched for Hasso, the commandant also treated him with tolerable respect.

Velona got the best guestroom in Castle Kalmar. Aderno's, down the hall, was only half as big. Hasso wasn't sure whether the Lenelli here thought he was Velona's aide or her lover or her pet. For that matter, he wasn't sure what she thought herself.

Her lover he certainly was. He'd never even dreamt of a woman like her before, brazen as a man, strong as a man, pretty in a way that made every movie star and chorus girl he'd ever seen seem insipid beside her. If you could trap fire and high explosives inside a sweetly curved skin, that was Velona. And she gave herself to him—and took from him—without the slightest reservation.

Heart slowing in the afterglow, he asked her, "Why?" There was another Lenello word he'd picked up.

"Why what?" Velona asked, her candied mouth only a few centimeters from his.

"Why—this?" Hasso's wave encompassed everything from Castle Kalmar as a whole to her naked thigh still splayed over his. She smiled when his hand came to rest there. He smiled, too, but at the same time he marveled at the firm power of the muscles under his fingers.

"Why not?" she answered, which annoyed him more than it helped. Then she said something else, too fast and complicated for him to follow. He shrugged. She tried again, more slowly this time. He caught Aderno's name and a couple of other words. She was asking if he wanted the wizard to translate.

He shook his head, started to realize how very little he wanted that. "No, dammit. I need to talk to *you*," he said in German. He couldn't put that into her language yet. He pointed at her to get the idea across even without words she could understand.

She grabbed his hand and set it on her breast. It tightened automatically. Her nipple stiffened. Her breath sighed out. She kissed him. Things went on from there. They didn't talk, which didn't mean they didn't communicate. You could say an amazing number of things with touches and caresses and sighs. Maybe the things you said that way mattered more than the ones that needed words.

But Hasso was stubborn. After they gasped their way to a second completion, Velona turned her back on him and started to breathe deeply and regularly. She even fell asleep afterwards like a man. Hasso asked, "Why—this?" again

She swung toward him again. "Because it feels good. Because I like it. Because I like you," she said, using gestures to eke out the words. Then she said something else. He wasn't sure whether it was, "Are you happy?" or, "Are you satisfied?"

He was still too perplexed to be perfectly happy. He couldn't deny he was satisfied, though. He mimed limp, boneless exhaustion. Velona laughed and poked him in the ribs. Then she rolled back onto her other side. He got the unmistakable impression *she* wouldn't be happy if he bothered her again.

So he didn't. He listened to her fall asleep instead. It didn't take long. And it didn't take long for his own eyes to slide shut, either.

When he woke the next morning, his legs ached. He moved like an arthritic chimpanzee. His thighs weren't hardened to riding. Velona quickly figured out what was wrong with him, and he learned how to say *saddlesore* in Lenello.

Breakfast was smoked sausage, hard bread, cheese, onions, and sour beer. Hasso missed coffee or tea or even the nasty ersatz products Germany had used since the start of the war. He tried to explain what they were like to Aderno, and ran into a blank wall of incomprehension.

"We make hot infusions from leaves and roots to fight fevers or ease toothache or soothe a sour stomach," the wizard said. "Is that what you mean?"

"Well, no," Hasso answered with a mournful sigh. He would have missed his morning jolt of energy even more if he hadn't had to do without it as shortages squeezed the *Reich*. Beer was all right in its way, but it didn't pry his eyelids apart like a big, steaming cup of coffee.

"If you can conjure some out of the world from which you came, we might be able to use the Law of Similarity to make more for you," Aderno said.

"Fat chance," Hasso said. "I'm no wizard."

"You may not have the training, but the power lies within you." Aderno sketched the sign he'd used when he first came to Castle Svarag. Again, it glowed gold in the air between them. "You saw that?" Aderno asked. Hasso nodded. The wizard set a reassuring hand on his shoulder. "Yes, the power is there. That is what seeing—especially seeing gold—means. You are no mindblind savage like these." Aderno pointed to a couple of Grenye dumping garbage on the midden. He might have been talking about a yoke of oxen.

"It may be there, but I don't know how to use it. Even if I did, *could* I reach back into my old world, like that?" Hasso asked.

"I don't know," Aderno admitted. "If your world is so inimical to sorcery, maybe not. Maybe a wizard in the capital will have a better notion than I do." He shook his head. "He *may* have a better notion. There aren't many wizards, even among us. Whether any of them will know of your world and what it is like … well, who can say?"

The commandant at Castle Kalmar gave the travelers fresh horses to speed them on their way. Hasso took that as a mixed blessing; he'd started getting used to the animal he was riding. His new mount seemed more spirited, which was the last thing he wanted. Trucks and cars didn't vary so much.

He found out that Drammen, the name of the capital, meant something like *high and mighty* in the Lenello language. Aderno was ready to go on and on about the place, but Hasso didn't want to listen to him. He tried his few words of Lenello with Velona instead. He might not follow her, but he enjoyed trying.

She used gestures to show him Drammen was big, and opened and closed her hand many times to show him it was populous. "How many people?" he asked. When they stopped, he drew in the dirt with a stick to show her he understood the idea of written numbers. To show one was easy. Five and ten weren't hard, and fifty and a hundred just took patience.

Velona got excited when she saw what he was doing. She called Aderno over. The wizard was chewing on something; the peppery fumes he breathed into Hasso's face proved it was a chunk of sausage. "Well, well," he said, examining the numbers. "Those aren't what we use, but you'll follow ours, all right."

To the Lenelli, one was a horizontal slash. Ten looked like a plus sign. A hundred was a square with a horizontal line through the middle. If you put the symbol for three—three horizontal slashes piled on one another—to the left of the symbol for ten, it meant thirty. If you put it to the right of the symbol for ten, it meant thirteen. The Lenelli didn't use a zero. The system struck Hasso as better than Roman numerals, not as good as Arabic.

To show him how many people Drammen held, Aderno needed to teach him one more symbol: a square divided into quarters by vertical and horizontal lines. The wizard seemed impressed when he didn't boggle at the idea of a thousand.

Drammen, by what Aderno wrote, held somewhere between thirty and forty thousand people.

With a patronizing smile, Aderno asked, "And how many people in the town you come from, Hasso Pemsel?"

Hasso had to think about his answer. He took the stick from the wizard and wrote the symbol for four and the symbol for a thousand. Aderno's smile got wider. Then Hasso wrote the symbol for a thousand again, to the right of the first quartered square.

Velona blinked. Aderno stopped smiling. "No, that can't be right," he said impatiently. "You have written the numbers for four thousand thousand—we would say four million. But that is obviously impossible."

"Four million, *ja*," Hasso said. "That's about how many people there are in Berlin." *At least till the Russians get through with it,* he thought glumly. *God only knows how many they'll leave alive.*

"You can't expect me to believe you," Aderno said.

"You asked me. Now you don't like the answer," Hasso said.

"Only a madman would like it," the wizard insisted. "No one could keep four million people fed. The idea is ridiculous. Even if by some miracle you could, their filth would pile up in mountains. You must be lying."

Hasso swung the Schmeisser's muzzle toward him. "What did you say?" he asked softly. "You may want to think about what comes out of your mouth."

Aderno had the courage of his convictions. "Do not act as if your honor is threatened if I challenge a clear lie," he said. "It will only make you look more foolish when I use the truth spell."

"Ah, the truth spell. I forgot about that," Hasso said. "Yes, go ahead."

"You really are a crazy man, outlander. If you want to prove it to the world, if you want to prove it to the woman who has taken a fancy to you … well, we can do that." Aderno aimed a long, lean wizardly forefinger at him. "Tell me again how many people live in this town of yours."

"About four million," Hasso answered stolidly.

The wizard sketched a star in the air between them. It glowed green. Velona clapped her hands together and laughed out loud. Aderno look as if someone had stuck a knife in him. "But it can't be!" he protested—to whom, Hasso wasn't sure. Most likely to the ghost of his own assumptions.

"You can apologize now," Hasso said. *Or you can kiss my ass. I don't much care which.*

Aderno had the air of a man who'd put out his foot for a step that wasn't there and fallen five meters. "I think I would rather believe you can fool the truth spell than believe in a city with four thousand thousand people in it," he muttered.

"Believe whatever you please," Hasso said. "You asked me, so I told you. If you don't like it, it's no skin off my nose. You wanted to brag about how wonderful Drammen is, and you got a surprise. Shall we ride now?"

They rode. As they went along, Velona and Aderno got into a screaming row. Every so often, one of them would point Hasso's way, so he figured they were arguing about him. Velona went on laughing, so he guessed she believed him, whether the wizard did or not. Hasso heard the words *four million* more than once. Maybe it would have been better if Aderno hadn't asked him. Too late to worry about that, though.

Hasso wondered what the ordinary Lenello troopers thought. He couldn't tell. Those proud faces might have been carved from stone for all they showed. SS recruiting posters with men like that on them would have pulled in twice the volunteers—or maybe none at all, since so many would have despaired of measuring up to that standard.

Still, men were men, horses were horses, pigs were pigs ... and Aderno's unicorn was a goddamn unicorn, and his magic was, without a doubt, real, live magic. Hasso didn't know much about this world, but he knew it was different from his. And his was different from this one, and the people here seemed to have more trouble than he did working that out.

***

Drammen lay on the Drammion. Hasso judged the river more impressive than the Spree, which ran through Berlin, but less impressive than the Danube or the Rhine. Barges and sailboats came down the river to the city; sailboats fought their way up to it against the current. No motors anywhere, which didn't surprise him. He didn't miss the stink of exhaust.

And if he had, there were plenty of other stinks to savor. He'd grown intimately familiar with horse manure and unwashed humanity during the war. The wind wafted those odors from Drammen to his nose. And with them came the stench of what might have been every sour privy in the world. He'd seen at the castles that the Lenelli didn't have much of a notion of plumbing. Now, approaching a city—not a large city, by his standards, but a city even so—he got a real whiff of what that meant. No wonder Aderno hadn't wanted to imagine the filth from four million Berliners.

Catching Velona's eye, Hasso screwed up his face and held his nose. She laughed and nodded, but then shrugged and spread her hands as if to say, *What can you do?*

"Cities always stink," Aderno said.

Sure they do, if there's no running water and horses shit in the streets, Hasso thought. He didn't want to think about the flies in Drammen. As if to mock him, a big shiny one lit on the back of his hand. He swatted at it—and missed.

"Stink or no stink, though, have you ever seen finer works than the ones protecting Drammen?" Aderno had his share of hometown pride and then some.

Artillery could have knocked down the curtain walls around the city in hours. The castle on a hill near the center of town would have taken a little longer, but not much. Hasso thought of G Tower again. That reinforced concrete could hold up against damn near anything. It wasn't a fair comparison, though, and he knew as much.

"They're very strong," he said, and by the standards of this world that was bound to be true. The wizard looked pleased, even smug, so he hadn't sounded too sarcastic. Good.

A group of Grenye leading donkeys were ahead of them at the gate. The sad little beasts were piled high with sacks of this and that, so high that Hasso marveled that their legs didn't collapse under them. The Grenye, seeing Lenelli behind them, made haste to get out of the way. The Lenelli accepted that as their due.

The guard who swaggered out to question Aderno had *top sergeant* written all over him, from that rolling, big-bellied walk to the double chin and the silver hair frosting gold. Most officers treated a senior noncom with the respect his position and his years deserved. Aderno didn't. He spoke more brusquely than Hasso would have in his shoes.

Whatever the wizard said, though, had enough oomph to impress the veteran. The fellow came to attention, saluted with clenched fist over his heart, and waved Aderno's party through. When Hasso looked up as he rode through the arched gateway, he saw more Lenelli staring down at him through murder holes. In case of trouble, what would they pour on attackers? Boiling water? Boiling oil? Red-hot sand? Something anybody in his right mind would rather give than receive—he was sure of that.

The gateway had two stout, spike-toothed iron portcullises, one near the outer end, the other near the inner. Would even a panzer be enough to smash them down? Hasso wasn't sure. They didn't have to worry about panzers here, anyhow.

Inside the wall was a clear space to let troops maneuver. That would be prime real estate. If the king kept people from building there, he had real power. He also had real worries, or worries that seemed real enough to him. Otherwise, he wouldn't have bothered to keep that area open.

The houses closest to the wall put Hasso in mind of the sorry Grenye huts he'd seen on the way to Drammen. And, as he and his escorts rode through the narrow, stinking streets, he discovered that almost all of the people living in those huts were Grenye. When he saw one obvious Lenello sitting on a front stoop with a jug of wine beside him, he was so surprised that he pointed to the big blond drunken man.

Two troopers' eyes traveled to the sodden Lenello. As soon as they saw him and recognized him for what he was, they looked away, pretending that they didn't. After a moment, Hasso realized it went deeper than that. The men on horseback weren't pretending. They were denying. Were he able to ask them if they saw their compatriot, they would have said no. And they would have meant it, all the way down to the depths of their souls.

Hasso started to ask Aderno why that should be so. Something in the set of the troopers' jaws, something in the ever so slight narrowing of their eyes, told him that might not be a good idea, especially when he noticed that same existential disapproval clotting the wizard's features. Aderno must have noted the derelict Lenello, too.

How did the British in India react to one of their own who went native? How had Americans responded to a trader who stayed with the redskins and preferred a squaw to a white woman? A lot like this, unless Hasso missed his guess.

A dumpy Grenye woman came out of the hut and took the jug from the Lenello. She wasn't trying to keep him sober; she wanted a drink for herself. The blond man gave her a slack-jawed grin and patted her on the ass.

Comparing her to Velona and the other Lenello women Hasso had seen was almost like comparing a gorilla to human beings. That fellow could have had one of those, but he'd ended up with—that? *No wonder he drinks*, Hasso thought.

Shabby shops and taverns and eateries lay within the first ring of huts. Again, all the proprietors and most of the customers were Grenye. When they bargained, they gesticulated and shouted and jumped up and down and did everything but poke each other in the eye. They reminded Hasso of the Jews in the villages in the east that the *Wehrmacht* had overrun.

When the shouting got especially raucous, Aderno stuffed his fingers in his ears. The racket had to drive him nuts. Maybe it also damaged his sorcerous sensitivity. Hasso just found it annoying. Velona caught his eye. She pointed to the Schmeisser he wore slung across his back. Then she pointed to eight or ten Grenye, one after another, and made guttural noises in her throat to suggest many rounds going off. And then she laughed and brought a forefinger up to her red lips in a gesture he couldn't misunderstand. Mischief glinted in her eyes. Without a word, she was saying shooting Grenye was the only way to make them shut up.

A man with an unkempt beard and a mop of curly, dark brown hair came over to the Lenelli riding past. He held up a little jar—what was in it? salve? perfume? fish paste?—and went into a passionate, practiced sales pitch.

"No," one of the troopers with Hasso said. The Grenye followed, still yakking a blue streak. "No!" the Lenello said again, louder this time. The Grenye had to be used to rejection, because he went right on with his spiel, coming ever closer as he did.

"No!" the Lenello shouted. He lashed out with his right foot. With a kick a World Cup footballer might have envied, he booted the jar out of the Grenye's hand and sent it flying into a dungheap six or eight meters away.

The Grenye yelped in surprise and pain. All of Hasso's escorts, even Aderno, laughed at him. Plainly, he was used to that. But his own people laughed at him, too, maybe for pushing too hard, maybe for not getting out of the way fast enough. His head hung as he trudged over to retrieve the jar from its noisome new home. He brightened when he discovered it wasn't broken, and wiped it off on his tunic so he could try to sell it to some friendlier customer.

Inside the ring of shops, closer to the castle, dwelt the Lenelli. Had Hasso not already known, one glance at their homes would have told him who was on top here and who was on the bottom. Wide, well-kept lawns separated one Lenello home from another; the overlords weren't packed cheek by jowl the way their subjects were. Each Lenello home was at least six or eight times as big as a Grenye hut. The buildings were solidly made of stone or brick. They weren't built from wattle and daub and whatever scraps a Grenye could beg, borrow, or scrounge. They had roofs of red tile or gray or green slate, not tired thatch and bits of planking. The Grenye would have fallen in love with corrugated sheet iron if only they'd heard of it. Most of the Lenello homes could have doubled as fortresses. Even their stables and other outbuildings were far finer, far sturdier, than anything the Grenye lived in.

Velona saw Hasso eyeing the Lenelli's houses. "Aren't they good?" she said.

He understood that, and nodded. "Yes. Good," he said. There was a word you soon learned whenever you picked up a new language.

"Lenelli are good," Velona said. "Grenye…" Hasso had already seen she was a good mimic. Now he discovered she could do an uncanny impersonation of a grunting hog. It startled a laugh out of him. She pointed ahead. "And the king lives—there," she said.

The gesture was nicely timed. They'd just come round a corner. An avenue—or as close to an avenue as Drammen boasted—led straight to the royal palace. If the avenue was muddy and rutted and odorous … well, what streets in this world weren't? The palace was an impressive piece of architecture, no two ways about it.

A moat surrounded the gray stone outer walls. Soldiers on the walkway atop the outwalls surveyed the city between chest-high crenelations. Hasso had seen the towers of the keep even from outside the city walls. A red flag floated from the tallest of them. His lips quirked in a mirthless smile. He couldn't hold that banner against the Lenelli, even if he'd been fighting one very much like it for almost four years. Yeah, artillery could have breached the walls and knocked down the towers in jig time. But he wouldn't have wanted to try taking the place without it.

They rode down the avenue. It wasn't the same as parading under the Brandenburg Gate after France fell. It *really* wasn't the same as parading under the Brandenburg Gate would have been after Russia fell. Hasso feared only the Red Army was parading through Berlin these days. Was anything left of the Brandenburg Gate?

He shrugged. He'd never know. And a glance at his comrades said they all thought approaching the royal palace was a pretty big deal. Even Aderno looked like a second lieutenant about to get the Knight's Cross straight from the *Führer* himself.

What would happen to Hitler with Berlin falling? Hasso tried to imagine him in Russian captivity. The picture didn't want to form. The *Führer* would do anything, anything at all, before he let himself turn into Stalin's plaything. Why couldn't England and the USA see that, if Germany went down, the last dam against the spread of Bolshevism fell? It was as if they thought the *Reich* even worse, which struck him as insane.

He shrugged again. He would never know the answer there. As soon as his backside touched the Omphalos, he'd put his own world behind him forever. He didn't have many answers here, either, but he could hope he would one of these days.

Velona caught his eye and winked. She blew him a kiss. "You will see the king. He will like you." She made it sound simple and inevitable. She didn't seem so overawed as the wizard and the troopers.

If you can keep your head when all those about you are losing theirs ... chances are you don't understand the situation. Hasso knew too well that he didn't.

He found out how much he didn't understand in short order. Another man—another wizard?—rode a unicorn up to the guards at the outer end of the drawbridge just ahead of the group of which the *Wehrmacht* officer was a part. The guards talked with him for a moment, then stood aside and let him through.

Then Hasso's group approached. When the guards saw them, they stiffened to attention and saluted. Then they bowed themselves almost double, and then, straightening, they saluted again. They bawled out some sort of honorific or another—Hasso didn't understand it, but he heard the fervor with which they shouted it. SS troopers yelled, "*Heil* Hitler!" the same way.

The fuss wasn't for Hasso. Nobody at the castle knew him from the man in the moon. It wasn't for Aderno. Hasso *had* figured out the wizard's place in the scheme of things: he was hired help. He was high-class hired help, entitled to some respect, like a first-rate dentist back in the *Reich*. But nobody jumped through hoops for a dentist there, and nobody was likely to jump through hoops for Aderno here. The mounted soldiers? They were exactly what they looked like—muscle, nothing else.

No. The guards were having conniptions because Velona was back. She said something to them, then pointed toward Hasso. As soon as she did that, they saluted him, too.

Uneasily, he returned the salute. "Hello. Good day," he said, a couple of phrases in Lenello that couldn't land him in too much trouble.

"Good day," they chorused, and then something he didn't understand.

"What does that mean?" he asked Aderno. He wanted to learn Lenello on his own. If he had the wizard magically translating for him, he wouldn't. And he didn't like Aderno all that much, and he didn't think Aderno fancied him, either. Put all that together and he didn't want much to do with the wizard. Once in a while, though, he needed a shortcut.

"They said, 'Good day, savior of the priestess!'" Aderno told him.

"Priestess?" Hasso hadn't known she was one. He chuckled. No nun he'd ever heard of would have said thank-you the way she did.

"Priestess, yes." But Aderno didn't seem quite happy with the German equivalent Hasso offered for what he said. "You might also think of her as the goddess on earth."

Hasso glanced over at Velona. She smiled and fluttered her fingers at him. Priestess? Goddess on earth? *What the hell have I got into?* he wondered. But he liked what he'd got into just fine. Along with Velona and the escort, he rode across the drawbridge and into Castle Drammen.

III

After laying a goddess on earth, getting presented to a mere king was a piece of cake. King Bottero was a great big man, as so many Lenelli seemed to be. Hasso didn't feel much shorter after he went to his knees in front of the massive, blocky throne than he did before. The king's guards murmured when Bottero rose and set a hand on Hasso's shoulder; maybe he didn't do that for every Hans, Franz, and Dietrich who got an audience.

Bottero gestured. Hasso got to his feet. Even standing, the top of his head came up to about the bottom of the king's nose. In Germany, he'd got used to looking at the tops of other people's heads. Most of the Lenelli could do it to him. He didn't like that, especially since his sandy hair was beginning to thin up there.

When the king said something, Hasso had to shrug. "I'm sorry, your Majesty. Don't speak much Lenello yet," he said. Velona had taught him *your Majesty* just before he went into the throne room. What was he supposed to call her? Your Divinity? She was divine, all right, but not in the theological sense of the word.

Bottero looked annoyed—not at Hasso, but at himself. He said something else. Then he called Aderno's name. The wizard came up and went to his knees. Bottero spoke to him, impatiently. *Get up! Get up!* It had to mean something like that. As Aderno rose, he said, "His Majesty says you look like one of us, so he forgot you weren't."

If I'm a Lenello, I look like a damn runt, Hasso thought. They couldn't shoot you for thinking, not if you kept your big mouth shut. Not even the *Gestapo* or the NKVD did that. "Tell his Majesty I'm glad to be here." *I'm glad to be anywhere. I wasn't a good bet to still be breathing now.*

As usual, Hasso heard the Lenello words without understanding them when the wizard spoke to the king. He couldn't follow Bottero's reply, either. But when Aderno spoke to him, he heard Lenello in his ears and what might as well have been German in his mind. "His Majesty says he is glad to have you—all the Lenelli are glad to have you—since you saved the goddess on earth from the Grenye savages."

"I was glad to do it," Hasso said. He'd been glad to do it even before Velona offered him what maidens—not that she was—used to call their all. After that…

After that, he would have followed her to Siam, or maybe to the moon.

What would he have done if she were small and dark and plain—*Jewish-looking* went through his mind—and the men chasing her were perfect Aryans? Would he have opened up on them anyway? Or would he have waited to find out what the hell was going on? He had no idea.

King Bottero spoke again. "Not half so glad as we were to have it done," Aderno translated.

"Where do we go from here?" Hasso asked. He'd seen the *Führer* a couple of times, but never spoken to him. He would have been awed if he had. Talking to a king didn't awe him a bit. Talking to *this* king didn't, anyhow. If a Kaiser still ruled Germany, or even if he'd met George VI of England, that might have been different. But Bottero seemed no more than an ungodly tall man in odd fancy dress who wore a gold circlet with ball-topped knobs sticking up from it.

He did have an impressive bass rumble. Aderno's lighter voice turned his words into ones that made sense to Hasso: "You did us a service. I hope you will take service with us. I have heard you know fighting tricks we would all do well to learn, and I have also heard the power dwells in you."

Hasso started to say he didn't know anything about the power. At the last second, he clamped down on that. The less he gave away, the better off he was likely to stay. And so all that came out was, "I'll be happy to join you, your Majesty."

After the wizard turned that into Lenello, King Bottero's ice-blue eyes suddenly twinkled. A grin pulled up the outer corners of his mouth. He set a massive hand on Hasso's shoulder and said something in what could only be a man-to-man tone. Hasso figured out the likely translation even before Aderno gave it: "I'll bet you will. She's quite a woman, isn't she?"

"Yes, your Majesty." Hasso could say that in Lenello. He would have meant it no matter what language he used. Then he eyed the king's roguish expression in a different way. Was he imagining things, or did Bottero sound as if he knew exactly what he was talking about?

The *Wehrmacht* officer didn't see any polite way to ask the king. Maybe he would be able to find a polite way to ask Velona. Or maybe he didn't want to know.

Then Bottero spoke again, and Hasso found out whether he wanted to or not. "His Majesty makes himself remember you are a foreigner, and so you are not used to our ways," Aderno said. He waited for Hasso to nod, then went on, "He will borrow the goddess for the coming summer solstice, as he does each solstice and equinox. No doubt, he says, you have some such customs in your own land."

"No doubt," Hasso said tonelessly. He'd heard of pagan fertility rites, but he'd never dreamt they might matter to him. And what the hell was he supposed to say when the king told him, *Hey, I'm going to borrow your girlfriend for a night?* If he said, *No, you're not,* chances were he'd be shorter by a head. And if he said no to Velona, she was liable to laugh at him. If she was the goddess on earth, wasn't this part of her job requirement?

"You don't say much," King Bottero observed through Aderno. He might be the size of a draft horse, but he was no dummy.

"What am I supposed to say?" Hasso made himself shrug. "If it doesn't bother Velona, how can I squawk?"

Bottero laughed when he heard that. "I knew you were a sensible fellow," he said, and gave Hasso a slap on the back that almost knocked him sprawling. "When you get right down to it, the women do the deciding."

"Ja," Hasso agreed with a crooked smile. Pagan fertility rites or not, this world and the one he'd escaped weren't so very different. He turned to Aderno. "If I take service here, I know whose service I'm joining. Who's on the other side?"

"A wise question. You should always know your foes at least as well as your friends," the wizard said. The *Wehrmacht* officer grunted. Hitler should have thought about that before he got into a war against both the USA and the USSR. If the *Führer* had, Hasso wouldn't have been standing here right now. Aderno went on, "You would serve his Majesty against the other Lenello kingdoms, except the ones that are allies."

Hasso nodded. "That makes sense."

But Aderno wasn't done. "And you would serve him in ensuring that the Grenye in his kingdom know their place—know it and keep it."

"Fair enough." If you were going to rule people you'd conquered, they had to respect you. Hasso had seen that in Russia. Let them think they were as good as you were and there'd be hell to pay. The Germans had paid it, too.

"And"—now Aderno seemed like someone holding his nose against a bad smell that wouldn't go away—"there is Bucovin." When King Bottero heard the name, he made a horrible face, too.

"Bucovin?" Hasso echoed, as he was no doubt meant to do.

"The heart of the Grenye infection," Aderno said grimly. He pointed. "It lies to the east."

Bottero spoke. "His Majesty says the Grenye lie all the time, and from any direction."

"Heh," Hasso said. How close to the border was Castle Svarag? Had Velona been escaping from Bucovin? If she had, why didn't the people on her heels carry anything better than peasant weapons? All kinds of interesting questions. But a bigger one occurred to Hasso: "You have magic and the Grenye don't?"

"Certainly." Aderno drew himself up like an affronted cat. "We are Lenelli, after all, and they are only Grenye." When the wizard translated the question for the king, Bottero's big head bobbed up and down.

"Right," Hasso said. He hoped the sarcasm wouldn't make it through the translation spell. To try to blunt it if it did, he went on, "What I don't understand is, if you can work magic and they can't, why didn't you beat them a long time ago?" He thought of the conquistadors with their guns and horses and dogs and iron armor, and of the Indians who'd gone down in windrows before them.

Again, Aderno turned the question into Lenello for his king. "We're getting there," Bottero said. "Our ships only found this land two centuries ago. We've pushed the savages back a long way from the sea. But Bucovin ... Bucovin is difficult." He nodded again, seeming pleased he'd found the right word.

Hitler would have said that about the Russians in 1942. And he would have been right—much righter than he knew then, in fact. The *Reich* and the Russians were both behind Hasso forever now. *So I'm in the New World, am I?* he thought. Bottero didn't look a bit like Franklin Delano Roosevelt, and probably nothing like what's-his-name, Roosevelt's replacement, either.

None of that brainfuzz mattered a pfennig's worth to the Lenelli. "Difficult how?" Hasso asked, as any soldier might. Aderno didn't look happy about translating the question. King Bottero didn't look happy about answering it, either. He bit off some harsh-sounding words. "When we attacked the Grenye there, we had a couple of armies come to grief." Aderno echoed what the king said so Hasso could understand. "We don't know exactly why."

"Did they somehow learn magic on their own?" Hasso thought about Indians learning to ride horses and shoot guns.

But the wizard shook his head. After he translated the question, so did the king. This time, Aderno showed no hesitation in answering on his own: "It is not possible. They are Grenye, and mindblind. There are no wizards among them. There never have been. There never will be. There never can be."

Slavs are Untermenschen. *All we have to do is hit them a good lick and they'll fall over,* went through the German's mind. How much baggage he brought from the world he'd fled! Would he ever escape it? How could he? It made him what he was.

Something he'd seen in this world occurred to him. "When we rode into Drammen, do you remember that drunken Lenello with the Grenye girlfriend we saw?"

By Aderno's expression, he might have stuck pins under the wizard's fingernails. Very unwillingly, Aderno nodded. Even more unwillingly, he said, "I remember." The king barked a question. Most unwillingly of all, Aderno translated Hasso's question. What Bottero said after that should have scorched paint off the walls. When the king ran down, Aderno found a question of his own: "Why do you ask?" In contrast to his sovereign's words, his might have been carved off a glacier.

"I was wondering whether some Lenello renegade might have made magic for Bucovin if the Grenye couldn't do it on their own," Hasso said.

Again, King Bottero had to ask his wizard for a translation. When he got one, he did some more cursing, but then shook his head and answered the question. "There was no magic used against us," he said flatly. "None. We failed anyhow, failed twice, failed badly. Our own magic faltered there. Other Lenello kingdoms have failed, too. Bucovin is ... difficult. We have not sent an army there for a while. Maybe we will try again before too long—there has been talk of it. But we will be wary if we do."

"I see." Hasso wasn't sure he did. Plainly, though, the Lenelli didn't see what had gone wrong against the ... difficult Bucovin, either.

Bottero gave him a crooked grin. "Now that you know my realm's old shame, outlander, will you still take service with me against my enemies, whoever they may be?"

What would the king and the wizard do if he said no? They'd throw him out on his ear, that was what. And so would Velona, and he'd deserve it. What would happen to him them? Would *he* end up a drunken stumblebum in the Grenye part of town?

He hadn't crossed worlds for that. He gave Bottero his own salute, arm thrust out ahead of him. "Yes, your Majesty!"

The ritual that followed came straight from the Middle Ages. Following Aderno's instructions, Hasso dropped to both knees again and held out his hands clasped together. King Bottero enfolded them in his own big mitts. "I am your man," Hasso said, prompted by Aderno. "I pledge you my full faith against all men who may live and die, so help me God." A Lenello would have sworn by the goddess, he supposed. He wondered if Aderno would correct him, but the wizard let it go.

Bottero hauled him to his feet with effortless ease. The king wasn't just a big man; he was strong, too. He leaned forward and kissed Hasso on both cheeks. They were big, smacking kisses, the kind a Russian might have given—no French sophistication here.

"You are my man. I accept your homage. By the goddess, I will do nothing to make myself not deserve it," Bottero said through the wizard. "I welcome you to my service."

"Thank you, your Majesty." Hasso felt better because of the oath he'd sworn. Now he had a real place here. He belonged. He didn't know all of what that place entailed yet, but he could find out. He wasn't just somebody who'd fallen from nowhere. He was one of King Bottero's men. All the Lenelli would understand that. So would the Grenye.

A couple of small, dark servants came into the throne room. They started sweeping and dusting. None of the Lenelli paid any attention to them; they might have been part of the furniture. As they worked, they chattered in low voices in a croaking, guttural language that sounded nothing like Lenello.

"What are they saying?" Hasso asked Aderno.

The wizard shrugged. "I have no idea. It could only matter to another Grenye."

"Doesn't your translation spell work on their language?" Hasso couldn't imagine why it wouldn't. Why have a translation spell if you weren't going to use it to understand a tongue you didn't speak?

"It would," Aderno said with the air of a man making a great concession. "But why would I care to listen to Grenye grunting? I'd just as soon listen to what the king's hunting hounds had to say."

Hasso would have been interested to hear what dogs had to say, too. All the same ... "Bottero's hounds won't plot to murder you in your bed one fine night." He knew the risk of keeping Russian servants on the Eastern Front. Some Germans got by with it. A lot of Russians hated Stalin worse than Hitler. But Hasso had never been tempted. It would have been just his luck to draw somebody who was playacting.

King Bottero laughed when the wizard told him what the German's words meant. "These are also my dogs," the king said, waving toward the Grenye. "They will not bite."

He seemed very sure of himself, and of his servants. Hasso glanced at the Grenye again. They went about their work with their heads down, and seemed to pay little more heed to the Lenelli than their masters did to them. But a certain slight stiffness in the way they moved made Hasso sure they understood Lenello, even if the Lenelli didn't bother to understand them.

***

"Goddess on earth?" Hasso asked Velona, the Lenello words strange in his mouth.

They lay side by side on the bed of his small chamber in Castle Drammen. No matter what Velona was, he was only a new vassal of ambiguous rank. Chances were he got a chamber of his own only because she fancied him. Otherwise, he would have drawn a cot or a straw pallet in the common room with the belching, farting, snoring ordinary soldiers.

He wouldn't have minded. He'd done that often enough. But this was much, much better.

The bed was small, too, which meant he and Velona touched even when they lay side by side. The tip of her breast just brushed the skin of his arm. She smelled of clean sweat and cinnamon. If she was a goddess, she was a very human one.

She nodded, which made shadows swoop across the promontories of her face. The only light in the room came from a lamp that sputtered and added the odor of hot mutton fat to the air. "That's right," she said.

"What does it mean?" Hasso asked the question a dozen times a day.

Velona looked surprised when he asked now. "What it says, of course."

"What is that?" Things Hasso wanted to say bubbled up inside him: how in his world there were no goddesses on earth, or even gods; how God Himself seemed far away, if He was there at all; how the age of miracles, or the age when people believed in miracles, was long gone.

And yet a little miracle, or something a hell of a lot like one, had brought him here from burning Berlin. But even if the *Führer* was as close to a god on earth as people knew in these grimly rational days, it would have taken more than a little miracle to save the *Reich* from the clutches of the Russian bear, the American eagle, and the British lion.

Speaking German, all that would have burst free in a torrent of words. In Lenello, he was limited to questions that made him sound like a *Dummkopf*. Sooner or later, he would understand more. He'd been through enough to teach him patience the hard way.

"You really don't know." Velona sounded amazed.

"I really don't know." Hasso hoped he got the conjugation right.

She laughed—not at him, he didn't think. "The goddess lives in me," she said, touching the inside of her left breast to show what she meant. "Sometimes I am Velona, sometimes I am the goddess, sometimes I am the goddess and Velona at the same time." She spoke slowly and simply to give him a chance to understand.

"How to know —how I to know—which?" he asked.

He wondered if she would laugh again, but she didn't. "When I ran out of Bucovin, the goddess filled me. I could not have run like that if she hadn't. Those Grenye you saw chasing me, those weren't the first ones who came after me. I left the others in the dust."

"I understand," he said after a bit. Her explanation wasn't smooth. She backed and filled and used different words and gestured and sat up in bed and acted out what she meant. He never got tired of watching her. Goddess or Velona, she was the most *alive* person he'd ever met, and it wasn't even close.

"Good!" Her eyes flashed brighter than the feeble rays from that smelly mutton-fat lamp should have let them do. "But even the goddess fills only a woman. Those churls would have caught me if you hadn't—" She imitated the noise from the Schmeisser again. She kissed him. "Thank you."

"Happy. Glad." Hasso drew her to him. "Big glad!" She laughed. Then he asked, "Make love with goddess? Or make love with Velona?"

"Oh, that was me," she said, and pointed at herself to make sure he got it. "The goddess went out of me when I didn't need her any more. That was one reason I was so worn there for a little while." Again, she worked at what she was saying till she was sure he followed. She was a good teacher … and learning a language from a lover had incentives a tutor with a mustache and a tweed jacket couldn't hope to match.

If the goddess possessed her some of the time, what was it like when possession ended? In his own world, he would have taken her talk for metaphor. Here? He kept an open mind. He'd seen enough strange things to make him unsure where metaphor left off and magic began. And if magic worked, why couldn't there be a literal goddess?

No reason he could see, no reason at all.

"What about with King Bottero?" he asked. He hoped he didn't sound too jealous. He didn't feel *too* jealous, but he wasn't altogether easy about it.

"Oh, with him I am the goddess and me both," Velona answered matter-of-factly. "The seasons need renewing, and this is how we do it. And he is a man, and I am a woman, and that is how men and women do it. You ought to know." She poked him in the ribs.

"Well, yes," he said. She made it sound so reasonable. The only thing wrong was that what happened between men and women *wasn't* reasonable. No matter how people tried, they couldn't make it reasonable, either. They couldn't in the world he came from, anyhow. He didn't think the Lenelli and Grenye were much different.

Velona laughed. "In fact…" she said. Sure enough, he'd just bumped her belly. They started all over again. He hadn't thought a man his age could perform the way he did. But then, he hadn't had inspiration like this, either.

Afterwards, he wished for a cigarette. Even the ones the German quartermasters doled out, that tasted of hay and horseshit instead of honest tobacco, would have been better than nothing. But he'd had them in the back pocket of his trousers when he landed in the swamp here, and they got ruined. Too damn bad.

"Is it better now?" Velona might have been soothing a little boy. Her methods were different—were they ever!—but not her tone.

"Well, yes," Hasso said again. And it was, too, and it would stay that way till the summer solstice, or till he thought about the summer solstice, or till he ran into King Bottero, or for a little while, anyhow.

What could he do about it, any which way? Tell the goddess not to do what the goddess did? Velona would laugh in his face. He'd be lucky if Bottero only laughed. He could go from vassal to victim in the time the king took to snap his fingers.

And so… *And so what?* he wondered. If he couldn't stand the idea, the only thing he could do was break off with Velona. The king would still keep him around, as a soldier, as an unarmed-combat instructor, and maybe in the hope that he could teach the Lenelli to make firearms. They wouldn't turn out Schmeissers any time in the next few hundred years. If he could make black powder, though, they might manage cannons and matchlock muskets. And cannons ought to be plenty to win him a field marshal's baton, or whatever they used here instead of one.

So he could make his way here without Velona if he wanted to. He thought so, anyhow. But did he want to? If he did, he figured he needed to check his brain for working parts. If she had to do what a goddess had to do, he figured he could live through it.

"It'll be all right," he told himself.

"What?" Velona asked, and he realized he'd spoken not only out loud but in German.

"All good," he said in Lenello, and hoped he meant it.

***

The master-at-arms at Castle Drammen was a fellow named Orosei. He wasn't particularly big for a Lenello—only a couple of centimeters taller than Hasso—but he was in perfect shape. As they faced each other in the courtyard, stripped to the waist, the German could see as much. He wasn't bad himself, but Orosei had not a gram of fat and muscles like steel bands.

Soldiers watched the faceoff. Hasso was starting to understand bits of Lenello. They figured he was crazy—nobody in his right mind messed with Orosei. Eyeing his opponent, Hasso thought they had a point.

He'd done this at Castle Svarag, but Orosei looked like a much rougher customer than Sholseth or his buddies. This guy didn't just have muscle. He had technique, too. Hasso could see that at a glance.

"So you know tricks, do you?" Orosei said. His gaze went here, there, everywhere. He wouldn't give himself away by eyeing his target before he went after it.

Hasso shrugged. "Maybe a few."

"Well, let's get on with it," Orosei said. "Nothing personal, you understand." *I make my living squashing people. You're just another one.*

"Nothing personal," Hasso agreed. *If I can beat you, I look like a big deal. You're in the way—like Poland.*

They circled warily. Hasso took it on faith that Orosei was good. The master-at-arms didn't seem inclined to take chances on anybody. Once things started happening, fights could—often did—end in seconds. Someone would make a mistake or just move an instant slower than he should have, and that would be that.

"Did you come here to fight or to dance?" Orosei asked. In the middle of the question, without warning or even raising his voice, he sprang.

The next few seconds were one of those frantic flurries that happened when two pros went at each other without any rules. One of Orosei's boots thudded into Hasso's chest—not quite in his solar plexus and not quite hard enough to break ribs. The Lenello's thumb didn't quite take out Hasso's left eye, either—and Hasso didn't think he quite broke it when he bent it back. He got in some licks of his own, too.

They broke apart again. Orosei would sport a mouse under one eye, and he definitely had hurt that hand. He saluted Hasso Lenello-style, clenched fist over his heart. "You're good, all right," he said. "We can use you."

"You are good, too." Hasso didn't like plodding through a language he barely spoke, but he had no choice.

They circled some more. Hasso fired a kick at Orosei's knee. Orosei grabbed his foot and launched him, then jumped on him like a starving tiger. But Hasso had expected to get thrown, and greeted him with a boot in the belly. It was like kicking planks, but it got the master-at-arms off him.

Orosei bounced to his feet. He saluted again, saying, "You're *bloody* good. Show me those flips I've heard about."

"We go slow?" Hasso asked, and the master-at-arms nodded. Hasso knew a moment's relief that he'd proved himself without getting maimed and without wrecking the other guy, who was bound to have friends in high places. He said, "Come at me—not very fast."

Orosei did. He made a perfect practice partner. Hasso grabbed his outthrust arm, twisted, got him on his hip, and flipped him over his shoulder. Orosei thudded down on his back with a big grin on his face. He sprang up. "That's good, by the goddess! Do it again!"

Hasso sent him ass over teakettle a couple of more times at half speed, and then at something closer to full speed. Orosei was a glutton for getting things right. If he took some bruises doing it, he didn't care.

"Let me try," he said when he thought he had it.

"Half speed," Hasso said, and the master-at-arms nodded. Hasso approached. He extended his arm. Orosei twisted and flipped him smooth as could be. Hasso hadn't expected anything different—this guy *was* a pro.

He proved what a pro he was a moment later. After he'd tossed Hasso around three or four times, he said, "That is the move, and it's very fine. What is the counter?"

"Ah!" Now Hasso gave him a German-style salute. "Good question! Right question! I come half speed. You—" He mimed doing the flip. "You see."

Some of the soldiers drifted off when they found that Hasso and Orosei weren't going to ruin each other for their entertainment. Others crowded closer to watch Hasso show the master-at-arms how not to get thrown. A lot of them wanted to try the moves themselves, on one another and on the men who really knew how to do them.

"You're better than I am," Orosei said after a while. "I have to think about it, and you just do it."

"Practice," Hasso said with another shrug. How many times had he done those flips? On the other hand... "Me and sword? Bad." He made a face to show how bad.

"But you've got that fire-spitting pellet crossbow," Orosei said: a pretty good description of a Schmeisser from somebody who'd never heard of the Industrial Revolution. "Do all the soldiers where you come from carry those?" Orosei asked. When Hasso nodded, the master-at-arms winced. "You must kill each other before you get close enough for swords."

"Mostly." Hasso nodded again. Orosei wasn't just a hardnose with quick reflexes. He had brains. That figured. He was more or less a regimental sergeant major, so he'd better not be a dummy—especially right under the king's eye.

The Lenello tossed him a spearshaft with a bundle of rags at the end instead of a point. "You know what to do with this?"

"Some," Hasso answered.

"Let's see." Orosei took a practice pike, too, and did his best to stick Hasso like a pig. When Hasso showed he could handle himself, Orosei whacked him on the back. "Yeah, you're pretty decent. How come, when you don't know what to do with a blade?"

As best Hasso could, he explained about bayonets. Then he said, "Wait, please," and hurried back to his chamber. He returned with his entrenching tool. "Fight with this, too." He demonstrated some of the unkind things you could do with the metal blade.

Orosei watched with interest, then hefted the entrenching tool himself. "Nice little thing," he said with an appreciative nod. "You dig holes so the pellets don't dig holes in you?"

"Yes," Hasso said. Orosei got it, all right.

"And it's a fine close-in weapon, too," the master-at-arms said. "Handy to have both in the same package." He handed the entrenching tool back. Hasso was beaming as he took it. He and Orosei didn't have many words in common, but they spoke the same language anyway.

***

By the time the summer solstice rolled around, Hasso could read and even write a bit. His progress amazed the lame, white-haired Lenello who taught him. But old Dastel was used to teaching people who'd never met letters before. Hasso understood the idea that each sign stood for one sound just fine. So what if the Lenelli used thirty-four characters? So what if they wrote from right to left like Semitic *Untermenschen*? As soon as Hasso memorized which squiggle sounded like what, he could read as well as anybody—and better than most, because people here had a habit of muttering their words as they read them. His biggest problem was his limited vocabulary. Learning to read helped there, too. Words on a page didn't vanish into thin air the way spoken ones did.

Pages were parchment or something like that. Words were written by hand, with reed pens or goose quills. No Gutenberg here, not yet. *I could do that, too,* Hasso thought. *Or would the wizards get mad at me for unfair competition?*

As the longest day of the year drew close, anticipation built in Castle Drammen and in the city surrounding it. In the castle, Grenye servants lugged casks of wine and barrels of beer up from the cellars. The cellarmaster, an immensely fat Lenello, kept a stern eye on things to make sure the casks and barrels didn't get broached too soon.

More Grenye dug trenches in the courtyard and chopped wood to fill them and set up enormous spits to turn roasting carcasses above them. The swarthy little natives seemed as excited about the upcoming holiday as their overlords. Why not? They'd be able to get drunk and make pigs of themselves. They didn't get to do that very often.

As the solstice approached, Hasso got drunk several times. He tried giving Velona hints that he wasn't happy. She had to know why; she was nobody's fool. But she affected not to understand, no doubt thinking that better than a raging brawl. And she showed no sign whatever that she didn't intend to lay King Bottero.

Some of the Lenelli chased Grenye women more as the solstice neared. The big blond men seemed to do a bit of that all the time. The Grenye had a hard time saying no, and their menfolk took their lives in their hands if they presumed to challenge their superiors. The Lenelli had the power of law behind them, and the power of size, and the power of military training.

And a good many Grenye women didn't want to say no. Hasso had seen that before, in France and in Russia. Losers' women were often easy. Sometimes they saw the other side's victorious soldiers as, literally, meal tickets. You could do better for yourself in an occupier's bed than in one where you slept all alone. Occupiers also had a kind of glamour because they *were* victorious, in stark contrast to your own worthless odds and sods who couldn't defend the country against them.

Sometimes, also, people fell in love, and who'd been on which side to start with hardly seemed to matter. Those were the affairs that turned out best—and worst. They could lead to marriages, despite regulations. Or they could lead to disaster when a soldier got transferred or when somebody decided who was on which side counted after all.

Hasso wondered what would happen if Velona caught him with a little dark Grenye. Actually, he didn't wonder. She would scream. She would break things. She would throw things. She would throw him—out.

To him, her joining Bottero seemed as much a betrayal as that would have been. But she couldn't see it from his point of view. If he tried to tell a Catholic woman not to take communion, she'd spit in his eye. And Velona wasn't just a woman taking communion. She was a priestess giving communion, too. She was the deity for whom communion was given. No wonder she wouldn't listen to him. He could see that.

He hated it anyway.

Much good it did him. Horns and drums woke him at sunrise, welcoming the longest day of the year with a raucous racket. He hadn't got too smashed the night before. His head didn't hurt or anything. But he wasn't thrilled about rising with the birds—and he was, because he could hear them chirping somewhere not far enough away.

The alleged music woke Velona up, too. Seeing her smile at him from a few centimeters away went a long way toward reconciling him to being awake. "Big day today!" she said, the way anyone back home might have on a holiday morning.

"Yes." Hasso knew he sounded grumpy—hell, he sounded downright dismal—but he couldn't help it.

Velona laughed and poked him. "I do know what's bothering you," she said, and then she made damn sure it wouldn't bother him for a while. Afterwards, she kissed him and asked, "There—is it better now?"

"Yes." This time, he sounded happier about things. Velona kissed him again before she got out of bed. Even so, the real answer was *yes and no.*

He had that whole long day to brood about her going off to Bottero's bed-chamber.

But it turned out to be even worse. Grenye servants set up a bed in the middle of the courtyard. *They aren't going to—?* Hasso thought, scandalized.

But they were. As sunset neared, an enormous crowd gathered around the bed, eating and drinking and talking and waiting expectantly. Bottero came out of the castle and pushed his way through. He was naked as the day he was born, but much bigger. "Goddess!" he boomed, standing by the bed. "I summon you, goddess!"

Velona came out, too. The crowd cleared by itself for her. Her golden nakedness might well have been divine; it seemed to draw all the fading light to itself. "I come, your Majesty!" she answered. "I come!"

They lay down on the bed together, right there in front of everybody. They did, and then she did, loudly. Hasso got very drunk.

IV

Hasso woke the next morning with a colossal hangover and an inferiority complex the headache did nothing to dispel. He'd figured Bottero would be big—large men usually were large all over. But *that* big? The king had to have a horse lurking somewhere not too far down his family tree. No wonder Velona didn't want to miss their date.

She wasn't in bed with him. All things considered, that might have been just as well. He got out of bed, pulled the chamber pot out from under it, and took an enormous leak. Then he put on his clothes and went to the buttery for something to eat—and for something to drink, to dull the pounding between his ears.

He wasn't the only one badly the worse for wear that morning. Passed-out Lenelli and Grenye sprawled together in the courtyard. The overlords and their subjects didn't show that kind of camaraderie when they were conscious. Men who were up and about moved slowly and carefully, as if afraid their heads would fall off if they hurried. Hasso knew just how they felt—he felt that way himself.

A cook standing behind a bubbling pot of porridge was taking pulls at a mug of beer. Hasso pointed at the pot. "Give me some of that," he said. Then he pointed to the mug. "And give me some of that!"

"Barrel's over there. Help yourself." The cook gestured with the ladle before filling a cheap earthenware bowl and plopping a horn spoon into it. "Here you go. Say, you're the foreigner who sleeps with the goddess most of the time, aren't you?"

"That's right. What about it?" If this guy was going to tease him about sharing her with the king, Hasso aimed to clean his clock. He was feeling just rotten enough to welcome a fight.

But the cook only grinned at him. "You're a lucky dog, you are. His Majesty gets your sloppy seconds."

He'd been worrying about getting Bottero's. He hadn't even thought it worked the other way around, too. Not knowing what to say, he didn't say anything. He just went over to the beer barrel and dipped out a mug.

The hair of the dog that bit him took the edge off his headache. The porridge—he thought it was barley, but it might have been oats—had bits of greasy, salty sausage in it. It helped coat his stomach and put some ballast in there. He got up and went back for a refill. He started feeling human again, but still wished he had some aspirin. *Wish for the moon, too,* he thought.

He was almost done with the second bowl when King Bottero walked in. Along with everybody else sitting on the benches, Hasso jumped to his feet. He didn't hurl himself at the king's throat. Maybe the remains of a hangover had their uses after all.

Bottero waved the warriors back to their seats. "As you were, men. As you were." He seemed careful not to talk too loud. Maybe he was feeling it from the night before, too.

Feeling it or not, the first thing Bottero did was dip himself out a mug of beer and drain it. He filled it again before he went up to the cook for some porridge. Then he ambled over and sat down by Hasso.

"Your Majesty," Hasso said unwillingly.

"Morning," Bottero said. "Quite a night last night, eh? Do they have holidays like that in the land you come from?"

"Well … no." Try as he would, the German couldn't imagine the *Führer* playing the starring role in a fertility rite. Göring, on the other hand … Hasso swigged from his mug. The *Reichsmarschall* was too damn fat to do it as well as King Bottero had.

The king's eyes were tracked with red, but shrewd all the same. "Didn't think so," he said. "Velona tells me you aren't too happy about the rite. I didn't do it to spite you. I don't go around stealing my men's women. But the rite … We need the rite. Enjoying it is part of the rite."

"I understand, your Majesty." Hasso tried not to sound too stiff. The king was going out of his way to be decent. He could have just ordered this foreigner with the funny ideas knocked over the head. Hasso didn't think his skill at unarmed combat was keeping him breathing. Maybe the Schmeisser had something to do with it. More likely, Velona really was fond of him, and Bottero was stretching a point for her sake.

"Hope so," the king said. "I don't want that kind of trouble. I don't need it." He drained the mug again. "What I need is another beer. Can I get you one?"

Hasso started to tell him no thanks. Then he realized Bottero was honoring him by asking. You *didn't* turn your sovereign down, not if he needed to borrow your woman (who just happened to be his goddess) for a ritual, and not if he offered to dip you out a beer with his own big, meaty hand. "Thank you, your Majesty."

That was the right answer. King Bottero heaved his bulk up off the bench and went over to the beer barrel. Everybody watched him when he moved. Some men had that ability to draw eyes. Hitler had far more of it than Bottero, but the king was a long way from going without. And everybody watched him fill two mugs and bring them both back with him. He set one in front of Hasso and raised the other. "Piss in the river," he said.

"Piss in the river," Hasso echoed, and he also drank. Americans said, *Mud in your eye*. This was the same thing.

People buzzed in the background. Hasso couldn't make out much of what they were saying, but he didn't need to understand them. They'd be talking about how Bottero was going out of his way to show the weird foreigner favor, and about what that might mean. Courts were courts, whether they revolved around a general, a petty king, or a *Führer* with a continent at his feet (or, not much later, at his throat).

"Is it all right, then?" Bottero asked.

In his mind's eye, Hasso saw the king piercing Velona, saw her face slack with pleasure in the fading twilight. It didn't make him happy, but it didn't make him want to murder the king, either. And in another three months, Bottero would be doing it again.

Of course, in another three months Velona might have decided she was sick of the weird foreigner herself. In that case ... Hasso supposed he would get drunk anyway, watching the king lay her and thinking he used to do the same.

And a different question occurred to him: "What does the queen say?"

Bottero blinked. His queen was a Valkyrie with a wrestler's build. Her name was Pola, and she was the daughter of the king whose realm lay just north of Bottero's. They didn't get on badly, but they sure hadn't married for love. She couldn't hold a candle to Velona—not even close.

With a sour chuckle, Bottero said, "She knows we need the ritual. What can she do?"

"I understand, your Majesty," Hasso said. "I feel the same."

***

"Bucovin." King Bottero made a fist and slammed it down on the map spread out on the table in front of him. "By the goddess, we really are going to do something about Bucovin this time around. We've put up with the miserable place too long already."

Blond heads bobbed up and down, Hasso's among them. He'd got invited to the meeting not because of his own rank but because Velona wanted him there with her. Otherwise, he would have been as welcome as ... *as a no-account* Wehrmacht *captain in the* Führer's *bunker*, he thought. Yes, the comparison was apt enough.

Looking at a map like that, even a no-account *Wehrmacht* captain would have wanted to hang himself. How could you make war without decent maps? This one didn't have any kind of scale. It didn't have any kind of projection. As far as he could tell, the Lenelli had never heard of such things. This was just a rough sketch of the lands that centered on Drammen.

There was the marsh where Hasso had come into this world, pictured with a stippling of dots. There was the road on the causeway—at least, he presumed that was what the thin, straight red line meant. And there was Bucovin, to the east. The capital was a place called Falticeni; Hasso sounded it out a syllable at a time. Lenello used one character for a sound that needed four in German. Had Hasso been writing it, he would have spelled it *Faltitscheni.*

One of Bottero's marshals stabbed a forefinger at the place. He was a middle-aged fellow named Lugo. By local standards, he was short—about Hasso's height. But he was almost twice as wide through the shoulders. If you hit him and he decided to notice, he'd rip your spleen out.

"We'll burn it and sow salt so nothing grows there again," he rumbled, his voice half an octave lower than even the king's basso.

A Grenye servant came in, set a tray full of mugs of beer and wine and a plate of sausages baked in dough—a local delicacy—on the table, and then strolled out again. Hasso pointed to him as he went and asked, "Why he listen?"

"Who? Sfintu? What's wrong with Sfintu?" Bottero asked, genuine puzzlement in his voice.

Hasso wanted to bang his head against the wall. They'd never heard of security. They didn't even suspect they'd never heard of it. How to spell things out in words of one syllable, especially when words of one syllable were almost the only kind he knew?

"Sfintu is a Grenye." He stated the obvious. "Bucovin is Grenye. If Sfintu listens, if Sfintu talks to someone from Bucovin, they know what you do before you do it."

"A spy!" Velona got it. "He's saying Sfintu is a spy."

"Well, Sfintu bloody well isn't," Bottero declared. "He was born here. He's as loyal as the day is long. He likes Lenelli better than his own grubby kind."

Maybe that was true. Hasso wouldn't have bet anything he cared about losing on it—his neck, for instance. It wasn't what he wanted to argue about, though. Patiently, he said, "Even if Sfintu is loyal, he can talk to someone not loyal. Not even know someone he talk to is not loyal. But Bucovin learn things anyway."

Bottero and Velona and Lugo and the other big shots in the Kingdom of Drammen thought about that. Hasso could almost hear wheels turning and gears meshing. The Lenelli weren't stupid, even if they were naive. "You don't trust anyone, do you?" Bottero said.

"No," Hasso answered. "War too big—too, uh, important—for trust."

"Your kingdom must win a lot of wars," Lugo remarked.

That hurt too much to laugh, and Hasso didn't want to cry in front of the Lenelli. Germany had twice astonished the world with what her armies could do—and she would have been better off never to have fought at all. What would happen to her after this war was finally lost hardly bore thinking about.

Instead of thinking about it, Hasso said, "Keep secrets, better chance. Tell enemy, not better chance." He was pretty much stuck in the present indicative. Sooner or later, he would figure out other verb forms. He was starting to understand them when he heard them. Using them himself was a different story.

King Bottero plucked a hair from his beard. "You know some things we don't, plainly. How would you like to be in charge of keeping things quiet?"

How would you like to be security minister? Bottero didn't even have the words to say what he meant. *How would you like to be Heinrich Himmler?* Bottero didn't have the name, either, which probably wasn't the worst thing in the world.

"Can I do job?" Hasso asked. "Not know magic."

Several of the marshals sneered at that. "You'd be worrying about the Grenye," Lugo said. "They don't know any more about magic than pigs know about poetry."

The *Reich* had learned some bitter lessons about underestimating its enemies. Operation Barbarossa should have knocked the Soviet Union out of the war by the first winter. And it would have, too, if only the Russians had cooperated. They hadn't.

"Two things," he said in his slow, bad Lenello. "One thing is, if Grenye have no magic, why Lenelli not conquer Bucovin before this? Two thing is, Lenelli have Bucovin for enemy. King Bottero have—uh, has—also other Lenelli for enemy. I keep things quiet, I keep things quiet from Grenye and from other Lenelli. And Lenelli have magic for sure. Bucovin?" He turned to Velona. "What has Bucovin?"

She'd gone in there. She must have hoped magic would protect her. It hadn't done the job, or she wouldn't have been running for her life when Hasso splashed into the swamp. If whatever gave her away to the Grenye in Bucovin wasn't magic, what the devil was it?

"I don't know what they have there," she answered, her voice troubled. "Whatever it is, it doesn't show. The countryside looks like our countryside, with the Grenye on little farms. They keep ducks and partridges. They don't have many big animals—we brought those here when we landed. The ones they do have, they mostly stole."

"Talk about magic," Lugo said impatiently. "Uh, goddess." Even if he was impatient, he remembered to be polite. Had he watched Bottero screw her? Or had he been screwing a mere mortal himself right then?

"You can't talk about magic in Bucovin without talking about Bucovin," Velona said, and then, to Hasso, "You have to understand what a funny place it is. They have castles like ours along the roads—a lot like ours. They model theirs after the ones we build." Her mouth twisted. "Sometimes they have renegades helping them, too."

Hasso thought again of the drunken Lenello in the Grenye section of Drammen, the one his escorts hadn't wanted to see. He wondered if he ought to haul the fellow in and grill him. Then he wondered something else. "They have renegade wizards help them?"

Several men swore, including the king. So did Velona. Women here didn't have to speak modestly. He got the idea she would have sworn even if women were supposed to stay modest. It wasn't just that she was the goddess and could get away with it, either. It was her style.

"There *have* been renegade wizards," Bottero said heavily. "We make examples of them when we catch them. We don't want that kind of nonsense"—he used a barnyard word instead—"spreading. But they aren't the problem, not in Bucovin."

"No, they aren't," Velona agreed. "It's something else. I got into Suceava—"

"Where?" Hasso asked.

She showed him on the map. It was the nearest town east of the marsh. *I might have known,* he thought. "Their towns, now, their towns are truly strange. They're more like overgrown villages than proper cities. But they aren't like that, either. They're … different."

One of Bottero's officers nodded. Hasso thought his name was Nolio. "I've been into Bucovin pretending to be a trader," he said. *They do know something about spying, then,* Hasso thought. Nolio went on, "You just feel wrong going there. Out of place. Like even the walls and the floor are staring at you, let alone the people. And the people are worse. They don't respect you the way Grenye are supposed to. They think they're as good as you are, the dogs."

"They are free," Hasso said.

"Wild," Bottero corrected. All the Lenelli around the table, Velona included, nodded solemnly. That was how it looked to them. How it looked to the Grenye… they didn't care. *And if you've got any brains, you won't care, either—or you won't let on that you care.*

"What goes wrong when you visit Bucovin?" Hasso asked Velona. He'd tried to ask before, but he was getting better at the language now.

Not good enough, though. "What went wrong when I visited, you mean?" she asked. That *was* what he meant. He was starting to recognize past tenses when he read them and even when he heard them, but they wouldn't come out of his mouth with any reliability. But Velona sounded as sheepish as she ever did when she said, "What went wrong? Everything, near enough." She threw her hands wide, and almost knocked a mug of beer out of Nolio's hand.

"Why? How? You have magic. You are the goddess."

"It's like Nolio says. In Bucovin, everything watches you. The towns, the people, I don't know what, but *something* there seems to suck the life out of magic. It works, and then you get deeper in and it doesn't work so well, and then it just… stops. Almost makes you think Grenye have their own magic. But they don't—they can't," Velona said.

"That's so," King Bottero said. "When we fight there, it's us against them. Spells mostly fail—and the more we depend on them, the worse the time they pick to fail. One of us, mounted, in armor, is worth, four, five, six, eight of those stinking churls on foot. But they're starting to use more horsemen, and Bucovin's a big place, too." He pointed to the map again. "They have big armies, and they don't fight fair. They mostly won't give us standup battles. They skulk and they raid and they burn our wagons and—" He broke off, an angry flush rising all the way up to his scalp. "What's so cursed funny?"

"Sorry, your Majesty." Despite the apology, Hasso had to work to make himself quit laughing. It was either laugh or cry, which would have surprised the king even more. Bottero's complaints sounded much too familiar. How many German generals had said those exact same things about the Russians? One *Landser* was always worth a couple of Ivans, sometimes more than that. Throw enough

Ivans into the fight, though... Stalin put out a fire by smothering it in corpses. If you had enough corpses, it worked, too. Picking his words with care, Hasso said, "My people fight a war like that, too."

"Ah?" the king said. "With all your tricks and ploys, I bet you had better luck than we ever managed to find."

"Well," Hasso said, "no." He bit down hard on the inside of his lower lip. Tears bubbled very close to the surface. He turned back to Velona. "The goddess not help the, uh, the plain you?" He hoped she would follow what he meant.

And she did, for she answered, "Even her power seems less there. Not gone, but less. To use it to go on—I couldn't. They sniffed me out as being something that didn't belong there. Maybe as a danger. I'm not so sure of that. When they were going to seize me, though, when I had to flee, then she gave me what I needed." Her smile almost dazzled him. "Then she led me to you."

One of Bottero's officers swore softly. Hasso knew why. Any man who wasn't dead or a fairy would want that woman smiling at him that way and saying those things to him. And Hasso was convinced that even a fairy, seeing Velona, would reconsider. Seeing her smile that way, hearing her talk that way, to someone else had to burn like acid.

"So," the king said, "will you help us keep secrets? You want help with the wizardry, I'll give you Aderno."

The proud wizard would no doubt pitch a fit at working for a foreigner who'd literally fallen out of the sky. Hasso liked that idea. It wasn't what swayed him, though. The job needed doing, and he could likely do it better than any Lenello. "Yes, your Majesty," he said.

* * *

Aderno was as thrilled about working under Hasso as the *Wehrmacht* officer figured he would be. Thanks to his translation spell, the wizard didn't have to pull any punches, either. "If you weren't sleeping with the goddess, King Bottero never would have given you this post."

"I know," Hasso said calmly. That made the wizard's jaw drop. Still calmly, Hasso went on, "If I hadn't rescued the goddess, I wouldn't be sleeping with her. I didn't see you anywhere around when I did it, either. So why don't you just shut up?"

"I ought to turn you into a—" Aderno broke off most abruptly, as any man with a gram of sense would do when somebody aimed a Schmeisser at his belly button. Unlike people from Hasso's own world, he didn't know exactly what the weapon would do, but it had killed three Grenye, after all, so he was convinced it would do something dreadful. And he wasn't wrong, because it would.

"Don't mess with me," Hasso told him. "If you really can't stand this, go talk to the king. He gave you the job. Maybe he'll take you off it and assign me somebody civilized instead. But if you stay, you'll do what needs doing, and you'll do it the right way. What'll it be?"

Sometimes the Lenelli reminded Hasso of Germany's Balkan allies—a well-timed show of arrogance would put them in their place ... for a while. "I don't want to bother the king," Aderno said. "I'll do what you ask of me."

"Good." Hasso hid a smile. He hadn't even had to threaten to sic Velona on the wizard. "First thing I want to do is talk to that drunk who lives with the Grenye."

Aderno blinked. "Why?" he squawked, quite humanly surprised.

"Because chances are he knows more about them than any three so-called experts here at the castle," Hasso answered. "And he'll know things they'd never think to try and find out."

By the look on Aderno's face, he found that none too wonderful. But then he remembered his promise and nodded. "Whatever you want," he said with a shrug. "I'll send some soldiers to haul him out of his sty and drag him over here. He'll likely think we aim to throw him in the dungeon—but the scare will serve him right."

Hasso shook his head. "No. I don't want to scare him. I want to win him over. No hauling, no dragging. I'll go to him."

"Into the Grenye quarter?" The wizard looked revolted.

Hasso only nodded. "Why not?" he said, and meant it. The Lenelli had fleas and lice, too. The Grenye were grubbier, but it was a difference of degree, not of kind. Before the war, Hasso would have hated how grubby he was himself. But after what he'd been through in the *Wehrmacht*, it was just one of those things.

Not to Aderno. "They are *Grenye*," he said, as if that explained everything. Velona had been just as thrilled about wearing Grenye boots, Hasso remembered. He couldn't have disgusted an SS man more by suggesting a walk through a ghetto.

He shrugged now. "The more we learn, the better the chance we have when King Bottero moves against Bucovin." Would Aderno be able to come up with an argument against that? Hasso would have bet the wizard couldn't, and he would have won his bet.

They plunged into the Grenye quarter that very afternoon. They went on foot; Hasso wanted to be as inconspicuous as he could. That wasn't very easy. He was fairer than any Grenye, and at least fifteen centimeters taller than most of them. And Aderno, who was both fairer and taller still, walked on tiptoe all the way, as if afraid he would pollute himself if he planted his feet squarely.

Here in their own district, the Grenye were bolder and noisier than at Castle Drammen. There they got very quiet whenever any Lenelli came into sight. Part of that was deference; part, Hasso judged, was fear. Among their own kind, the short, swarthy natives chattered and chaffered, both in the Lenello tongue and in what sounded like two or three of their own languages.

Hasso stopped in front of a plump man who was selling wickerwork baskets. "Where can I find Scanno?" he asked—that was the drunken Lenello's name.

The Grenye had been crying his wares in the blond men's tongue. Hearing the question, though, he looked elaborately blank. "What do you say?" he asked.

Patiently, Hasso repeated himself. The basket-seller shrugged a fancy shrug. "I don't understand you." He added something in a language that wasn't Lenello and spread his hands as if in apology.

"He's lying," Aderno said from behind Hasso.

"Yes," Hasso agreed, because the phrase for *No kidding* didn't spring to mind.

"I can make him sweat." Aderno sounded as if he looked forward to it.

"No," Hasso said; Lenello could make him laconic. He turned back to the Grenye. "By the goddess, no harm to Scanno. Where can I find him?"

"By the goddess?" the man said, watching his eyes.

"By the goddess," Hasso said again. "Her name is Velona when she dwells in a woman. I know the woman."

"Ah," the Grenye said, suddenly able to understand him—or more willing to admit he did. "You're that one. I wasn't sure before." *What's that supposed to mean?* Hasso wondered. The basket-seller went on, "He mostly drinks at Negustor's tavern." He rattled off directions too fast for Hasso to follow.

Turning to the wizard, Hasso asked, "You have that?"

"I have it," Aderno said grimly, sounding as if he wished he could throw it away. "We go there, we're asking to get knocked over the head."

"Tell me—slow—how to go. I go by myself, then. You stay behind," Hasso said.

"I ought to," Aderno exclaimed. But Hasso shamed him into leading the way, as he'd thought he might. When they left the road to the east gate, everything got even smellier and dirtier and more crowded than it had before. The muddy streets were hardly wide enough to let Hasso stretch out his arms without hitting buildings to either side. He had to flatten himself against a wall when two Grenye led several heavily burdened donkeys up one alley.

"Excuse us, masters," the men said, doffing their lumpy brown wool caps. The things reminded Hasso of cowflops.

"We shouldn't get out of the way for Grenye," Aderno said.

"Not do that. Get out of the way for donkeys," Hasso said, which left his companion scratching his head.

Negustor's tavern stood next door to what seemed to be a pawnshop and across the street from what was undoubtedly a brothel. A bare-breasted Grenye woman in an upstairs window shouted an invitation to Hasso and Aderno, then mocked their manhood when they ignored her. Hasso thought it was a good thing the day was clear; had raindrops hit the wizard's skin, they probably would have burst into steam.

Inside the tavern, Hasso had to duck his head. The ceiling was plenty high for Grenye, but not for him or Aderno. It was dark and gloomy and smoky enough to make his eyes sting. Along with the smoke from the torches, the place smelled of stale beer and sour piss.

Hasso looked around. Grenye drank at the bar, and at several tables. They were looking at him, too, and not with anything approaching warmth. A new dog in the neighborhood would have got the same kind of once-over. He wondered whether somebody would be drunk and angry enough to pick a fight.

Meanwhile, there was Scanno. He wasn't a big Lenello, which meant he was about Hasso's size. But, even sitting down, he was noticeably bigger—to say nothing of noticeably blonder—than the Grenye at the table with him. And he was also noticeably drunker, swaying on his stool as he poured down what was obviously at least one too many large mugs of beer.

One of his small, dark drinking buddies left as soon as Hasso and Aderno came far enough into the tavern to give him a clear path to the door. Hasso wondered who wanted him, and for what, and how badly. But that was a question for another day. He went up to the Grenye behind the counter—Negustor himself?—set a small silver coin on the counter, and said, "Beer, please."

The tapman blinked. Had he ever heard *please* from a Lenello? Even from Scanno? Or from anyone at all? He made the coin disappear, then dipped up a mug, filling it quite full. "Here you go."

"Thanks." Hasso turned. "Want something, Aderno?"

To get out of here. Every line of Aderno shouted it. But the wizard just said, "Wine." He set down a coin, too. The tapman took it and gave him a smaller mug. Aderno tasted, made a sour face, and sighed.

Hasso dug out another coin. He pointed to Scanno. "One for him, too, please."

"He needs more beer like a drowning man needs a boulder," the tapman said, but he dipped out one more mug.

Hasso took it and carried it over to Scanno's table. "Here," he said, setting it down in front of the Lenello. "Join you?"

"Hang on." Scanno drained the mug he already had. Then he patted the stool to his left that that Grenye had hastily vacated. "Anybeery who buys me bod's a friend of mine." He frowned, knowing that wasn't right, but fixing it seemed too much trouble.

Aderno, disapproval sticking out of him like a porcupine's quills, perched gingerly on another stool. The Grenye next to whom he sat down upended his mug and also made a quick exit. The one on Hasso's left stayed where he was. Innocent? Curious? Dangerous? *I'll find out,* Hasso thought.

Scanno's eyes had as many red tracks as a railroad map of the *Reich*. God only knew when he'd last combed his beard. He stank of sweat, alcohol, and stale hops. "Well, friend, waddaya want?" he asked, slurring his words so Hasso could barely understand him. "You out slumming?"

"We want to talk to you," Hasso answered.

Scanno took a pull from the fresh mug of beer. "Piss in the river." He eyed Hasso, blinking blearily. No matter how bleary he was, his ears still worked. "You're no Lenello," he said. "I've heard plenty of Grenye who talk our lingo better'n you. Who are you? Where are you from?"

"My name is Hasso Pemsel." *And now you know as much as you did before.* "I am from a different world. Magic. I am in King Bottero's service now."

That might have been the funniest thing Scanno ever heard. He laughed till tears ran down his cheeks and into his matted beard. "You came from another world and you couldn't do any better'n joining up with Buttfart? The goddess must hate you bad, pal."

Aderno audibly ground his teeth. Hasso kicked him in the ankle under the table. He said, "The goddess does not hate me." There, at least, he could be positive. Then he asked, "What is better than to serve the king?"

"Anything short of an arrow in the ass," Scanno answered. That was plenty for the last Grenye at the table, who got out while the getting was good. Scanno went on, "I mean, look at me." He jabbed a thumb at his chest. "I serve myself, nobody else. I'm better off than your shadow here any day of the month, 'cause I'm free."

"Your so-called freedom is a recommendation for slavery," Aderno said icily.

"Hush," Hasso told him. The wizard looked not only affronted but alarmed. Was he wondering whether Hasso was about to join the forces of drunken lawlessness? It looked that way to the German.

He'd succeeded in surprising Scanno, too. "What's with you?" the renegade said. "You look like a Lenello, but you sure don't act like one."

"Is better to act like Grenye?" Hasso asked. That made Aderno perk up, deciding Hasso likely was on King Bottero's side after all.

And Scanno, drunk and hoping he'd found a friend, wasn't on his guard. "You're cursed well right it is," he said. "Would I be here if it wasn't?" He drained the mug Hasso had bought him. Hasso signaled to the tapman, who carried over another one. Scanno would have a head that pounded like a drop-forging plant when he came down from this bender, but that was his worry.

He seemed to think the fresh beer had got there of its own accord. "What do you have against your own folk?" Hasso asked him.

"Waddaya think?" Scanno said. Since Hasso had no idea, he kept quiet and waited. Scanno got to his feet and staggered over to a corner, his gait like a ship at full sail on a rough sea. After easing himself, he lurched back. For a wonder, he remembered where he'd been going before the interruption: "Ever watch a twelve-year-old steal a ripe pear from a kid half his size?"

"I know what you mean," Hasso said. And he did. The image held a lot of truth. Aderno looked as if he were about to burst. Hasso kicked him under the table again. Aderno's idea of gathering intelligence was tearing what you wanted to know out of whoever had it. Teasing it out seemed beyond his mental horizon.

"Well, that's what we're doing here," Scanno said. "By the goddess, it *is*! I couldn't stand it any more, so I said a plague on it—and here I am."

"What about Bucovin?" Hasso said. "Bucovin not so small. Not so..." He looked for a word, and was glad to find one without needing help from the wizard: "Not so easy."

"Bucovin had time to figure things out, see?" Scanno said. "The little Grenye kingdoms, the ones by the sea, they went down bam, bam, bam like nobody's business. They never knew what hit 'em. But Bucovin watched and started figuring stuff out."

"Like what?" Hasso asked. "Bucovin full of Grenye. No magic in Bucovin. How to fight against Lenello wizards?"

"Magic? Magic—" Scanno spat on the straw-strewn dirt floor. "*That* for magic! That's about what it's worth."

"Shall I sing you up a case of boils, wretch?" No, Aderno wouldn't keep his mouth shut even when he needed to. "Shall I show you what magic's worth?"

"You've got emerods on your tongue, Turdface," Scanno said. Hasso had spent enough time in Lenello barracks to have no trouble with the insult. Scanno aimed a shaky finger in Aderno's direction. "I knew what you were before you started bragging. I could smell it, I could. Do your worst. You're not such a big pile of shit as you think you are."

Holding Aderno back after that would have been impossible. Hasso didn't even try. The wizard snarled his spell—plainly one he knew well—rather than singing it. "Skin break, skin bubble, skin burn!" he cried, and aimed his finger the way Hasso would have aimed his Schmeisser: with purpose and with malice. "Transform! Transform! Transform!"

And nothing happened.

Aderno stared at Scanno, who was drunk and surly but not disfigured. He stared at his finger as Hasso would have stared at the submachine gun after a misfire. Hasso could hope to clear a jam. What did you do when magic misfired?

The first thing Aderno did was try the spell he'd used on Hasso when they met in the courtyard of Castle Svarag. He sketched a star in the air between himself and Scanno. Hasso saw him do it, but didn't see the star glow on its own, as it had when the wizard did it with him.

Aderno did some more staring, this time at his own index finger. He tried the spell with Hasso, who saw the same golden star he had before. After Aderno made sure he had, the wizard shook his head. "The magic seems to be in order. But—"

"It doesn't work," Hasso finished for him.

"It doesn't work," Aderno agreed. "And I don't know why not. This miserable sot has no magic, used no magic. And yet my spell would not bite. And I don't know why." A German engineer couldn't have sounded any more upset if he'd watched a book fall up instead of down.

"Told you so, know-it-all," Scanno jeered.

Lenello magic, from what Hasso had heard, grew weak and erratic in Bucovin. Scanno was right here, but Aderno's magic didn't want to work against him, either. What did that mean? Hasso had no idea. Plainly, neither did Aderno.

V

Aderno wanted to take Scanno back to Castle Drammen to experiment on him. The wizard didn't put it in quite those words, but that was what it boiled down to. Scanno, not surprisingly, didn't want to go. "You aren't going to play games with me," he said.

"It's for the good of the Lenelli," Aderno said.

Scanno blew beer fumes in his face as he laughed. "Like I care!"

"Come on," Aderno said to Hasso. "We can get him there."

Hasso didn't feel like fighting a drunk who was unlikely even to notice if he got hurt. He also didn't want to wreck whatever chance they had of getting voluntary cooperation from Scanno. "Forget it," he said—in Lenello, so Scanno could follow. "We come back a different time."

"I wouldn't come back here for half the gold in the treasury!" the wizard exclaimed.

"Fine," Hasso said. "*I* come back a different time."

"You're a peculiar one," Scanno said. "You belong with me, not with this tight-arsed twit."

"No." Hasso let it go there. He didn't want to tell the renegade that he'd killed Grenye. He didn't want to tell him he was sleeping with the goddess on earth, either. If Scanno asked around, he could hear it for himself. Hasso got to his feet. "Come on. We go."

The tapman gave him a polite nod as he left. He nodded back, which seemed to surprise the Grenye again.

Out on the street, Aderno lost his temper. "What do you think you're doing, taking that lout's side? Are you crazy? Are you a traitor, too?"

"Shut up," Hasso said in Lenello, an officer's snap in his voice. He went on in German, knowing the wizard would understand and the Grenye all around wouldn't: "Let him think I'm on his side, or I might be. Let him think that, and who knows how much we may learn from him? Get rough now, and we end up with nothing."

Aderno gaped. "Maybe you're playing your own game. Maybe you think all of us are children."

"You act like it sometimes." Hasso said that in Lenello. Aderno flushed, for he used the second-person singular, not plural.

A Grenye with a pheasant feather stuck in his cap said something about his nice, clean sister and pointed to the brothel across the street. Hasso shook his head. The Grenye didn't want to take no for an answer. He reached out to tug at Hasso's arm. Aderno said something too fast for the *Wehrmacht* officer to follow. The Grenye got it, though. He disappeared in a hurry.

"If our magic fails against the Grenye, how are we supposed to conquer Bucovin?" Aderno said.

"Maybe you do it one bite at a time," Hasso answered. "Maybe you go on to Falticeni and take it away from their king."

"Their chief, you mean," the Lenello said scornfully.

"Whatever he is." It didn't matter to Hasso. "Or maybe you decide it's too much trouble and you leave them alone. We had a big neighbor who we thought would be a pushover, too. That's why I was fighting in what was left of my own capital." If the *Führer* had gone after England instead of trying to knock out Russia … Well, things could hardly have turned out worse.

"This whole land is ours. It is our destiny. If the savages don't bend the knee to us, we'll push them aside like the dirt they are." Aderno didn't care who was listening to him.

Sometimes disasters followed talk like that. Hasso had seen as much at first hand. But sometimes they didn't. The Americans hadn't worried about Indian raids for a lifetime. The aborigines in Australia had even less left to them than the redskins in the New World. Europeans ruled India and Africa. Conquest *could* work.

"Come on," Hasso said. "Let's get back to the castle."

* * *

Aderno went off to commune with a fellow wizard and try to figure out why his magic failed. Hasso thought about telling King Bottero what he'd done, but decided not to. This kingdom was tiny by the standards of the *Reich*, but not so tiny that the man at the top would want to hear every little detail. Chances were he'd listen politely—once. Hasso didn't care to burn up his credit like that.

He asked one of the guards where Velona was. The fellow shrugged, which made his mailshirt clink ever so slightly. "Don't know," he answered. Maybe he really didn't. Or maybe he didn't care for a jumped-up foreigner. His tone wasn't rude enough to be insubordinate.

Hasso asked the same thing of a Grenye maidservant carrying a heroic amount of laundry wrapped in a sheet. "She is in the chapel, my lord," the woman answered. Her Lenello was fluent, but flavored with an accent that said she'd be more at home in one of the swarthy natives' languages.

"Thank you very much," Hasso said. The maidservant looked as startled as the tapman at Negustor's had. Lenelli didn't waste much politeness on their social and political inferiors.

The chapel wasn't so fancy as its name suggested. Hasso heard it with Christian ears, which gave him expectations the Lenelli didn't have. The room was small and simple and spare. It had an altar with a low relief of the goddess carved into soft golden limestone. The lithe silhouette might have been taken from Velona's—except that the altar had crossed with early Lenello settlers.

But for the altar and a few stools, the chapel was bare. Maybe Christianity needed more in the way of display because, in Hasso's world, miracles were hard to come by. Here, with magic working and the goddess taking possession of her mortal acolyte, the impossible was as real as a punch in the nose.

Velona had prostrated herself before the altar. She didn't notice Hasso come in. Was that a faint radiance hovering around her? He wouldn't have sworn it wasn't, not after the way she seemed to glow as she strode naked toward Bottero on the night of the solstice. Hasso grimaced, not wanting to remember the rest of that night.

He wondered if he ought to cough, or if it would break some kind of spell. Erring on the side of caution, he stood and waited. After a couple of minutes, Velona stood up and turned toward him. When she did, her eyes flashed fire like a wild animal's. Human eyes didn't do that ... except hers did. Hasso had no doubt of what he saw.

"Who disturbs the goddess?" The voice wasn't quite hers. It was deeper, more reverberant, as if it came from deep inside her—or maybe from far beyond her. Either way, the hair at the back of Hasso's neck wanted to stand on end. "Who dares?"

"I is sorry," he said, startled out of his grammar. He didn't care to admit, even to himself, that he was scared out of it.

She recognized his voice. He could tell the moment she did: it was the moment her aura died away. Suddenly she was just a woman, just his woman, again. "Oh. Hasso," she said, and her voice was the one he knew. "You ... surprised me."

"Sorry," he said again, now certain to whom—and to what—he was apologizing. "Not mean to bother."

"It's all right. You didn't know any better. I was almost done communing anyhow." She made him feel like a kid who'd interrupted something very important that he wasn't big enough to understand. The more she pretended it was all right, the more certain he got that it wasn't. She tried to be brisk: "Well, you must have had a reason to come looking for me. What was it?"

In his halting Lenello, he told her about the curse Aderno had tried to drop on Scanno, how he'd failed, and how, despite failing, he'd seen that no magic protected the renegade. "I think you need to know this," he finished.

"Well, you're right," she said. "I do. Thank you. The goddess needs to know it, too." She kissed him. For a split second, the tingle that shot through him seemed even more than the high voltage Velona put into whatever she did. Imagination? In the world he came from, he would have thought so. Here? He had no way to know.

"What do you do about it?" he asked. "What does goddess do?"

She set a forefinger between her breasts. "*I* will take the word to the king. It marches too well with what happened to me when I went into Bucovin. One by one, my disguises and wards failed, but not for any reason I could find."

"The wizard tell—tells—he, too," Hasso said.

"No doubt. But Bottero will take it more seriously from me, because I am who I am and what I am," Velona said. "As for the goddess…" Hasso could see the deity come forth in her. Her eyes brightened and focused somewhere not of this world. Her hair spread and thickened till it reminded him of a lion's mane. She seemed altogether larger; though he still looked down at her, he felt as if she were peering down at him from a considerable height. She went on, "The goddess will deal with it in her own way." Then divinity disappeared, and she was Velona again.

What is the goddess' way? Hasso wondered. He didn't ask, though. He didn't have the nerve.

Her gaze sharpened in a merely human way. "If Aderno's spell won't bite on this wretch of a Scanno, what does that say? That he's in Bucovin's service, most likely. That he's a spy, a viper. You should have brought him here. Pins and pincers would tear the truth out of him even if magic failed."

If the Grenye in Bucovin couldn't find a better spy than a man busy drinking himself to death, they were in more trouble than they knew what to do with. But that thought led Hasso to another: "Can—how you say?—test Grenye? If magic works, ordinary, safe people. If magic does not work, maybe they have to do with Bucovin. Yes? No? Maybe?"

Velona thought about that. Her eyes glowed in an entirely human fashion. The way she showed she liked an idea was more drastic than he'd known from any other woman, to say nothing of more enjoyable. Was it sacrilege on a stool in the chapel? Not, he supposed, if your panting partner was a part-time goddess.

"What if someone comes in?" he asked afterwards, but only afterwards—he didn't worry about that, or anything else, while she straddled him.

She only laughed. "You ask the strangest questions. No one would come near the chapel while I was in it. No one but you, I mean, because you don't know our ways."

"Oh." How big a blunder *had* he made? A good thing she was fond of him, or even standing in the doorway might have been dangerous.

Velona had no trouble figuring out what he was thinking. "Don't worry about it. You told me things I needed to know. I did and the goddess did. Who knows? Maybe she even led you here."

Even though he'd begun to realize they didn't always fit in this world, Hasso clung to the rational, orderly patterns of thought he'd brought from the one that bred him. "How can she did that if she is here with you? If she is here *in* you?" he asked.

By the way Velona looked at him, the question had never occurred to her. The idea that there *could* be a question had never occurred to her. "She is the goddess. She can do anything she pleases," she said, as if stating an axiom of geometry.

How am I supposed to argue with that? he wondered, and then, *Why do I want to argue with it?* What would have happened to someone who argued about the Virgin Birth with a bishop in the tenth century? Hasso didn't know, not in detail, but it wouldn't have been pretty. He was sure of that. "All right," he said quickly.

Too quickly. Velona knew he wasn't in the habit of backing down. "You don't believe it," she said.

"I not say that," Hasso protested.

"I didn't say you said it. I said you believed it." Velona turned toward the altar. "If the goddess wanted to make that rise up in the air, she could."

It weighed several hundred kilos. If it was going to rise up in the air, the goddess had to lift it. If she didn't, nothing this side of a massive block and tackle would. Hasso was going to make a polite noise of agreement and escape the argument when he realized Velona wasn't paying any attention to him. Again, he had the feeling he was standing too close to where lightning had just crashed down. Power filled her. He watched it happen, as if he could watch a battery taking a charge. She pointed at the altar again, this time with an air of command.

And it rose about half a meter into the air.

That was impossible. Hasso knew as much. He also knew that what he knew wasn't worth as much as he thought—convoluted, but true. Velona lowered her hand, and the altar descended, too. The stones under it creaked as they took up the weight again.

"You see?" Velona said. Did the goddess still resonate in her voice? Maybe a little.

"I see," Hasso agreed. Did astonishment still resonate in his voice? He knew damn well it did. Fear sweat prickled at his armpits. Velona was a hell of a high-powered woman all by herself. When you added in the other…

"If you see, what do you have to say now?" She sounded like herself again. Like herself, yes, but proud of what she and the goddess had done.

"Why she not do that to Bucovin?" Hasso asked. "Pick up, then drop and smash?"

Velona started to answer, then suddenly stopped. She looked very human then, human and confused. "I don't know, Hasso Pemsel," she said after that longish pause. "That is the goddess' truth, and she keeps it to herself. I've prayed. All the Lenelli have prayed. The power to do that doesn't seem to be there. Maybe she wants us to overcome the challenge on our own. Some people think so."

"Maybe Bucovin has a power, too," he suggested.

By the way she looked at him, he'd said something stupid. "Bucovin is full of Grenye. Grenye have no power. That's what makes them Grenye." Again, it sounded like a geometry lesson.

"Why Lenelli not beat Bucovin by now, then?" Hasso asked.

"Some of it's bad luck," Velona answered. "Some of it … Well, we've been on this side of the sea a while now. The Grenye in Bucovin have had all that time to learn to fight the way we do. And some of it … some of it, I can't tell you the reason. That's why I went to Bucovin—to try to find out."

"But no luck?" Hasso said.

"Well, some luck," she said. "I found you, didn't I? If you're not a gift from the goddess, I don't know what you are."

"I am a man," Hasso said.

She kissed him. "I should hope you are, sweetheart. But you're a gift from the goddess, too." He wasn't sure he liked that. He wanted to count for himself, not for any … theological reasons. By the way she said it, though, he didn't get a vote.

***

King Bottero's mounted lancers and archers were pretty good. Hasso enjoyed watching them practice on the meadows outside of Drammen. The lancers tore bales of straw to shreds. The archers pincushioned targets. He wondered how he would handle the Schmeisser from horseback. He could ride, but he was no cavalryman.

"Lancers tear hole, then archers and foot soldiers go through?" he asked Lugo, who was also watching the soldiers drill. Panzers opened the way for infantry in his world. He figured knights would do the job here.

But the Lenello didn't understand what he was talking about. "Lancers fight on the line," he said. "Archers on the wings, to harry the enemy. Infantry in the rear, to try to protect if things go wrong."

Haven't they ever heard of the Schwerpunkt? Hasso wondered. The French had scattered their panzers all along the line. They'd paid for it, too, when German armored divisions punched through them. Hasso thought the same thing could work here, too. Why wouldn't it?

He tried to explain, using pebbles and twigs to show what he meant. Lugo looked at what he was doing, looked at him, and shook his head. "This is how we've always fought," he said. "I don't see any reason to change."

That pissed Hasso off. "You not want to win? You not want to beat Bucovin? You not want to beat other Lenello kingdoms? Why not?"

"This is how we've always fought," Lugo repeated. "It works fine."

For ten pfennigs, Hasso would have blown his brains out, assuming he had any. To Lugo, Hasso was a no-account foreigner to be tolerated as the goddess' bed-warmer but not taken seriously. Maybe letting the Lenelli think the goddess sent him wasn't such a bad idea after all. "We see what the king thinks," he said.

"If his Majesty wants to let you waste his time, that's his business." The marshal looked down his nose at Hasso. Since he was a short Lenello, he had to tilt his head back to do it, which didn't stop him.

"I hope he listens. Why not? You not win with what you do now. Maybe you win with a different thing, a new thing," Hasso said.

"And maybe we lose, too." By the way Lugo said it, that blew up a mine under the idea right there.

"Maybe," Hasso said, and the Lenello gaped in amazement that he would admit the possibility. He added, "How are you worse off to lose new way, not old way?"

Lugo didn't answer him. Hasso chose to believe that was because he couldn't answer him. The marshal took himself off, leaving the twigs and pebbles behind like untranslated hieroglyphics. Hasso wanted to kick him in the ass to speed him in the air, but feared giving him a brain concussion if he did.

What would the lancers think of being used as a breakthrough group? *Only one way to find out*, he thought, and walked over toward them. Their leader was a captain named Nornat. *Captain*, here, more or less equaled lieutenant colonel. The Lenelli had soldiers and sergeants and lieutenants—who were kids getting their feet wet—and captains and marshals, and that was about it. Who ranked whom depended far more on prestige than on a table of organization. The system caused more friction than Hasso liked, but he had more urgent things to worry about.

Where he fit himself was an interesting question. He was a captain of sorts, but only of sorts. Velona's favor helped. Surviving against Orosei—who, like a lot of very senior noncoms, had more clout than most captains—helped more. Whatever he was, he wasn't just someone who'd fallen off the turnip wagon.

Nornat led another charge. After his line of lancers shredded some more bales of straw, he guided his dappled gray up to Hasso. Mail jingled on his shoulders. Sweat ran down his face from under his conical helm. The bar nasal on the helmet didn't protect his face as well as the German would have liked. "What do you think, foreigner?" Nornat asked. By the pride in his voice, Hasso had better not think anything bad.

"Strong. Tough," Hasso said. Nornat's grin showed a couple of missing front teeth. A scar twisted his upper lip. No, a bar nasal didn't cover everything. *We shredded Polish lancers*, went through Hasso's mind. *You wouldn't have lasted any longer.* But that didn't matter here. Hasso cast his line: "Want to be more tougher?"

Nornat snapped like a trout. "How?"

"I show you," Hasso said.

When Nornat saw that he meant it literally, he swung down from his mount. The animal lowered its head and started cropping grass. Nornat crouched by Hasso. The Lenello smelled of sweat and leather and iron and horse—all familiar military scents. Hasso made lines of pebbles and twigs. Then he made a column and aimed it at a line. "You charge, and—" He stopped, waiting to see whether Nornat would get it.

And Nornat did. His eyes lit up. "We charge, and we smash right through, and we tear the guts out of whatever's in our way!" He straightened up in a single smooth motion, which impressed the hell out of Hasso—that mailshirt wasn't light. "Carsoli! Sanfrat! Come over here! You've got to take a look at this!" he yelled.

Carsoli was a big man. Sanfrat was bigger, so big that only a brewery-wagon horse could haul him around. Hasso didn't like feeling like a dink among the Lenelli, but he didn't know what the devil he could do about it, either.

Nornat explained his idea at least as well as he could have himself—probably better, because Nornat was a working cavalry officer with a working cavalry officer's appreciation of problems. "What do you think, boys?" he asked when he finished.

"I don't know," Carsoli said; by his tone, he didn't like it but didn't want to stick his neck out, either.

"Stinking Grenye won't be looking for it—that's for sure," Sanfrat said. "Ought to win us a battle or two just from surprise." He might be big—hell, he was enormous—but he wasn't slow or stodgy.

"What did Marshal Lugo have to say? You were talking about it with him, weren't you?" Nornat was quick on the uptake, too.

Hasso wished he could lie, but knew he'd get found out if he tried. "He does not like it. He says the old way to fight is good enough."

Sanfrat snorted. "I'm surprised he ever lost his cherry. He would've said playing with himself was good enough."

Nornat laughed. So did Hasso. He'd never known any soldiers who didn't have pungent opinions about their superiors. Even the Ivans joked about their commissars after they got captured. Carsoli bared his teeth in a sort of a smile, but that was all. Hasso feared the marshal would hear about the gibe in nothing flat.

"How do we" —Hasso gestured— "get around the marshal?"

"Just talk to the king," Nornat answered. "He'll listen to you, or I think he will. I'll talk to him, too, by the goddess. And you're friends with Orosei, right?"

"Mm—maybe." Hasso didn't know if he would go that far. He and the master-at-arms had a strong mutual respect, the kind two tough men who knew each could maim the other tended to acquire. Whether that equaled friendship wasn't so obvious.

"Well, try him," the cavalry captain said. "He likes your throws. I was watching when the two of you tangled. I lost some money, because I thought he'd pound you into the ground. But he's game for new things, so chances are he'd go for this column fighting. And I don't care what his rank is—he has Bottero's ear."

Carsoli looked about ready to burst, like a man who needed to run for the jakes. Hasso caught Sanfrat's eye, then flicked his gaze back to the dubious officer. Sanfrat got it without anything more than that. He didn't even nod. He just smiled a little, crookedly. *Something* would keep Carsoli from blabbing to Lugo right away. Something immense and muscular and blond, most likely.

Hasso's smile was as crooked as Sanfrat's. He would have handled things the same way in the *Wehrmacht*. Yes, people were people, whether they carried Schmeissers or lances, rode horses or panzers.

Were the Grenye people, too? Hasso hadn't worried about Jews in his own world; he didn't worry much about the Grenye here. They were the enemy. What more did a soldier need to know about them?

***

Orosei lifted his mug of beer in salute to Hasso, who sat across the table from him in the buttery. Hasso had been using bits of stale bread and raisins to demonstrate his idea. "I like it," Orosei told him. "You can stab right through the line that way. And once you do, the bastards on the other side won't know what the demon to try next."

"That is how I see it," Hasso agreed. "Marshal Lugo does not think so, though."

"Lugo doesn't think, and that's about the size of it." The master-at-arms didn't bother lowering his voice. If Lugo decided he was insulted, he would have to challenge. Here as in the *Reich*, the challenged party got to choose the weapons. Orosei was sudden death on two legs with any weapon or none. Lugo was brave enough and tough enough, but he wasn't in the master-at-arms' class. Orosei went on, "We can do this. It wouldn't be hard. We really can—and we ought to."

"We see things the same way, then," Hasso said.

Orosei drained his mug and waved for a refill. A Grenye serving girl came over with a pitcher. "Thanks, sweetheart," Orosei said, and swatted her on the backside. She squeaked, but she was smiling as she scurried away. Chuckling, Orosei went on, "Let's both talk to his Majesty. Lugo's a marshal, but he isn't a god. The two of us can cancel him out."

"I would love to," Hasso said.

"You're all right. By the goddess, you are," the master-at-arms said. "I wasn't sure Velona knew what she was doing till I got to know you, but she did. She usually does. You've got your head nailed down tight, bugger me if you don't." Hasso would have said Orosei had his head on straight, but it amounted to the same thing.

"I thank you," the *Wehrmacht* officer answered. "You, too."

"Well, I try," Orosei said. "Some of the people in this castle don't know enough to squat before they shit, if you know what I mean. But you aren't like that. You've got your fancy weapon, but it doesn't mean you don't know how to fight."

"I thank you," Hasso said again. Praise from a soldier as capable as Orosei really meant something to him.

"I don't waste time buttering people up," Orosei said. "Life's too short for that crap. So we'll go to the king and see what he says, and then we'll go from there."

"What if he says no?" Hasso asked.

The master-at-arms shrugged. "Then it's better luck next time, that's all. What his Majesty says, goes. But the idea's too good not to try it out. It isn't like we've had much luck against Bucovin. Everybody knows how things keep going wrong there. Maybe this will make them go right instead. Here's hoping." He raised his mug again.

In the hallway outside the buttery, a woman said, "No! No! No! No! No!" Her voice got higher and shriller every time she repeated it. Hasso didn't wait to hear any more. He bounced to his feet and ran out to see what was going on. Orosei was right behind him.

Aderno was dragging a Grenye woman, a serving wench, along by the wrist. She didn't want to come, but he was much bigger and much stronger. "By the goddess, wizard, can't you find a willing woman?" Orosei didn't bother hiding his scorn.

"I don't want her for that," Aderno said.

"What, then?" Hasso demanded. Everything about the scene, from Aderno's grip to the woman's eyes, so wide with fear that you could see white all around the irises, looked like a prelude to rape.

"It was your idea," Aderno answered. "I want to try that spell on her, the one that didn't work on Scanno. If it doesn't work on her, either, then Bucovin's got claws in the palace. That's something we need to know."

Orosei relaxed. "Ah. All right. Makes sense."

Hasso didn't. "Can't you use a different spell? A spell that doesn't do what the one with Scanno would?"

"No." The wizard shook his head. "I want everything to be the same except for the person I'm aiming at."

A *scientific sorcerer*, Hasso thought. "Can you cure the spell once you cast it?" he asked. He didn't like the idea of slagging her face with boils and carbuncles and whatever else Aderno would conjure up.

"Maybe." Aderno didn't sound as if he cared, or as if he intended to try. "Any which way, I'll learn something."

"She do something to deserve something bad happen to her?" Hasso asked. The Grenye woman started shrieking and wailing again—now she knew something bad *would* happen.

"She walked by when I needed somebody. That's all that matters," Aderno replied.

"No. Let her go," Hasso said.

"What? Are you out of your mind? I'd just have to go and catch another one." The wizard might have been talking about rabbits.

"Let her go," Hasso repeated. "Find a Grenye who does something bad. Find one who … should have it happen." He couldn't come up with the word *deserve* in Lenello, but he got his meaning across.

"Listen, Hasso, take it easy. She's only a Grenye," Orosei said.

"In Bucovin, do they say, 'He is only a Lenello'?" Hasso asked.

The master-at-arms bristled. So did Aderno. "They'd better not," Orosei growled. "They're only Grenye, sure, but they're not that stupid."

"Come on." Aderno tugged at the woman. "We've already wasted too much time on this nonsense."

Hasso realized he would have to hurt the wizard, maybe kill him, to make him stop. He hesitated before doing that. The way Orosei went along with Aderno made him hesitate more. They'd lived here all their lives. They knew how things were supposed to work. He hadn't, and didn't. With a disgusted noise, he turned away.

Aderno dragged the Grenye woman down the hall. As she went, she stretched out a hand to Hasso. "You tried, lord. Thank you for trying. Nobody ever did before." Then she was gone.

"Jesus!" Hasso kicked the wall as hard as he could. Pain shot up his leg. He hadn't thought he could feel any worse, and didn't like finding he was wrong.

"What are you throwing a fit for?" Honest puzzlement filled Orosei's voice.

"Anybody'd think you were laying her or something. If you were, you should've said so. The wizard would've snagged somebody else. But if you were, you'd better light out for the tall timber starting yesterday, on account of the goddess won't be very happy with you."

"Not laying her," Hasso said. The master-at-arms was right; Velona wouldn't be happy with him if he were, and that was putting it mildly. "Just ... bad to take advantage of weak."

"Why? What else are they there for?" No, Orosei didn't get it. Would Hasso, had he come here flush with victory in 1940? He didn't think so. Defeat was always so much more instructive than victory. Germany had learned a lot from World War I, France next to nothing. What would the *Reich* learn this time around?

Not to mess with the goddamn Russians, that's what, he thought. *Not messing with the USA looks like a pretty good idea, too. And messing with both of them at once is really, really dumb.*

"Things you do, sometimes they come back and—" Hasso mimed biting.

Orosei threw his hands in the air. "Oh, by the goddess! She's only a Grenye. She's not even a cute Grenye. I'm glad you're not screwing her—I wouldn't think much of your taste if you were. I mean, sure, pussy's pussy, but you can do better than that. Demons! You have done better than that, way better."

"You think Grenye don't remember everything Lenelli do to them?" Hasso asked.

"Let 'em remember. They can't do anything about it. They're—"

"Only Grenye," Hasso finished for him. How many times had he heard that since finding himself here? The Lenelli sure believed it. Did the Grenye? If they did, how come Bucovin stayed on its feet?

"That's right. That's all they'll ever be." Orosei thumped him on the back. "Come drink some more beer. You look like you could use it. You're kind of green around the gills. You fit in so well here, sometimes I almost forget you're a foreigner with funny notions. Every once in a while it comes out, though—no offense."

A foreigner with funny notions. Hasso found himself nodding. He was that, all right. Back in the *Reich*, he'd taken things for granted. Why not? They were what *he'd* grown up with. Here, unfairness struck him like a poke in the eye.

Or was it unfairness? What if the Grenye really were ... only Grenye? Then wasn't it natural for the Lenelli to ride roughshod over them? Natural or not, it was what the Lenelli were doing. And, with his plan for a striking column of lancers, it was what he was helping them to do.

He let Orosei steer him back to the buttery. A Grenye servant brought him more beer. The swarthy little curly-haired man stared at him out of eyes as big and wide and dark as a deer's. How much of what went on out in the hallway had he heard? What kind of gossip would wildfire through the servants in Castle Drammen by this time tomorrow? How much trouble would Hasso land in because of it?

Off in the distance—but not nearly far enough off in the distance—a woman screamed, and went on screaming. Orosei pretended not to hear, the way someone who'd done a lot of interrogations might pretend not to hear a prisoner's screams from the next room. Hasso tried pretending, too, but didn't have much luck. Getting smashed let him forget about the noise—and, eventually, about everything else.

***

When he woke up, he had no idea how he'd got to his own bed. Velona made a face at him. "Was she worth it?" the goddess on earth asked, a certain malicious glee in her voice.

Things came back in a hurry in spite of Hasso's headache. "I don't touch her," he said. "I don't even know her name."

"Her name is Zadar. And I know you didn't touch her, or" —Velona's eyes flashed— "you'd be roasting over a slow fire right now." Hasso didn't think she was using a figure of speech. She went on, "You were stupid even trying to get in Aderno's way."

"Aderno is a beast," Hasso said. "He likes hurting people. He does it for fun." He got out of bed, grabbed the chamber pot, and pissed and pissed and pissed. He didn't bother turning his back. The gurgling stream was part of his opinion of Aderno, too.

Velona understood as much. "If he hurts our enemies, more power to him," she said.

"If you get in his way, he hurts you, too," Hasso said.

Those perfect blue eyes widened. Velona's nostrils flared. Then she relaxed and started to laugh. "Oh, I see. You mean Aderno would hurt anyone who got in his way. You didn't mean he'd hurt *me*." She didn't believe anyone—except the Grenye, who were beyond the pale of civilized behavior—would want to hurt her.

But Hasso shook his head even though it hurt. "I mean you, sweetheart. Aderno wants what Aderno wants. Anyone who wants something else? Something bad happens to him—or to her."

"The goddess would not allow it." Velona sounded certain.

After some of the things Hasso had seen, he wasn't sure she was wrong. But he wasn't sure she was right, either. "The goddess almost lets the Grenye catch you," he pointed out.

"So she did." Trouble flicked across Velona's face for a moment, but then it blew out like a candle in a hurricane. "Instead of letting them catch me, though, she sent you here. You saved me—or she saved me through you. And now Orosei tells me you've got a fine new scheme for smashing Bucovin."

Orosei made a pretty fair politician. Hasso supposed that was part of the master-at-arms' job, too. "Smashing? I don't know." He shrugged like a Frenchman, because the Lenelli liked overacting. "I hope we can win some battles with it. King Bottero has to say yes first."

"Oh, I think we can arrange that." She sounded confident again. How would she go about persuading the king, if that was what she needed to do? *Do I want to know?* Hasso wondered, and needed no more than a heartbeat to decide he didn't.

VI

Hasso used coins on a tabletop to show King Bottero what he had in mind. He didn't do much talking. He didn't have to; Orosei, Nornat, and Sanfrat did it for him. They were more enthusiastic about his idea than he was, seeming filled with converts' zeal.

Marshal Lugo stood by Bottero, listening to the cavalry officers bragging about what they'd do to Bucovin if the king turned them loose to fight the way they wanted to. The marshal looked like a man who'd just taken a big bite out of a horse-manure sandwich.

"You can do this?" Bottero asked when the officers finished their excited exposition.

"Yes, your Majesty!" Nornat and Sanfrat chorused. Carsoli wasn't there. Maybe he'd go along if the king ordered it, but he was no convert.

King Bottero turned to Orosei. "What do you think?"

"It's something we haven't tried before, anyhow," the master-at-arms answered. "What we *have* tried against Bucovin hasn't worked real well, so why not trot out something different for a change?"

"We can use this against Lenelli, too," Nornat said. "Once the lancers break the enemy line, it's like breaking a turtle's shell. What's inside is meat. Our meat."

"Mm." The king plucked at his beard. "How about you, Lugo? You haven't had much to say."

"Everything sounds wonderful when you're drinking beer," the marshal said. "How well it'll work when we really try it out … That's liable to be a different story, and not such a pretty one."

The crack held just enough truth to sting. Hasso gnawed on his lower lip. Perhaps noticing him look unhappy, Bottero asked, "What do you have to say to that, outlander?"

"Nothing is perfect, your Majesty. Some things is—uh, are—better, some worse," Hasso said. "How good is what you do now? Bucovin is still here, so maybe not so good. Maybe try something different, something new."

"A good answer," King Bottero replied.

"No, not so good!" Lugo cried. "The foreigner will risk our men, risk good Lenelli. But where will he be? Someplace safe, that's where. Someplace where he

61

doesn't need to take chances."

"I am no lancer," Hasso said. The marshal sneered. Hasso held up a hand. "Not done yet. I am no lancer, but I ride at the front, when the column charges." He bowed to Lugo and clicked his heels. The Lenelli didn't do that, but they recognized the formality of the gesture. "I ride there, yes. You ride beside me?"

Nornat and Sanfrat sucked in their breath together. Orosei chuckled and then politely tried to pretend he hadn't. *I'll put my money where my mouth is*, Hasso might have said. *Have you got the balls to ride along?*

Lugo looked as if he hated him. He likely did. But he was ruined if he looked like a coward in front of his sovereign. "If the king orders this foolish scheme to go forward, you will not see me hang back," he said. "No miserable outlander will ever say he dares to go where a Lenello dares not come with him."

"Good." Hasso ignored the insult. "We ride together. Together, we crush the Grenye. Nothing else matters. You do not have to love me, Marshal. You only have to want to win. That is all I want."

"Ha!" Lugo said. "You want to make a big name for yourself, to show everyone how smart you are. Be careful you don't outsmart yourself."

He wasn't wrong there, either, no matter how little Hasso felt like admitting it. The German only shrugged. "What can I do? Where can I go? This is my land now. I want to see King Bottero win. If the king wins, I win. If the king loses, I lose. Better for everyone if the king wins."

That last should have been a subjunctive. Hasso realized as much after the easier, more common indicative came out of his mouth. The grammatical error wasn't all bad, though. It made King Bottero's triumph sound more nearly inevitable, less doubtful, than the subjunctive, a mood made for showing uncertainty, ever could have.

Orosei winked at him. Maybe the master-at-arms thought he'd made the mistake on purpose. Or maybe Orosei thought he'd said the right thing, even if his grammar was bad. He could hope so, anyhow.

By the way Bottero's eyes lit up, Hasso *had* said the right thing. "I *am* going to win," the king boomed. "The kingdom is going to win. We will drive the Grenye before us like chaff on the breeze." But that seemed to remind him of something else. "You got silly about some Grenye wench not long ago, didn't you, Hasso Pemsel?"

Except for Velona, the Lenelli mostly used his full name when they weren't happy with him, the way a parent might have. Hearing it used that way put his back up. "Silly? I don't think so, your Majesty. Does Aderno treat a horse or a dog bad on purpose? Not likely. Why treat a Grenye bad on purpose, then? Just make trouble with no need. Plenty of trouble already, yes? Why make more if you don't have to?"

"This will help our folk," Bottero said in that-settles-it tones.

Marshal Lugo was no fool—or, at least, was not the kind of fool who made a bad courtier. "Yes, your Majesty," he intoned. If *his* tone suggested he would sooner go on the rack than do anything Hasso proposed ... well, how could you prove that? You couldn't, and Hasso knew it too bloody well.

If King Bottero found anything wrong with the way his marshal agreed, he didn't let on. He made a fist and slammed it into his other hand. "We march against Bucovin," he declared, and that was that. The *Führer* could have been no more decisive.

***

As Bottero's realm readied itself for war, Hasso found himself wondering whether the king might not be *too* decisive. It struck him as late in the year to start a major campaign. Germany had moved against the Ivans on 22 June after delaying six weeks to squash Yugoslavia and Greece. That delay probably kept the *Wehrmacht* from taking Moscow. And 22 June was right at the summer solstice. They were well past it here; Hasso grimaced when he remembered how they'd celebrated it.

So much he didn't know about the way things worked here. How big exactly *was* Bucovin? Bottero's maps had no reliable scale of distances. And how bad were the local winters? Hasso had no idea. He'd never been through one.

He could find out. Velona's eyes got wide when he asked whether rivers or lakes froze over. "No," she said. "Farther north, maybe, but not around here. Do they do that where you come from?"

"Sometimes." *Too damned often, in Russia*, Hasso thought. Then he asked, "Does it snow here?" Only trouble was, he didn't know how to say *snow* in Lenello. The question came out as, "Does ice fall from the sky?" He used fluttering fingers to show snowflakes dancing on the breeze.

Velona laughed after she understood what he meant. "Oh, yes," she said, and taught him the words he needed to ask the question the right way. She kissed him when he showed he remembered them and could pronounce them. If he'd got rewards like that in school, he figured he would have grown up to be a genius.

"How often does it snow in the winter?" he asked.

"Sometimes," Velona said with an enchanting shrug. *Don't get too distracted*, Hasso reminded himself. She went on, "It snows every winter—sometimes more, sometimes less."

"You make war in the wintertime?" Hasso persisted.

"Not so much as in the summer, but we do," Velona answered. "We aren't peasants, the way the Grenye are. Fighting in the winter is harder for them. It takes them away from their farms."

Maybe there was method in Bottero's madness after all, then. Hasso could hope so, anyhow. "Your harvests the past few years are good?" he asked.

"Good enough." Velona started laughing again, this time at him. "Good heavens, darling, are you going to count every ear of wheat in the granary and every arrow in every horse-archer's quiver?"

"Someone should," Hasso said stubbornly. Man for man, panzer for panzer, the *Wehrmacht* was better than the Red Army. Everybody knew that, even the

Ivans. But when they could mass five times the men, eight times the panzers, twenty times the guns, quantity took on a quality of its own. Bucovin wouldn't have that big an edge—or he hoped it wouldn't. Even so … "Lots of Grenye."

"Too many. That's why we're going to war." It all seemed simple to Velona. "The goddess wants us to rule them."

"She tells you that?" In Hasso's world, the question would have floated on a sea of sarcasm. Not here. He'd seen enough to make him shove sarcasm aside. If Velona told him the goddess possessed her now and then, he couldn't very well argue. He had no better name for what happened.

Velona nodded now. "She wouldn't have led us here if she didn't."

God wills it! The Spaniards had believed the same thing, and conquered most of two continents before they paused to wonder. And the Lenelli had a lot more evidence going for them than the Spaniards ever had. "The goddess says Bottero beats Bucovin this time?" By now, Hasso recognized the future and the various past tenses when he heard them. Before long, he would have to start using them himself. People understood him when he stayed in the present, but he was starting to sound stupid in his own ears.

"She hasn't said one way or the other," Velona answered. "But why would she let us go forward if something bad would happen when we did?"

One more question Hasso couldn't answer. Not having been devout back in Germany put him at a disadvantage here. You could argue about religion in the world he came from. Not in this one, not the same way. Spiritual things were as real here as Wednesday or a poke in the eye.

In his own world, he would have asked if the ambassador from Bucovin had been sent packing. Things worked the same here … to a point. The Lenello kingdoms exchanged envoys among themselves, and gave them safe-conduct home when they went to war. But no Lenello kingdom exchanged ambassadors with Bucovin. Recognizing the Grenye as equals would have been beneath the Lenelli's dignity. They talked with Bucovin when they had to, but always unofficially, so they could pretend to themselves that it didn't really count.

He found a different question instead: "Is the eastern border sealed?"

Velona looked blank. "What do you mean?"

Hasso wanted to bang his head against the stone outwall of Castle Drammen. Being security minister in a kingdom that didn't know anything about security gave him unending frustration. Things he took for granted had never yet crossed the Lenelli's minds. As patiently as he could, he explained: "Grenye go out of Drammen. They go out of Bottero's kingdom. They go into Bucovin. They tell the Grenye what the king does. If we seal the border, they can't cross and tell."

"That wouldn't be easy," Velona said with a frown.

"No, not easy," Hasso agreed. "But worth trying, yes? Stop some of them from going to Bucovin, Grenye there know less. The more we stop, the less Bucovin finds out." *I hope.*

Velona couldn't issue the orders. Neither could Hasso, not by himself. The Lenelli who knew him personally took him seriously. To the ones who didn't, he would never be anything but a jumped-up outlander. So he took the idea to King Bottero. The King got it faster than Velona had. When he did, he kissed Hasso on both cheeks. He'd been eating onions, so Hasso appreciated the sentiment more than the kisses themselves.

"Who would have imagined such a thing?" Bottero boomed after releasing Hasso from his embrace. "The goddess knew what she was doing when she sent you to us, all right."

To Hasso's way of thinking, anyone who *didn't* take those elementary precautions was asking to have his head handed to him. Were his own fourteenth-century ancestors this naive? If they were, it was a miracle any of them lived long enough to reproduce. Of course, the soldiers on both sides must have been equally inept, or somebody would have wiped the floor with somebody else.

"I'll send the order out to the east by sorcery, so we don't waste any more time," Bottero said—yes, he did get it.

"Not just to the east. To the north and south and west, too," Hasso said. "Seal the whole border." Now the king looked blank. "Grenye can go up or down to another Lenello kingdom, one without a closed border. Then they go to Bucovin," Hasso pointed out.

That got him kissed again. "You are as slippery as a slug, as sneaky as a serpent!" Bottero said. Hasso supposed those were compliments. The king went on, "I never would have thought of that—never, I tell you!"

Suppose Heinrich Himmler came from the Philippine Islands. That would probably make him more valuable to the *Führer*, not less. He would still make a dandy security chief. But, as a manifest foreigner, he could never think of grabbing the topmost job for himself.

In Bottero's kingdom, Hasso was far more foreign than a Filipino in Berlin. Another country? He was from another world! He would never be king, not even with the goddess at his side and at his back. Security minister and technical adviser was as high as he could rise. He had the post. Now he needed to deliver the goods.

"Can magic help to find Grenye who want to go east?" he asked. "Grenye who go through the swamp, say, not by the built-up road?"

"Grenye who *sneak* through the swamp." Bottero tiptoed with his fingers on a tabletop to show what *sneak* meant. Hasso nodded his thanks; that was a useful verb for a security man to know. The king went on, "I'm no wizard myself, so I can't really tell you. Aderno could."

"Aderno and I, we are not happy with each other." Sometimes Hasso came out with phrases he'd read. They often made people smile. In Lenello as in German, the written language wasn't just the same as the spoken one.

Bottero smiled now... for a moment. Then he looked severe—and a man as large and tough as he was could look very severe indeed. "You serve the kingdom. You serve it well. Aderno was doing the same thing with that Grenye wench."

"Aderno serves Aderno with that Grenye wench," Hasso said stubbornly. "Aderno likes to hurt people. Fight with Grenye gives him a reason." He shook his head. That wasn't the word he wanted. "Gives him an excuse." That was what he wanted to say.

"He serves the kingdom." Bottero couldn't see anything else.

Hasso shrugged, seeing no point in arguing with his sovereign. National Socialist doctrine shouted that that psychiatrist in Vienna was nothing but a crazy damn Jew. All the same, Hasso would have bet Deutschmarks against dung that Aderno had a big old bulge in his pants when he dragged Zadar off to what might literally have been a fate worse than death.

"You serve the kingdom, too," Bottero reminded him. "You and Aderno both serve the same goal. So you should get along with each other."

That was logical. As far as Hasso was concerned, it was also next to impossible. "I would rather kill him than get along with him ... your Majesty," he said.

The king stared at him. At first, Hasso thought he'd badly offended Bottero. Then he realized Bottero was fighting hard not to laugh. The king lost the fight. "You fell from beyond the moon," he said between snorts. Hasso nodded. That wasn't so very different from his own thought of a little while before. Bottero went on, "You fell all that way—and you're just as touchy and proud as a Lenello born a short spit from my palace."

Hasso clicked his heels, which showed once more how foreign he was. But his words said the opposite: "I am a man, your Majesty."

"Well, Velona told me the same thing," Bottero said.

"What? That she is a man? Don't believe her."

Bottero snorted again. "If she told me that, I *wouldn't* believe her. I know better, and so do you." He grimaced; he must have remembered that his sharing Velona didn't make Hasso happy. Before the German could say anything, Bottero continued, "No, she told me *you* were a man, and it's so. And you're a man I need. That's so, too."

"And Aderno?" Hasso asked.

"Is also a man I need," the king said. "Don't try to kill him unless you really have to. If you do try, you may find that wizards take a deal of killing, and sometimes they aren't dead even after they die."

Thinking fondly of his Schmeisser, Hasso said, "I take the chance."

* * *

Detachments from west of Drammen, and from north and south, flowed into the capital, some by river, others by road. Soldiers camped inside Castle Drammen, and on the wide grounds of the Lenello estates around it. They swarmed into the Grenye districts closer to the walls. When they came back, most of them were drunk. Some had unfortunate diseases. Several got their belt pouches slit.

A couple of them got their throats slit instead. Several Grenye also ended up dead, some in fair fights, others, by all appearances, slaughtered for the sport of it. Hasso had seen that the Grenye districts had plenty of brothels. Not all the Lenelli bothered going to them. If some warriors saw a short, dark woman whose looks they liked, they went and took her. If she wasn't a whore, she was only a Grenye.

How many times had Hasso heard that phrase since coming here? More often than he wanted to: he knew that. He didn't bother taking his worries to Bottero; the king wouldn't do anything about it. Instead, he talked to Velona, asking, "Does the goddess like what the soldiers do to women who don't want it or deserve it?"

"They're soldiers," she answered with a shrug. "They act that way because that's how soldiers act. What can you do about it?"

"Me?" With a sour laugh, Hasso jabbed a thumb at his own chest. "I can't do anything. I am only a man, and only a foreigner at that."

"Not *only a man*. Quite a man," Velona purred.

"I thank you." Hasso hoped she'd talked to Bottero that way. He tried not to let her distract him now. It wasn't easy, but he managed. "*I* can't do anything, no. But can you? You are the goddess. Does the goddess care for women, or not?"

"Of course she does." Velona paused. "I am not the goddess. Sometimes the goddess is me. It's not the same thing." Now Hasso shrugged. It came close enough for him. He knew he would never understand the difference, not unless or until a god possessed him. He didn't think that was likely. It might not be impossible here, but even so…. Velona went on, "If she wants me to do anything about those Grenye sluts, I'm sure she'll tell me about it."

Some of them weren't sluts. That was the point Hasso kept trying to make, the point none of the Lenelli wanted to see. Instead of banging away at it, he tried a different tack: "Next time she is in you, maybe you should ask her. Maybe she needs a question to think about it."

"Maybe I will." Velona sounded more as if she was humoring him than as if she really intended to do it, but he couldn't do anything about that. He'd done what he could do. If it wasn't enough … Well, when had the Grenye ever caught anything close to an even break? If they didn't catch one now, it wouldn't change the way the world worked very much.

When enough of his soldiers came into Drammen to satisfy him, King Bottero started east, toward the border with Bucovin. Hasso gathered that some units were late, and that the king wasn't about to wait for them. That made sense to the German. Despite his own best efforts, surprise was bound to be gone. All the same, you didn't want to waste time on campaign and let the enemy get ready for you. The *Wehrmacht* waited around at Kursk, and how the Ivans made them pay! Fewer men on time were often better than plenty a few days too late.

Plenty of men on time were better still, but Hasso had realized he couldn't expect too much from the Lenelli. They knew nothing about Germanic efficiency. He hoped to teach them, but Rome wasn't built in a day.

Everything pointed to their being more efficient than the Grenye, and not just because of magic. That would probably do. When civilized soldiers attacked barbarians, the barbarians usually lost. That was how civilization advanced.

Hasso thought of Arminius. He thought of three Roman legions cut to pieces in the Teutoberg Wald. Germany stayed outside the Roman Empire because the barbarians won that time. What would his world look like if they'd lost? Nobody would ever know now.

He'd watched and ridden along when the *Wehrmacht* roared into Poland, into France, into Russia. Because he'd done all that, watching and riding along when the Lenelli moved out of Drammen impressed him less than it might have. It felt more like a scene from a historical movie with plenty of extras than the start of a real campaign.

The stinks of sweat and horse manure said it was real enough. Foot soldiers trudged along in loose order, shields and quivers on their backs, unstrung bows in their right hands, shortswords on their hips. Almost all of them wore iron helms. A few had mailshirts. The ones who did wore surcoats to keep the sun from cooking them in their own juice.

Teamsters kept wagons rolling. Ungreased axles screeched. Horses and mules strained in the traces. Choking clouds of dust rose. Hasso knew all about unpaved roads—one more thing the Russians had taught him. He hoped it wouldn't rain. This particular unpaved road would turn to rutted mud, and then to glue.

Barges and boats came up the Drammion alongside the marching men and noisy wagons. Moving bulky supplies by water was easier, cheaper, and faster than it was by land. When the river turned to marsh, as it would, the Lenelli would have to unload the vessels. In the meantime, they took advantage of them.

Companies of mounted archers and lancers rode along as if everything depended on them alone. In a way, the armored men were right. They were the strike force, the spearpoint, of Bottero's army. They could crack the enemy line, the way panzers could in the other world. But if the archers ran out of arrows, if the lancers were reduced to scattering over the countryside to scrounge for food, they wouldn't be able to fight the way they should. The Lenelli understood that ... up to a point.

Bottero's army had one accompaniment the *Wehrmacht* wouldn't have: Aderno and six or eight other wizards on unicornback. Hasso would have preferred Stukas and Messerschmitts overhead, or even a hot-air or hydrogen-filled observation balloon. He knew he would never get the airplanes; they were much too far over the technological horizon. A balloon might be possible ... one of these years.

His own horse was a good, steady gelding. He could hope it wouldn't go mad with fear when he started shooting from its back. He did envy the wizards the elegance and beauty of their mounts. He also envied them the unicorns' horns, some silvered like Aderno's, others gilded. Not only were they splendid; they looked to be formidable in battle, too.

"A pity lancers and archers don't ride unicorns," he said when they stopped for supper the first evening out of Drammen.

Aderno looked through him. Since they almost came to blows over the Grenye serving woman, the wizard barely bothered staying polite. "For one thing, unicorns are rare, and so deserving to carry on their backs men with rare talent," he said. "For another, they will not suffer men without sorcerous talent to mount them. Anyone but an ignorant newcomer would know as much."

It wasn't quite, *Screw you, stupid*, but it came close enough. "I bet I can ride one," Hasso said.

The rest of the wizards laughed till they had to hold their sides. "You want to be thrown and stomped and gored, don't you?" said one of them, a beanpole of a man named Flegrei.

"No. I want to ride a unicorn." Hasso reached into a pocket—he was wearing his *Wehrmacht* trousers, which boasted such refinements—and pulled out a goldpiece. "This says I can do it."

"You're on!" Flegrei shouted, and showed off his own shiny coin.

All the wizards except Aderno clamored to bet Hasso. He had to check whether he had enough money with him to cover them. As it turned out, he did. He thought they really wanted not just his gold but to watch him get thrown and stomped and gored. Since he figured Aderno had more reason to want that than any of the others, he asked, "You, too?"

Aderno bit his lip. Yes, he wanted to watch the foreigner fail, too. He just wasn't so sure as the rest of the wizards that Hasso would. In the end, though, he nodded. "Yes, me, too. Why not?"

Hasso turned out not to have one more coin. "If the unicorn kills me, tell Velona I say she should pay you," he said. Aderno nodded. Hasso bowed to the other wizards. "Whose unicorn do I ride?"

"You mean, whose unicorn *don't* you ride?" Flegrei jeered. "You can try with mine. Once you get what you deserve, maybe you won't strut so tall."

That gibe stung. Hasso didn't like being short among the Lenelli. He briefly wondered how the Grenye, most of whom were much shorter than he was, enjoyed looking up to the big blond men from out of the west. But then the Grenye slipped from his mind. He bowed again. "Shorten the stirrup leathers, please," he told Flegrei, whose legs were much longer than his.

Flegrei's answering bow was scorn personified. "At your service, my prickly little hedgehog," he said. Hasso watched him closely as he adjusted them, but he did an honest job of it. That had to mean he really didn't believe Hasso could stay on the unicorn. When Flegrei finished, he stepped away from the beautiful snowy beast. "All yours."

"*Danke schön.*" Hasso forgot Lenello for the moment. He walked up to the unicorn. It looked at him sidelong out of an eye as blue as Velona's. A low snort, more curious than anything else—he hoped—came from it. The wizards murmured among themselves. Maybe they'd expected the unicorn to run him through with its horn as soon as he got anywhere near it.

Before he could think about what he was doing, he swung up into the saddle. The unicorn snorted again, this time sounding distinctly surprised. It started to buck.

"Cut that out," he said, and went to work calming it as he would have with a restive horse. And the unicorn, sensing that the new rider, though a stranger, had some notion of what he was doing up there, *did* calm down. He rode it in a slow circle around the staring wizards and halted directly in front of Flegrei.

Dismounting, he bowed yet again and held out his hand. "Nice animal. Now pay up, you cocksure bastard."

Goggling, Flegrei paid. "How did you do that?" he choked out.

"Easy." Hasso jabbed a thumb at his own chest. "I'm magic. You're smart, you stop screwing with me." He went around to the other wizards, collecting a goldpiece from each of them. He saved Aderno for last. "You, too."

"Here." Aderno gave him the coin. "You *are* magical, or you can be. If you saw the gold star, you certainly can be. But I didn't think potential would satisfy a unicorn—which shows I don't know as much as I wish I did. There is more to you than meets the eye, Hasso Pemsel. How much more keeps surprising me, and not always happily."

Back in Germany, Hasso thought, *I'd have to be a virgin to ride a unicorn.* But there were no unicorns in Germany. And, with the Russians rampaging through the country all hot with vengeance, there probably weren't a hell of a lot of virgins left there, either.

The wizards squabbled furiously. "He saw *gold*?" Flegrei shouted at Aderno. "Why the demon didn't you say so? You would have saved us all some money!"

"You would have saved us from looking like idiots, too," another sorcerer said.

"Nothing could save *some* people from looking like idiots." Aderno could be bitchy.

"You must be one of them," the other wizard retorted. "If he saw gold and you bet against him, you deserved to lose, by the goddess."

"It's not just the talent—it's the training. Or I thought it was," Aderno said. "But it seems I was wrong."

"Yes, it seems you were." Flegrei sounded disgusted. "And it cost all of us gold, and now the goddess-cursed foreigner will be more puffed up than ever."

Hasso felt like making his chest swell up and strutting around like a pouter pigeon. He decided not to, though; Flegrei was already angry enough at him. And Aderno said, "Watch your mouth, you blockhead! Whatever the foreigner is, he's not goddess-cursed. Velona will put your ears on a necklace if she hears you go around saying he is."

"Ha! I'm not afraid of her," Flegrei declared.

"Well, if that doesn't prove you're a blockhead, I don't know what would," Aderno said. By the way the rest of the wizards stepped back from Flegrei, they agreed with Aderno. That was one more sign of the power of the woman Hasso had taken up with—or rather, the woman who'd taken up with him.

As for his own power ... Security minister wasn't bad. *De facto* General Staff officer wasn't bad, either. And showing up a bunch of haughty wizards, and making money while he did it, was a hell of a lot better than not bad.

***

Coming back to Castle Svarag wasn't quite like coming home for Hasso. He wondered if he would ever feel at home anywhere here. He doubted it. Giving up the sense of home was the émigré's curse. But he'd spent some time at Mertois' castle, and he'd got to know a good many of the castellan's soldiers. He felt less not at home here than he did most other places in this world. The convoluted thought made one corner of his mouth quirk up in ironic amusement.

"Good to see you, little man. Good to see you," Sholseth boomed. The clout on the back he gave Hasso almost knocked him over. "I hear you and Orosei couldn't take each other out."

"After a while, we stop trying," Hasso answered. "We decide, why bother? One of us could get hurt bad."

Sholseth nodded. "Makes sense. I tell you, I felt better when I heard Orosei didn't beat you. He's as good as we've got. I know I can't take him, even though I'm bigger. So if you're as good as he is, no wonder you knocked me for a loop."

"Maybe I'm just lucky," Hasso said.

"Nah." Sholseth shook his head. "You're good. When you threw me over your shoulder, I thought, *What the demon am I getting into?* Then I went wham, and I pretty much stopped thinking after that." He thumped Hasso again, still good-naturedly. He seemed to take a perverse pride in being the first Lenello to discover what a formidable fellow this foreigner could be.

Hasso was glad enough to drink and talk with his old acquaintances. But he also found he had serious business at Castle Svarag. Mertois was keeping close to a dozen Grenye who'd got caught slipping east toward Bucovin in his dungeon. Hasso had them brought out one at a time. "If you lie to me, you be sorry," he told the first one, a stocky man named Magar. He nodded to Aderno. "And the wizard, he knows if you lie."

"I didn't do anything," Magar said stolidly.

"No one ever does anything," Hasso answered with a weary sigh. "Everyone is always so innocent, it makes you cry. Why you run off to Bucovin?"

"I wasn't going to Bucovin," Magar said. "I had a fight with my woman. I was going away when these Lenelli on horseback grabbed me and hauled me back here."

"Well?" Hasso asked Aderno.

The wizard used the little truth spell Hasso had seen before. Then he frowned. "I'm not sure. It doesn't say yes or no." His head came up and his nostrils twitched; he might have been a hunting hound taking a scent. "This reminds me of how that goddess-cursed Scanno masked his taste for Grenye-loving."

"Does it?" Hasso eyed Magar. "Where do we go now?"

"Where else? The torturers. They'll pull the truth out of him," Aderno answered.

Magar let out a horrified yowl. "I didn't do anything!" he wailed when he found words. "Don't hurt me! I didn't do anything!"

Aderno waited to see what Hasso did next. If Hasso didn't go along, the wizard would suspect *him* of liking the Grenye too well. But that wasn't what decided him. Bucovin was the enemy. If Magar worked for the Grenye there, he would know useful things, things King Bottero needed to find out. "Yes, we give him to them,"

Hasso said. Magar howled again. Ignoring him, Hasso went on, "They need to go after truth, not to hurt for the fun of hurting. They know the difference?"

"They know," Aderno assured him. He couldn't help adding, "I wasn't sure you did."

"Oh, yes," Hasso said. Like any army, the *Wehrmacht* squeezed enemy prisoners when it had to. So did the *Waffen*-SS, often more enthusiastically. "Sometimes prisoners say anything just to stop hurting," he warned. "Have to be careful, keep him away from others, weigh what he says, what they say." He used his hands as a set of scales coming into balance.

"Yes." Aderno nodded. "You *do* know something about this business. I wondered how soft you were."

"Because sometimes I think you are a jackass, that makes me soft?" Hasso asked. Aderno blinked. Hasso went on, "I know sometimes you think I am a jackass, too. I do not think that makes you soft." He jerked a thumb at Magar. "Have them work on him where the ones we question can hear him yell. When they hear that, they want to tell us everything we need to know, yes?"

Magar quailed from the wizard's smile. Hasso didn't blame him; he would have quailed, too, were those teeth and that twist of lip aimed his way. "A good thought, outlander. Yes, a very good thought."

Sure enough, the Grenye's shrieks pierced the interrogation chamber like so many spearthrusts. The other little dark men quivered whenever a new one rang out. Hasso let a couple of them go free after Aderno's magic showed they really were hunting or fishing when the Lenelli scooped them up. "If you are not King Bottero's enemy, I am not your enemy," he told them. "But if you are the king's enemy, my job is to make you sorry. I do—I *will do*—my job."

The ones he turned loose blubbered their thanks. Some of the ones he didn't turn loose went on claiming they had nothing to do with anything. Aderno's spell didn't always prove they were lying. It didn't exonerate them, either. It did… nothing. The ambiguity, the blankness, were plenty to make Hasso and Aderno suspicious. Those Grenye went to the torturer, too.

One peasant sang like a goldfinch. His name was Lupul, and he admitted everything as soon as he heard another Grenye yell in torment. Hasso could almost watch his ballocks crawl up into his belly. "Yes, I wanted to tell Bucovin what you were doing," he gabbled. "Why not? My people rule Bucovin. You blond robbers don't."

"We will," Aderno said. He turned to Hasso. "Now what do we do with him?"

"He should have a quick end, anyway," Hasso said. "Give him to the headsman." Lupul wailed. Hasso felt like wailing himself, though he didn't show it. If the Grenye were still clan against clan, tribe against tribe, beating them in detail would be easier. If they saw the struggle as all of them against the Lenelli… well, it sure didn't help.

VII

King Bottero didn't invade Bucovin along the causeway road through the swamp. He sent soldiers along it, but only to hold it against any counterthrusts from the Grenye to the east.

"Once we drive the savages back, we can send supplies and reinforcements up the causeway," he said.

Hasso nodded along with Bottero's marshals. The men of Bucovin could have blocked an advance along the causeway for a long time with only a handful of men. Hasso was relieved that the Lenelli could see as much for themselves. He didn't like having to point out their stupidities and blindnesses to them. Some of it was necessary—hell, a lot of it was necessary—but he recognized the difference between gadfly and pain in the ass.

He felt Orosei's ironic eye on him. The master-at-arms was no marshal, but Bottero would have had a mutiny on his hands if he tried to keep him in the dark. Did Orosei know what Hasso was thinking? It looked that way to the *Wehrmacht* officer.

Some of the lighter boats could go out into the marsh, at least partway. The rest unloaded their supplies, which went into more wagons. That made the army slower and more unwieldy than it had been, but Hasso didn't know what anybody could do about it. You needed *things* to fight, and you needed to haul them to where you fought.

His horse's hooves drummed on the planks of a bridge that took him over the Drammion to the south bank. Grenye farmers looked up from their fields to stare at the Lenelli riding by. In their dull homespun, the peasants seemed hardly more than domestic animals themselves. Looks could deceive, though—and probably did.

In Russia, the Germans hadn't paid much attention to the peasants. Once the Red Army was beaten, the new overlords would get around to the *muzhiks*. Then the partisans started dynamiting railroad lines and sniping from the woods.

How many of these Grenye would try to slip off and let Bucovin know which way the Lenelli were going? Too many—Hasso was sure of that. His security cordon had stopped a lot of the natives from succeeding as spies. Had it stopped all of them? Could it? He knew better.

He rode up alongside the king. Pointing out the peasants in the fields, he said, "More spy trouble."

"Well, we'll deal with it," Bottero answered. "By now, we're moving as fast as they are. They won't get to Bucovin much ahead of us."

"Yes, your Majesty," Hasso said—that was true. "I wished they like Lenelli better than they do."

"I don't care what they think about us. As long as they don't make trouble, they can think whatever they want," the king said.

In a way, he made sense. That offered the Grenye a safety valve. In another way, though ... "If they think bad things about Lenelli, maybe they try to do bad things, too," Hasso said.

"Let them try. We'll squash them. We've done it before—we can do it again." Bottero didn't lack confidence. From everything Hasso had seen, Lenelli rarely did. But the Germans had been sure they would have no trouble ruling Russia. Maybe they wouldn't have, had they won.

The Lenelli would be fine, too—as long as they kept winning. So it seemed to Hasso, anyway. If they ever started to lose...

With magic on their side, could they lose? Were the Grenye really forever barred from it? What about halfbreeds? There had been renegade wizards—Bottero had spoken of them. What if another one arose?

Hasso laughed at himself. Was he trying to see how much trouble he could borrow? The laughter died. Every time he'd done that in the *Wehrmacht*, there always turned out to be even more than he thought.

He had a tent for himself and Velona. He wondered why she'd come along. Was she a mascot for Bottero's army? Did she intend to fight? He knew she was strong enough and skilled enough to do that if she wanted to. She'd gone into Bucovin all alone, without an army at her back.

She'd gone in alone, yes, and she'd barely come out alive. If not for somebody literally falling into the swamp from another world, she wouldn't have. The Grenye would have caught her and killed her. What did that say?

Whatever it said, she didn't want to talk about it. All she wanted to do was joke. Holding her nose, she said, "You smell like a horse, my dear."

"So do you," Hasso answered. She did, too. But she also smelled like her-self—better than any other woman Hasso had ever known. Still bantering, he went on, "I love you anyhow."

That sobered her as effectively as a bucket of cold water in the face. "Be care-ful, Hasso Pemsel," she said, her voice altogether serious. "It is dangerous to love me too much. Deadly dangerous for a Lenello. Deadly dangerous for you, too, unless you're much more different from us than I think you are."

"How can anyone help it?" he asked.

"Men can't help it," she answered, without modesty and also without doubt. "That's part of what makes it so dangerous."

"Only part?" He kept trying to tease.

But Velona's nod was the next thing to somber. "Yes, only part. Remember, I am the goddess, too. A man, a mere man, who loves me is like a moth that loves a torch. He flies too close—and he burns."

"What about King Bottero?" No, the night of the summer solstice wouldn't go away. And the autumn equinox was coming. Would Bottero and Velona—and the goddess—celebrate it in front of the army? If they did, Hasso expected another drunken night and another painful morning.

In the dim lamplight, Velona's eyes went even wider and bigger than they were already. "By the goddess, no!" she exclaimed. "He enjoys me. I know that. But love me? He's not so foolish—he knows better."

"But I don't? Is that what you mean?" Hasso didn't try to hide his bitterness.

"Some of what I mean." Velona was nothing if not blunt. Maybe some of that had to do with the indwelling divinity she carried. More, though, Hasso judged, came from her own nature. She went on, "The other difference is, I like Bottero, but I really care for you. I don't want anything bad to happen to you because of me, but it may."

"If you care for someone" —he stayed away from the explosive word *love*— "you worry about things like that. I thank you." He gave her a gesture that was half a nod, half a salute.

She sighed. "You don't know what you're talking about. You're thinking of a broken heart. You can get a broken heart if you fall in love with a milkmaid. Even a Grenye in love with another ugly little Grenye can get a broken heart. But if the goddess ever has reason to be angry at you..." She left it there.

Hasso started to ask her what might happen. Maybe she'd already answered him, though. *Like a moth that loves a torch.* In his world, it would have been one more figure of speech. Here? He wasn't so sure he wanted to find out.

"Have to keep the goddess happy with me, then," he said, and reached for Velona. "Even if she does smell like a horse."

Laughing, Velona kissed him. But then she said, "Oh, no—that's just me." He thought about teasing her some more. It didn't seem like a good idea. Making love, on the other hand ... never seemed like a bad idea. He blew out the lamp.

***

Castle Pedio, hard by the border between Bottero's kingdom and Bucovin, was less a fortress than an observation post. It had the tallest towers Hasso had seen since coming to this new world. The reason was simple: those towers let the Lenelli see as far into Bucovin as they could.

Half a kilometer east of Castle Pedio rose another structure, one that looked a lot like it. Castle Galats, that one was called. The Grenye had built it. It was clumsier, heavier—the Grenye didn't have the tools or the skills the Lenelli did. But Castle Galats served its purpose: a signal fire at the top warned Bucovin that King Bottero was on his way by this route.

Hasso swore when he saw the fire. "Should take that castle by surprise when you decide to go to war," he told Bottero. "Then signal doesn't go out."

The king frowned. "You tell me that *now*. I see it makes sense, but why didn't you suggest it before?"

"I don't know this castle is here then," Hasso answered with a shrug. "Why don't you tell me about it?"

"Everyone must have thought you did know," Bottero said. "Anybody who knows anything about the border would." He stopped and sighed. "But you don't know anything much about the border, do you?"

"Only what I hear," Hasso said. "I don't hear about watchtowers—I'm sorry. But this is the first time I am here, your Majesty. I am stranger here. This place can still surprise me. It still *does* surprise me every day."

"Well, you surprise us, too—mostly in good ways," King Bottero said. "Except when you show you don't belong here, we think you do."

"Thank you," Hasso said, even if the king meant, *You don't seem* too *barbarous most of the time.* He pointed toward Castle Galats. "Do we take that place, or do we just mask it?"

"Mask it," Bottero said at once. "The men from Castle Pedio can do that. Neither place has a big garrison."

"However you like," Hasso said. "I just don't want any nasty surprises when we go by. I don't like getting nasty surprises. Giving is better." He pointed toward the beacon fire in the Grenye tower. "We don't give any for a while now."

"Sooner or later, we will." As usual, the king sounded confident. "When the Grenye try to face us, we'll make them pay. Your striking column will help, by the goddess."

"I hope so." Hasso had all kinds of reasons for saying that. He wanted to make Marshal Lugo look like the stick-in-the-mud, the French general in Lenello's clothing, that he was. He wanted to make his own stock rise. And he wanted to beat Bucovin, which would help him reach both those other goals.

The Grenye in Castle Galats jeered at the Lenelli as the invaders went by. Bottero's men stayed out of arrow range of the watchtower, so Hasso couldn't get a close look at the barbarians' equipment. Some of the Grenye seemed to be wearing iron, while others made do with bronze.

"They know iron when Lenelli come here?" Hasso asked Aderno.

"Yes, but they were just learning to use it." The wizard looked as if he'd just bitten down on a particularly sour pickle. "They've learned a lot more since—from us. They buy as much as they make themselves—from us."

"Why sell to them?"

"Some people care more about money than anything else, and don't care how they get it," Aderno replied. "Is it not the same in your world?"

Since it was, Hasso nodded and let it go. He looked around. "So we are inside Bucovin now?"

"Oh, yes." Aderno nodded, too. "Can't you see how shabby everything looks?"

To Hasso's eyes, the land on this side of the border seemed no different from the land on the other side. The peasants in Bottero's kingdom were also Grenye. The thatch-roofed cottages here looked the same as the ones farther east—to the *Wehrmacht* officer, anyway. "How do you mean?" he asked.

Aderno made an exasperated noise. "Anyone with eyes to see would know… Well, maybe you don't have eyes to see. All right, then." He started ticking points off on his fingers. "A lot of their crops here are native weeds. They don't grow the fine vegetables and good grains we brought with us from across the sea. You can live on millet and sorghum and squashes, but why would you want to?" He made a face.

Were the Grenye slobs, or was Aderno a snob? Some of both, probably, Hasso judged. He and his buddies had sneered at the Ivans for eating kasha and sunflower seeds … till they gradually realized that sneering at the Ivans wasn't such a good idea any which way. "I see," he said slowly.

"Do you? I hope so," Aderno said. "I was just getting started, though. Their livestock is inferior, too. They had no chickens before we came, only ducks—miserable things, too—and half-tame quail and partridges. Their pigs are only a short step up from wild boars. The sheep and cattle they breed, they stole from us. Their native horses are barely even ponies. And they have no unicorns at all. They can't ride them, and unicorns also come from across the sea." He laid a hand on the side of his mount's white neck.

Europeans would have said the same kinds of things about Red Indians. But how much of what the Grenye had was really that much worse than its Lenello equivalents, and how much just seemed unfamiliar to Aderno and his folk? Hasso didn't know the answer. He did know Aderno didn't even see the question.

"Are you sure the Grenye can't ride unicorns?" he asked. An edge came into his voice as he added, "Remember, not long ago you say that about me."

This time, Aderno might have been sucking on the mother of all lemons. "I was wrong about you, and it cost me. I am not wrong about the Grenye, by the goddess." He paused thoughtfully. "Maybe I was wrong when I said they had no unicorns. They've stolen a few from us, the way they steal big horses to improve their herds, and it's possible that they've bred the unicorns, too. But no one has ever seen a Grenye on unicornback, not in all the years since Lenelli crossed the sea."

He sounded positive. Hasso, who'd been here a matter of months, was in no position to contradict him. "I see," the German said again—let Aderno make whatever he wanted of that.

Before long, Hasso saw something else, too: the first armed Grenye he'd spotted in the field. They weren't an army, only scouts—a handful of men on horseback who kept their eye on King Bottero's army but stayed as far away from it as they could while still doing their job. Every so often, one of them would ride off, no doubt to report to their superiors, while another took his place.

"We should catch some of them," Hasso said. "We should find out what they know. We should find out what they think."

"We should find out *if* they think," Aderno said scornfully. "Besides, they'll just scurry off into the woods if we chase them. You see how close to the trees they stay?"

"Yes." Hasso *had* noticed that. "Can't you bring them in by magic, though?"

He'd rarely seen any Lenello at a loss. He did now with Aderno. "By the goddess, I don't know," the wizard said. "It would be child's play on the other side of the border. Here? Well, I can find out."

Back in his own world, Hasso might have asked a radio technician to find the direction from which a Soviet signal was coming. Aderno set to work with that same kind of unflustered competence. He rummaged first in his belt pouches and then in his saddlebags for what he needed. He found a chunk of amber, a small stone that showed different colors depending on how the sun struck it—an opal, Hasso realized—and a smooth, rounded pebble that looked thoroughly ordinary.

"What is that?" Hasso asked, pointing at it.

"A capon's gizzard stone. A five-year-old capon's gizzard stone," Aderno answered with relentless precision. "It aids in gaining one's desire from any man. The other two, taken together, will make you victorious against your adversaries."

Oh, yeah? Hasso thought. Back home, he wouldn't have believed it, though he knew plenty of high-ranking Nazis were gaga for the occult and the supernatural. Much good that had done them, or the *Reich*. The way Germany was collapsing seemed to him the best argument in the world—in that world—against sorcery.

But things were different here. On the back of his unicorn, Aderno started juggling the three stones. Hasso Pemsel thought that was the funniest thing he'd ever seen, especially when the wizard thrust out his right index finger at a Grenye rider while all three stones were in the air at the same time.

It might have looked ridiculous. Hell, it *did* look ridiculous. That didn't mean it didn't work. The Grenye from Bucovin—the wild Grenye, the Lenelli would have called him—didn't want to ride up to King Bottero's army. He didn't want to approach the wizard on the unicorn. Hasso could see that more and more plainly as the fellow rode closer and closer. No matter how unwilling he was, he did what Aderno required of him, not what *he* wanted to do.

"Well, well." Aderno sounded pleased with himself. "Isn't that nice. Isn't that something?"

"Something, yes." Hasso wasn't sure what. He was sure it made his hackles rise. But as long as it worked, how much did that matter?

"Here you are, Grenye," Aderno said as the horseman came up alongside him and Hasso. "Do you speak Lenello?"

"Yes, I speak it." The Grenye's accent was thicker than Hasso's, but he made himself understood.

"Tell me your name," Aderno said, and then, in an aside to Hasso, "One more sorcerous hold on him."

Again, the Grenye didn't want to but found he had no choice. "I am called Nebun," he said.

Instead of a Lenello-style conical helm, he wore a leather cap strengthened with iron strips. His mailshirt showed less skill than the elegant armor Lenelli wore.

His sword, though … Hasso would have guessed a Lenello smith forged it, for it seemed the same as the ones Bottero's soldiers carried. What had Lenin said about capitalists selling the Soviet Union the rope it would use to hang them? No, some things didn't change a bit from one world to another.

"What are your orders, Nebun?" Aderno asked, and twisted his fingers in a certain sign. Again to Hasso, he added, "Keeps him docile."

So it did—or it seemed to, anyhow. Nebun answered readily enough: "To spy out your force. To see how strong you are."

"Tell your superiors we have twice the numbers you really see," Hasso put in. "Tell them you fear for your land. Do not let them persuade you of anything else no matter what they say. Do you follow me?"

"Yes, sir." Nebun might have been talking to a superior. "I will obey you as I would obey my own father."

Hasso glanced over to Aderno. "Can I rely on that?" he asked—in German, so the Grenye wouldn't understand.

Aderno's magic let him follow the alien tongue. He nodded. "I think so. You might almost have set a spell on him." He glanced over at Nebun. "For all I know, you did. You are not without power, as my lost goldpiece reminds me."

The idea that he might be able to work magic made Hasso want to laugh. The extra gold jingling in his belt pouch was a good reason to take the notion seriously, though. "Go, Nebun," he said. "Go back to your chiefs. Tell them how strong we are. Tell them we are very strong. Tell them you see all this with your own eyes. Go now."

"I go." Nebun booted his pony up into a walk, and then into a trot. He wasn't such a smooth rider as most of the Lenelli, but he got the job done.

"That should confuse them," Hasso said. "If they think they know things that are not so, they get confused. They make mistakes."

"If they think they know…" Aderno raised a wry eyebrow. "I get confused, too."

"Finding out what is really so is important," Hasso said. "The one who knows that better usually wins."

Inevitably, the German invasion of Russia came to mind again. The *Wehrmacht* thought Stalin had far fewer divisions than he proved able to pull out of his hat. By the time the first winter's fighting was under way, the Germans had destroyed as many divisions as they'd believed the Russians could raise. But more Ivans kept coming at them, and more, and still more … and now, if Hasso were magically transported back to Berlin, it would be a Berlin under the Hammer and Sickle. Anything was better than that.

"One thing that is really so I already told you—we can work magic and the Grenye can't," Aderno said. "Now you see it with your own eyes."

"I see that you can work magic and that that Grenye can't," Hasso half-agreed. He said nothing about his own magical abilities, if any. "But if this is so wonderful, why don't Lenelli take Falticeni a long time ago?"

The wizard gave him a dirty look but no answer. Not even Velona had an answer for that, or so it seemed. *If your men are so much better, why didn't they take Moscow?* How many times would people throw that in Germany's face? The surviving veterans would blame the winter, the Russian T-34 tank's wide tracks, the Siberian troops brought in to stiffen the Soviet line… everyone and everything but themselves. No, some things didn't change a bit from one world to another.

***

"Do the Grenye in Bucovin worship the goddess?" Hasso asked Velona at breakfast the next morning. "Or do they have their own gods, the ones they have before you Lenelli come here?"

She sipped from a mug of beer. Hasso still missed coffee and tobacco. This was this world's New World, wasn't it? Why didn't it have tobacco in it? Whatever the reason, it didn't. After swallowing, Velona said, "Some worship the goddess. They've seen she has true power. Their old gods are just statues of stone or wood. Some of them look pretty, but what do they do?"

She might have been a Hebrew prophet mocking the local Baals. No sooner had that thought crossed Hasso's mind than he laughed at himself. If the prophets had any descendants, the *Reich* would have settled most of them once and for all. You didn't ask questions about what the *Einsatzgruppen* were up to. You didn't really need to ask. The big wheels were serious about making sure the lands they ruled were *Judenfrei*.

But the goddess here wasn't sleepy like the long-ignored Baals of Palestine. She didn't ignore her worshipers, the way the Jews' God forgot about them. She was as real as a river. No wonder the Grenye started bowing down before her. The wonder was that any of them stayed stubborn enough to keep on following whatever gods they'd had before.

That brought up another question. "What goed—no, *went*, curse it—wrong when you went into Bucovin before?" Hasso asked.

Before answering, Velona smiled at him. "Your Lenello is getting better all the time."

"Baptism by total immersion," Hasso said in German. It wouldn't have meant anything to Velona even in her language. But when he needed to use Lenello to talk at all, he had the biggest incentive in the world for getting fluent as fast as he could. He could have used Aderno to translate … if he and the wizard didn't rub each other the wrong way all the time. He'd learned the language faster because he was doing it on his own. With an effort, he brought his mind back to the business at hand. "Bucovin."

"Yes, Bucovin." Velona stopped smiling. "I don't know what went wrong. I told you that before, I think. Things … stopped working, that was all. The whole country might have been trying to see through me, and finally it did."

"How do you stop it?" Hasso asked.

"If I knew, I would tell you," she answered. "Once we settle our knights on the land, once we have our wizards in the towns, things should take care of themselves. I hope so, anyhow."

Hasso didn't know what to say to that. The Germans had been sure that, once they seized Moscow, things would take care of themselves. Then, after Moscow didn't fall, they'd been just as sure that grabbing Stalingrad would set everything right. Then, after Stalingrad didn't fall … Hasso forced his mind out of that unhappy groove.

Saddling his horse and getting going did the job. The tackle the Lenelli used wasn't the same as what he'd known in Germany. The way horses and people were made dictated a lot about bits and reins and saddles and straps and stirrups, but not everything. He had to think about what he was doing here, more than he would have with familiar equipment.

The land was new, too. Far off to the east, he saw mountains against the horizon. Were they visible from Castle Svarag? If they were, he didn't remember them. A Lenello told him that was the Palmorz Range. "What is on the other side of it?" Hasso asked.

"Well, I don't exactly know," the horseman answered. "Not many Lenelli have been over it, and you know what liars travelers are. Could be anything." He shook his head. "Well, I don't think there's mermaids. Dragons, though, maybe."

"Dragons?" Hasso had seen them on everything from banners to belt buckles. But he could have seen them on things like that in Germany, too. "Are they real?"

"I hope to spit," the Lenello said, or words to that effect. "Didn't one burn down a village in King Cherso's realm three winters back? Wouldn't he have burned another one if a catapult didn't get lucky and put a bolt through his wing and make him fly away?"

King Cherso's realm lay well to the north of Bottero's. That was all Hasso knew about it. No, now he knew one thing more: it had a dragon problem, or had had one three winters back. "If the catapult missed, what would the dragon have done?" he asked—he was starting to get the hang of the subjunctive.

"Torn up everything in sight, I expect," the Lenello said. "That's what dragons do when they get pissed off, right?"

"I suppose," Hasso answered—a handy phrase that could mean anything or nothing. Hasso approved of clichés. They helped him get his meaning across, even when he hardly had one.

By the way Bottero's army behaved in Bucovin, it might have been an angry dragon. A lot of Grenye farmers fled before it, taking as much of their livestock with them as they could. The Lenelli grabbed everything the locals left behind. The pigs and occasional cattle and sheep went into the army's larder. So did the ducks and odd chickens and geese. So did all the grain the soldiers could find, regardless of type. The horses and donkeys were mostly too small for Lenelli to ride, but the invaders took them anyhow, to help haul wagons and carts.

And farmhouse after farmhouse, village after village, went up in flames. Bottero's soldiers took a childlike delight in arson. Hasso hadn't known any soldiers, Germans or Russians or Poles or Frenchmen or British, who didn't. He would have bet the Grenye got hard-ons watching things burn, too. But there was more to it than that.

The way the Lenelli went about torching houses and smithies and taverns and shops, they might have felt the Grenye had no right to build such things. No, it wasn't that they might have felt the Grenye had no right to do it—they *did* feel that way, and weren't shy about saying so.

"Goddess-cursed savages," a sergeant growled as he touched a burning brand to the overhanging thatch of a farmhouse roof. He swore some more when the thatch, which was damp, sent up a cloud of thick gray smoke without catching the way he wanted it to. In the end, persistence paid, and he got the farmhouse blazing. "They've got their nerve, pretending to be as good as we are."

"Where do you want them to live?" Hasso asked, genuinely curious. "In holes in the ground?"

The sergeant spat. "They'll be in holes in the ground when we're done with 'em, all right. Only thing is, they won't be living."

Bucovin affronted Aderno at least as much as it did the underofficer. The wizard was more articulate about it—or at least mouthier. "Do you know what this land reminds me of?" he said as the Lenelli rode past the funeral pyre of a village.

"No, but you're going to tell me, aren't you?" Hasso said.

Aderno missed the sarcasm. "Yes, I am," he said, and Hasso carefully didn't smile. "You've seen the paintings we do, haven't you?"

"Oh, yes. Fine work." Hasso sounded more enthusiastic than he was. Some of the canvases he'd seen in Drammen did show talent, but the Lenelli were just starting to understand perspective. To someone who'd admired work by Raphael and Rembrandt and Rubens, among many others, these people were no better than promising amateurs.

"I should hope so." Confident of his own folk's superiority, Aderno heard enthusiasm whether it was there or not. "Well, the Grenye remind me of a twelve-year-old trying to copy, say, Tibero's *Coming Ashore*. You know the painting I mean?"

"Oh, yes," Hasso said again. To his eye, the artist had tried to do too much in not enough space. Ships and heroic Lenelli and savage Grenye and waves and animals peering from the forest … and the naked goddess watching everything next to the sun. Sometimes art was more about knowing what to leave out than about what all to put in. Tibero wasn't a bad artist, but he'd never figured that out.

"Well, if a child tries to copy a masterpiece, all you get is a sorry mess," the wizard said. "And that's what Bucovin is—a sorry mess."

Hasso nodded. And the Lenelli were making it a worse mess. They didn't care what the Grenye thought of them because of their fondness for arson. The *Wehrmacht* hadn't cared what the Ivans thought when it marched into Russia, either. Later… Later turned out to be too late.

***

A Lenello died of lockjaw not long after Bottero's army entered Bucovin. Hasso wondered how the warrior managed to puncture himself. With so much manure around, a tiny wound was all it took. No vaccine or antitoxin here—even the idea for them was a universe away. Hasso hadn't seen or heard of smallpox in this world, for which he was duly grateful. He did know that cowpox could keep you from coming down with the horrible disease. And, except for first aid, his knowledge of medicine started and stopped right there.

He wondered when the Grenye would try to fight back. Or would they at all? Would they try to suck the Lenelli into their heartland and let winter deal with them, the way the Russians did with Napoleon? How bad were winters here, anyway? Milder than Russia's, anyhow, from what Velona said.

"Cursed Grenye are cowardly scuts," King Bottero said when Hasso asked him what the enemy was up to. "If they can keep from fighting us, chances are they will."

Not half an hour after the king said that, an excited courier brought word that a Grenye scout had popped up from behind a bush, shot an arrow into the unarmored leg of a Lenello scout, and managed to get away in the confusion that followed. "Miserable skulker!" The man who brought the news sounded furious at the native. "Stinking sneak!"

Remembering how the partisans went about their business in German-occupied Russia, Hasso said, "Teamsters need to be careful. Outriders need to be careful. The Grenye may go after people who don't expect to fight."

"Only proves they're cowards," the king said.

"If they hurt us, how much does that matter?" Hasso asked. "War is not about being brave. Not all about that, anyway."

Bottero stared at him, an uncomprehending gape he'd seen too many times. "What *is* war about, then?" the king demanded.

"Winning." Hasso's one-word answer came without the least hesitation. It was the answer of a man who'd seen his comrades show more courage than humanly possible in the grinding retreat across Russia and Poland and Germany itself. It was the answer of a man who'd seen that courage on display in Berlin, where in the end it would do no good at all. "Winning, your Majesty," the *Wehrmacht* officer repeated. "In the end, nothing else counts."

King Bottero still didn't get it. "Well, of course we'll win," he said. "How we do it counts, too."

Hasso saw only one thing to say to that, and he said it: "Yes, your Majesty." He didn't believe it for a minute. A few Lenelli—Orosei sprang to mind—knew better. The rest of them were full of chivalric nonsense ... except when they were pillaging Bucovinan farmhouses and firing Bucovinan villages. That was the small change of war, though. In battle, they could show their style.

His deep attacking column let the Lenelli show their style. Bottero had probably said he could try it out for just that reason. After everything Hasso had seen on all the fronts of Europe, he'd given up on style. Only results mattered.

The natives seemed to agree with him. They dug pits in the road ahead of the advancing Lenello army and mounted sharp stakes in the bottom. Those killed one horse and wounded a rider. Then Bottero's men started to be more careful.

When they saw that the roadway looked suspicious, they pulled off into the fields to either side of the dirt track.

Before long, the Grenye started digging pits in the fields, too. Those were harder to spot than the ones in the road. They killed several horses and a couple of Lenelli. They also infuriated the survivors.

Some of the Lenelli wanted to kill all the Bucovinans they found from then on to warn the others not to do such things. Velona was in that camp, which worried Hasso. She did make it plain she was speaking for herself, not for the goddess. That being so, Bottero had the nerve to say no. "After we conquer this country, who will till the land if we use up all the peasants?" he demanded, and no one had an answer for him.

Frightfulness ... Hasso had mixed feelings about it. The Germans had used it widely, of course. Sometimes it intimidated people into behaving. Other times the hatred it stirred up only made occupied areas boil with resistance. You couldn't know which ahead of time.

Frustration and anger built up in Bottero's army because there were no enemy soldiers to attack. And then, all at once, there were. Lenello scouts reported a large force of Grenye ahead, blocking Bottero's advance deeper into Bucovin.

When the news came back, the Lenelli burst into cheers. "Now they'll pay for screwing around with us!" a horseman yelled.

"Now we'll see how well your famous attacking column works," Marshal Lugo told Hasso. The German had no trouble understanding the words behind the words. *Now we'll see how smart you really are*, the marshal meant.

VIII

Battle came early the next morning. The Lenelli eagerly pushed forward. King Bottero didn't have to harangue them to get them moving. They *wanted* to hit the Grenye. They were champing at the bit for the chance. They seemed more enthusiastic about fighting than any *Wehrmacht* or even *Waffen*-SS troops Hasso had ever seen.

He wondered why. Arrows and swords weren't bullets and shell fragments, but they could still dish out some pretty horrendous wounds. But nobody in this world looked forward to dying at a ripe old age. Dying, however you did it, was commonly slow and painful here, the way it had been in Europe up until not long before Hasso's time. If you died on the battlefield, at least it was over in a hurry. That was bound to have something to do with things.

Hasso got a glimpse of the rest when the Bucovinan battle line came into sight. The natives didn't seem eager for battle. They hadn't rushed forward the way the Lenelli had. They aimed to defend, not to attack.

Just seeing them infuriated Bottero's men. It was as if the Germans had faced an army of chimpanzees or Jews. "Think they can stand against us, do they?" Aderno growled. "Well, they'd better think twice, that's all."

Velona didn't say anything at all. She stared out toward the assembled Grenye, stared and stared and stared. Her eyes showed white all around the iris. Her breath rasped in her throat; each inhalation made her chest heave, and not in any erotically exciting way. She looked like a woman about to have, or maybe in the throes of, an epileptic fit.

She looks like a woman the goddess is about to possess, Hasso thought, and gooseflesh prickled up on his arms.

Then—anticlimax—the Bucovinans sent a rider forward under sign of truce. They didn't use a white flag here. Instead, the horseman carried a leafy branch, which he waved over his head. He paused right at the edge of bowshot.

King Bottero leaned over to speak to a herald: a man who'd got his job with leather lungs. "Come ahead and say your say!" the herald bawled. "We won't kill you ... yet."

The Bucovinan envoy rode closer. Was he here to get a good look at the Lenello line of battle? Hasso had disguised the assault column as well as he could; lancers

85

were deployed all along the line, and the ones at the front rode with lances raised. The men farther back in the column kept their lances down so they would be harder to notice from a distance.

"Why have you invaded our land?" the native asked in good Lenello. "We are not at war. Go back to your own homes. Leave us alone. Leave us at peace."

How many nations that found themselves suddenly at war made the same agonized request? Almost all of them, chances were. Hasso had heard that, when German invaded Russia on 22 June 1941, a Soviet diplomat plaintively asked, "What did we do to deserve this?" The Ivans had done plenty; no doubt about it. But Hasso's wry amusement lasted no longer than a heartbeat. How could it last, when things turned out so disastrously different from what the *Führer* had in mind? If anyone in his own world asked that question these days, it was the Germans themselves.

King Bottero had never had to worry about godless Russian hordes killing and raping their way through his country. Because he hadn't, he laughed in the Bucovinan herald's face. "This is not your land, little man," he said. "It is ours, and we have come to take it."

The native's mouth tightened. A flush further darkened his already-swarthy cheeks. By the standards of the Lenelli, he *was* a little man; he was at least twenty centimeters shorter than Hasso, and Hasso was a shrimp next to Bottero and a lot of his warriors. But the Grenye's voice remained calm as he answered, "It is not yours till you take it, your Majesty … if you do."

Bottero laughed again. "Oh, we will, little man. We will. Tell me your name, so that after the fight I can claim you for my personal slave."

"I am called Trandafir, your Majesty," the Bucovinan replied. "You need not tell me your name—I already know it. I will take your words back to my lord." He turned his pony and rode off toward his own line.

Bottero stared after him—stared and then glared. The king needed longer than he should have to realize the native had given him the glove. Maybe he had trouble believing a Grenye would have the nerve to imply he'd take Bottero as *his* personal slave.

"By the goddess, that wretch will be no bondsman," Bottero snarled. "I will make sure he is dead, the way I would with any snapping dog."

"And well you should, your Majesty," Marshal Lugo said. "He offered you intolerable insult." He didn't seem to notice that the king had insulted the herald first. The Lenelli weren't good about noticing such things. The Germans hadn't been good about noticing them in Russia, either. Why bother? The Ivans were nothing but *Untermenschen*, weren't they?

Four years earlier, the answer to that question would have seemed obvious. As a matter of fact, it still did. But the obvious answer now wasn't the same as it had been in 1941.

To keep from thinking about that, Hasso watched Trandafir ride back to his line. Bucovin used banners of dark blue and ocher. The *Wehrmacht* officer wasn't surprised to see their envoy ride over to where those banners clustered thickest.

The Grenye king or general or whatever he was would be there.

Passing on Bottero's reply took only a moment. The natives couldn't have expected anything else. The Lenelli wouldn't have come here in arms intending to turn around and go home again. But here as in the world from which Hasso came, the forms had to be observed.

Horns blared along the Bucovinan battle line, first in that center group of banners and then up and down its whole length. The timbre wasn't quite the same as that of the Lenelli horns; even summoning men to imminent battle, it sounded mournful in Hasso's ears. The horns themselves looked different. They had a strange curve to them, one that didn't look quite right to the German.

Regardless of whether the horn calls seemed strange to him, they did what they were supposed to do: they roused the enemy army to defiance. The Bucovinans shouted their hatred and derision at the oncoming Lenelli. When they brandished their weapons, sunlight and fire seemed to ripple up and down their ranks. They might be barbarians, but they looked and sounded ready to fight.

And so were the Lenelli. Their trumpets roared forth familiar notes. These tunes weren't the ones the *Wehrmacht* used, but they were ones the *Wehrmacht* might have used. They did the same thing German trumpets would have done: they got Hasso ready to fight. Bottero's men were ready, too. The threats they shouted at the Grenye would have horrified the men who framed the Geneva Convention.

Velona rode out ahead of the Lenello battle line. She pointed toward the Grenye. "Forward!" she bugled. "Forward to victory!" Was she talking, or was the goddess speaking through her? Hasso thought he heard the goddess, but he wasn't sure.

As soon as Velona gave the war cry, she galloped straight at the Bucovinan line. The rest of the Lenelli—and Hasso—thundered after her.

***

A cavalry charge! There'd been a few even in the war from which Hasso had contrived to extract himself. He'd never imagined he would take part in one, though. He looked back over his shoulder at the striking column. Could he really translate panzer tactics into ones knights and swordsmen could use? He was going to find out.

He'd hoped the Bucovinans would stand there and receive the charge. No such luck—they knew better. They'd been fighting the Lenelli for a long time now. They'd learned a lot from the invaders from overseas. They had armored men on horseback, too—not a lot, but some—and sent them forward to blunt the big blonds' onslaught.

And they had a devil of a lot of infantry waiting there behind their horsemen. Some of the foot soldiers had spears. Some had swords. Quite a few carried what looked like scythes and pitchforks. Most of the men with real weapons wore helmets and carried shields. The rest had no more than they would have worn in the fields. Maybe that would have been enough against other Grenye. Against Bottero's hard-bitten professionals? Hasso didn't think so.

The Bucovinan knights were a different story. They were pros themselves. Their horses were smaller than the ones the Lenelli rode, but they knew what to do with them. They handled their lances as well as the Lenelli did. Seeing a three-meter toothpick aimed straight at his chest gave Hasso the cold horrors.

He rose in the stirrups and gave the enemy knight a short burst from his submachine gun. The Grenye's lance went flying. He threw up his hands and pitched from the saddle. He was probably dead before he hit the ground.

Hasso almost got pitched from the saddle, too. Staid gelding or not, his horse didn't like a gun going off right behind its ears. But the German had expected that. He hadn't ridden much, but he knew enough to fight the horse back down onto all fours when it tried to rear. He wished he'd had enough ammunition to familiarize the beast to the dreadful noise, but he didn't. Once his cartridges were gone, they were gone forever.

He'd better get the best use from them he could, then. He shot the next Bucovinan in front of him. Then he shot one of the natives who was bearing down on Velona. She rode into battle with a goddess' confidence—with *the* goddess' confidence?—that nothing could hurt her. That Grenye hadn't seem convinced. But Hasso made as sure as he could that Velona stayed right.

He shot two more lancers in quick succession. After that, the Bucovinans got the idea and stayed away from him—which helped open a gap in their line of horsemen. "Come on!" Hasso yelled, and rode through it. The rest of the striking column followed him. He aimed just to the left of the thicket of enemy banners. "There!" He pointed. "That's where we'll break through!"

The Bucovinan foot soldiers saw the column coming. They couldn't very well not see it, and they couldn't very well not understand what a breakthrough there would mean. Shouts in that guttural, unintelligible—at least to Hasso—language filled the air. The natives who had spears lowered them in a desperate effort to hold off the onrushing knights.

Back in the Middle Ages, the Swiss hedgehog—rank on rank of long pikes, a new version of the Macedonian phalanx—could hold knights at bay. The men of Bucovin were trying to improvise that kind of defense on the fly. It didn't work. Hasso would have been surprised if they really expected it to work. If you were a brave man in a bad spot, you did whatever you could and hoped for the best. He knew all about that.

A shouting little man set himself, pointing his spear in the general direction of Hasso's gelding. The *Wehrmacht* officer shot him in the face from less than ten meters away. The Bucovinan didn't even have time to look surprised before he toppled. The spear hit the ground before he did, but only by a split second.

Hasso shot three more Grenye, one after the next. Then he changed magazines on his Schmeisser again. He was down to his last one, the last one in all this world. But he'd done what he needed to do—he'd breached the Bucovinan line. And the Lenelli poured into the gap he'd made.

No denying the natives were brave. They swarmed toward the lancers, trying to spear them, to slash them, to pull them out of the saddle and stomp them to death. They didn't have a chance. Maybe they didn't realize it. Maybe they just didn't care. The Lenelli spitted them like partridges or knocked them over the head with the shafts of their lances or cut them down with long straight swords. Warhorses smashed dark faces and dashed out brains with iron-shod hooves.

Aderno's unicorn had blood on its horn.

Where was the King of Bucovin or the chief or whatever he called himself? Hasso looked to the right. He saw a man in fancy regalia, and fired several shots at him. With luck, he could decapitate the enemy army, the enemy state, on the spot and make everything that came afterwards a hell of a lot easier.

He couldn't tell whether his bullets struck home. After a moment, not just Bucovinans stood between him and the man he thought to be their sovereign. Hard-charging Lenello knights also blocked his view. The Grenye went on fighting as ferociously as the Poles had in the first few days of the war.

All the ferocity in the world hadn't done the Poles one goddamn bit of good. The harder they fought, the faster they died. And all the courage in the world wouldn't help the Bucovinans, either. Hasso shot one more man. Then he let out a wordless whoop.

"We're through the savages!" a Lenello shouted—all the words that mattered.

"Now we swing in!" Hasso called. Even if he hadn't shot the Bucovinan leader, King Bottero's men might capture him. That would do the job just about as well. "Swing in!" he yelled again, and pointed to show what he meant.

The striking column had practiced this maneuver over and over on the meadows outside of Drammen. The Lenelli should have been able to bring it off in their sleep. And about half of them did turn in against the enemy center. But the other half turned out, against the wing they'd cut off.

Hasso screamed abuse at the Lenelli. He called them every kind of idiot under the sun. They paid no attention to him. German troops probably wouldn't have screwed up like that. If they had, their officers would have straightened them out in a hurry.

Here, the officers didn't seem to see the problem. "The fighting's good every which way," Marshal Lugo yelled—he was there, all right, and battling hard.

"Yes, but—" Hasso did some more swearing. Were they all blind?

He didn't need long to realize blindness wasn't the problem. His own medieval ancestors probably would have fought the same boneheaded way. *There's the enemy*, they would have thought. *Let's go bash him over the head.* And if the battle might have turned out better had they bashed him here instead of there, they wouldn't have got all hot and bothered about it. They were having a good time fighting any old way.

And so were the Lenelli now. The rest of their line had come to grips with the Grenye, which meant the enemy couldn't turn and give all his attention to the riders who'd broken into the rear. As Hasso had hoped, the men of Bucovin were getting smashed between hammer and anvil.

But they weren't getting smashed as thoroughly as he'd had in mind. Sure, Bottero's warriors were chewing up that cut-off wing. The center, though, held longer and more stoutly than he'd thought it could. When people there did start to flee, a stubborn rear guard made sure they had an open escape route.

"Don't worry—we'll get 'em," a Lenello said when Hasso swore again. "See? The lord's banners are still in place."

Dear God in heaven! Which side is supposed to be the barbarians? Hasso wondered. "The banners are there, *ja*," he said with more patience than he'd thought he had in him. "But does that mean the lord is still there under them?"

"Huh?" The Lenello trooper really was slow on the uptake. After much too long, he went, "Oh." Then he got angry—not at himself, but at the Bucovinans. "Why, those cursed, sneaky sons of whores!"

"Right," Hasso said tightly. If you expected the enemy to act dumb all the time, you'd get your head handed to you. The Ivans had driven that lesson home with a sledgehammer.

A Bucovinan pikeman, seeing Hasso on a horse without a lance, rushed at him shouting something unintelligible that probably wasn't a compliment. As so many of the men from Bucovin had found out the hard way, being without a lance didn't mean he was unarmed. He shot the Grenye down. By now, his horse didn't jump out of its skin every time he fired.

But the Schmeisser ran dry just then. Automatically, Hasso reached for another clip. That was when he remembered he didn't have one. He felt much more naked without the submachine gun than he would have without his mailshirt and the *Wehrmacht* helmet with a nasal riveted on. He slung the Schmeisser over his back; even though it was useless now and would be forevermore, he couldn't stand to throw it away. Out came his sword. With it in his hand, he looked every inch the warrior. Maybe that would be enough to keep the Bucovinans from harrying him. After all, they couldn't—he hoped to God they couldn't—tell at a glance what a lousy swordsman he was.

Velona's sword was red with blood. Scarlet drops flew from the blade as she brandished it. Her face bore the same intent, inward, seeking expression it did just before she came. Was she communing with the goddess, or did she *really* enjoy fighting? Hasso wondered whether he wanted to know.

More and more Grenye broke away from the battle and made off toward the east. Some went singly, others in knots of five or ten or twenty. The men who stuck together and still showed fight had a better chance of getting away in one piece. The Lenelli were like any soldiers in any world—they went after what looked like easy victims first. Why chance getting hurt when you didn't have to?

A Bucovinan came up to Hasso with his helmet hanging on the point of his spear. "Peace," he said in halting Lenello. "Peace, please."

Hasso realized he didn't know the rules for taking prisoners here. But that question no sooner formed in his mind than it got answered. Not ten meters away, a Lenello tapped a surrendering Grenye on the shoulder with his sword.

In Hasso's world, he might have been knighting the enemy warrior. Not here. Here, with a doglike grin of relief, the Grenye threw down his weapons and kissed his captor's hand. Then, hands clasped behind his head, he shuffled off toward the rear.

Now that Hasso knew how to do it, he did it. The Grenye in front of him also looked massively relieved. He understood that. Deciding to give up wasn't the hard part. Getting the guys on the other side to accept your surrender was. Plenty of would-be POWs got killed. It wasn't always ill-will. Sometimes the winners were just too busy to bother with prisoners, so they disposed of them instead.

"Thank you! Thank you! I is your slave!" the Bucovinan said as he fervently kissed Hasso's hand. Did he mean that, or was he only being polite? In his own world, Hasso would have known the answer. Here ... Well, he'd worry about it later.

He jerked his thumb in the direction the other captive had taken. "Go there," he said. Away the Grenye went. He too put his hands behind his head. It wasn't quite the same as raising them high, but it evidently meant the same thing.

Hasso looked around to see if any more fighting was left. There wasn't much. As he watched, a Lenello used the broken shaft of his lance to smash in a Bucovinan's skull. No, surrendering here was no easier than it was in Hasso's world. The big blond knights with the brutal one laughed and cheered him on.

Lenello foot soldiers and dismounted lancers walked over the field. Every so often, they stooped to plunder or to finish off a wounded Bucovinan. Hasso's men had done that with the Ivans often enough. Here, a knife across the throat did duty for a bullet in the back of the neck.

The Lenelli also gave the *coup de grâce* to some of their own wounded men: those too badly hurt to have any hope of recovering. Hasso had seen that happen, too. It happened more often here. German doctors could do things nobody here had ever dreamt of. He made a note to himself not to get wounded here. Then he laughed. If he knew how to guarantee that...

Somebody slapped him on the back, almost hard enough to pitch him off his horse. "We did it!" Nornat yelled. "The column worked. Your scheme worked!" He sounded overjoyed and surprised at the same time.

"Good men make it work," Hasso said. The Lenello cavalry captain grinned and bowed in the saddle. Hasso wouldn't have wanted to try that himself. He hadn't been kidding, though. Grinning back, he went on, "Commanders get the glory. Lancers do the hard part and make commanders look good."

"Goddess only knows that's the truth," Nornat said. "Too many marshals can't see it, though. They think the sun rises and sets on them. I could name names, but...."

But you'd put your ass in a sling if you did, Hasso thought. But if Nornat wasn't thinking of brave but hidebound Marshal Lugo, Hasso would have been mightily surprised. "We could do better," he said. "We should do better. Column should all turn in on center, not out on wing." He gestured with his hands. "We do that, maybe we catch enemy, uh, lord. He can't get away."

"Well, yes." Nornat sounded as if he was humoring him. "Don't get too upset, though. We walloped the snot out of the savages the way it was."

Somebody—a Frenchman?—said the good was the enemy of the best. A solid victory satisfied Nornat. Hasso wanted more. He wanted to annihilate the enemy, the way Hannibal annihilated the Romans at Cannae.

Ever since before the First World War, German officers made that battle their model. Hasso understood why—who'd ever done better? But despite the triumph, Carthage lost the war. How many officers who carefully memorized every detail of Hannibal's double envelopment remembered that?

Hasso got down from his horse. "You! Come here!" he called to the first foot soldier he saw. When the man obeyed, Hasso tossed him the reins. "Here. Hold these for me till I get back."

"Yes, lord," the foot soldier said—the only possible answer. But then he went on, "What about my chance to loot?"

That was a fair question. Hasso dug in his belt pouch and pulled out one of the gold coins he'd won from the wizards. It bore the jowly image of Bottero's father. "Here. You might do better than this, but you might not, too."

The Lenello made the goldpiece disappear. Grinning, he said, "You may be a foreigner, and you sure talk funny, but you're a sport."

"Thanks," Hasso said dryly, and began his tour of the battlefield.

He'd walked plenty of fields in his own world, wherever victory let him do it. The last year and a half of the war, he thanked God every time he got away from a battlefield in one piece. He hadn't had many chances to look around afterwards, not unless he wanted the Russians to leave his body there along with too many others wearing *Feldgrau*.

Here, though … The Bucovinans had stood more bravely than he'd thought they could. Even after they had to know they were beaten, they went on doing as well as they could for as long as they could. They fought like soldiers, not like savages fierce in victory who panicked and broke the minute things went wrong.

A dead native clutched the shaft of the spear that pinned him to the ground. The horrible grimace he'd worn when he died was relaxing towards a corpse's blankness. His eyes stared sightlessly up at the sky.

Not far away, a dead Lenello sprawled in a pool of blood. His left hand clutched the stump of his right arm. He'd lost his right hand, and bled to death before a surgeon or a wizard could do anything to help him. Flies buzzed around the blood. A big one landed in the blood-streaked, callused palm of the severed hand.

You had an easier time telling how hard and how well someone fought on this field than on a lot of them on the Russian front. Artillery and bullets could be nearly random in how they killed and maimed. But if a sword or spear went in from the front, the dead man faced his foe when he died. If he had a wound in the back, he was likely trying to run away when he died.

The Grenye killed from behind almost all lay at some distance from where they'd posted their line. Those were the men who'd tried to escape, most of them after the fight was irretrievably lost. Yes, they'd fought hard, all right.

King Bottero rode up to Hasso. The king had a cut on the back of his right hand; he'd been in the thick of the fighting himself. The edge of his shield was as notched as a saw blade. His horse limped.

"You did what you said you'd do," Bottero declared. "Have you got any idea how unusual that is?"

Hasso saluted Lenello-style, his fist over his heart. "Your Majesty, I am a stranger, a foreigner, at your court. I don't dare fail."

"Why not? My own people do, all the time."

"They *are* your people," Hasso replied. "You forgive them because they are. But if I go wrong, you say, 'He is a foreigner trying to fool us. Off with his head!'"

Bottero threw back his head and laughed. "Are you sure you were never a king yourself?"

"Never!" Hasso pushed away the words with both hands, which set Bottero laughing again. The German went on, "Never want to be a king, either."

"You're smart," Bottero said. "You don't have everybody below you looking up at you and thinking what an idiot you are."

"Not me, your Majesty," Hasso said, which was plenty to make Bottero almost fall off his horse with mirth. Hasso spoke as innocently as he could—with exaggerated innocence, in fact. He was glad he'd amused his new sovereign. He was also glad Bottero believed him when he said he had no royal ambitions. It was true. Even if it weren't, he had to act as if it were. Confessing that you did want to wear a crown was apt to be more hazardous to your life expectancy than a Russian armored division.

"Find any loot worth keeping?" Bottero asked.

Soldiers here made a big part of their living from booty. Hasso, used to regular pay, had to remind himself of that. He had picked up one nice dagger with gold chasing on the blade. He showed it to the king.

Bottero nodded. "That's not bad. It's one of our patterns, but it looks to me like a copy by a Grenye smith. The chasing is very nice—I like that dragon—but the work on the blade itself is cruder than what we'd do."

Hasso didn't have the eye for such fine details. He'd kept the dagger because of the gold. He didn't expect to use it as a weapon. He had nothing against war knives; he carried one of his own. But it was just a tool, not a fancy Solingen blade like the ones SS men were so proud of.

"Where do we go now?" Hasso asked. "We should push after the Bucovinans. Not let them come back together, get ready to fight again." He wanted to say *regroup*, but he couldn't come up with the word in Lenello. He was a lot more fluent than he had been even a month before, but talking still sometimes felt like wading through glue.

"You *have* been eating meat, haven't you?" King Bottero smiled at him like a father smiling at an adventurous little boy. "We need to get ready to fight again ourselves, you know. Do you think your striking column will work as well now that they know we use it?"

That was a genuinely shrewd question. "I don't know, your Majesty," Hasso replied. "You know the Bucovinans better than I do, so you are a better judge. How fast do they learn? Will they have an assault column of their own in the next battle?" The possibility hadn't occurred to him till now.

"No." The king shook his head. "They aren't *that* quick. But they'll look for ways to stop the column from breaking through. And they'll have their own soon. You can bet on that. When the other Lenello kingdoms hear about what we're doing, they'll start using these columns, too."

"Defense," Hasso muttered. Did he know enough about the Swiss hedgehog to teach it to Bottero's men? He had to hope he did, because they were going to need it, if not at the next battle then before too long. He could see that coming.

"All this is worry for another time," Bottero said. "You kept your word to me. I won't forget, and you won't be sorry." With the wave of a gauntleted hand, he rode off.

Not far away, a Lenello foot soldier was slitting the throat of a feebly writhing Bucovinan. Still holding the bloody knife, he nodded to Hasso. "Boy, I wish the king would talk to me that way," he said.

Everybody had problems. The foot soldier thought his were worse than Hasso's. Maybe he was even right. All the same, Hasso knew his own weren't small. He also knew they wouldn't go away any time soon.

***

Back in Germany, women prided themselves on how little they ate. A birdlike appetite was a sign of femininity. After the battle, Velona ate enough for two troopers, maybe three. "Where do you keep it?" Hasso asked. He was hungry, but not *that* hungry. "Have you got a hollow leg?"

The joke was old in German, but new in Lenello. Velona laughed so hard, she almost spat out the swig of beer she'd just taken. "No, no, no," she said. "You have to understand—I'm eating for two."

"You're going to have a baby?" Hasso took the phrase to mean what it would have in his native tongue. The next question that ran through his mind was, *Is it mine?* He didn't ask that one, not least for fear she would up and tell him no.

But she laughed again, this time at him, though as far as he could tell without malice. "No, not a baby. I'm sure I'm not pregnant," she said. "I just stopped flowing a couple of days before the battle, remember, and I'm glad I did, too. What I meant was, I'm eating for me and the goddess both."

"Oh." Feeling like a fool, Hasso thumped his forehead with the heel of his hand. It hurt more than it should have; somewhere in the battle, he'd got a bruise there, even if he couldn't remember how or when. And he found himself nodding. No wonder Velona never gained a gram! But carrying a goddess around wasn't the sort of diet likely to become popular in Berlin or Cologne or Vienna... even if the German women in those towns were free of invaders, which they weren't.

How big a toll *did* the goddess take on a mere mortal's metabolism? Hasso had no idea, but Velona knew the answer from the inside out.

Her smile, he judged, held more than a little relief. "I could feel the goddess' power running through me," she said. "The savages could feel it, too, when I struck and even before that, when I bore down on them. I could tell."

"I believe you," Hasso said, which was nothing but the truth. When the goddess manifested herself in Velona, she definitely seemed more than human. Just being near her at such times made your hair prickle up, as if lightning had crashed down close by. Then, several beats more slowly than a Lenello would have, Hasso saw what she was driving at here. "We are in Bucovin, but the power still runs through you."

"The goddess is still with me," Velona agreed. But then her smile slipped. "It was like this the last time I came into Bucovin, too. At first, it was like this. After that … It wasn't that the goddess left me, or not exactly like that. When she tried to speak, though, I couldn't make out what she was saying. The land in these parts was thinking about something else."

How did she mean that? Never having had any kind of divinity speak to him or through him, Hasso couldn't know, not the way Velona did. He thought of a bad telephone connection. Then he laughed at himself. What good did a thought from his own world do him? He couldn't make Velona or anyone else here understand it. What would telephones seem to the Lenelli but magic?

Crystal balls, now … They had crystal balls, or something like them. "Wizards can talk back and forth from far away, right?" he asked, an idea starting to sprout in his mind.

"Yes, that's true." Velona nodded. She laid her hand on his in what was, he realized a moment later, a gesture of sympathy. "I can guess how strange that must be to you, coming from a world with so little magic in it."

Hasso didn't laugh. If he started, he feared he wouldn't be able to stop. *Stick to business*, he told himself. And so he did: "All right. If we split our army in two, the Grenye would also have to split their army in two, wouldn't they?"

"I'd think so, but I'm no Grenye general, goddess be praised," Velona said. "Where are you going with this?"

All at once, the sprouted idea flowered and fruited. "We can keep track of our two armies with magic, always know where they are, move together thanks to magic. We can come back together when we need to, and defeat the Grenye in detail." For once, he found the technical term he needed right on the tip of his tongue. If that wasn't a good omen, what would be?

Would Velona get it? Was it, in fact, a thought worth getting? Or was he misunderstanding the way things worked here? He waited to see how she responded.

He started to worry when she didn't answer right away. Her brow creased in serious thought. Seeing those tiny wrinkles reminded him she was human as well as divine. Were these human, normal moments the ones Jesus' followers had cherished most? Hasso wouldn't have been surprised, though none of the Gospels talked about anything so completely mundane.

"It could work," Velona said at last. "It could well work. We didn't need such tricks when we fought the Grenye after we first came across the sea. We knew so much more than they did, the fights were walkovers. A ploy like that wouldn't work when Lenelli fight Lenelli, because there's magic on both sides then. But against Bucovin ... Yes, it might be just the thing." A slow smile spread across her face. "And how fitting to turn their mindblindness against them, to use it as one of our weapons of war."

She kissed him. It didn't go any further than that, not then. They were both weary from the fighting. Hasso stank even in his own nostrils: of horse, of sweat, of fear, and of the blood that splashed his mailshirt and his skin. He didn't think Velona smelled of fear. That was a pretty good sign she had the goddess dwelling in her. After a battle, few people could avoid the sour stink of terror.

"You will tell the king tomorrow," she said, as if she were an officer giving a common soldier his orders.

Does she have the right to tell me what to do like that? Hasso wondered. In her own person, she probably didn't. But that was the point, as he'd realized a moment before. She wasn't just in her own person, not when she had the goddess for company. And the goddess could tell King Bottero what to do, let alone a newly arrived foreigner like Hasso Pemsel.

Automatically, Hasso's arm shot out in the salute he was more used to than the one the Lenelli used. "*Zu Befehl!*" he said, German tasting strange in his mouth. He turned it into Lenello: "At your command!"

"Well, all right," Velona said. "I didn't mean it quite like that. But for now, let's get some sleep." There was an order Hasso was glad to obey.

IX

"I am your slave," the Grenye prisoner insisted.

Hasso had never expected to see the warrior he'd captured again. But there the fellow was, helping one of the cooks dole out bowls of porridge flavored with salty, fennel-filled sausage and onions. It wasn't delicious, but it filled the belly. On campaign, that counted for more.

"Is he yours, sir?" the cook asked. "I didn't mean to take him if he really belonged to somebody, but you know how it is. We can always use an extra pair of hands."

"What is the custom?" Hasso asked in return. "He did surrender to me yesterday."

"Then he's yours if you want him," the cook said. "If you don't, I'll go on using him—he seems willing enough. Or you can feed him to the water snakes—but if you wanted to do that, you could have done it when he tried to give up."

The Bucovinan pointed to Hasso. "You spared me. I work for you now. I am Berbec." He jabbed a thumb at his own chest. "You are a great lord, yes? A great lord, sure, but you never have man like me before."

"That's what I'm afraid of," Hasso said dryly. Berbec laughed louder than the joke deserved … if it was a joke. Was taking a prisoner as a batman, as a valet—hell, as a slave—clasping a water snake to his bosom? The cook didn't seem to think so. Hasso found himself nodding. "Well, come on, then, Berbec. What can you do for me that I can't do for myself?"

"All kinds of things." Berbec bowed to him, then also bowed to the cook for whom he'd been working. The motion was different from the stiffer one the Lenelli—and the Germans—used. It might almost have been a move from a dance. "You don't have any other slaves?"

"Not right now," Hasso said.

Berbec clicked his tongue between his teeth. "You poor fellow." He cocked his head to one side, eyeing Hasso with sparrowish curiosity. "You look like a Lenello, but you don't talk like. Where you from?"

"A faraway country," the German replied, which was true but uninformative. He still didn't trust Berbec not to disappear the minute he turned his back. "Can you take care of a horse?"

"I do that." Berbec nodded eagerly. He might have picked the next thought out of Hasso's mind, for he went on, "Not steal him, neither. You could kill me, but you spare. I owe you my life. I pay back."

Maybe he meant it. Some people, and some peoples, were punctilious about their honor, to the point that looked like stupidity to anyone with a less rigid code. Whether the Grenye of Bucovin were like that, whether Berbec himself was … *I just have to find out*, Hasso thought. *In the meantime, I have to be careful.*

"You have funny helmet," Berbec remarked. His hands shaped the flare of the German *Stahlhelm.*

"In the style of my country," Hasso said. The Lenelli wore plain conical helms, more like those of the Normans than any others he knew. So did the Bucovinans, probably in imitation of the blonds from overseas.

"Not bad. Maybe turn sword better." Berbec might be a little man, but he was a warrior. "But nasal is new. Not have before?" He was a warrior with sharp eyes, too. That nasal was riveted on. The Lenelli couldn't weld steel, and Hasso didn't trust solder to hold. Berbec chattered on: "Why you not have before? Keep face from getting split open."

"War in my land doesn't usually come down to swordstrokes," Hasso replied. And wasn't that the sad and sorry truth? A helmet wouldn't stop a rifle round, though it would keep out some shell fragments. High-velocity bullets made most body armor more trouble than it was worth. Only if you were fighting with bayonets or entrenching tools would a nasal matter. Once in a blue moon, in other words. German armorers didn't see the point of adding one, and who was he to say they were wrong … for the kind of war they fought?

Berbec stared at him. Hasso thought the Bucovinan would call him a liar. But then Berbec thrust out a stubby, accusing finger. "You have the thunderflasher," he said. That wasn't a word in Lenello, but it was a pretty good description of a firearm. "You point it at someone, and it goes boom, and he falls over. All soldiers in your country carry thunderflashers, then?"

No, he was nobody's fool. "That's right," Hasso said.

"The Lenelli have all kinds of things. They are clever, the Lenelli." Maybe Berbec felt he could talk freely about them because Hasso wasn't one. "But they don't have thunderflashers." He eyed Hasso again, this time, the *Wehrmacht* officer judged, apprehensively. And why not? If the Lenelli all carried Schmeissers, Bucovinan resistance would last a minute and a half, tops.

"Can't make them here." Hasso wanted the words back as soon as they came out. Some Intelligence officer he was, blabbing like a fool!

Velona came up to the two of them. As soon as she saw Berbec, she understood what was going on. "He's one you caught yourself?" she asked. When Hasso nodded, she went on, "Good. You've been doing too much for yourself." She brushed her lips across his and walked on.

Berbec stared after her—not as a man will watch a good-looking woman, but more as anyone might stare at a lightning bolt smashing down close by. "That was—the goddess—the woman who, uh, carries the goddess." He might be a slave, but this was the first time Hasso had seen him without his self-possession.

"Yeah." Hasso nodded.

"She doesn't need a thunderflasher to cut through us," Berbec said sadly. "Only a sword—and herself."

Hasso nodded again, not without sympathy. What was it like for the Grenye, without magic of their own, to try to stand against Velona when the goddess was strong in her? Like a lone rifleman against a King Tiger panzer? Worse, probably, because the panzer and the infantryman belonged to the same world. The Grenye had to feel the very heavens were fighting against them—and they wouldn't be so far wrong, would they?

Berbec's stare swung back to Hasso. It was as if he could still see the mark of her kiss glowing on the *Wehrmacht* officer's face. "She is ... your woman?" He sounded like someone afraid to be right.

"Yes, she's my woman." Hasso felt the irony in his voice. Berbec might not understand, but, to the Lenello way of thinking, Hasso was Velona's man and not the other way around.

He succeeded in impressing his new servant, anyway. "I knew you were a great lord. I already told you that," Berbec said. "But I didn't know you were *such* a great lord." He bowed himself almost double. "I cry pardon. Forgive me."

He wouldn't straighten till Hasso touched him on the back. "It's all right. Forget it. I still put on trousers like anybody else. I still shit. I still piss. I still need you to see to my horse. That's what you say you do." He was getting better with past tenses, but he still wasn't good enough to feel comfortable using them.

"I do it," Berbec said. He seemed mostly stuck in the present indicative, too. For no sensible reason, that made Hasso feel better.

***

King Bottero's army pressed deeper into Bucovin. The natives didn't stand and fight again. They didn't go away, either. Raiders picked off Lenello scouts. Horsemen attacked the wagons that brought supplies forward. And, to Hasso's dismay if not to his surprise, flames and clouds of smoke rose up in front of the invaders.

"They burn their own crops," he said. The Russians had scorched the earth in front of the oncoming *Wehrmacht*. Later, moving from east to west instead of from west to east, the Germans used the same ploy to slow down the Red Army. The Ivans screamed about war crimes. They hadn't said a word when they used those tactics. Winners said what they pleased. Who could call a winner a liar?

King Bottero eyed the smoke and sniffed the breeze. Hasso couldn't smell the burning, not yet. Maybe the enormous Lenello could. "They think they'll make us too hungry to go on," the king said.

"Are they right?" Hasso asked.

"Not yet," Bottero said, an answer that struck the German as reasonable.

Aderno and the other wizards put their heads together. They worked a spell that might have come straight out of *Macbeth*. They danced; they chanted; they incanted. Dark clouds filled the sky. Rain came down—rain poured down, in fact. It drenched the fires. Whether it did the Lenelli any good was a different question, and one harder to answer. The roads got soaked, too, and turned to mud.

Hasso remembered the first Russian *rasputitsa*, the time of rain and muck. He remembered motorcycle drivers, their mechanized steeds hub-deep—sometimes headlight-deep—in muck, their rubberized greatcoats ten or twenty kilos heavier than they should have been, their goggles so splashed that they were almost useless (or, sometimes, worse than useless), the eyes behind those goggles gradually growing alarmed as one rider after another began to see it wouldn't be as easy as the High Command claimed. He remembered bogged-down panzers and artillery pieces, half-drowned horses, the sucking goo trying to pull the marching boots off his feet with every step. He remembered bone-crushing exhaustion at the end of every day—and well before the end, too.

Yes, the mud slowed down the Ivans. But they weren't trying to go forward, not that first autumn, anyhow. They were just trying to hold back the Germans, to keep the *Wehrmacht* out of Moscow. And they did, and blitzkrieg turned to grapple and slugging match ... and Hasso found a magical way to escape from burning, pulverized Berlin, but not one the rest of the city would ever be able to use.

And so he was here in western Bucovin, listening to the rain patter down. Soldiers greased their mailshirts every morning and night and draped themselves with cloaks. They swore when they found tiny tumors of rust anyhow—as of course they did. The horses that squelched through the deepening ooze couldn't swear, but the men on their backs made up for that. And the teamsters who fought to keep supply wagons moving cursed even harder than the knights.

By the time it had rained for a couple of days, Hasso began to think the wizards' spell might be worse than the scorched-earth disease. By the time the rain had poured down for a week, he was sure of it. He rode up alongside Aderno, whose unicorn was so splotched and spattered with mud that it looked to have a giraffe's hide.

Hasso waved his arms up toward the weeping sky. "Enough!" he said. He waved again, like a conductor in white tie and tails pulling a crescendo from a symphony orchestra. "Too much, in fact! Call off your storm!"

Aderno's answering glance would have looked even hotter than it did had water not dripped from the end of the wizard's long, pointed nose. "It's not our storm any more," he said. "It's just ... weather now."

"Well, work another spell and turn it into *good* weather, then," Hasso said.

Were there any justice in the world, the water on Aderno's nose would have started to steam. "What do you think we've been trying to do?" he said pointedly.

"I don't know," Hasso answered. "All I know is, it's still raining."

Aderno's gesture was as extravagant as the ones the German had used not long before. "Weather magic is never easy. We'd do a lot more of it if it were," he said. "And trying it here in Bucovin was worse. We were glad when we got what we wanted. Now—"

He broke off when a raindrop hit him in the eye. "Now you've got too much of what you want," Hasso finished for him. The wizard nodded unhappily. "And you can't close the sluice, either," Hasso said. In German, it would have been something like, *And you can't turn it off, either*. The Lenelli didn't have enough machinery to make phrases like that a natural part of their language.

"Air and sky and land in Bucovin don't want to listen to us," Aderno said. Hasso would have thought he was making excuses if Velona hadn't said the same thing.

Thinking of Velona, though, inspired him, as it often did—though not in the same direction as usual. Instead of erotic excess, his mind swung toward military pragmatism. "Do the air and sky and land here listen to the goddess?" he asked.

"Sometimes." Aderno's attention sharpened. "Sometimes, yes. And if the goddess' person begs her…"

Did Velona beg the goddess the last time she went into Bucovin? What did the goddess do for her then? Anything? Hasso's first, rational, inclination was to say no. But he realized Velona didn't see things that way herself. As far as she was concerned, the goddess gave her just what she asked for: a rescuer from another world, one Hasso Pemsel.

"I speak to her of this," Hasso said. He didn't think of himself as anybody's answered prayer, but in this crazy world he might be wrong, and he knew it.

As he made his way through the mud to the tent he shared with Velona, he reminded himself that he would have to grease his boots. If he didn't, the leather would turn hard as stone when it dried … if it ever dried. It would also start to rot. The Lenelli made boots at least as good as the ones he'd worn when he got here, but he'd got used to the idea of not wasting anything.

He wondered if he would be wasting his time talking to Velona. Try as he would, he didn't have a real feel yet for how things worked here. Maybe he was only suggesting the obvious. Maybe his idea wasn't obvious but was stupid.

Or maybe you're a goddamn genius, he told himself. That made him laugh. He sure as hell didn't feel like a genius. Back in Germany, he bloody well wasn't. But the things he knew from there often made him seem smarter than the locals here. *Don't believe your own press clippings*, he thought. Wasn't that one of Hitler's big mistakes? He was so convinced the Ivans were bums, he went after them without thinking about what a *big* bunch of bums they were.

Here heading toward the middle of Bucovin, Hasso could have done without that thought.

Velona took him seriously. That a woman like her might take him seriously was just about enough to make him believe in her goddess, or at least in miracles. When he finished, she said, "I will do what I can. I don't know how much that will be. The goddess didn't seem to hear me when I was in Bucovin before. I feared she'd abandoned me … and then there you were, on the causeway."

"There I was," Hasso agreed. *Was* he the answer to Velona's prayer? Or had the Omphalos stone sent him here of its own volition? Or was it just dumb luck, with nobody responsible one way or the other? The goddess and whatever powered the Omphalos might know. Hasso didn't believe he ever would.

When Velona decided to do something, she didn't do it halfway. Beseeching the goddess proved no exception to the rule. She carried a statuette of the deity with her. The bronze—about a quarter of a meter tall—was nothing fancy. Had Hasso seen it in a museum back in Berlin, he would have walked past it without a second glance.

Velona set it up on the muddy floor of the tent with a candle burning to either side: a makeshift altar. Then she stripped herself naked and prostrated herself before it. Hasso's admiration for her beauty was almost entirely abstract, his pleasure at seeing her long, smooth length esthetic rather than lustful. She seemed as much in the divine world as in the material, which had a lot to do with that.

Or maybe she just intimidates the crap out of me, he thought—not a reflection likely to have crossed his mind for any ordinary woman. Whatever else you said about Velona, ordinary she was not.

"Hear me!" she said, as if the statuette were an equal. "Hear me!" Hasso wondered whether the bronze image would answer, but it didn't—at least not so he could hear. Velona went on, "Enough of rain! Enough of mud! Enough of barbarism! Time for Bottero's troopers to storm forward!"

Hasso wanted to go outside and look at the weather. If it wasn't changing right then ... If it wasn't, then Velona would have to give the goddess another talking-to.

One of the candles flared up. Maybe that was what made the statuette's eyes flash. The rational part of Hasso could believe it was, anyhow. That way, he didn't have to believe he was watching the goddess' response to a petitioner who was fully entitled to treat with her.

He didn't have to believe that, no, but believing anything else wasn't easy. And Velona only made it harder when she said, "Well, I should hope so! It's about time, don't you think?" She might have been talking to a neighbor woman about reining in the neighbor's unruly children.

The bronze goddess' eyes flashed again. This time, Hasso didn't notice any candle flare to cause it. He tried to convince himself that he didn't see the statuette nod in response to Velona's urging. He tried, but he didn't have much luck. His eyes saw what they saw. What it meant ... was probably about what it looked like. If he had trouble believing that, wasn't it because the God he was used to worshiping was so leery of doling out miracles? Things were different here.

With an athlete's grace, Velona got to her feet. Hasso had never seen such an... inspiring votary of any god. He tried to imagine her arising, naked and beautiful, from in front of the altar in a Catholic or Lutheran church. The picture didn't want to form. In a way, that was hardly surprising, however rough her presence would have been on a celibate priest. In another way, though, wasn't the impossibility of such a scene too damn bad? If Velona didn't make you want to worship, weren't you already dead inside?

Beaming, she said, "I think that took care of it. Thank you for giving me a push there."

"Any time." Hasso reached out and cupped her left breast in his right hand.

"A push, I said." Velona tried to sound severe, but didn't have much luck. "What would happen if your slave walked in here right now?"

"Berbec? He'd be jealous." Hasso didn't let go. "And he'd think I was the bravest man in the world, for daring to touch you."

"I like it when you touch me." Velona set her hand on his, which made his breath come short. But she went on, "If I didn't like it and you touched me, *then* you would be the bravest man in the world. And the stupidest."

"I believe you," Hasso said. Men had amused themselves with their enemies' women since the beginning of time. The Germans had done their share of it in France and in Russia. And now the Ivans were paying the *Wehrmacht* back with their trousers down around their ankles.

Things in this world were bound to be the same. Not all the halfbreeds here had happened because Grenye women welcomed Lenello men with their legs open. But if anyone tried to force Velona to do anything she didn't want to do when the goddess was with her... Hasso didn't know what would happen to a bastard dumb enough to try that. He did know he wouldn't care to find out.

Instead of drawing him down to the cot with her, she slipped away. "I'd better get dressed," she said. He must have looked like a man who'd just bitten down hard on a lemon, because she started to laugh. "*Not now* doesn't mean *never*, my dear," she reminded him, wagging a finger under his nose. "We both have other things to worry about, though. Why don't you see what the weather's doing?"

Because I'd rather lay you, he thought grumpily. But, after what he'd been thinking, he couldn't very well say that. And if a woman decided you only wanted her for her twat, you were in trouble, big trouble. If a woman like Velona decided that...

If that happened, what the two of them had was dead. And if it was dead, Hasso figured his own chances of ending up literally dead got a lot higher. The Lenelli cut him extra slack because he was the goddess' boyfriend. If anybody picked a fight with him with swords, though, he was in big trouble. He'd got a lot better with a blade since coming here, but he knew enough to understand the difference between better and good.

Since he didn't want to worry about that, he stepped outside. The rain was gone. A brisk breeze blew the dark clouds across the sky. In the west, the sun poured wet, buttery light across the landscape. A slow smile spread across Hasso's face. The Lenello wizards had started the rain. Now the goddess had ended it.

And the Bucovinans would have a tough time setting their fields aflame for a while—things would be too wet to catch easily. If the roads dried out enough to keep foot soldiers and horses and wagons from bogging down, King Bottero's army could press a lot deeper into Bucovin.

Then what? Hasso wondered. The question wouldn't have occurred to the

Lenelli, but the Lenelli had never tried invading the Soviet Union. Hasso looked around their encampment and slowly shook his head. *Goddamn lucky bastards.*

***

Bottero's army did push deeper into the barbarians' country. A day and a half after Velona and the goddess persuaded the rain to clear out—Hasso had no other explanation for what happened there—Aderno rode up to him and asked, "Have you seen Flegrei?"

"No." Hasso shook his head, which meant the same thing to the Lenelli as it did in Germany. "Should I see him?"

"Well, I was hoping *somebody* had." Aderno didn't sound happy. "I wanted to ask him something. Nobody's set eyes on him since not long after we got moving this morning."

"He's a wizard. He rides a unicorn. He should be easy to spot," Hasso said.

"I know," Aderno answered, and Hasso realized he was working hard not to show how worried he was. "He should be ... but he isn't. I'm afraid something's happened to him."

"*Scheisse,*" Hasso muttered. He could swear in Lenello to let the people around him know he was pissed off, but he got no satisfaction from it himself. For that, he still needed his native speech. "Do you think the Grenye used to ambush him?" He muttered to himself again—that was the wrong form of the past tense, and he knew it. Now, too late, he knew it.

Aderno was too rattled to sneer, though. "I'm afraid they did. I'm afraid they must have," the wizard replied. "We need to take enough men down our trail so we can be sure we don't get bushwhacked looking for him."

"*Scheisse,*" Hasso repeated, louder this time. The word wouldn't mean anything to Aderno unless he had his translating spell working, but the tone was bound to get through. Hasso added a few more choice opinions *auf Deutsch*. But Aderno was right. They needed to find out what had happened to Flegrei. If the Grenye suddenly had a wizard working for them—maybe with a knife at his throat, but even so—the Lenelli needed to know about that. And if the knife had gone into Flegrei instead, the invaders needed to know that, too.

Hasso had enough clout to pull a troop of horsemen out of the line of march on his own hook and start them back the wrong way. A couple of captains asked him what the demon he thought he was doing. When he told them he was looking for a missing wizard, they did some swearing of their own.

"You shouldn't let some of those people run loose," one Lenello opined. "They just get into trouble."

Aderno looked highly affronted. He might have had more to say to the soldier if traveling in opposite directions hadn't swept them apart. Later ... Hasso shook his head. He'd worry about that later, by God.

"Look for the unicorn," he told the men with him. "We have a better chance of spotting the animal than we do of spotting the wizard."

The troopers nodded. Aderno looked surprised, as if that hadn't occurred to him. Maybe it hadn't; he didn't always operate within the restrictive confines of the real world himself. After a moment, he added, "The Grenye may have taken Flegrei away, too. It's possible that they can get him to do what they want if they hurt him enough. But no Grenye can ride a unicorn. So they'd likely kill it first—they can't deal with it any other way."

That made sense to Hasso, who gave the wizard a mental apology. He didn't waste time on a spoken one. He was too busy trying to look every which way at once. Out away from the Lenello army, he felt the way he had behind the front in the Soviet Union. Every tree, every rock, every bush was liable to be dangerous. And you'd never know which one till too late. How many eyes were watching him and his comrades right now? How many Bucovinan fists tightened on weapons? Hasso couldn't see anybody, but that didn't mean nobody could see him. Oh, no.

But would the men of Bucovin have enough soldiers back here to take on so many Lenelli? He could hope not, anyhow.

The farther from the security of Bottero's main force he got, the more he worried, the more his head swiveled back and forth, back and forth. He watched the Lenelli with him. The big blond knights also seemed to be trying to grow eyes in the backs of their heads.

"I wouldn't want to do this when the sun was going down, not for all the beer in Bari," one of them said. Several others nodded. Hasso had no idea where Bari was, but he understood the sentiment just fine.

Not far from the road, a farmhouse was charred wreckage. Had the Lenelli torched it, or did the retreating Bucovinans do it themselves? Whatever the answer was, would that matter to the peasants whose home was only a ruin? Hasso had trouble making himself believe it.

Fire had also run through the fields, which inclined him to believe the incendiarism was Bucovinan work. King Bottero's men would have taken the nearly ripe millet for themselves ... if they had the time, and if flames from the burning buildings hadn't got loose. So hard to be sure about anything you didn't see for yourself. Too damned often, it was hard to be sure about things you *did* see.

A Lenello stabbed out a pointing forefinger. "What's that behind the barn there? Something white, I think."

Hasso hadn't noticed it till the soldier pointed it out. It wasn't much more than a flash; the barn hid it pretty well. That made him apprehensive. So did the fruit trees within easy bowshot of the barn. All the same, he said, "We have to check it out." The knights nodded with the air of men who knew they were liable to be sticking their dicks in a meat grinder and also knew they had no choice. Or did they? Hasso turned to Aderno. "Do you sense an ambush?"

After a few passes and a murmured versicle, the wizard shook his head. "I sense no enemies close by," he said. But he didn't sound happy about his own judgment, either, for he added, "If we were in Lenello-ruled land, I would be surer."

It wasn't magic. The Lenelli swore it wasn't, anyway. But the countryside of Bucovin liked the Grenye better than it liked their foes. The blonds had been grumbling about that ever since they crossed the border. "We go like we expect an attack," Hasso said.

Nobody quarreled with him. One knight said, "You may be a foreigner, but you've got your head nailed on tight, by the goddess." That made Hasso feel good.

That good feeling didn't last long—only till he got a closer look at the flash of white the alert Lenello had spotted. It was a unicorn; it was on the ground; and it was dead. Blood marred the pristine perfection of its coat: blood from at least a score of wounds. Hasso saw some that came from arrows, others from spears, and a few sword cuts as well. The unicorn's silvered horn wasn't bloodied; the beast hadn't had the chance to fight back.

"You hate to see them hurt," Aderno said. Hasso found himself nodding. Seeing a unicorn brought down that way was like looking at the corpse of a beautiful woman caught in a bomb blast. Hasso had had to do that more often than he cared to remember. In a way, this was even worse. A beautiful woman could be a deadly enemy. The poor unicorn didn't know anything about the war between Lenelli and Grenye.

Somehow, Hasso didn't think the Grenye of Bucovin would have appreciated the distinction.

"Here's the wizard," a Lenello knight called, pointing into the woods.

Hasso swung down from his horse and tossed the reins to another Lenello. There didn't seem to be any Bucovinans close by. He drew his sword anyway.

Because of the unicorn, the smell of blood was already thick in his nostrils. It got thicker. He walked around a scrubby oak sapling and got a good look at what the enemy had done to Flegrei.

He swore softly, in Lenello and then in German. He'd seen such things on the Eastern Front, when the Ivans got hold of some Germans. He'd seen his countrymen do the like to Russians they caught. It jolted him here all the same. The men who started seeing how clever they could be with their knives always aimed to make their foes afraid—if they aimed at anything past a little sport and revenge. They commonly made those foes more determined than they would have been otherwise.

The first thing that came out of his mouth was, "Well, now we know."

"Now we know," Aderno agreed in a voice like ashes. "I hope he was dead before they did ... some of that, anyway."

"Yes." Hasso nodded. Flegrei couldn't have lived through everything the Bucovinans did to him... could he? Hasso didn't like to think the wizard had been alive when they.... He didn't cross his hands in front of his crotch, but he had to make himself hold still. "He is a wizard," he said. "How do they do this? Why doesn't he hit them with spells?"

"If they tied his hands, he wouldn't have been able to make passes. Maybe he was stunned when the unicorn went down," Aderno said. "And then after that, of course…" He pointed to one of the creative things the Grenye had done.

"Yes. After that." Hasso wanted to look away, but he didn't. He couldn't remember the Ivans coming up with that particular mutilation and insult. If the Bucovinans were more inventive than Stalin's soldiers … He wouldn't have believed it if he hadn't seen it with his own eyes. He didn't like believing it now.

"They aren't usually this bad," a knight said. "Of course, I don't suppose they catch a wizard very often."

"I wonder what made poor Flegrei ride back of that farmhouse," Aderno said. "Maybe he just wanted to ease himself away from everybody else. Whatever it was, he should have known better."

"Do Lenelli do … this to Grenye, too?" Hasso asked.

"To avenge him, we will," the knight answered. "Those bastards have to know they can't get away with this crap. We haven't done anything this bad in a while, and they had it coming then."

Would they have thought so? Hasso wondered. But that was a pointless question. He found one that wasn't: "What do we do with him?"

"Two choices I see," the knight answered. "Either we burn him here or we take back the pieces so the king and the army find out what kind of war we're fighting."

Hasso couldn't see anything else to do, either. He didn't feel the call was his to make, even if he held the highest rank here. As a foreigner, he would be missing too many nuances. He turned to Aderno. "You follow the same craft," he said. "What would he want?"

The wizard plucked at his neatly trimmed beard. "I don't think he would want to be a spectacle, not … the way he is," he answered. "Better we make a pyre for him here."

"All right. We do that, then." Hasso waved at the forest. "Plenty of branches, as long as we cut them. Can we get them dry enough to burn well?"

"I know a spell for that," Aderno said. "It's mostly used to get enough wood for campfires, but I can make it bigger."

Hasso started hacking at branches with his sword. "Let's get to work, then." The Lenelli joined in. Maybe they wouldn't have done it of their own accord; like the knights of medieval Germany or France, they thought a lot of physical labor was beneath their dignity. But seeing the man set over them go to work without hesitation brought them around. If he didn't hold back, how could they?

They got enough for a pyre in less than an hour. Aderno murmured and swayed in front of the pile. Steam rose from the rain-soaked wood. When it stopped, the wizard nodded to Hasso. "This magic worked, anyhow. We can burn him now. Lay him on the pyre."

"Me?" Hasso hoped he didn't squeak too much.

"Of course," Aderno said. "You command here. Who else?"

Hasso had dealt with enough corpses that one more didn't really faze him, but it wasn't a duty he would have wanted. He had to make sure he had all of Flegrei; the Lenelli wouldn't have liked it had he left any of the cut-off bits behind. After he finished, he scrubbed his hands on wet grass. That got most of the blood off, but not all of it. The knights gathered around the pyre nodded to one another. They would have done the same thing. Then they would have forgotten about it. Hasso still wanted to get his hands really clean, which showed he came from a different world.

"May the life to come prove kinder to Flegrei than this one did," Aderno said.

"So may it be," the knights intoned.

"May he have joy of all his friends to come, and overcome all his foes," the wizard went on.

"So may it be." This time, Hasso joined the chorus. It wasn't the funeral service a German chaplain would have read, but it wasn't so very different, either.

"May the goddess avenge him against the barbarians who wickedly stole his life."

"So may it be."

"As the smoke of the pyre rises to the sky, so may Flegrei's spirit rise to the heavens beyond the sky."

"So may it be."

One of the knights had used flint and steel to get a small fire going. The Lenelli carried their firestarters the way *Wehrmacht* men carried matches and cigarette lighters. Aderno lit a small branch and used it to touch off the pyre. His magic had done what it needed to do; the flames took hold with no trouble. Hasso smelled wood smoke, and then the stink of burning meat. Flegrei might have been—was—a bastard, but they were on the same side. You never wanted to see one of your guys get it. That reminded you your number might come up next. You knew anyway, sure, but who needed reminding?

X

Stories were enough to get out the word about how Flegrei died. Before long, everybody in Bottero's army seemed to be talking about it. Not all the stories had much to do with what really happened. Hasso heard Lenelli talking about how a squadron of sorcerers had been ground up in a mill and fed to Grenye hogs.

"You gonna quit eating spare ribs?" one knight asked another.

His friend thought about it, but not for long. "Nah," he said. "They probably won't be from the same pigs. And if they are … Well, shit. If they are, I won't *think* they are, so that's jake."

"Sounds right," the first knight agreed, and they rode on.

Since they were arguing about the shadow of an ass that wasn't there, Hasso didn't waste his time trying to set them straight. Crazy rumors were part and parcel of war. Some of the stories he'd heard on the Russian front … There, they didn't talk about feeding dead Germans to pigs. They talked about Ivans eating German corpses, and their own. He'd believed those yarns, too. As a matter of fact, he still did believe some of them. If you got hungry enough, you were liable to do anything.

If you got mean enough, you were liable to do anything, too. Three days after Flegrei's untimely and unpleasant demise, the Lenelli came to a place big enough to show up on their map. It was called Muresh, and it was bigger than a village, even if it didn't make much of a town. Behind it, a bridge spanned the Oltet River; the bridge was probably the reason Muresh had been founded, and the reason it had grown.

The place didn't boast a wall. It did have a Bucovinan garrison, in a small, sad imitation of a Lenello castle just in front of the bridge. The soldiers in there couldn't have held the place more than a few hours against everything King Bottero had to throw at them. They weren't idiots. They could see that for themselves.

So they got out. They hurried across the bridge, tipping its timbers into the Oltet as they went. Another castle, none too big and none too strong-looking, stood on the far bank. The Lenelli wouldn't have a whole lot of trouble repairing the bridge… till they came within bowshot of that other castle. Then things wouldn't be so much fun. Fixing bridges while the bastards on the other side took potshots at you was nobody's idea of fun, not in any army.

A few ordinary Bucovinans escaped from Muresh, too, fleeing with the men who were there to guard the bridge and not them. Most of the locals stayed where they were, though, either because they couldn't get away or because they didn't think anything bad would happen to them.

Most of the time, they would have been right. The Lenelli hadn't struck Hasso as wantonly cruel. Maybe he just hadn't watched enough. Maybe he hadn't seen them when their blood was up.

King Bottero looked at the peasants and craftsmen of Muresh, at the women and children. He folded his thick arms across his broad chest. "Boys, these stinking Bucovinans killed Flegrei filthy," he shouted to his men. "I want you to go in there and pay the bastards back!"

The soldiers roared, a deep, baying sound that put Hasso in mind of the wolves he'd heard in Russian woods. The locals knew what a noise like that meant. They made a noise of their own then: a cry of horror and despair. Some of them tried to run away. Laughing at the joke, the knights rode after the running men and women and speared them from behind.

Then they swarmed into Muresh, and things got worse.

Some of the Grenye went down on their knees and begged for their lives. Most of them were, on the whole, lucky. The Lenelli killed them quickly. What happened to the men who tried to fight back...

No one could say the Lenelli didn't have imagination. A gray-bearded cook had used a big two-pronged fork and a knife to try to keep them out of his tavern. It didn't work—the Lenelli laughed as they beat down his unskilled defense. One of Bottero's soldiers smeared cooking oil into the Bucovinan's beard while three more knights held him. The native snapped like a dog, which only made the Lenelli laugh harder.

Then the fellow who'd used the oil lit a stick at the tavern's cookfire. The Bucovinan must have known what was coming next. Hasso feared he did, too. "No!" the cook howled—it might have been the only word of Lenello he knew. "No! No! NO!"

His howls did him no more good than his tries at biting had. Stretching out the moment, enjoying every bit of it, the Lenello slowly brought the flame closer to the oil-soaked beard. Then he set the cook's face on fire. "Fight us, will you, you stinking, scrawny savage!" he shouted.

The men who had been holding the Grenye didn't just let go of him. They shoved him away, so that he ran down the streets of Muresh screaming and beating at his burning hair and skin. The Lenelli thought he was the funniest thing they ever saw. "Look at him go!" they yelled.

"Maybe he'll burn this louse-trap down," one of them added.

"Serve them right if he does," another said. "Serve them all right if he does, by the goddess!"

In the sack and massacre that followed, Hasso might as well have been ... a man from another world. He didn't hate the Bucovinans enough to want to kill them for the fun of it, though he'd done that to Russians a time or two. But he knew the Lenelli wouldn't listen to him if he tried to stop them. And so he walked through the narrow, stinking, muddy streets of Muresh as if he were a camera.

All the Lenelli who saw the cook with the burning beard liked the idea. They set the faces of several other Bucovinans on fire. One of them torched a woman's hair. Her shrieks were even higher and shriller than those of the men. Some of Bottero's troopers laughed at that. But others shook their heads. "Waste of pussy," one of them declared.

"Still plenty to go around," said a knight who thought the woman with her hair ablaze was funny.

He wasn't wrong. Even more than the Germans in Russia, the Lenelli in Bucovin lived by the law of the jungle. Winners did whatever they wanted, and the enemy's women were fair game. The Lenelli raped with the practiced efficiency of men who took it for granted. A gang of them would catch a woman, throw her down on the ground, force her legs apart and hold her arms, and then mount her one after another, roughly in order of rank.

Some of them let the women shriek; maybe they thought the noise added spice to the game. Others used rough gags of cloth or leather to cut down the din. Sometimes, when they were finished, they would send the woman off with a pat on the backside or even a coin. Sometimes they would get a final thrill by cutting her throat and leaving her there to die in the mud.

One Lenello tried to gag a screaming woman with his member instead of a crumpled rag. A moment later, he was screaming himself, and pouring blood— she bit down, hard. It did her no good, of course. Another blond soldier thrust his sword up where he and his friends had taken their pleasure. She died, slowly and agonizingly, while they tried to bandage their wounded buddy.

Velona watched the rapes as she might have watched animals rutting in the farmyard. "What does the goddess think of this?" Hasso asked her.

For a moment, the incomprehension with which she greeted the question made him wonder if he'd asked it in German by mistake. But no—he'd spoken Lenello. Even if he had, Velona didn't understand him. "Why should the goddess care about Grenye?" she said.

A potbellied Lenello missing half his left ear flung himself onto a wailing Grenye woman spreadeagled on the ground in front of them and started pumping away, his heavy buttocks rising and falling. "Does the goddess care about women?" Hasso asked. "She is one, yes, in a way?"

"She is a Lenello woman." Velona set a finger between her breasts. "She is, some of the time, *this* Lenello woman. And the Grenye… are only Grenye. When I say she doesn't care about them, I know what I'm talking about."

"All right. I only wonder—wondered." Hasso didn't feel like quarreling. If she did care anything about the natives, she might have done something about the sack. The soldiers would have listened to her. If they didn't, the goddess might have come to her… and it would have taken a bold—and a foolish—Lenello to gainsay her when the goddess made herself manifest.

He looked across the river. The Bucovinan soldiers in the castle on the other side of the Oltet had to be watching—and listening to—the ruination of Muresh. Did they have wives or sweethearts or sisters in the town? What were they thinking? Hasso knew too well the bitter mix of fury and despair and impotence that descended on the *Wehrmacht* as the Ivans started raping their way through Germany. Were the little swarthy men draining that cup to the dregs right now? How could they be doing anything else?

The Lenello sergeant or whatever he was grunted and pulled out of the Grenye woman. A last few thick drops of semen trickled from the head of his cock as he did up his trousers again. A younger Lenello took his place and began to thrust like a man possessed.

Somebody handed Hasso a big jar of beer. He drank—and drank, and drank. That way, he didn't have to think. And maybe, just maybe, he'd forget some of the things he'd seen.

***

Come morning, he wasn't sure whether King Bottero's men had deliberately torched Muresh or the fires they set got out of hand. What difference did it make, anyhow? The place was just as gone either way.

He woke with a bursting bladder, a pounding headache, and a mouth that tasted like the bottom of a latrine trench. The stink of smoke and burnt flesh assailed his nose when he left the tent he shared with Velona to ease himself. He looked around for the cookfires—maybe porridge would settle his sour stomach. He didn't see them anywhere, though. The cooks still had to be sleeping off the previous day's orgy of slaughter and lust.

He looked across the Oltet again. The Bucovinans had men on the battlements of their keep. The place would be easy to take even so—once the army got across the river. With the planking down from the bridge, that might not be so easy. He shrugged and winced, wishing again for aspirin.

As far as the Lenelli were concerned, what they'd done was all part of a day's work. They hardly looked at the smoldering ruins of Muresh. Instead, they started yelling for the cooks. Burning the place and massacring the people only seemed to have given them an appetite.

They hadn't killed everybody. A few Bucovinan men survived as slaves, a few women as—Hasso supposed—playthings. Some of the locals had the dazed look of people who'd lost everything in a natural disaster but somehow come through alive. Others seemed more calculating, perhaps trying to figure out how to make the best of what had happened to them. Seeing that thoughtful gleam in some of the women's eyes made Hasso want to cry and swear at the same time.

Berbec clung close to him—close enough to be annoying, like a dog that always stayed at his heel. "Why don't you get lost?" Hasso snapped when he'd had enough.

"If I leave you, master, I *am* lost," the captive replied. "I think someone will do for me." He hacked at his throat with the edge of his hand to leave no doubt about what he meant.

And he was right enough to embarrass the German. "All right. Stay with me, then," Hasso said roughly. "Enough killing."

"Too much killing," Berbec said.

King Bottero took matters into his own hands—or rather, used his own foot. He booted the cooks out of their cots and bedrolls. They grumbled, but they came. When the king woke you up, you either got to work or tried to assassinate him. None of the cooks seemed ready for anything that drastic.

Across the river, the Bucovinans in their castle would be eating breakfast, too. They had to know the Lenelli would try to cross the Oltet as soon as they could. They also had to know that, if Bottero's men made it across the river, their own chances weren't good. Hasso had seen and joined in more rear-guard actions than he liked to remember. Recruiting sergeants with medals and campaign ribbons all over their chests didn't talk about that kind of soldiering.

He was spooning up porridge when Bottero came over to him. Berbec tried to disappear without moving a muscle. He needn't have worried; the king either truly didn't notice him or affected not to. It amounted to the same thing either way. To Hasso, Bottero came straight to the point: "Do you know any easy way to get across the Oltet?"

"Is there a ford close by?" Hasso asked.

Bottero shook his big head. "No."

The *Wehrmacht* would have used rubber rafts to seize a bridgehead. No such items were part of the Lenello logistics train. "Have we got boats? Can we make rafts?"

"We don't have boats. How could we carry them along?" Bottero said. With ox-drawn wagons as his main supply vehicles, he had a point. "Building rafts would take too cursed long. The weather won't get better. I want to hit the Grenye again, just as soon as I can."

That made good sense. Even if the winter here wouldn't turn Russian, it wouldn't be a delight, either. Hasso shrugged. "Sorry, your Majesty. Then we have to do it the hard way—or can your wizards knock down that castle for you?"

What did the Americans call that? Passing the buck, that's what it was. King Bottero, who had been scowling, brightened. "I'll find out," he said, and stomped off.

Hasso carefully didn't smile. Even if the wizards told Bottero no, he'd get angry at them, not at his military adviser who'd fallen out of the sky. That suited Hasso just fine.

Berbec might have tried to disappear, but he'd kept his ears open. He sketched a salute. "You are not just a bold warrior, my master," he said. "You are sly, too."

"*Danke schön,*" Hasso said, perhaps with less irony than he'd intended. He studied the Grenye he'd vanquished and then acquired. How much of that did Berbec mean, and how much was the grease job any slave with a gram of sense gave his master? Some of each, the German judged: the best flattery held a grain of truth that made all of it more likely to be believed.

"What do you say?" Berbec scratched his head over the sounds of a language only one man in this world would ever speak.

"I say, 'Thank you,'" Hasso answered, and then, "How do you say that in your language?" Berbec told him. When Hasso pronounced the words, Berbec's dark eyebrows twitched, so the German judged he'd made a hash of things. "Tell me when I am wrong," he said. "I want to say it right. Repeat for me, please." He'd had plenty of practice saying that in Lenello.

"You sure you want me to say you are wrong?" Berbec understood the dangers inherent in that, all right.

But Hasso nodded. "By the goddess, I do. I am angrier if I make mistake than if you tell me I make mistake."

"Hmm." The native's eyebrows were very expressive. Frenchmen had eyebrows like that. So did Jews in Poland and Russia. Their eyebrows hadn't done them any good. Neither had anything else. Berbec's … made Hasso smile, anyway. "Well, we see." The Bucovinan still seemed anything but convinced.

"If you tell me sweet lies and I find out, I make you sorry." Hasso tried to sound as fierce as … as what? As a Lenello who'd just sacked a town in Bucovin, that was what. Yes, that would do, and then some.

It would if it convinced Berbec, anyhow. "Hmm," he repeated. *Next to the Lenelli, maybe I'm not such a tough guy after all.* He'd spent five and a half years in the biggest war in the history of the world, most of the last four on the Russian front—and in spite of everything he'd seen and done, he was still a softie next to Bottero's knights and foot soldiers. Maybe that said something good about the civilization that had blown itself to smithereens from the Atlantic to the Volga. He smacked Berbec on the back, not too hard. "You listen to me, you hear?"

"You are my master. You could have killed me, and you didn't. Of course I listen to you," Berbec said. Something in his deep-set dark eyes added, *If I feel like it.*

Hasso did him a favor: he pretended not to see that. He just laughed and slapped the Bucovinan on the back again and got ready for another day of warfare, for all the world as if there hadn't been a sack and a slaughter here the day before. He'd done that kind of thing back in his own world, too.

***

King Bottero's artisans started gathering lumber from what was left of Muresh to resurface to bridge across the Oltet. That told Hasso the king's wizards hadn't come up with any brilliant ideas on their own. The artisans had to do considerable scrounging, too, because not much *was* left of Muresh.

Orosei came over to Hasso as the *Wehrmacht* man watched the artisans at work. "You didn't have any sneaky schemes for getting across?" the master-at-arms asked.

Hasso shrugged and spread his hands. "No miracles in my pockets. No ford.

No boats. I think we have to do it the hard way."

"Oh, well." Orosei shrugged, too. "I told the king to ask you. It was worth a try."

"So you're to blame, eh?" Hasso made a joke of it. Orosei might have been doing him a favor.

"That's me." Orosei grinned. Either he wasn't trying to screw Hasso or he had more guile in him than the German guessed.

"I say to King Bottero, try the wizards." Hasso shrugged. "They have no miracles in their pockets, either."

"Too bad," Orosei said. "They talk big. I'd like 'em better if they delivered on more of their promises, though. That poor bastard the Bucovinans caught … If he was hot stuff, why didn't he turn 'em into a bunch of trout before they got to work on him?"

"Swords are faster than spells," Hasso said. So everybody had told him. Like a lot of things everybody said, it must have held some truth, or Flegrei would still be around. Hasso suspected it wasn't the last word, though.

Bottero's master-at-arms let out a sour chuckle. "Yeah, they are. A good thing, too, or clowns like you and me'd be out of work. When kings wanted to fight wars, they wouldn't use anybody but those unicorn-riding nancy boys." He spat in the mud to show what he thought of wizards.

Hasso had seen his share of homos in the *Wehrmacht*, and maybe more than his share in the *Waffen*-SS, where they seemed to gravitate. Yeah, sometimes you could blackmail them. But when they fought, they fought at least as well as anybody else. Some of them, in fact, made uncommonly ferocious soldiers, because they didn't seem to give a damn whether they lived or died.

More boards thudded onto the stone framework of the bridge across the Oltet. The Bucovinans in the keep on the far bank watched the Lenelli work without trying to interfere … till Bottero's men replanked about half of the bridge. That brought them into archery range, and the Grenye started shooting as if arrows were going to be banned day after tomorrow.

A Lenello shot through the throat clutched at himself and tumbled into the turbid green water five meters below. He wore a heavy mailshirt; he wouldn't have lasted long even without a mortal wound. Another big blond warrior came back cussing a blue streak, an arrow clean through his forearm.

"You're lucky," somebody told the wounded man. "Now they can get it out easy—they won't have to push it through."

"Bugger you with a pinecone, you stinking fool," the bleeding Lenello retorted. "If I was lucky, this goddess-cursed thing would've missed." Good grammar would have called for a subjunctive there. None of the soldiers seemed to miss it. Like any language, Lenello spoken informally was a different beast from the one the schoolmasters taught. Hasso smiled reminiscently, remembering all the German dialects he'd coped with. He wouldn't have to worry about that any more.

The archery on the bridge was a different story. Other Lenelli fell, a few dead, more wounded. Some of the hurt men made it back under their own power; others needed buddies' help. Every soldier who helped a wounded friend was a soldier who wasn't retimbering the bridge. That work slowed to a crawl.

Bottero sent archers out onto the span to shoot back. They were bigger, stronger men than the Bucovinans in the castle. But most of their arrows fell short. The natives, shooting down from a height, had gravity on their side. Working against it was a losing proposition.

The Lenelli didn't need long to see as much. They quit shooting at the Grenye, and brought a troop of men with shields forward to protect the soldiers moving the planking forward. That wasn't perfect, but it worked well enough.

Meter by meter, the planking advanced. As it neared the east bank of the Oltet, the Bucovinans in the castle tried something new. They stopped shooting at the men setting the planks in place and sent volley after volley of fire arrows at the lumber itself. Some of the long shafts with burning tow and tallow attached near the tip fell into the river and hissed out. But the Lenelli had to stomp out lots of others or drench them with buckets of water dipped up from below. One soldier, in a display of bravado, dropped his trousers and pissed a flame into oblivion.

Here and there, though, the fire arrows started blazes before the Lenelli could suppress them. If those had spread, they might have driven King Bottero's men from the bridge. But some of the wood the Lenelli used was wet, which slowed down the flames. And the blonds managed to keep ahead of the fires in spite of everything their enemies could do.

When it became clear that the Lenelli *were* going to make it over the Oltet, the Bucovinans in the castle fled, as they'd abandoned Muresh. They left Bottero nothing he could use. Not long after they abandoned the tower, smoke started pouring from it—they'd fired whatever was left inside.

"Miserable bastards," Orosei grumbled.

"Good soldiers," Hasso said. "They do their job, then they pull out. They hurt us, they delay us, they deny us the tower. Good soldiers."

"They've got no business being good soldiers," the master-at-arms said. "They're nothing but a pack of Grenye savages."

He sounded personally affronted that the enemy should do anything right. Some Germans in Russia had sounded the same way about the Ivans in 1941. After that, such expressions of amazement came a lot less often. The *Wehrmacht* was the best army in the world—which meant the Red Army had the best schoolmasters in the world. The same was bound to be true here.

"How much do the Bucovinans learn from you?" Hasso asked.

"Too bloody much, if you want to know what I think." No, Orosei didn't want to take them seriously.

After the defenders fled, replanking the last bit of bridge went fast. With typical Lenello swagger, an officer leaped from the bridge onto the riverbank. He leaped—and he vanished. A moment later, a shriek rang out that Hasso could hear all the way across the river.

"What the—?" he said. Orosei spread his hands and shrugged, as baffled as the man from another world.

Before long, the story came back across the bridge. So did the officer's body. The Bucovinans had dug themselves a mantrap on the riverbank: a cunningly concealed pit, with upward-pointing spikes set in the bottom. They knew their foes' habits, all right. They made the trap, and the Lenello jumped into it.

"I've heard of them doing things like that before," Orosei said. "You've got to watch out for the spikes they use. They smear shit on them, to poison the wounds they make."

"No matter here," Hasso said. He'd got a look at the dead officer. One of those spikes had gone through his chest, another through his throat. He'd bled like a stuck pig, which he might as well have been. His wounds wouldn't have time to fester.

More Lenelli stepped onto the eastern bank of the Oltet. They moved more cautiously than that first luckless officer had, and probed the ground in front of them with spears. They found another mantrap a few meters farther in from the water's edge. The Grenye had used the night well indeed.

Hasso wondered whether watchers would be waiting to harass the Lenelli as they filled in the pits. But the natives seemed to think they'd done everything they could to slow down Bottero's men here. The Lenelli crossed the Oltet with no further trouble.

***

Orosei pointed to smoke rising up in the east. "They're burning things again," he said. "Do they really think that will slow us down?"

"Yes," Hasso answered. "They're liable to be right, too. Where's the wagon train that should be here yesterday?"

"Should have been—you talk funny, you know that?" the master-at-arms said. "I don't know where the miserable wagons are. We can't detach enough men to cover all of them."

"I know," Hasso said. "Do you think the Bucovinans don't know, too? Without the wagons, without foraging on the country, what do we eat?"

Orosei looked around. "Mud. Rocks." He rubbed his belly. "Yum."

He startled a laugh out of Hasso. "All right—you have me there. But what do we do when we get hungry?"

"Eat the goddess-cursed Bucovinans, for all I care," the Lenello answered. For all Hasso knew, he meant it. The Germans thought the Ivans were *Untermenschen*. The Lenelli thought the same thing about the natives here, only more so. Did they think the Grenye were far enough down the scale to do duty as meat animals? Hasso decided he didn't want to find out.

He didn't want to let go of his own worries, either. "If the Bucovinans burn their crops, what do *they* eat?"

"Their seed grain," Orosei answered. "Then they starve along with us, but they take longer."

Bucovin was a big place—Hasso remembered the maps Bottero used. They weren't anywhere near so good as the ones the *Wehrmacht* used, but they showed that well enough. Could the natives bring in enough food from places where they weren't burning it to supply the ones where they were?

He had no idea. When he asked Orosei, the master-at-arms only shrugged his broad shoulders. "Beats me," he said. "You're the spymaster, right? You're the one who's supposed to find out stuff like that, right?"

"Right," Hasso said tightly. Orosei made intelligence work sound easy, which only proved he'd never done any. By the end of 1941, the Germans were sure they'd knocked out as many divisions as the Red Army had at the start of the war—but the Russians weren't within a million kilometers of quitting, or of running out of men.

King Bottero sent out raiding parties to the north and south of his main line of march. They drove some pigs and a few cattle and sheep back to the army—and a few horses and donkeys as well. Those were riding or draft animals, but you could eat them if you had to. Though not a Frenchman who did it by choice, Hasso had chewed gluey horseflesh plenty of times on the Russian front. He'd been glad to get it then; if the Lenello cooks served it up, he'd eat it again now.

The raiders also brought back some grain the Grenye had already harvested. It didn't make up for the wagons that weren't going to get to the army, though. Had the Bucovinans burned that grain or captured it? Only they knew.

But they left no doubt about what had happened to the Lenello teamsters. They left a bloated, foul-smelling blond head in the road in front of Bottero's oncoming army. Someone had written a message in Lenello on a sheet of bark and put it by the head. Even Hasso had no trouble sounding out the two words: *YOU NEXT.*

When King Bottero saw that, Hasso thought he would have a stroke. Hitler's rages were the stuff of legend in Germany; Bottero's fury now matched any fit the *Führer* could have pitched. For a little while, the German didn't understand just why the king was going off like a grenade. Yes, the warning in the road was grisly, but it was no worse than a hundred things the Lenelli had done when they sacked Muresh.

But then Bottero roared, "My horse—my *horse*, I tell you!—has more business pushing me around than these goddess-cursed, mindblind, soul-dead Grenye! They'll pay! Oh, how they'll pay!"

That made the *Wehrmacht* officer nod to himself. It came down to the business of who were *Untermenschen* again. Bottero really would have taken it better had his horse tried to tell him to go back to his own kingdom. For the Bucovinans to assume equality with the invaders, even an equality of terror, was a slap in the face to everything the Lenello kingdoms stood for.

And it wasn't just Bottero. All the Lenelli who saw the head and, even more important, who could read the crude threat by it, quivered with outrage. Velona was quieter than the king—Krakatoa erupting might have been noisier than Bottero, but Hasso couldn't think of anything else that would—but no less angry.

"They dare," she whispered, as if speaking louder might make her burst. "They truly dare to try conclusions with us, do they? Well, his Majesty has the right of it—we'll teach them a lesson they'll remember for the next hundred years. The ones we leave alive will, anyhow."

Germans had talked like that in Poland in 1939, and in Russia in 1941. Poles and Russians by the millions had died, too. The Germans had expected nothing less; those deaths were reckoned a prerequisite for clearing the *Lebensraum* Germans needed in the fertile croplands of the east.

What the Germans hadn't expected was how many of their own number would die. The Slavs were uncommonly stubborn about refusing to be cleared, and now Hasso's folk fled before them instead of driving them away.

Could that happen here? He had trouble believing it. The Bucovinans were brave, and there were lots of them, but they were outclassed in ways the Ivans hadn't been. Still, that head and the warning by it spoke of more implacable purpose than Hasso had looked to see from the natives.

They spoke of such things to him, anyhow. King Bottero took another message from them. "Burn the head," he commanded in a voice like iron. "His soul will ascend to the heavens." He looked around. Had he spotted any Bucovinans, he probably would have ordered them sacrificed to serve the Lenello teamster in the world to come. His face had that kind of intense, purposeful stare, anyhow. But, since he didn't, he pointed to the bark with the writing. "Dig a hole and throw that in. Don't cover it over yet, though, by the goddess."

His men sprang to obey him. That was partly their own anger working, and partly their fear. Anyone who tried standing against Bottero in that moment would have been a dead man in the next. The dirt by the side of the road was soft and easy to dig up. One of the Lenelli picked up the piece of bark with his fingertips, as if it were unclean. After he dropped it into the hole, he scrubbed his hands on the dead grass and then spat after it.

Spitting wasn't enough to satisfy Bottero. He dismounted from his great warhorse, walked over to the hole, undid his trousers, and took the most furious and majestic leak Hasso had ever imagined, let alone seen.

Even that didn't suffice, not for the king. He gestured to the leaders around him. Hasso didn't care one way or the other about pissing on an offensive sign. If Bottero wanted him to, he would. The king did, and so he did. Other officers' efforts made a pretty fair puddle in the hole in the ground.

Hasso *was* taken aback when Bottero waved Velona up to the hole. He could see why Bottero wanted to show the goddess' utter contempt for the Bucovinan warning, but.... Velona didn't seem embarrassed; she just squatted and pissed. If it didn't bother her, Hasso told himself it shouldn't bother him, either.

After that, the Lenelli shoveled in some dirt, too. The army rode on. Velona looked … maybe unhappy, maybe just distant. "You don't like what you just did?" Hasso asked, guiding his horse up alongside hers.

"Oh," she said in some surprise, as if recalled to herself. "No. It isn't that. The natives deserve what we gave them. But … I wish he hadn't buried it, that's all.

The earth here fights for Bucovin."

She'd said that before, about her last visit to the Grenye land. What did it mean here? Did even she know? Hasso thought about asking, and then thought again.

XI

Bucovinan raiders hit harder at Bottero's scouts and supply wagons once the Lenelli got over the Oltet. They didn't stop the king's army, but they harassed it and slowed it down—the last thing it needed as fall moved on toward winter. Falticeni, the capital of Bucovin, lay ... somewhere up ahead, anyhow.

As winter snow came down, a few German units fought their way into the suburbs of Moscow and, in the distance, got a glimpse of the Kremlin. Then the Ivans threw them back, and they never came so close again. Hasso wished he hadn't thought of that, even if the weather here was milder.

The king's temper frayed. He gathered his generals and wizards together so he could shout at them all at the same time. "Why aren't you keeping the outriders safe, curse you?" Bottero bellowed.

"We're doing everything we know how to do, your Majesty." An officer named Nuoro had charge of the supply train. "But there aren't enough of us, and there are too stinking many Bucovinans. Things go wrong sometimes, that's all."

"That's all, he says!" King Bottero rolled his eyes. "If things go on like this, we'll be eating our belts and our boots before too long."

He exaggerated—by how much, Hasso wasn't sure. Nuoro gave him a stiff, almost wooden, salute. "What would you have me do, your Majesty?"

"Push the supplies through. Don't let the teamsters get massacred. How hard is that?" Bottero demanded.

"In a land full of raiders and bushwhackers, sire, it's not so easy. How many more soldiers will you give me to keep the wagons safe?" Nuoro asked.

"Well, maybe a few," the king said. "I can't give you *too* many more. We need them to beat the savages back. That's what we're here for, you know."

"Maybe we haven't got enough soldiers for everything we need to do ... sire," Nuoro said. How many times had the Germans worked through the same agonizing choices in the vastnesses of the Soviet Union? How much good did their agonizing do them? Not bloody much.

But Bottero had options that weren't available to the *Wehrmacht*. He turned to his wizards. "If I string you out along the route back to the border, you can smell out ambushes, right? You can stop them?"

121

"Well, yes, your Majesty," Aderno said. "But then we won't be here with the striking force in case of battle."

"What?" Now Bottero looked—and sounded—highly offended, so much so that he might almost have struck a pose. People in a position to know said the *Führer* did stuff like that. Acting had to be one of the things that went into ruling. Still offended, the king went on, "You think we can't beat the barbarians by ourselves?"

That question had only one possible answer, and Aderno gave it: "Of course you can, your Majesty. We might make it a little easier for you, that's all."

"By the goddess, we'll manage on our own," Bottero said. "But if you can't conjure up the grub we need to keep going—and it doesn't look like you *can* do that—the next best thing for you is to make sure the plain old ordinary grub from our own kingdom gets here safe. How does that sound?"

Aderno saluted. "As you wish it, your Majesty, so shall it be."

A German would have shot out his arm and said, "*Heil* Hitler!" An Ivan, no doubt, would have nodded and said, "Yes, Comrade General Secretary!" It all amounted to the same thing in the end.

Then Hasso had a disconcerting thought. Stalin had almost led his country right off a cliff in the early days of war on the Russian front, but the Ivans went right on saying, "Yes, Comrade General Secretary!" And the *Führer* damn well *had* led the *Reich* off a cliff as the war ground on, but the Germans went right on saying, "*Heil* Hitler!" Obedience was all very well, but didn't it have limits somewhere?

Somewhere, certainly. Here? No. Bottero had given a reasonable order. It might not work out, but chances were it would. And Hasso also thought the Lenelli could beat whatever Bucovin threw at them. The natives were brave, but all the courage in the world didn't matter when it ran into technique.

So the *Wehrmacht* taught, anyhow. But who wasn't in Moscow, and who was in Berlin? So what if one German was worth three Ivans? If every *Landser* knocked down his three Russians, and then a fourth Russian showed up, and a fifth....

Exactly how big was Bucovin? How many swarthy little men did it hold, swarthy little men who didn't want to live under a big blond king who could roar like a lion? Enough for their numbers to cancel out the huge advantage in weapons and skill the Lenelli had? Hasso didn't know.

He hoped like hell Bottero did.

***

Off rode the wizards on their gleaming unicorns. Hasso was sorry to see them go, not so much because he'd miss them—they were a contentious, bad-tempered lot—but because he'd miss their mounts. The unicorns were marvelous and beautiful. Without them, the army seemed only ... an army. Its glamour was gone.

Well, almost. Velona still rode with Bottero and his soldiers. Her glamour was of a different sort from the unicorns', which didn't make it any less real. Most of the time, she was just herself, not a woman in whom the goddess dwelt. Even as herself, she was striking, of course, but there was more to it than that. She held the memory of the goddess whether touched by the deity or not.

Hasso sometimes wondered if he was imagining that, but never for long. He knew better. That doubt was just the sputtering of his rational mind, here in a world where rationality mattered so much less than it did in the one where he grew to manhood.

As if to prove as much, two wagon trains in a row made it through to King Bottero's army. The teamsters were full of praise for what the wizards had done to help them on the way. "They sent them savages running with lightning singeing the hair off their balls," one driver said enthusiastically. "I'll buy those bastards a beer any day of the week, twice on Sundays."

Weeks here had ten days, and Sundays were feast days instead, but Hasso tried to turn Lenello into idiomatic German inside his head. Most of the time, he did pretty well. Every once in a while ... Every once in a while, he might as well have been in another world. *Funny how that works*, he thought with a sour smile.

Things didn't get better the next day. The Lenelli were marching near a river—the Aryesh, it was called—that ran north and east. It should have shielded their left from any trouble from the Bucovinans. It should have, but it didn't. Somehow, a raiding party appeared at dawn where no raiding party had any business being. The enemy soldiers shot volleys of arrows into the startled Lenello infantry, then galloped off before King Bottero's horsemen could harry them.

Bottero, predictably, was furious. "They have no business doing that!" he shouted. "They have no *right* to do that! How did they get there? They came out of nowhere!"

"They must have crossed the river, your Majesty," said the infantry commander, a stolid soldier named Friddi.

"Brilliant!" The king was savagely sarcastic. "And how did they do that? No bridge in these parts, and it's too deep to ford. Maybe they had catapults fling them across!"

"Maybe magic flung them across, sire," Friddi said.

"Don't be any dumber than you can help," Bottero said. "They're Grenye, by the goddess! They can't do that. And we don't *think* they've got any renegades doing it for them. If they do, those bastards'll be a long, hard time dying, I promise you that."

Hasso thought of Scanno, back in Drammen. Scanno liked Grenye better than his own folk, and made no bones about it. *Dammit, we never did pick him up and grill him about how he beat Aderno's spell*, he thought—there was something that slipped through the cracks as the campaign revved up. But he was a drunk, a ruin of his former self. He wouldn't make a wizard if he lived to be a thousand, and Hasso wouldn't have bet on him to last another five years.

Stubbornly, Friddi said, "Well, your Majesty, unless it was wizardry, I don't know how the demon they got there."

However the men of Bucovin managed to cross the Aryesh, they threw the Lenello army into enough confusion to make it halt for the day. Hasso hunted up Orosei. "You know some men who are good trackers?" he asked.

"Oh, I might. I just might." The master-at-arms' eyes gleamed. "You've got an idea."

"Oh, I might. I just might." Hasso mimicked Orosei's tone well enough to send the Lenello into gales of laughter.

The half-dozen soldiers Orosei told off had the look of hunters, or more likely poachers. "You do what our foreign friend says," Orosei told them. "We've got some tricks he doesn't know about, but I expect he's got some we don't know about, too."

"What's on your mind, lord?" By one tracker's tone of voice, he was suspicious of Hasso on general principles first, then because the German was trying to order him around.

"Take me to where the Bucovinans cross the river. Track them back to there for me," Hasso said.

"If they *did* cross it," the Lenello said. "If they didn't just show up, like. I don't *suppose* Grenye can do magic, but you never can tell, now can you?" He seemed a lot less convinced than King Bottero. What that meant ... Well, who the hell knew what that meant? Hasso had more urgent things to worry about.

"Track them back," he said. "Then we see. Till we try to find out, we can't really know." That was true in his world. Here ... *It had better be true here*, he thought.

"You don't need us for this," another tracker said as they all set out. "A blind man could follow these hoofprints."

"A blind man, nothing," still another Lenello put in. "A dead man could."

"Fine. Pretend I am blind. Pretend I am dead," Hasso said. "But remember one thing, please. If you make a mistake, I haunt you." That got some grins from the men Orosei had picked, and one or two nervous chuckles. Back in Germany, he would have been joking. Here, as the first Lenello tracker said, you never could tell.

Back through the bushes and saplings the train led, back to the Aryesh. The trackers were right; Hasso could have done this himself. He shrugged. He hadn't known ahead of time. But now he had witnesses if his hunch turned out to be right. And if it turned out to be wrong, they would see him looking like a jerk.

He shrugged again. *If you're going to try things, sometimes you damn well* will *look like a jerk, that's all.*

The Aryesh was muddy and foamy. It looked almost like Viennese coffee. Hasso sighed. Along with tobacco, that was something he would never enjoy again. Nothing he could do about it. No, there was one thing: he could do *without*.

He unsheathed his belt knife and trimmed a sapling into a pole about a meter and a half long. "Nice blade," one of the trackers said. "Where'd you get it?"

"I have it with me when I come from my world," Hasso answered.

"How about that?" the Lenello said, and then, in a low voice to one of his pals,

"Never seen one like it before. Almost makes you believe that cock-and-bull story, doesn't it?" Hasso didn't think he was supposed to overhear that, but he did.

"What's he going to do now?" the other tracker said, his *voce* also not quite *sotto* enough. "Dowse with that stick? We already know where the cursed river is."

Hasso hadn't even thought of dowsing. In Germany, that was an old wives' tale. It probably wasn't here. If any kind of magic was practical, finding water fit the bill. But, as the tracker said, he already knew where the water was here. He was after something else.

He thrust the pole into the Aryesh. He wasn't enormously surprised when only the first twenty-five or thirty centimeters went in. After that, it hit an obstruction. His grin was two parts satisfaction and one part relief.

Orosei was only confused. "What's going on?" he asked.

Instead of answering with words, Hasso probed with the pole again. Then he stepped out into—or onto—the river. Walking on the water, he felt like Jesus. The Aryesh didn't come up to the tops of his boots. He strode forward, probing as he went.

"What the—?" one of the trackers exclaimed.

"They don't put their bridge where we can see it," Hasso said, turning back toward the Lenelli. "They build it underwater, build it sneaky, so they can use it and we don't know."

"Well, fuck me," the tracker said. If that wasn't his version of coming to attention and saluting, Hasso didn't know what would be.

"I don't know, not till I see," Hasso answered. "But I think maybe. In my world, the enemies of my land use this trick." The Russians used every trick in the book, and then wrote a new book for all the tricks that weren't in the old one. The *Wehrmacht* used this one, too. A bridge that was hard to spot was a bridge artillery wouldn't knock out in a hurry.

Artillery couldn't knock this one out—no artillery here. Hasso looked across the Aryesh. He didn't see anybody, which was all to the good.

"What we need to do is, we need to pull up ten or fifteen cubits of this tonight," he said. He almost said *five or six meters*, but that wouldn't have meant anything to the blonds with him. They used fingers and palms and cubits, and weights that were even more cumbersome. What could you do? Since he couldn't do anything, he went on, "Then the Bucovinans ride across, go splash."

Orosei grinned at him. "If that doesn't make those bastards turn up their toes, I don't know what would!"

"That's the idea, isn't it?" Hasso said.

Even the trackers, who had been dubious about him, laughed and nudged one another. "He's not so dumb after all, is he?" one of them said.

"Not *so* dumb," another agreed, which struck Hasso as praising with faint damn. But he would take what he could get.

He made the trackers love him even more when he said, "You stay here and keep an eye on things. Orosei and I, we go back to the king and let him know what needs doing."

"What if the savages come across the river at us now?" a tracker demanded.

"Not likely, not in the daytime. They want to keep this a secret, right?" Hasso said. Before the trackers could answer or complain, he added, "But if they do, then you bug out." They couldn't very well bitch about that, and they didn't.

"An underwater bridge?" King Bottero said when Hasso brought him the news. "How the demon did they do that?"

When Hasso hesitated, Orosei took over. The German's Lenello wasn't up to technical discussions of pilings and planking. Bottero's master-at-arms finished, "I never would have thought of it. I didn't know *what* to think when I saw him walking on the water." (Yes, that was funny, though only Hasso in all this world knew why.) "But he says they use this trick in war where he comes from, so he was ready for it."

Nice to know Orosei doesn't try to hog credit, Hasso thought, *or not when the guy who deserves it is around to hear him, anyway.*

"What do we do about it?" the king asked. Hasso told him what he had in mind. Bottero stroked his beard. A slow smile stole over his heavy-featured face. "I like that, fry me if I don't. We'll do it tonight, and we'll watch the Grenye go *sploot.*" Hasso didn't think *sploot* was a word in Lenello, but he had no trouble figuring out what it meant.

"Send a good-sized band of men, your Majesty," Orosei suggested. "If the barbarians decide to bring more raiders across tonight, they might swamp a little party of artisans."

Hasso hadn't thought of that. Plainly, neither had King Bottero. He nodded. "You're right. I'll do it." He turned and shouted orders to the officers who would take charge of that. Then he nodded again. "There. I've dealt with *something*, anyhow." A frown spread across his face like rain clouds. "Or have I? Have the Bucovinans built more of these underwater bridges, ones we don't know about yet?"

"A wizard could—" Hasso broke off, feeling stupid. All the wizards were scattered along the army's long supply line. Now that the main force needed one, it didn't have any.

Then he noticed that Bottero was eyeing him. "Didn't Aderno say *you* had some of the talent?" the king rumbled.

"He says it, but I don't know if I believe it." Hasso's voice broke as if he were one of the fifteen-year-olds to whom the *Volkssturm* gave a rifle and a "Good luck!" as they sent them off to try to slow down the Red Army. "And even if it's true, I don't know how to use it."

"About time you find out, then, isn't it?" Bottero said. "If you *can* do it, you'll give us a big hand."

"But— But—" Hasso spluttered.

"His Majesty's right," Orosei said. "Magic isn't a common gift. If you've got it, you shouldn't let it lie idle. The goddess wouldn't like that."

Did he mean Velona or the deity who sometimes inhabited her? Hasso didn't know, and wondered whether the Lenello did. "But— But—" he said again. He hated sounding like a broken record, but he didn't know what else to say.

The king slapped him on the back, which almost knocked him out of the saddle. If he'd fallen off the horse and landed on his head, it would have been a relief. "Talk to Velona," Bottero said. "She'll give you some pointers, and you can go from there. It doesn't sound like the kind of magic that can kill you if you don't do it right. Give it your best shot."

Hasso hadn't even thought about the consequences of a spell gone wrong. He wished his new sovereign hadn't reminded him of such things, too. But what were his choices here? He saw only two: say no and get a name for cowardice—the last thing he needed—or give it his best shot.

He'd long since decided that a big part of courage was nothing more than a reluctance to look like a coward in front of people who mattered to him. And so, reluctantly, he said, "Yes, your Majesty."

***

Velona came up and kissed him, which was a hell of a distraction for somebody contemplating his very first conjuration. "You can do it," she said. Her voice was full of confidence—and perhaps some warm promise, too. "I'm sure you can do it. The goddess wouldn't have brought you here to let you fail."

He didn't know why the goddess had brought him here. He didn't even know *that* the goddess had brought him here. King Bottero had a point, though. Velona knew a lot more about magic than he did. *Christ! My horse knows more about magic than I do,* he thought. Between her suggestions and his own few feeble ideas, he'd come up with what might be a spell.

It turned dowsing upside down and inside out. He wasn't trying to find water flowing underground—he was looking for unmoving objects concealed beneath running water. If everything went exactly right, the forked stick in his hands would rise when he pointed it at a submerged bridge.

The not-quite-dowsing stick was carved from one of the timbers the Lenelli had torn from the first underwater bridge. Velona said that would give it a mystic affinity with the other bridges ... if there were others. The idea seemed reasonable, in an unreasonable kind of way.

Even so, he let his worry show: "If I find no bridges, does that mean there are no bridges? Or does it mean I can't find them? If I am no wizard, casting a spell does not help. Will not help." He remembered how to make the future tense. He didn't need to worry about the future, though. He was tense right now.

"Cast the spell. Then see what happens," Velona said. That also seemed reasonable—if your view of reason included spells in the first place. Hasso's didn't. Or rather, it hadn't.

Fighting not to show his fear, he started to chant. Velona had come up with a lot of the spell. Hasso would never make a poet in Lenello—come to that, he'd made a lousy poet *auf Deutsch*. What he had to remember here was to get the words right. He understood what the magic ought to do, even if he didn't perfectly follow all the phrases in the charm. Poetry was supposed to be challenging ... wasn't it?

Velona gestured. That reminded him to move the not-dowsing rod. He swung it slowly from southwest to northeast, paralleling the course of the Aryesh. All of a sudden, it jerked upwards in his hands. He almost dropped it, he was so surprised. He'd no more thought he could truly work magic than that he could fly.

"There!" Velona said. "Go back, Hasso Pemsel. Go back and get the exact direction, so the artisans can find the hidden bridge."

He did, and damned if the rod didn't rise again. His own rod rose, too. He remembered how she'd called him by his full name when they met, there on the causeway through the swamp. He remembered what they'd done right afterwards, too, and he wanted to do it again.

His thoughts must have shown on his face, for Velona laughed, softly and throatily. "Soon," she promised. But then she tempered that, adding, "But not yet. First we see where the savages can sneak across the river."

"Oh, all right." Hasso knew he sounded like a petulant little boy who couldn't have what he wanted just when he wanted it. (*Quite a bit like the* Führer, *in fact*, he thought.) Velona, who knew nothing about Hitler except that he was the man who ruled the country Hasso came from, laughed again, this time with rich amusement in her voice.

Hasso wished he had a compass, to give him a precise bearing on where that bridge lurked under the water. Nobody here had any idea what a compass was. If he could float an iron needle in a bowl of water ... But he had too many other things to worry about right now.

Velona marked off the bearing as best she could. Hasso decided it would probably serve; they weren't very far from the Aryesh. "Go on," she urged him. "See if there are any more."

He wished she were urging him on while they were doing something else, but he saw the need for continuing with this. That need might not delight him, but he did see it. And working magic had a fascination, and an astonishment, all its own. He didn't think he'd been so delightfully surprised since the first time he played with himself.

And ... "I'll be a son of a bitch!" he muttered. Damned if the rod didn't jerk up in his hand again. Chanting the charm over and over, he fixed the precise direction. Again, Velona marked it.

He found one more bridge after that, or thought he did. Part of him—a good bit of him—still wondered whether this wasn't some kind of delusion. But even in his world dowsers could—or claimed they could—find water. Maybe there was something to it.

Velona had no doubts. As soon as the spell was done, she plastered herself against him tighter than a coat of paint and gave him a kiss that curled his ears and made steam come out of his hair. Before he could sling her over his shoulder and carry her off to their tent—the first thing that occurred to him, even if she didn't weigh that much less than he did—she broke free and called for the artisans. After a moment, regretfully, so did Hasso.

The men came up with astonishing haste. Hasso didn't flatter himself that his shouts had much to do with it. When your goddess yelled for you, you went to her first and then wondered why she wanted you. (Hasso sometimes wondered why Velona still wanted *him*, but in a much more pleasant way.)

"Follow these bearings to the river, one by one," she said, pointing at the lines she'd laid out. "When you get there, probe under the surface. You'll find hidden bridges in each place. Tear them up."

They saluted, clenched fists over their hearts. "We'll do it!" they said, and hurried off. Hasso hoped they weren't going off for nothing, not least because he would look like a jerk if they were.

They must have found what they were looking for, because that evening King Bottero summoned Hasso to dine with him. He hadn't done that since Hasso's striking column slammed through the Bucovinans in the first—and, so far, only—big battle the two sides had fought. Bottero poured wine for Hasso with his own hand. "You see?" he said expansively. "I told you you could do it."

"Yes, your Majesty," Hasso said, which was an answer as useful here as *Jawohl, mein Führer!* had been back in the *Reich*. And it wasn't even a lie this time around. Bottero did say so, and he was right.

"Why did you have any doubts?" the king asked. "If Aderno said you had the power, you did. Aderno may be a pain in the fundament sometimes, but he knows the difference between a snake and its cast skin."

"No magic in the world I come from," Hasso said. "Hard for me to believe anyone has it." He jabbed a thumb at his own chest. "Extra hard to believe I have it."

"Well, you do," Bottero said. "Get used to it. The artisans came back all excited about how you knew exactly where to send them. They said you made their work easy. One of them asked why our regular wizards couldn't do so well."

Hasso winced. "They shouldn't say that." He didn't want the regular wizards angry at him. Maybe he could work a little magic, however crazy that seemed. But he wasn't a pro, and he knew it. If somebody who *was* a pro decided to turn him into a prawn, he didn't know how to defend himself or fight back.

A pretty young Grenye woman brought in a platter of pork ribs and roasted parsnips. The robe she wore was so thin, it wouldn't have kept her warm long outside. The king ran his hand up her leg. Was her smile forced or real? Was she glad to be getting off as easy as this, or did she hate him for groping her—and, no doubt, for taking her, too? Hasso had no way to know, which might have been—surely was—just as well.

He concentrated on the food. After a while, he asked, "How far to Falticeni, your Majesty?"

"We're getting there," Bottero answered. "Pretty soon, the savages will have to fight us again. We'll whip them, and then we'll go on and take the place."

The woman stood by the king, waiting for anything he might want—for anything at all, plainly. "Should you talk with her here?" Hasso asked.

"Why not?" Bottero asked. "She knows how to say, 'Yes,' in Lenello, and that's about it. And she's not going anywhere anyhow. She's hot enough to keep around for a while." He fondled her again, then asked, "You want her to suck you off? She's good."

Hasso might have enjoyed that if he'd found the girl himself. With Bottero watching, as he plainly intended to do? "No, thanks, your Majesty. I just came from Velona."

"Ah." The king leered. "She can wear anybody out."

"Yes." Hasso left it at that, and hoped Bottero would. He wasn't lying; Velona had helped him celebrate his successful sorcery. He also feared being unfaithful to her. As a woman? No, not so much, though she would be incandescent enough if scorned. But as a woman with the goddess indwelling? The last thing Hasso wanted to do was face an irate deity.

He didn't say that to King Bottero. It didn't seem manly. Then Bottero said, "You're pretty smart. If she found out about you and some chit, she'd fry your nuts off, I bet. Forget I asked you."

So the king respected—if that was the right word—Velona, too? Well, he would. He really believed in the goddess, believed in his belly and his balls. (Hasso tried not to think of his belly on Velona, his balls slapping the inside of her thighs.) To Hasso, belief like that came much harder, no matter what he'd seen here.

"How do we make the Bucovinans fight us?" Hasso asked. "If they stand, we can beat them, yes?"

"We'd better!" Bottero said. "That's what I'm trying to do—take a big bite out of them. Instead, they've been nibbling on us … and I don't mean like Sfinti here." He swatted the Bucovinan woman on the backside. She smiled at him again. Again, Hasso wondered what went on behind her eyes.

But only for a moment—he had other things to think about. The *Wehrmacht* had wanted to get the Red Army to stand and fight, too. Instead, the Russians traded space for time, drawing the Germans on till they got overextended and then hitting back. The Bucovinans looked to be playing the same game against Bottero.

Would it work here? If the Lenelli took Falticeni, obviously not. Otherwise? Hasso shrugged. He was too much a stranger here to be sure of much. Hell, he hadn't even been sure he could do magic. He still had trouble believing it.

He didn't want to think about that now. He gnawed on ribs and drank beer and tried not to watch Bottero pawing Sfinti. It wasn't that he hadn't seen plenty worse, most recently at Muresh. But the way she just stood there and let the king do what he wanted raised Hasso's hackles. He wouldn't have wanted to sleep with her, not literally, even if she kept on smiling. Wouldn't you be much too likely to wake up slightly dead the next morning?

King Bottero didn't seem to worry about it. Bottero didn't seem to worry about much of anything. "The rest of the Lenello kingdoms will be so jealous of us once we've cut off Bucovin's head," he boasted.

"Jealous enough to gang up on you?" Hasso asked. That would be all Bottero needed: getting through one war only to end up in another that was worse. Against other Lenelli, he wouldn't have any special edge.

"Don't think so." No, the king didn't worry about much. "What it will do, though, is it'll draw us more people from across the sea. They'll know we'll have lands to hand out, lands with plenty of Grenye on 'em to work and to have fun with." He pulled Sfinti down onto his lap.

Hasso got to his feet. "Maybe I'd better go, your Majesty," he said. King Bottero didn't tell him no. He bowed his way out of the tent. As the flap fell, Bottero laughed and the Bucovinan woman giggled. The guards outside grinned and nudged one another. One of them winked at Hasso. He had to make himself grin and wink back.

He also had to make himself hope Bottero knew what he was doing in there. The king pretty obviously thought so. Were the Bucovinans smart enough to leave a pretty assassin behind to be captured? Or would an ordinary Grenye woman pull out a knife if she saw the chance?

And even if the answer to both those questions was no, what would happen to Bottero's kingdom after this campaign? Hitler's biggest mistake was thinking he could take on almost the entire rest of the world. Was the local king doing the same stupid thing? Again, Hasso had to shrug. He didn't know enough to judge—just enough to worry.

"You're back sooner than I expected," Velona remarked when he ducked into the tent they shared.

"His Majesty has other things on his mind." Hasso shaped an hourglass in the air with his hands.

The Lenelli didn't use that gesture, and Velona needed a moment to realize what it meant. When she did, she laughed ... for a moment. "He didn't want to share with you?" she asked ominously.

He could, to his own relief, answer with the exact truth: "I don't want to share with him. I have better here."

He wasn't afraid of facing the Bucovinans in battle. He wasn't afraid of trying to work magic, either—though maybe he needed to be, now that he'd discovered he could do it. But facing an angry Velona ... That scared him green. He would rather have jumped on a Russian grenade.

Her eyes flashed as she inspected him. It wasn't just a figure of speech; the spark in them seemed to light up the gloom inside the tent. Maybe he was imagining things, but he didn't think so. Her gaze didn't probe him the same way a wizard's would have, which was not to say it didn't probe him.

At last, grudgingly, she nodded. "All right. I believe you. But if you ever waste your seed with a Grenye woman..." She didn't go on, not with words. She did create the strong impression that that wouldn't be a good idea. And Captain Hasso Pemsel, veteran of five and a half years of war in Europe and a campaign season's worth in this strange new world, shivered in his boots.

He didn't shiver only because Velona intimidated him. (He tried not to admit to himself that she did—he tried for a good second and a half, and then gave it up as a bad job.) It was bloody cold in there. Winter was coming on, and the tent walls were about as good at keeping the chill out as they would have been on the Eastern Front. He threw more charcoal on the brazier, which might have raised the temperature half a degree: from arctic all the way up to frigid.

He breathed easier when Velona relented enough to ask, "Does the king think he can make the Bucovinans stand and fight?"

"He wants to." Hasso was glad to talk about the campaign instead of anything that had to do with Sfinti's charms. "Can't conquer them unless they stand—or unless they let us walk into Falticeni."

"They won't," Velona said flatly, and Hasso nodded. He didn't think the Bucovinans would, either; they were fighting the Lenelli every way they knew how. And they had sense enough to see that pitched battles weren't the best way to do it. Her gaze went far away. "It won't be easy." Her voice might have been coming from Beyond, too.

Was that prophecy? Could there be such a thing in this world? Once more, Hasso didn't know. He did know his shiver, this time, had nothing to do with the cold outside.

XII

Two mornings later, a Bucovinan—noble?—approached the army to parley. He did it formally, with an escort of a dozen or so horsemen with armor as good as any Hasso had seen on a Bucovinan. As usual, they carried greenery in lieu of the white flags that served as truce signs in Hasso's world.

Some of the Lenelli muttered at that. "Who do they think they are, acting like civilized men?" Marshal Lugo grumbled. "We ought to run this beggar off just to teach him proper manners."

"Better to hear him," Hasso said. "Let us find out what he and his master have in mind." *Hortatory subjunctive*, he thought, pleased with himself. He hadn't needed to come out with one of those since he was taking Latin a hell of a long time ago.

"Bring him here," Bottero decided. "Listening to him doesn't cost us anything, and we can always run him off later if we don't like what he says."

The Bucovinan envoy bowed in the saddle to the king. "I am Otset, your Majesty," he said in excellent Lenello. "I bring you the words of Zgomot, Lord of Bucovin." He didn't claim Zgomot was a king; any Lenello sovereign would have either laughed or got furious at such presumption. "Hear my lord's words and marvel at how generous and full of forbearance he is."

King Bottero's face turned the color of brick dust. "Do you want us to horse-whip you home, little man? You sound like you do."

Otset bit his lip. He *wasn't* very big, especially when measured against the enormous Lenelli. But he answered calmly enough: "If someone invaded your kingdom, your Majesty, would you greet him with cheers and flowers and bread and salt?"

When the *Wehrmacht* rolled into the Ukraine in 1941, some of the locals had greeted the Germans just like that. If the Germans had treated them better, the Ukrainians and other Soviet subjects might have stayed friendly, which would have made an enormous difference in the war. The measure of Stalin's damnation was that close to a million of his citizens fought on Hitler's side in spite of everything. And the measure of Hitler's damnation was that almost the whole goddamn world fought on Stalin's side in spite of everything.

Bottero rumbled, deep down in his chest. He could not and would not see any Grenye ruler as an equal. With the air of one making a great concession to a churl who didn't come close to deserving it, he said, "Well, say your worthless say, and then you can go and get lost."

"Thank you so much for your gracious kindness, your Majesty," Otset said, deadpan. He might be a shrimp, but he had nerve. Bottero rumbled some more, but he didn't seem to realize he'd been one-upped. The ambassador or herald or whatever he was went on, "Lord Zgomot says, you have his leave to return to your own realm. His brave armies will not harry you if you turn around and go home."

That set not only Bottero but most of the high officers who rode at the fore with him laughing their heads off. "What a generous worm your so-called lord is," the king said. "We thought we didn't see your armies because they didn't have the nerve to stand against us." He mockingly bowed in the saddle. "So thanks for telling us they're brave. Without you, we never would have known."

Most of the Lenelli went right on laughing. Hasso didn't. Bottero was pushing it, and had to know he was. The Bucovinan army the Lenelli had beaten didn't fight badly. The Grenye had no magic working for them, and they'd never had a striking column shatter their line before. Under those circumstances, no wonder they lost. But they didn't disgrace themselves.

Otset only shrugged his narrow shoulders. He wore a dark blue woolen cloak with a hood over a linen shirt brightened with embroidery. His breath smoked as he replied, "Plenty of other Lenello armies have come into Bucovin out of the west. We still stand. We will go on standing after you have to leave our land, too."

King Bottero went brick-red again. "By the goddess, little man you will not!" he shouted. "We'll burn Falticeni around your heads, savage, and when we catch *you* we'll throw you on the fire. Now get away from me, before I kill you on the spot for spewing shit at your betters!"

"Word of your charm has preceded you, your Majesty," Otset said. This time, Bottero did recognize the sarcasm. He bellowed wordless fury, like a bull. Otset took no notice of it, but continued, "The folk of Bucovin will fight you. The land of Bucovin will fight you, too. And the last time the goddess visited us, she barely got free with her life." He nodded to Velona, who rode not far from the king—he knew her for what she was. "If you persist, if she persists, luck may be different this time."

Bottero bellowed again. Hasso paid him little heed, but eyed Velona instead. She jerked in the saddle as if taking a wound, then pretended, not quite well enough, that she'd done no such thing. "You may mock me," she said, "but you scorn the goddess at your peril."

Otset shook his head. "I do no such thing, lady. But this is not the goddess' land. Better for you to go back to places she has taken for her own."

"She will take this land, too," Velona said. "She will take all this land, however far it reaches. It will be hers. It *is* hers, and her folk will settle it."

Lebensraum, Hasso thought, not for the first time. Velona put it differently from the way the *Führer* had, but it amounted to the same thing. The only trouble was, the Ivans had the *Lebensraum* now, and the Germans damn well didn't. All kinds of things were different here, though. Chances were that one would be, too.

"You say it, lady, but saying it does not make it so." Otset sketched a salute to Velona, a courtesy he omitted with King Bottero. He spoke to his escort. They turned their horses and rode off in the direction from which they'd come.

Several Lenelli nocked arrows, ready to shoot Otset and the rest of the Bucovinan riders out of the saddle. Bottero did not a thing to stop them. But Velona, her face troubled, raised a hand, and none of the big blond men let fly. "The goddess would not want us to slay an envoy," she said.

"Even an envoy who knows her not?" Marshal Lugo sounded scandalized.

"He knows her." Velona's voice was troubled. "But he denies she has power here. It is up to us to prove him wrong."

That stirred the king. "Right!" he shouted. "We'll smash them!" How the Lenelli cheered!

***

After Otset's warning about the land, Hasso more than half expected blizzards to start roaring down out of the north. He'd been through that in Russia in 1941, and had a Frozen Meat Medal to prove it. Not many of the old sweats who'd earned that one were still in one piece; he was, as those things went, lucky.

When he worried about blizzards out loud, the Lenelli laughed at him. "We don't get weather like that, goddess be praised," Orosei said.

"Even if we did, the stinking Grenye couldn't bring 'em down on us," King Bottero added.

And they turned out to be right. No stormwinds full of snow blew in the advancing soldiers' faces. But that didn't mean the Lenelli advanced very far or very fast. No snow came, no, but rain fell in buckets, barrels, hogsheads. The muddy road turned to swamp. The invaders started getting hungry, too, because they couldn't forage widely, and the supply wagons had even more trouble moving than did men mounted or afoot.

"We whipped the weather once," Bottero told Hasso. "Why don't you cast a spell so we can do it again?"

Why don't I? Hasso thought wildly. *Because I don't have the faintest idea how, that's why.* He tried to put that less blatantly: "Your Majesty, I work one spell my whole life. You want me to get rid of *this*?" He looked up at the gray, gloomy sky, and got a faceful of rain for his trouble.

But the king only nodded. "Yes, that's what I want. You're what I've got. I'm going to use you, or else use you up."

A *Wehrmacht* colonel ordering a platoon to stay behind as a rear guard so the rest of the regiment could get away from the Ivans couldn't have been more brutally blunt. Soldiering was soldiering, no matter which world you wound up in. Sometimes you got the shitty end of the stick, that was all.

Hasso found himself holding it here. He saluted. "I do my best, your Majesty."

"Never mind your best. Just do what I tell you." Sure as hell, Bottero thought like a king.

Rain, rain, go away. Come again some other day. That was the only charm Hasso knew along those lines. Just on the off chance, he chanted it up at the heavens, first in German and then in Lenello. The rain kept right on falling. He hadn't expected anything different. He sighed. It would have been nice if things were simple.

Since they weren't, he went to talk with Velona. She wore a thick wool cloak with a hood, not very different from Otset's. It smelled powerfully of sheep, and so was probably good and greasy—better than the one he had on, anyhow. She heard him out, her face getting graver and graver as he went on. Then she said, "Well, you can try."

"What's that supposed to mean?" Hasso asked.

"Weather magic is never easy," she answered, her tone as somber as her expression. "And weather magic in Bucovin will be harder yet. That wretch of an Otset wasn't wrong. I've seen it for myself, and I've spoken of it with you—there is a bond between the Grenye and the land here. It isn't magic. I don't know what the right name for it is. But it is real."

"What can I do about it? How can I beat it?"

She shrugged, which made water bead up and run down the cloak. "Do the best you can, Hasso Pemsel. I will pray to the goddess to grant you favor and lend strength to your spell. Back in our own lands, I am sure she would hearken to me. Here—" Velona shrugged again and spread her hands. Raindrops splashed off her palms, which did nothing to encourage Hasso.

He scratched his beard. By now, he was used to wearing it. It had got long enough not to itch any more. Back in the *Wehrmacht*, he'd had to shave it off when he found the chance. The only problem with it was that it gave lice more room to roam when he got infested.

What was the opposite of rain? Sunshine. *Brilliant, Hasso,* he told himself. He couldn't pull the sun out of a pouch on his belt. He could, he supposed, make a fire and use that to symbolize the sun. Maybe it would serve, if he could get a fire going in this dripping, puddle-filled land. And the opposite of wet was dry. If he could find a dry sponge or even a dry cloth to symbolize soaking up the rainwater, he could try his magic.

Maybe it would work. Even if it didn't, King Bottero would know he'd tried. Sometimes making the effort counted as much as succeeding or failing. The Germans had put in plenty of pointless attacks against the Russians to keep Hitler happy, and then gone back to what really needed doing. Hasso understood how that game was played.

As she had with his first spell, Velona helped him here. He was convinced he had even fewer poetic gifts in Lenello than in German. But she nodded as they worked together. "You've got a good notion of how magic is supposed to work," she told him.

"You say the sweetest things, darling," Hasso answered, deadpan. Velona's face lit up like a flashbulb—a comparison that, in all this world, would have occurred to him alone. He added, "If only it were true." The subjunctive was for talking about conditions contrary to fact. He used it here without the slightest hesitation.

Bottero's army slogged and sloshed forward, not going anywhere very fast. In Russia, even tracked vehicles bogged down in mud like this. The Ivans had light wagons with enormous wheels, wagons that almost doubled as boats, that could navigate such slop. Every German outfit tried to lay hold of a few of them. Hasso hadn't seen anything like them here. He could describe them to Lenello wainwrights, but they wouldn't get built in time to do any good on this campaign. And so … *So I get to work magic*, he thought. *Again.*

He waited till the army stopped to encamp for the evening. That was in midafternoon, not only because darkness came even earlier with the clouds but also because the Lenelli needed extra time to set up an elaborate web of sentries. The Bucovinans liked to sneak in a few marauders to hamstring horses and murder men in their tents. If the raiders died instead, that might discourage them. It would certainly discourage the ones who got killed.

"You're ready, are you?" Bottero boomed. "Good. That's good, Hasso."

"I don't know how good it is, your Majesty," the German answered. "I can try, that's all."

"You'll do fine. You did before." The king didn't lack for confidence.

Maybe I will, Hasso thought. He hadn't dreamt he would be able to divine where the Bucovinans' underwater bridges lay. No matter what he hadn't dreamt, he'd done it. *Why shouldn't I do it again? No reason at all.*

After Poland and France and the Balkan campaign, that kind of reasoning took the *Führer* into the Soviet Union. The German gamble there *almost* paid off. The *Wehrmacht* came so close to knocking the Ivans out of the fight. But what did they say? Close only counted with horseshoes and hand grenades.

Hasso wished he had a few potato-mashers on his belt, They wouldn't help with his rain magic, but they made a damn fine life-insurance policy.

But he didn't, and he didn't like to dwell on things he didn't have. Velona had warned him more than once that you had to pay attention when you cast a spell. If you didn't, the magic could turn and bite you. Hasso wished she hadn't told him that. The magic could also turn and bite you if you screwed up your chant. For somebody with a still uncertain grasp of Lenello, that was also less than encouraging news.

Velona chose that moment to ask him, "Are you ready?"

"No," he answered honestly. She blinked—that wasn't what she'd expected to hear. He went on, "But I don't get—I *won't* get—any readier if I wait. So I try the spell. We see what happens."

She kissed him, which was distracting in a much more pleasant way than his own gloomy and uncertain thoughts. "You can do it. I've seen that you can."

Maybe she'd been listening to Bottero.

"Well, I hope so." He got a little fire going in the bottom of a pot that he put under an awning made of tent cloth. He set another pot upside down under the awning and put the dry cloth under it. He couldn't help thinking that a real wizard would have used far more elaborate preparations. Aderno probably would have laughed his ass off at what Hasso was doing. But Aderno wasn't here, and Hasso damn well was. Like those kids who found themselves in the *Volkssturm,* he had to do the best he could.

He wished he hadn't thought of it like that. The Ivans and the Amis and the Tommies slaughtered the poor damned kids in the *Volkssturm* in carload lots. A few lived long enough to learn how to soldier. Most got wounded or killed before they could. Was that true of wizards, too? There was another cheerful notion.

No time for it now. "Give me the parchment," he told Velona. She did, and held her cloak over it so the rain wouldn't wash away the words before he could chant them. He called on the goddess. He called on the heavens. He called on the sun and the clouds. Once, when he stumbled over a word, the fabric of the world seemed to stretch very tight. Sudden frightening heat built up inside him. He got the next word right, and the one after that, and found his rhythm again. The heat receded.

His fear didn't. He wondered if it ever would. Yeah, you could blow yourself up with this stuff if you didn't know what you were doing. And he didn't. Worse, he knew he didn't.

Recognizing his own ignorance made him want to race through the spell, to get it over with as fast as he could. That probably wasn't smart—it made him more likely to screw up. *Tortoise,* he told himself. *Not hare. Tortoise. You have to do it right. That's more important than doing it fast.*

Making himself believe it wasn't easy.

At last, he got through it. He didn't burst into flames or explode from water buildup inside him or dry out as if he'd been stuck in the Sahara for a million years or do any of the other interesting and horrible things his overactive imagination came up with. He just said, "So may it be," one more time and slumped down, exhausted. Was that rain soaking him, or sweat? Did it matter?

Velona straightened him up. She had strength for two, or maybe for an army. "There," she said. "You did it. You did everything a man could do. But I already knew you did everything a man can do." To leave him in no possible doubt of what she meant, she kissed him again.

He was sure she would have taken him to bed if he'd shown even the slightest interest. Just then, though, he was so weary, he didn't think he could have got it up with a crane. "Wine," he croaked. "Or beer, anyhow."

Velona didn't get angry, which had to make her a princess—no, a goddess— among women. "I'll get you some," she said, but she didn't. Instead, she shouted for Berbec. The captured Bucovinan obeyed her faster than he followed Hasso's orders, and with less back talk. By the standards of this world, Hasso was probably a softy. He shrugged. He couldn't do much about that, and he was too damn tired to care right now, anyway.

Berbec came back with wine. Hasso wondered where he'd got it. From the king's cooks, maybe? If Berbec said the goddess wanted something, who would have the nerve to tell him no? Even Bottero would think twice before he did that.

The wine was thick and sweet, like all the vintages here. Anybody with a sophisticated palate would have thrown up his hands in despair. Hasso didn't give a damn. The alcohol gave him a jolt, and the sugar gave him another one. By the time he'd downed a big mug, he'd improved all the way up to elderly.

Velona drank some, too. Then she kissed him one more time. He didn't know about kisses sweeter than wine, but kisses sweetened with wine were pretty nice. And he remembered Berbec, and the line in the Bible about not binding the mouths of the cattle that thresh the grain. He sloshed the wine jar. It was almost empty, but not quite. He gave it to the Bucovinan. "Here," he said. "Finish this."

"Me?" Berbec sounded astonished. Velona looked even more astonished, and angry, too. Hasso nodded, pretending he didn't see the storm on her brow. Berbec gulped hastily, then gave a sort of half-bow. "Much obliged, master," he said, and scurried away before that storm burst.

It did, as soon as he was gone. "Keeping slaves content is one thing. Wasting wine on them is something else," Velona said pointedly.

"So I'm a crappy master. The world won't end," Hasso said. "I don't have it in me to fight right now, either. Let's see how the magic turns out, all right?"

He wondered if a soft answer *would* turn away wrath. Velona followed her own road, first, last, and always. If you weren't heading in that direction, you were commonly smart to stay out of her way. But she just said, "I'll try to talk sense into you later, then."

If those weren't words of love, Hasso didn't think he'd ever heard any.

***

Come morning, he looked up into the sky. It was still cloudy. It wasn't exactly raining, but it wasn't exactly *not* raining, either. A fine mist got his face wet.

He had the feeling someone was watching him. He looked around, but the only person he saw was Berbec. The servant had his tunic off. He was getting lice and their eggs out of the seams. Hasso wondered how many times he'd done that since 1939. More than he wanted to remember, anyhow. You never got ahead of the goddamn bugs. You had a bastard of a time staying even.

"Are you watching me?" Hasso asked. "*Were* you watching me?" Yes, pasts and futures were starting to come.

Berbec paused. After crushing something between his thumbnails, he said, "I try to keep an eye on you, see what you want." He had a mat of hair on his chest and belly. He also had some impressive muscles. He might be a runt, but he was a well-built runt.

And he and Hasso were talking past each other. "No," the *Wehrmacht* officer said. "I mean, were you watching me just now?"

"Not me." Berbec shook his head. "I was paying attention to these lousy things." He looked surprised, then started to laugh. His Lenello was also imperfect, and he'd made the joke by accident.

"All right. Maybe it isn't—wasn't—you, then." Hasso looked around again. He still didn't see anyone else close enough to have given him the willies that way. He looked up into the sky again. The mist kept coming down, but it was no more than mist.

And the feeling that he was being watched got worse. He remembered the Bucovinan envoy, and he remembered how Velona felt when she got deep into Bucovin. The land wasn't on the Lenelli's side here. Did the land include the sky? He didn't know. How could he? He was more foreign in these parts than the Lenelli were, a million times more foreign. His sorcery might not have stopped the rain, but did seem to have slowed it down. Would that be enough to get the countryside pissed off at him?

If it was, how worried did he need to be?

He was still chewing on that, and not liking the taste of it very much, when King Bottero strode over to him. The king paused every few steps to kick mud off his boots. Berbec saw him coming, too, and unobtrusively got lost. Bottero's smile almost made a substitute for sunshine. "You see? I knew you could do it," he said.

"Did I do it?" Hasso shrugged. "I don't know, your Majesty. Still some rain." He blinked as a drop got him in the eye.

"Not bloody much." King Bottero was inclined to look on the bright side of things. "It was coming down like pig piss" —which was what the Lenelli said when they meant it was raining cats and dogs— "but now we've only got this drizzle. We can cope with this. The other, that was pretty bad."

"I don't know if this is because of me," Hasso repeated. "If it starts raining hard again—"

"In that case, you'll work your magic again and slow it down." The king didn't have to listen to anybody if he didn't feel like it. The *Führer* hadn't had to, either. Hitler was still in Berlin when Hasso disappeared from that world. If he was lucky now, he was dead. If he wasn't so lucky, Stalin had him. Hasso had trouble thinking of anything worse than getting caught by Uncle Joe.

And Stalin didn't have to listen to anybody, either.

"It's still muddy." Bottero kicked glop off his boots again. "But if it doesn't get any worse than this, we'll manage. It's on to Falticeni."

"I hope so, your Majesty." Hasso meant that, anyway.

The king slapped him on the back. "You can do it. We can do it. And you will do it, and so will we." Off he went, pausing every now and then to clear those boots.

When the army set out, of course, the ground was still muddy from all the rain that had fallen before. That meant the Lenelli still had to move slowly. Hasso's horse probably felt like doing what Bottero had done. No matter what it felt like, it kept slogging forward.

One bit of good news: with all that rain, the Bucovinans couldn't burn everything in the path of the king's army. They did dig more camouflaged pits in the roadway, as they had when the Lenelli forced their way across the Oltet. A few unwary scouts rode their horses into them. The sharp stakes set up at the bottom of the pits pierced men and horses alike.

Bottero fumed when supplies didn't come up fast enough to suit him. "What are our wizards doing back there?" he complained. "Are they too busy screwing little brown women to pay attention to their proper business?"

He was screwing little brown women himself, or at least one little brown woman. No one seemed to want to mention Sfinti to him. Hasso, a near-stranger in these ranks, found discretion the better part of valor. Orosei did remark, "It's muddy behind us, too, your Majesty."

"Well, yes," Bottero said. "But we need the food, curse it."

"Jumping up and down about what you can't help won't make it any better," the master-at-arms said. Hasso would have liked to tell King Bottero the same thing, but didn't know how the monarch would take it from him. Orosei, more at ease in a society where he'd belonged since birth, didn't hesitate.

And the king did take it from him. A sheepish grin spread across Bottero's face. "It makes *me* feel better," he said.

"Hurrah." Orosei wasn't afraid to be sarcastic to his sovereign, either. And King Bottero laughed out loud, for all the world as if the soldier were kidding.

Somewhere up ahead lay Falticeni. Over the next set of hills? Past the next forest? Around the next bend in the road? The Germans had looked for Moscow like that in the winter of '41, and they knew exactly where it was. Half the time, the Lenelli seemed to think Falticeni lay somewhere over the rainbow. With the maps they had, who could blame them? They knew its direction, but not where along that line it was.

And, the farther east they went, the worse the rain got again. Hasso worked his amateur spell once more. He was smoother at it the second time around; he didn't come close to cooking himself in his own juices, the way he had the first try. But he couldn't see that the magic did much to the weather this time.

"We're deeper into Bucovin now," Velona said in what had to be meant for consolation. "The land *does* work against spells here."

"Why isn't that magic?" Hasso asked irritably. "It screws magic up."

"It's like trying to fight a battle in the rain and mud," she answered. "It screws up everything. It's just the way things are here. If the Grenye worked magic, they'd have trouble with it, too."

But the natives didn't, couldn't, work magic. The Lenelli sneered at them for that, and made them out to be, well, *Untermenschen* on account of it. If the big blonds' big advantage faded, though, the farther east they went...

"We just have to do it the hard way, that's all," Velona declared. "We can do that, too. We're better warriors than those scrawny little buggers ever dreamt of being. And speaking of doing it the hard way…" She looked at him sidelong.

That turned out to be better consolation than all the words in the world.

***

The Bucovinans didn't seem to know they couldn't stand up against Bottero's army. Raiding parties tangled with his scouts. No mystery about where these bands came from: they rode down from the northeast, shot arrows at the Lenelli or pitched into them when enjoying the advantage of numbers, and then rode off again.

Bottero thought about sending Hasso forward with the scouts. "A wizard could remind the little bastards why we're better than they are," the king said.

"I don't know how much I can do on this ground." Hasso left it there: any more and he would have looked bad.

"We'll save you," Bottero decided after some thought. "You go up with just a few of our men along, something stupid can happen. Don't want that, not when there's bound to be a big battle ahead. Chances are we'll need you more then."

"Whatever you say, your Majesty." Hasso was more relieved than he let on. The prospect of combat didn't faze him. After everything he'd been through, he had its measure. No, what did make him sigh (unobtrusively, he hoped) was the good sense King Bottero showed. He didn't throw away the potential of a large gain later for some small one—or the potential of that small one—now.

The striking column of Lenello knights practiced whenever it could. It had won a battle for the army, so even Marshal Lugo wasn't complaining about it any more. The big blonds did like to fight aggressively; the idea fit them well enough once they got used to it. Punch a hole in the other fellow's line, then pour on through. What could be better than that?

Nothing—as long as it worked.

"This time, the Bucovinans likely expect us to do something with the column," Hasso warned. "A surprise is only a surprise once. We need to watch their line, see where the weakness is. Then we hit there." He slammed his right fist into his left palm.

Captain Nornat got the idea. "They'll give us a hole to go through, sure as sure," he predicted. "They're nothing but Grenye, after all. They always make sloppy mistakes like that. It's one of the reasons we keep thrashing them."

"You don't want to have to count on the other guy doing something dumb," Hasso said. "You want to be able to beat him even if he does everything as well as he can."

"Well, sure," the Lenello officer said. "But when he does screw up, you want to make him sorry."

Hasso nodded; he couldn't very well disagree. In Russia, you could bet the Ivans wouldn't move as fast as they should have. Lieutenants didn't dare do much on their own—they had to get authorization from higher up the chain of command. For that matter, so did colonels. Again and again, the Germans made them pay for being slow.

Hasso's laugh was so bitter, Nornat raised a questioning eyebrow. "Nothing," Hasso said, which was an out-and-out lie. The *Wehrmacht* had taken advantage of the Russians time and again, sure. And in the end, so what? Stalin won the goddamn war anyhow.

The Bucovinans' faults were different from the Russians'. These guys were still trying to figure out how the Lenelli fought. They didn't have enough practice to be as good as the invaders from across the sea. No wonder they screwed up every once in a while.

"They fall to pieces when we take Falticeni?" Hasso asked.

"They'd better!" Nornat said. "We grab their stupid king or lord or whatever they call him, we hold his toes to the fire, they'll spread their legs for us, never you fear."

"Good." That was what Hasso wanted to hear. He remembered how Skorzeny's paratroopers had stolen Mussolini. What if some of those guys had managed to grab Uncle Joe? Wouldn't that have been something? The *Reich* would have got what it wanted then, by God!

Or would it? Would some other Moscow bureaucrat have grabbed the reins instead and gone on fighting? How could you know with Russians? Stalin was a strong leader, but he didn't personify things the way Hitler did in Germany. You couldn't imagine the *Reich* without the *Führer*. Russia might be able to go on without the tough bastard from Georgia.

What about Bucovin, which was the only enemy that mattered to Hasso nowadays? "What's the lord in Falticeni like?" he asked. "Can they find somebody to take over if we get our hands on him?"

"He's a Grenye," Nornat said. "He kind of pretends to be like a Lenello king, but it's just pretend. The savages used to think their lords were gods, like. That was before they found out we knew about the real gods and we could work magic on account of it. Now the poor stupid bastards don't know what the demon to think." His snort held more scorn than sympathy.

Magic here was like gunpowder in America: it not only gave the invaders an edge, it gave them a big, scary edge. But the Grenye were closer to the Lenelli than the American Indians had been to the Spaniards. They knew how to work iron, and they had had plenty of real kingdoms of their own.

If the Lenelli had guns as well as wizardry ... That thought had gone through Hasso's mind before. But it was one for another time, another war. Bottero wouldn't let him fool around with sulfur and saltpeter and charcoal now, or stand by while he tried to show local smiths how to make cannon that wouldn't blow up.

Nornat hadn't said anything about whether the Bucovinans could get along without their lord. That probably meant he didn't know. If the Grenye had decided their kings weren't gods after all, they had a better chance of doing without them.

I hope we get to find out, that's all, Hasso thought.

The Bucovinans hadn't given up. They didn't seem afraid of the Lenelli, either, even if they couldn't fully match them. The raiding bands they sent out against Bottero's army got bigger and bolder, and slowed the army's advance. Several times, the king had to send reinforcements forward to keep his scouts from getting overwhelmed. And, in spite of all of Hasso's magic, the rain got worse again.

He waited for Bottero to scream at him. To his surprise, the king kept quiet. Velona explained why: "I reminded him how deep inside Bucovin we are. We can't expect things like that to go our way here. We just have to win anyway."

Maybe the Grenye didn't think their rulers were gods any more. King Bottero had no doubt Velona was at least part goddess, and that what she said went. After some of the things Hasso had seen, he didn't have many doubts along those lines, either.

And then the rain blew away. Hasso would have taken credit for it if he'd worked a spell any time recently. Since he hadn't, he just accepted it along with the Lenelli. The weather stayed cool—it was November, after all, or something close to it—but it was crisp and sunny: the kind of weather that made having seasons worthwhile. It seemed as if he could see for a thousand kilometers.

One of the things he could see was a smudge of smoke on the horizon ahead, a smudge big enough to mark a good-sized city or a really big camp. "Is that Falticeni?" he asked Velona, pointing. *Are we there yet?*

She shook her head. "I don't think so. It looks like the Grenye are going to fight us again after all."

"It sure does," Hasso said. *It looks like they're going to throw the whole goddamn world at us, too.*

Velona looked at that differently. "We'll beat them here, and they won't be able to stop us again." If the goddess said it, didn't that make it true?

XIII

No matter what Velona—or maybe the goddess, speaking through her—said, the Bucovinans didn't think they were bound to lose. King Bottero's army found that out midway through the next morning, when they came upon their foes drawn up in line of battle ahead of them.

"They pick their ground well, anyhow," Hasso said to Orosei. Trees protected both sides of the enemy line, and the field in front of them sloped upward toward their position. A few bushes and a lot of calf-high dead grass covered the field. Hasso didn't think the Grenye could find enough cover there for ambushes.

"Even if they do, they aren't very smart. It's like I told you—look a little to the left of their center." The master-at-arms didn't point in that direction; he didn't want to show the foe he'd spotted anything out of the ordinary. "See that, outlander? They've left a gap between a couple of knots of horsemen. It's not a big gap, but—"

"We can pour through there," Hasso finished, excitement rising in him. Orosei nodded, a smug grin on his face. He'd spotted it, and Hasso damn well hadn't. Fine, then: let him take the credit. Hasso said, "We need to tell the king. The striking column goes in there."

"Just what I was thinking," Orosei agreed.

"They're standing there waiting for us to hit them, aren't they?"

"You bet they are," the Lenello said. "Whenever they try to take the lead in a big battle, we clobber 'em even worse than we do this way. They've figured that much out. I bet they're just trying to slow us down, waiting for snow to make even more trouble for us."

"I wouldn't be surprised," Hasso said. Tactics like that didn't surprise anybody who'd won the Frozen Meat Medal.

Hasso and Orosei rode over to Bottero. Hasso let the master-at-arms take the lead in showing the king the gap in the Bucovinan line. Orosei still didn't point. King Bottero needed longer to spot the opening than Hasso had, which made the *Wehrmacht* officer feel good. When Bottero did, a predatory grin spread across his face. "They're ours!" he cried. "The goddess has delivered them into our hands!"

He sounded like an Old Testament prophet. For a moment, that thought cheered Hasso. Then he frowned, wondering whether it should. After all, what were the Old Testament prophets but a bunch of damn Jews? Hasso hadn't done anything to Jews himself, not directly. But he had no great use for them, and he'd made sure to look the other way when the SS cleaned them out of Polish and Russian villages. Like the priest and the Levite, he'd passed by on the other side of the road.

Well, he didn't have to worry about Jews here. Things were simple. There was his side, and there was the other side, and that was it.

The guys on the other side were feeling pretty cocky, too. Even if the Grenye stood on the defensive, they waved their weapons and yelled what had to be insults at the oncoming Lenelli. They wanted Bottero's men to think they were plenty ready for a fight, anyway.

Orosei turned to the king again. "By your leave, your Majesty?" he murmured.

"Oh, yes," Bottero said. "By all means."

Leave for what? Hasso wondered. He understood all the words, but still had no idea what was going on. He supposed he ought to be glad that didn't happen to him more often here.

Orosei didn't leave him in the dark for long. The master-at-arms rode out into the open space between the two armies. He brandished his lance and shouted in the direction of the Bucovinans, challenging their champion to come out and meet him in single combat.

Hasso whistled softly. There was a grand madness to this. War in his own world had lost that personal touch; you seldom saw the men you fought. You didn't want them to see you, either. If they did, they'd shoot you before you knew they were around. This was a different kind of warfare. It was personal.

Would any of the Bucovinans dare to meet Orosei? If they were smart—from Hasso's point of view—they'd send out half a dozen guys at once and try to finish him off. Nothing degraded the idea of military honor like years on the Russian front.

But a single lancer rode out from the line waiting ahead. The natives cheered him like men possessed. He stopped a few meters out in front of them, turned in the saddle to wave, and then turned back and gave Orosei a formal salute. Damned if the master-at-arms didn't return it. Then they spurred their horses straight at each other.

Riding downhill give the Bucovinan a little edge: he could go faster and build more momentum. If that bothered Orosei, he didn't let on. He bent low over his horse's neck, his lance aimed straight for his opponent's short ribs. The other guy was aiming at his, too, but that didn't faze him a bit. From what Hasso had seen, nothing that had to do with battle fazed Orosei.

Clang! Both lances struck home. Both riders went off their horses and crashed to the ground. And both riders were up with swords drawn faster than their comrades could cheer and groan at the same time.

As lancers, the two champions proved evenly matched. As swordsmen ...

Orosei towered head and shoulders above his foe, who was good sized for a Grenye but nothing much against a big Lenello. Orosei's arm was longer, and so was his blade. If the Bucovinan turned out to be fast as a striking cobra, he might have a chance. Otherwise, Hasso guessed he was in over his head, literally and figuratively.

And he was. He had no quit in him. He ran straight at Orosei, probably figuring his best chance was to get in close and see what he could do. Iron belled on iron as they hacked away at each other. Orosei had no trouble holding off the Bucovinan champion. They were both well armored, so getting through with wounds that mattered took a while. The one that did the Grenye in never got through his mailshirt. It didn't matter. That stroke had to break ribs even through chainmail and padding. The Bucovinan staggered back and sagged to one knee.

He kept on trying to fight, though he must have known it was hopeless. Orosei approached him like a stalking tiger. The master-at-arms was a professional; he didn't take anything for granted. Sure as hell, the Grenye jumped up for a last charge. With his side so battered, though, he couldn't use the sword the way he wanted to. After a sharp exchange, it flew from his hand.

"Ha!" Orosei's shout of triumph echoed over the field.

The Bucovinan went to both knees this time, and bowed his head. How much chivalry was there here? Would Orosei send him back to his own side, especially since he couldn't fight in the battle ahead? The Lenello's sword rose, then fell with a flash of sunlight on the blade. Blood spouted. The body convulsed. Orosei picked up the head by the hair and turned to show it to the enemy.

Still carrying his trophy, he went over to his horse, which was cropping dead grass not far away. The stink of blood made the beast snort and sidestep, but he grabbed the reins and swung up into the saddle. He rode back toward the Lenello line. Bottero's men cheered wildly. The Bucovinans stood silent as the tomb.

"Toss me another lance, somebody," Orosei called as he drew near. "Mine cracked when I hit this bastard." He held up the head again.

"Use mine," King Bottero said. "I'll take another one. Now they've seen: victory will belong to us."

"So may it be!" Velona shouted.

"So may it be!" the Lenelli echoed. If the embodiment of their goddess said so, they thought it had to be true.

Hasso peered up the slight slope toward the Bucovinan line. "I don't see any striking column there," he said to Nornat, who rode beside him at the head of the one King Bottero would hurl against his foes.

"Neither do I," Nornat said. "They haven't put one together yet, I guess. They copy things from us all the time, but they need a while to work out what to do with them and how they go. They aren't real big, and they aren't real bright."

Bottero rode out in front of his army, not to challenge the enemy as Orosei had done but to harangue his own soldiers. "One more fight, boys!" he said. "One more fight, and then it's on to Falticeni. Then *we* take over Bucovin, and all the other Lenello kings turn green with envy and die. And we all get rich, and we all get estates, and we all get lots of slaves, and we all get plenty of pretty Grenye women to screw!"

The soldiers cheered like maniacs. Hasso yelled along with everybody else. No German officer's speech had ever been so direct. But this was what war was all about, wasn't it? You killed the other guys and you took away what they had. Whether you talked about estates and slaves and women or about *Lebensraum*, it boiled down to the same thing.

"All right, then!" King Bottero yelled. "Let's go get 'em! The goddess is with us!"

"The goddess is with us!" the Lenelli shouted. Hasso looked over to Velona. She blew him a kiss. He sent one back to her.

Bottero waved to the trumpeters. They blared out the charge. The Lenelli—and Hasso—set spur to their horses. They thundered forward. The striking column aimed straight for the little gap Orosei had noted in the Bucovinan line. Break through there and they'd cut the enemy army in half.

While Bottero heartened his men, some Bucovinan bigwig or another was doing the same with the small, swarthy natives. They'd shouted, too, but the lusty cheers of the Lenelli all but drowned them out. As Hasso galloped toward the Bucovinans' battle line, he knew the same feeling of invincibility, of playing on the winning team, he'd felt in France in 1940 and in Russia in the summer of 1941.

Once he'd been dead right to feel that way. Once...

To his surprise, the waiting Bucovinans just held their ground. They didn't gallop forward to meet the Lenelli with impetus of their own, the way they had the first time the armies met. That went dead against everything he thought he'd learned about cavalry. "Are they going to stand there and take a charge?" he shouted to Nornat, trying to pitch his voice to carry through the drumroll of hoofbeats all around them.

"Looks that way, the cursed fools," the Lenello answered. "They should have found out they couldn't do that a hundred years ago. Well, if they need a fresh lesson, we'll give 'em one." Below the bar nasal of his helmet, his lips skinned back in a predatory grin.

Closer ... Closer ... Along with the thuds of the horses' hooves, the Lenelli were howling like wolves, both to nerve themselves for the collision and to scare the living piss out of the Bucovinans. Would the natives break and run? If this kind of charge were bearing down on Hasso, he knew damn well he would think hard about running himself.

Here and there along the enemy line, archers started shooting at Bottero's soldiers. Beside Hasso, Nornat laughed what had to be the most scornful laugh the German had ever heard. "Do they think they'll even slow us down like that?" he said.

One or two riders clutched at themselves and slid from the saddle. One or two horses crashed to the ground. One or two more fell over them, spilling their riders. The rest of the charge rolled on.

Bucovinan foot soldiers set themselves, spears thrust forward in a forest of iron points to withstand the oncoming lancers. Did they really believe they could make the Lenelli stop that way? Could they possibly be so stupid? Hasso had trouble believing it.

For a moment, he simply accepted that. All right, he had trouble believing the Bucovinans *could* be so stupid. Then what? Only at that point did alarm bells start clanging in his mind. The natives had to know the Lenelli thought they were stupid and inept. If they could play on that, take advantage of it…

"Something's wrong!" Hasso shouted to Nornat. "They're trying to fool us!"

"What?" Nornat yelled back.

Before Hasso could say it again, the first Lenello horses fell into the lovingly concealed pits the Bucovinans had dug in front of their line.

The horses screamed. So did the men on top of them. Hasso and Nornat weren't in the very first rank of the charge any more; men on swifter horses had got a little ways ahead of them. But they were close, too close. Hasso reined in frantically. His horse saw the danger, too, and tried to swerve, but it was too near the edge. In it went, in and down. Hasso wasn't ashamed to scream, either.

Then another falling horse's hoof caught him in the side of the head. Blackness swooped down on him. How the fight went from there … he had no idea.

***

He came back to himself a little at a time. He was hearing things before he realized he was hearing them. He thought he made out words, but he didn't understand any of them. Had whatever happened to him—he didn't remember what it was, not yet—scrambled his wits for fair?

Lenello. He had to think of Lenello, not just German. He felt more than a little pride at recalling that. But it didn't help. He thought he could understand Lenello if he heard it. Whatever this was, it wasn't Lenello.

He felt as if he'd been dropped on his head from about five kilometers up. *Concussion*, he thought dully. He'd had a couple facing the Russians. Those damn *Katyushas* could pick you up and throw you around like nobody's business. He didn't think he'd ever had a headache like this one, though.

He didn't want to open his eyes. He feared his head would fall off if he did—this was much, much worse than any hangover he'd ever known. And he was afraid to open them for another reason: he feared he might not see anything at all, or might see only hellfire. He wasn't a hundred percent sure he was alive.

And when he forced himself to pull his eyelids apart, what he did see made him wonder and made him even more afraid: darkness shot through by the flickering flames of torches. If this wasn't hell, what was it? Were those demons gabbing not nearly far enough away? What language did demons speak? Hebrew, maybe?

That was the scariest thought yet.

But when Hasso sucked in a big breath of air that might have come out as a shriek, he calmed down instead of turning it loose. He smelled blood and shit and horses and unwashed men. That was the smell of a battlefield, not of the infernal regions.

Then he remembered charging forward with the Lenelli. He remembered going into the pit. "Good God!" he said. "Those little bastards did fool us!"

The Bucovinans must have won their battle, too, because those sure weren't Lenelli prowling through the pits right now. What happened to Orosei, and to Nornat, and to King Bottero?

Sweet suffering Jesus, what happened to Velona?

Sweet suffering Jesus, what's going to happen to me?

A couple of torches were coming closer. The figures they illuminated weren't red-faced demons with horns and spiked tails. They were Bucovinans in tunics and baggy trousers and calf-high boots. That wasn't necessarily reassuring. The little swarthy men carried the torches upraised in their left hands and long knives dripping blood in their right.

One of them stooped to cut a horse's throat. The beast sighed, almost as a man might have, and died. A moment later, the other one stooped, too, only the throat he cut belonged to a Lenello. The man's dying sound was on a slightly higher note than the horse's.

They *were* getting closer. Hasso thought about fighting them—for about a second and a half. The way he felt, he couldn't have fought off a puppy that wanted to lick his face. He wasn't even sure he could twist free of the dead horses that squeezed him—luckily, without quite squashing him.

What would they do if he played dead? Out of barely open eyes, he watched them finish another Lenello. Chances were they'd slit his throat on general principles. That seemed to be what they were here for.

Could he surrender? He hadn't wanted to give up to the Ivans, for fear of what they did to prisoners—and because of all he knew about what the *Wehrmacht* did to Russian POWs. He knew some of the charming things the Lenelli did to Bucovinans they caught. How did Lord Zgomot's men return the favor? *Do I want to find out?*

If he wanted to keep breathing, he did. The Bucovinans working their way through the pit killed another Lenello. They weren't especially malicious about it, which didn't mean they hesitated. And they were getting awful goddamn close now.

What have I got to lose? Hasso thought. *If I just lie here, they'll cut me a new grin any minute now. The best defense is a good offense ... I hope. Please, Jesus.*

"Do you speak Lenello?" he asked—croaked, really.

The little men started violently. One of them said something that had to be cussing. They both came toward him. He didn't like the smiles on their faces. Maybe just getting his throat cut was the best he could have hoped for. At least it was over in a hurry then. So many other interesting possibilities...

Interesting. Right.

"I speak your language, man out of the Western Sea," answered the native who hadn't sworn. He spoke it better than Hasso did, which still wasn't saying much.

"Tell me your name, so my gods can spit on it when they bury you in dung in the world to come."

He plainly still believed in their old-time religion, even if the Lenello goddess had given some Grenye different ideas. And he wanted to use Hasso's name to curse him. The *Wehrmacht* officer might have lied if he'd thought a Grenye curse would bite. He was sure he would have lied to Aderno. But he was also sure the natives couldn't work that kind of magic.

And so he gave the fellow the truth: "I call myself Hasso Pemsel."

It didn't mean anything to the one who'd asked for his name. The other one, though, said something else incendiary in his own guttural language. The two of them palavered, waving their arms—and those damn snickersnees. Finally, the one who admitted to speaking Lenello came back to that language: "We have orders to take you alive if we can. Do you yield yourself to us?"

"Do I have a choice?" Hasso asked.

"You always have a choice," the Bucovinan answered. "You can yield, or you can die right now."

"What happens if I yield?"

"Whatever we want." The native wasn't helping. But then, he didn't have to.

Hasso sighed. "I yield." His head hurt too much for him to argue. He tried to twist out from between the dead horses, and discovered he couldn't. He couldn't have put up a fight even if he'd wanted to. "Help me out, please."

The Bucovinan laughed, none too pleasantly. "Now I know you are the stranger we want. No Lenello would ever say *please*, not to the likes of us." Resentment—hatred?—simmered in his voice. He went back and forth with his buddy in their language. The other man gestured a fierce warning with his knife before going over to Hasso. They didn't believe in taking chances. In their boots, Hasso wouldn't have, either.

He took the Grenye's hand. Grunting, the native put his shoulder against the corpse of the horse pinning Hasso's legs and shoved. With some help from the native, Hasso managed to wriggle free. He discovered he couldn't have run, either: his legs were asleep.

Though small, the local was strong. He dragged Hasso out of the pit and laid him on the ground. There he relieved him of his belt knife. The other Bucovinan, the one who spoke Lenello, came over and peered down at him. "You have a holdout weapon?" the fellow asked, adding, "If you say no and we find it, you won't like that, I promise."

"My left boot," Hasso said. "And under my left arm."

They took the knives. "You're full of tricks, aren't you?" the one who spoke Lenello remarked.

"Oh, yes? What am I doing here, then?" Hasso said with a bitter laugh.

"Breathing," the Bucovinan replied, which echoed Hasso's own thoughts much too closely. "You want to keep doing it?" He didn't wait for an answer, but nudged Hasso in the ribs with a boot. "Can you stand up now?"

"I ... think so." The German sandbagged a little. He wanted to seem weaker and more harmless than he was. But he would have swayed on his pins any which way. The Bucovinans didn't instantly shove him into motion. More teams of little swarthy men with torches were moving over the battlefield, in the pits they'd dug and around them. Every so often, a native would stoop—and that, presumably, would be that for some luckless Lenello. "Do you—uh, *did* you—get the king?" Hasso asked.

"No, curse it." The Grenye sounded unmistakably disgusted. "He fought his way clear. But he won't be going forward any more, by Lavtrig." He and the other Bucovinan swirled their torches clockwise when he named the deity. "The rest of you big blond bastards won't, either."

I'm not one of those big blond bastards, Hasso thought. But he was blond and he was big by Grenye standards—and he'd fought for King Bottero. Keeping his mouth shut looked like a real good idea.

Keeping his mouth shut about that did, anyhow. He couldn't help asking, "What about Velona?"

"Who?" The native who spoke Lenello gave him a blank look.

"The goddess," Hasso said.

"Oh. *Her.*" The Bucovinan spoke to his buddy. They both swirled their torches again, this time counterclockwise. What was that supposed to mean? Reverence? Fear? Warding? All of the above? The native went on, "No, we weren't too sorry when she got away. If we could have killed her, fine. But how would we keep her prisoner? It would be like keeping the sun in a roomful of kindling."

He wasn't far wrong, not from what Hasso knew of Velona. No god or goddess possessed him, but he *was* a wizard … of sorts. Maybe that would do him some good. Maybe the land here wouldn't let him work magic. He'd have to see.

"Come on." The native shoved him. "Move." Hasso moved—slowly, but he moved.

* * *

They fed him. They gave him something that tasted like beer brewed from rye, which was just about as bad as that sounded. The native who spoke Lenello stuck with him as they took him to Falticeni. Hasso found out the fellow's name was Rautat, and that he'd worked in Drammen for several years before going home to Bucovin.

"Why did you go?" Hasso asked. "Why did you come back?"

"I had to see," the Bucovinan answered.

They were standing next to a couple of trees by the side of the road, easing themselves. Three soldiers in leather jerkins aimed arrows at Hasso's kidneys in case he tried to get away. The persuasion worked remarkably well.

"Yes, I had to *see*," Rautat repeated as he laced up his trousers. "You Lenelli can do all kinds of things we don't know how to do. You can make all kinds of things we don't know how to make. I worked for a smith. I wasn't even a 'prentice. I pumped the bellows. I carried things. I banged with a hammer. And I watched.

My uncle is a smith, so I knew something about it—the way we do it, anyhow. Now I know a lot of your tricks, too, and I use them, and I teach them to other people who want to learn them. Other Grenye, I mean. *My* people." He jabbed a forefinger at his own chest.

You were a spy, Hasso realized, buttoning his own fly. Rautat watched that with interest. He watched everything Hasso did with interest. The Lenelli didn't use a fly fastening. Hasso had on his old *Wehrmacht* trousers.

As they stepped away from the trees, the German nodded to himself. Rautat had been just as much a spy as an *Abwehr* agent who tried to steal the secrets of some fancy new British steel-manufacturing process. The only difference was, the Lenelli didn't seem to know their processes were worth guarding.

And I didn't think of it, either, he reminded himself as he swung up onto the scrubby little horse they were letting him ride. He muttered angrily in German. He'd been Bottero's spymaster, and he'd been better at the job than any Lenello ever born. But he hadn't been good enough. How many just like Rautat were there, in all the Lenello kingdoms? Hundreds? Thousands?

"What is that tongue you used? It's not Lenello," Rautat said. How many of those Grenye were as sharp as he was? Probably very few.

"No. It's my own language," Hasso answered. "I'm not a Lenello."

"You look like one," Rautat told him. Hasso shrugged. The dark little man plucked at his curly beard. "You don't sound like one, I will say." He took a scrap of parchment, a reed pen, and a little clay flask of ink from a belt pouch and scribbled a note to himself. Seeing Hasso's eyes on him, he said, "I learned your letters when I was in Drammen, too. We mostly use them now."

"Yes, I know that," Hasso said. The crude warning the Bucovinans posted had used Lenello characters and, indeed, the Lenello language.

"We had writing of our own before you big blond bastards came." Rautat sounded like a man anxious to prove he wasn't a savage and half afraid he was in spite of everything. "Your way is a lot quicker to pick up, though. It's mostly the priests who still write the old characters. They take years to learn, and who else has the time?"

How had the natives written in the old days? Hieroglyphics? Things like Chinese characters? Some slow, clumsy, cumbersome system, anyhow. One of these days, chances were even the priests wouldn't use it any more. And then who would be able to read the accumulated wisdom of Bucovin, assuming there was any?

Rautat cocked his head to one side and eyed Hasso like a curious sparrow. "So you're not a Lenello, eh? Where *are* you from, then? Some other kingdom across the sea, I suppose."

"No. Farther away than that." Hasso told how he'd come to this world.

What would the Bucovinan make of it? Hasso knew what a German *Feldwebel*—for he took Rautat to be a top sergeant, more or less—would have made of it, even if the fellow had worked in Cleveland for a while. The *Feld* would have laughed his ass off and said, "Bullshit!" Hearing a story like that, Hasso would have said the same thing himself.

But this was a different place. Rautat frowned. It wasn't that he disbelieved; he was trying to figure out how the pieces fit together. Well, Hasso had been doing that ever since he splashed down into the marsh. He didn't have all the answers yet, and he would have bet anything that Rautat wouldn't, either.

The native pointed at him. "So you're the whoreson who spat thunder and lightning at us in the first big battle! That's why we worked so hard to find your name!"

"*Ja*, that's me," Hasso said, and then, "*Ja* means *yes*."

"No wonder they want you in Falticeni," Rautat said. "Can you do that some more?"

"No. My weapon needs *cartridges*." Again, a word came out in German—it had to. "They come with me from my world. The Lenelli know more tricks of making things than you people do, yes? Well, the folk of my world know more than the Lenelli do. The Lenelli can't make these *cartridges*. No one here can."

"Ah." As a wily *Feldwebel* would, Rautat had a good poker face. He sounded almost artistically casual as he asked, "Can you teach us any of what you know and the Lenelli don't?"

"I don't know," Hasso answered, trying to keep worry out of his own voice. "I'm not sure."

He *could* show the natives this and that. He could show them most of the same things he would have shown to Bottero and Velona. He could, yes, but should he? He knew what he thought of Field Marshal Paulus, who'd surrendered to the Russians at Stalingrad and then got on the radio for them, telling the Germans they couldn't win and had better give up while they still had the chance. Maybe Paulus did persuade a few *Landsers* to desert. To Hasso and the rest, though, he was nothing but a goddamn traitor.

Of course, maybe the NKVD held Paulus' feet to the fire before he started broadcasting. *And maybe the Bucovinans will hold my feet to the fire. What do I do then?*

Hasso had an Iron Cross First Class. If you'd lived through the whole war, it was hard not to have one. He'd been put up for the Knight's Cross, but it didn't go through for some dumb reason or another. He didn't much care. He'd never thought of himself as heroic. He wanted to live. Would he have plomped his butt down on the Omphalos stone if he were bound and determined to die for the *Vaterland*?

He also wanted to be able to go on looking at himself in the mirror, even if mirrors in this world were sorry things of polished bronze. He'd taken service with Bottero, who could have carved a stranger into strips and fed him to his hounds. And he'd fallen in love with Velona, even if the word scared him and her both.

If any place in this world was, Bottero's kingdom was his country now. *I'll escape if I can*, Hasso told himself. *Even under the Geneva Convention, that's my duty*.

The Ivans hadn't signed the Geneva Convention. The Lenelli and the Bucovinans had never heard of it, never even imagined it.

Rautat took out a little knife and started cleaning under his nails with the tip. The watery late-autumn sun flashed off the sharp edge. What else could that knife do? Anything the bastard holding it wanted it to, that was what. The day wasn't too cold. Hasso shivered anyway.

***

He wasn't the only captive heading back to Falticeni. Every so often, he passed other big blond men on the road with large guard contingents. They traveled on foot, in small groups, hands tied behind them and left legs bound one to another. They eyed him as he rode past. Rautat wouldn't let him talk with them. He didn't suppose he could blame the Bucovinan, things being as they were.

"What do you do with these men?" he asked after his mounted party went by another group of Lenello prisoners.

"Use them," Rautat answered. "They work for us. They teach us things. If they settle down and behave, they live better with us than they would in their own kingdom."

At the price of exile, of course. Still, when the other choice was getting your throat cut or worse ... But Hasso also remembered Scanno, who even in Drammen preferred the company of Grenye to his own folk. Scanno wouldn't be the only Lenello who thought that way, either. There might not be many, but there were bound to be some.

And Hasso also thought about Japan after the Western powers made it open up in the nineteenth century. What did the world look like to the Japanese then? The little yellow men had to acquire all the skills they lacked, and in a hurry, too, or else go under like the Indians and Africans. And they did it. They smashed the Russians in 1905—which made Hasso jealous—and they were giving the Americans all they wanted now. The Grenye of Bucovin were in the same boat.

But the Japanese *could* acquire all the tricks the Americans and British and Russians and French and Germans knew. The Grenye found themselves behind the eight-ball in a way the Japanese didn't. "Have you got any Lenello wizards in Falticeni?" Hasso asked, not least to see if he could make Rautat twitch.

He didn't. The native just shook his head. "Not right now. For us, wizards are like holding a sword by the blade. We can cut ourselves, not just the enemy. Somebody who can make spells is liable to try to rule us, not to do what we want. It's happened before."

Obviously, it hadn't worked. "How do you—how *did* you—stop that?" Hasso inquired, genuinely curious.

Rautat shrugged. "We killed them. Not easy, not cheap, but we did it. Even a wizard has to sleep some of the time."

"Er—right," Hasso said. The Man Who Would Be King—he'd read the Kipling tale in translation—didn't have an easy time of it no matter who the natives were. *One of you, lots of them. As long as they don't believe you're a god, they can get you. And even if they start out thinking you are, pretty soon they'll change their minds.*

"What *can* you do for us?" Rautat asked.

"Don't know yet," Hasso answered uncomfortably. "I need to see what you can already do before I say."

Rautat grunted and left it there. That was a relief. If the natives decided Hasso couldn't do anything useful, wouldn't they just knock him over the head? But if he did show them things he knew about—gunpowder, say—he'd betray Bottero. And Velona.

He had to think their meeting on the causeway meant *something:* for him, for her, for the Lenelli, for this whole world. Could he turn his back on that and help these swarthy little bastards against the folk who were bringing civilization, *Kultur*, to this whole continent? How, if he wanted to be able to live with himself afterwards?

Well, if he didn't give the Bucovinans a hand, odds were he wouldn't live with himself afterwards for very long.

Smoke smudged the horizon to the northeast. Pointing to it, he asked, "Is that Falticeni?" If he thought about the landscape, he wouldn't have to worry about himself. Not so much, anyway.

"That is Falticeni," Rautat said proudly. "Soon you will see it with your own eyes. You will. Not King Bottero. He runs away like a beaten dog."

Back in 1941, after the *Wehrmacht*'s drive on Moscow faltered in the face of blizzards and Siberian troops and the men and panzers had to fall back, the Russians jeered about Winter Fritz, a poor, freezing starveling who was hardly worth the effort it took to shoot him. Rautat, naturally, had never heard of Winter Fritz. But he got the idea all the same.

Hasso's escort stopped at a farmhouse a few kilometers outside of town. The farmer turned out to speak a little Lenello. He'd never been to Drammen, but he'd visited Castle Svarag, closer to the border. He gave Hasso a bowl of stewed turnips and cheese, a chunk of black bread, and a mug of rye beer. It wasn't wonderful, but it filled the belly—and it was no worse than what his family ate.

At Rautat's order, Hasso slept in the farmhouse. That wasn't for the sake of comfort, but to make it harder for him to get away. The farmer and his wife and sons and daughters all snored. Hasso might have stayed awake an extra fifteen seconds because of it: maybe even thirty.

Breakfast the next morning was the same as supper had been. And after breakfast, it was on to Falticeni.

XIV

Something old, something new, something borrowed, something blue... Hasso had heard that somewhere, but damned if he could remember where. His first good look at Falticeni, even before he got inside the town, called the jingle to mind again.

The lower courses of stonework on the walls of Bucovin's capital looked half as old as time. The stones weren't shaped into neat square blocks; the idea didn't seem to have crossed the minds of the Grenye who'd put them there. The big gray masses of granite or whatever the rock was had just been trimmed to fit together. And they did. Despite the lichen and moss that had been growing on them for God only knew how many years, they looked sturdy and solid.

Then, suddenly, the wall got five or six meters taller. These stones *were* squared off. They looked much like the ones that formed the walls around Drammen and other towns in Bottero's kingdom. Plainly, the Bucovinans had realized the wall they had wasn't good enough to keep Lenelli out. Just as plainly, they'd learned from the men from overseas that squarish stones were a lot easier to handle than ones left in their original shapes.

And the towers that projected out from the wall might have been copied straight from Lenello fortifications. They gave defenders more places from which to shoot at attackers and to drop heavy things or hot things or pointed things on their unfortunate heads. Even the crenelated battlements were lifted from works farther west. The soldiers pacing those battlements, though, were indubitably Bucovinans.

"It is a great city, yes?" Rautat said proudly.

"It is a great city, yes." Hasso made it a point never to disagree with anybody who could order him chopped into cat's meat. It certainly was a big city, anyway. To his surprise, it looked at least twice the size of King Bottero's capital.

Its entryway boasted a stout iron portcullis. Like the towers, that was an obviously modern addition. Like all the entryways Hasso had seen here—and like all the ones he'd seen at castles in Europe—Falticeni's had a dogleg to the right. That made attackers trying to swarm through expose their left sides, the side on which their hearts lay, to whatever the defenders could do to them.

Hasso glanced up. No murder hole in the ceiling. The natives hadn't thought of such a thing when the entryway was built, and excavating one out of solid stone would have been too much work. He couldn't deny the position was plenty strong without one. Had Bottero's army reached Falticeni, it wouldn't have had such an easy time breaking in.

Rautat and the other Bucovinans escorting Hasso went back and forth with the guards at the entryway. The *Wehrmacht* officer understood not a word of what they said. Their language, of course, was no more related to Lenello than Cherokee was to English. He sighed mournfully. Just when he started getting fluent … he had to start over. Yes, some of these people spoke Lenello. Some Russians spoke German, too. That didn't mean they enjoyed doing it.

Rautat pointed to him and gave a pretty good impression of a Schmeisser going off. *He's the guy*—or maybe, *He's the son of a bitch—with the thunderstick.* Hasso could guess what the commentary meant, even if he didn't know words or grammar. The gate guards looked and sounded suitably impressed. Sure, they were natives, but they were also people. He could read their expressions and their tone of voice. *And a whole fat lot of good that may do me, too.*

"I take you to the palace," Rautat told him. "The lord will want to talk to you."

Hasso made himself nod, made himself seem calm. *But do I want to talk to him?* That would have been funny, if only it were funny. *Do I have a choice?* He had the choice the native named when capturing him: he could die. He didn't want to do that. Of course, the Bucovinans hadn't got to work on him yet, either.

The guards stepped aside, waving Hasso and his escorts around the last kink in the entryway and into Falticeni. Not without pride, Rautat gave a wave of his own. "This is *our* city," he said.

At first, it looked a lot like the Grenye districts in Drammen. Streets were narrow and winding and muddy, and they stank. Most of the houses and shops Hasso could see were of wattle and daub, with thatched roofs. Big ones sat next to small ones with no order Hasso could find. None seemed to be more than two stories high.

That meant Hasso could see what had to be the royal palace in the middle of town. As the reconstructed wall aped Lenello fortifications, so the palace imitated Lenello castles. Even the red clay semicylindrical roof tiles copied the ones the Lenelli used. The local lord might have been saying, *See? All the modern conveniences. We can do this stuff, too.*

Getting there was less than half the fun. Nobody already in the streets wanted to let newcomers by. Scrawny dogs yapped and snarled and made as if to bite the horses' fetlocks. Scrawny children of all sizes from toddlers on up raced around like maniacs, some wailing, others yelling at the top of their lungs. A few paused to stare at the spectacle of a big blond captive going through their streets. Hasso didn't think the things they shouted were endearments.

One kid bent to scoop up a handful of mud, or maybe manure, and throw it at him. Hasso ducked. The stuff flew over his head and splatted against a wall across the street. Rautat yelled at the kid. The brat bent over and showed off his bare backside, which was as skinny as the rest of him. Rautat made as if to kick it. He couldn't come close, not without dismounting. The kid scampered off.

"Thanks," Hasso said.

"Oh, I didn't do it for you," the Bucovinan replied. "I just want to make sure you're in one piece when I deliver you, so they can get the answers they need."

You're nothing to me but an interesting piece of meat. That was daunting. But if Hasso weren't an interesting piece of meat, Rautat would have slit his throat and gone on to the next one in the pit.

"Well, thanks anyhow," Hasso said.

Rautat gave him a long look. "You've got nerve, anyway," he said grudgingly.

Hasso shrugged. "Big deal."

"You talk like a soldier," the native remarked.

"I am—I was—a soldier before I came here, in a bigger war than this world ever saw," Hasso answered. "The tools of the trade were different. The life isn't, not very much."

Outside a tavern, a drunk in ragged clothes sprawled in the street snoring, a jug clutched tight to his chest. Hasso could have seen—hell, he had seen—the like in any number of Russian villages ... and, yes, in some German ones as well. People were people, in his own world or here, Lenelli or Grenye. Rautat scowled at the sot and rode a little faster to get by him. Hasso hid a smile. The native was self-conscious about his folk's shortcomings, as almost anyone from any folk would have been.

They rode past a brothel, too, with a couple of naked women displaying themselves in second-story windows. Hasso thought they were more likely to catch pneumonia than customers. They gaped at him, for a moment startled out of their cocked-hip, bosom-thrusting poses.

One of them called something to Rautat. He laughed and shook his head. Turning to Hasso, he said, "She wants to know if you're really big."

Hasso was made ... like a man. He said, "But you think all Lenelli are big pricks." The joke worked in Lenello the same as it did in German. Odds were it worked in most languages.

Rautat laughed and laughed. "You're a funny fellow, all right. Pretty soon, you'll find out whether it does you any good."

"*Ja.*" Hasso didn't like the sound of that.

In Drammen, the Lenello nobles had their fine houses in the center of town, near the royal palace. Broad lawns separated those mansions from the streets and from the lesser dwellings of *hoi polloi*. Again, the Bucovinans imitated the newcomers ... to a point. Their prominent people did have large houses. Sometimes the buildings even had stone ground floors. But the second story was invariably timber or wattle and daub, and almost all the roofs were thatched. Only a handful had tiles like the palace.

Almost all of them, though, had a garden rather than a lawn—or if they did have grass, a cow or a couple of sheep grazed on it under a herdsman's watchful eyes. The idea of bare ground for the sake of decoration or swank didn't seem to have got here from the west.

A plump man in a tunic with extra-fancy embroidery took a chicken from someone who looked poorer than he was. He wrung the chicken's neck and cast the carcass onto a brazier heaped high with glowing charcoal. "What's he doing?" Hasso asked.

"He's a priest making a thanks-offering or a sin-offering for that fellow." Rautat gave him a curious look. "Don't your priests do that?"

Hasso thought of the last *Wehrmacht* chaplain he'd talked to, a dour Lutheran who didn't even smoke (and, once again, the longing for a cigarette sneaked up and bit him in the ass). He tried to imagine Klaus Frisch sacrificing a chicken to propitiate an angry Jehovah. "Well," he said, "no."

"How do you know your gods pay any attention to you, then?" Rautat persisted.

"Good question," Hasso said, and then, counterattacking, "How do you know your gods do? Why don't you follow the goddess?"

Even riding through the streets of his own capital with the *Wehrmacht* officer a helpless prisoner, Rautat looked scared shitless. "The goddess hears Lenelli first," he said. "She wouldn't listen to the likes of me."

From what Hasso had seen, that might well be true. And yet … "Plenty of Grenye in King Bottero's realm worship her."

The most scornful majordomo in two worlds couldn't have let out a sniffier sniff than Rautat's. "There are Grenye who want to be Lenelli," he said. "*I* don't, thank you very much."

He spoke fluent Lenello. He wore Lenello-style armor. His city had Lenello-style fortifications grafted onto its older works. His sovereign's palace even had Lenello-style roof tiles. And he said he didn't want to be a Lenello?

Well, maybe he didn't. The Japanese wore Western-style clothes. They had Western-style industries, and a Western-style military, too. But did they want to turn into Americans or Englishmen or Germans? Hasso didn't think so. They used Western techniques to let them stay what they already were: Japanese. Maybe the Bucovinans could pull off the same stunt here.

But, if they couldn't work magic and the Lenelli damn well could, the odds were against them.

Still affronted, Rautat went on, "Besides, who knows what mongrel clans those Grenye come from? We're better people than that, we are."

Once more, Hasso carefully didn't smile. Had the plains Indians looked down their noses like that at the coastal Indians who quickly succumbed to the English colonizers? They probably had … till it was their turn.

When Hasso got a close look at Lord Zgomot's palace, he decided he wouldn't want to try to take it without heavy artillery. Yes, maybe Bottero was lucky he didn't make it to Falticeni. He might have thrown away a lot more men here than he did in the lost battle.

Or the goddess might have manifested herself through Velona and knocked the capital of Bucovin flat. If you had magic, if the gods really did take part in what happened on earth, maybe you didn't need 105s and 155s. After all, Joshua knocked down Jericho's walls without them.

Every time Hasso thought about anybody from the Old Testament, he started to look around nervously. *No, dummy*, he thought. *Nobody from the* Gestapo's going to haul you away, not here. You can let a Jew cross your mind every now and then.

Rautat shouted to the sentries in their own language. They yelled back. Hasso couldn't understand a word of it. His mind went back to wandering. If the goddess could come through here, why didn't she do it a long time ago? *The land fights for them.* Velona wasn't the only one who'd said it. What did it mean? It wasn't magic—the Lenelli insisted on that. But it was *something.*

One of the guards yelled some more, and gestured. Rautat and the other Bucovinan soldiers dismounted. A moment later, Hasso did the same. Grooms came out to take charge of the horses. Hasso's captors escorted him into the palace.

***

The palace was gloomy. It was drafty. It didn't smell very good. Of course, you could have said the same things about King Bottero's establishment. Everything here, though, seemed just a little worse, a little sloppier, than it had back in Drammen.

And Hasso found one danger here that he hadn't had to worry about there: doorways. Lots of Lenelli were taller than he was. Their lintels were high. The Bucovinans, on the other hand, mostly came up to his chin. And he banged his forehead twice in quick succession before realizing he had to watch—and duck—every goddamn time.

Getting one—no, two—right above the eyes did nothing for the headaches that still plagued him. He wished his head would come off. Inconsiderate thing that it was, it stayed attached and hurt.

Rautat spoke with a court official whose spiffy embroidery probably meant he was a big wheel. The fellow with the gaudy tunic looked Hasso over. *Him?* his glance said. Well, Hasso didn't think he cut a very fancy figure just then, either. The palace functionary asked Rautat a couple of questions. Hasso's captor answered with emphasis, jabbing a forefinger at the other man's chest.

With a sigh, the official yielded. He said something to Hasso in Bucovinan. "I am sorry. I do not speak your language," Hasso answered in Lenello.

He wasn't astonished when the native turned out to know that tongue. "Come with me," the fellow said. "Your name is on a list. Lord Zgomot wanted to see certain folk if we captured them. Here you are, so he will see you."

"Here I am," Hasso agreed, so mournfully that Rautat laughed and the court official smiled a most unpleasant smile.

They led him down a hallway decorated with art of a sort he didn't think he'd ever seen before. For lack of a better name, he thought of the pieces as feather paintings. Some of them were quite realistic, others bands or swirling lines of color. They must have taken enormous labor to create, first in finding the feathers and then in arranging them.

"Nice work." Hasso pointed at one—a picture of the palace, done all in feathers. "Very pretty."

Rautat and the functionary both stared at him, then started to laugh. "By Lavtrig, now I know you're no ordinary big blond bastard! They all think featherwork is stupid and ugly and foolish because they don't do it themselves," Rautat said.

He spoke in Bucovinan to the soldiers escorting the *Wehrmacht* officer. They gaped at Hasso, too. Hasso couldn't remember any Lenelli ever talking about featherwork. It really must have been beneath their notice. He wondered why. It sure looked good to him.

Then they led him past what he first took to be a small elephant's tusk. But it was shaped more like a sword blade, and had a formidable point on the end. "What is that? What beast does it come from?" he asked.

"A dragon," Rautat answered matter-of-factly. "That is the greatest fang of the Dragon of Mizil, which we slew when Bucovin was young. His bones lie under the walls of Falticeni, and under the palace here."

"A dragon? What does a dragon look like?" Hasso asked.

They went on a little farther. Then the court functionary pointed to a big featherwork on the wall. "Behold the Dragon of Mizil!" he said.

Hasso beheld it. He wondered from which birds the natives had got those iridescent green and bronze feathers, or the yellow and orange and red ones that showed the fire it breathed. He also wondered whether the artists had actually seen the dragon or limned it from the stories of those who came before them. And he wondered … "How do you kill something like that?"

Together, Rautat and the court official burst into something between verse and song. After a moment, the rest of Hasso's guards joined in. Germans might have launched into "*Deutschland über Alles*" or the "Ode to Joy" with as much ease and as little self-consciousness. Everybody in Falticeni had to know the story of the Dragon of Mizil.

Everybody but me, Hasso thought. And he didn't understand a word of Bucovinan. "Can you translate, please?" he said.

To his surprise, Rautat shook his head. "Not this," the soldier answered. "This is ours. This is special. This is not for Lenello dogfeet." He must have translated one of his own words literally, for he corrected himself a moment later: "Scoundrels." The palace flunky nodded agreement.

Hasso only shrugged. He was in no position to argue with them. They hadn't killed him. Except for when he went into the pit, they hadn't even hurt him. Yet. All things considered, he had to figure he was ahead of the game.

They turned a last corner. There was the throne room. There, on what looked like a dining-room chair wrapped in gold leaf, sat Lord Zgomot. The court official poked Hasso in the ribs with an elbow. "Bow!" he said.

***

Again, Hasso was in no position to argue. Bow he did. As he straightened, he sized up the ruler of Bucovin. King Bottero had put him in mind of Hermann

Göring, Göring the way he had been before defeat and drugs diminished him: big, bold, swaggering, flamboyant, enjoying to the hilt the power that had landed in his lap.

Zgomot, by contrast, wore a mink coat that would have made Marlene Dietrich jealous, but still looked like nothing so much as the druggist in a small Romanian town. He was small himself, and skinny, with a pinched face, a beak of a nose, and a black beard streaked with gray.

His eyebrows were thick and black, too, and almost met in the middle. The dark eyes under them, though, seemed disconcertingly shrewd. He was taking Hasso's measure as Hasso studied him.

"So ... You are the strange one, the one from nowhere, of whom we have heard." Unlike Rautat's or the functionary's, Zgomot's Lenello was almost perfect. The only hint that he wasn't a native speaker was the extremely precise way in which he expressed himself. He wasn't at ease in the language, as Bottero or Velona or Orosei would have been.

Poor Orosei, Hasso thought. He was glad the king and the goddess—the king and his lover—had got away. He wished like hell he'd got away himself.

But he damn well hadn't. And now he had to deal with this native—who was no doubt trying to figure out how to deal with him. "Yes, Lord," he said: he was who Zgomot claimed he was.

The Lord of Bucovin pursed his lips. He didn't look like a happy man, the way Bottero usually did. He had the air of someone whose stomach pained him. "Are you as dangerous as people say you are?" he asked.

"I don't know, your Majesty. How dangerous do people say I am?" Hasso answered.

"Don't you be insolent!" the palace official snapped.

"He is not being insolent," Zgomot said. "Most people never know what others say about them behind their back."

So there, Hasso thought. He got the idea lying to Zgomot wouldn't be smart, not if you had any chance of getting caught later on. "Lord, I don't know how dangerous I am. After I come here, I try to serve King Bottero as best I can, that's all," he said.

"You had the thunder weapon, yes?" Zgomot said. "You almost killed me with it in the first fight, yes?"

"Yes," Hasso admitted.

"And you're the one who came up with the column to strike with, yes?" the Lord of Bucovin persisted.

"Yes," Hasso said again, wondering if he was cooking his own goose.

"Then you're dangerous." Zgomot spoke in tones that brooked no contradiction. He eyed Hasso. "If you'd come here—to this place—in Bucovin instead of where you did, would you have served me as best you could instead of that big pig of a Bottero?"

You wouldn't have had Velona to persuade me. Persuade! Ha! That's a word! But if I'd come down by Falticeni, I wouldn't have known anything about Velona.

And what a shame that would have been! The thoughts flickered through Hasso's mind in a fraction of a second. "I don't know, Lord. Probably," he replied aloud. "Unless your people kill me for being a Lenello, I mean."

"Chance you take when you're big and blond," Zgomot observed, his smile thin to the point of starvation. How big an inferiority complex did the Grenye carry? How could you blame them if it was about the size of the dragon whose fang they so proudly displayed? The Lord of Bucovin went on, "Since you *are* here now, will you serve me the way you served Bottero even though he didn't deserve you?"

This time, Hasso didn't answer right away. The easiest thing to do was say yes and then do his best to get away or minimize his contributions. But he remembered again what he thought of Field Marshal Paulus. And he knew what *Wehrmacht* troops thought of the Russians who fought for the *Reich*. You might use them—you might use them up—but you'd never, ever trust them.

Slowly, he said, "Lord, I am King Bottero's sworn man. How can I serve his enemy?" He wondered if he'd just written his own obituary.

"A good many Lenelli have no trouble at all." Zgomot's voice was dryer than a sandstorm in the Sahara. "We do keep an eye on them, but they're mostly so happy to stay alive that they show us whatever they can. We've learned a lot from them."

"Would you let one of them do anything really important?" Hasso asked.

Now the Lord of Bucovin hesitated. "Mm—maybe not," he said at last.

"Then maybe you understand, sir. King Bottero lets me do those things. You don't—you won't—you wouldn't."

"Suppose your other choice is the chopper?"

"Suppose it is." Hasso hoped he sounded more nonchalant and less frightened than he felt. "How do you trust anything you chop out of me?"

"Oh, we have ways." That wasn't the Lord of Bucovin. That was Rautat, the practical noncom. He sounded very sure of himself, and probably with good reason. Zgomot said something in Bucovinan. Rautat answered in the same language. Hasso didn't like it when people hashed out his fate in a tongue he couldn't understand. Who would have?

"Well, nothing is going to happen right away," Zgomot said, returning to Lenello. "Maybe we can show you you made a mistake taking service with Bottero. Or maybe, if we decide you're too dangerous to keep alive, we'll have to kill you to make sure you don't go back. We'll just have to see."

"Whatever you say, Lord." *At least it's not the chopper right away!*

"Whatever I say?" Zgomot's laugh was hardly more than a token effort. "Well, stranger, you've never ruled, have you?"

***

Prison. It was about the most Hasso could have expected, but it was nothing to get excited about. He had a room with a window much too narrow to give him any chance to escape through it. He had a cot and a slops bucket. The bucket did boast a cover. For such refinements he was grateful.

The door was too sturdy to break down. The bar was on the outside. Guards always stood in the corridor—he could hear them talking every now and again.

They fed him twice a day. The food wasn't especially good, but there was plenty of it. He didn't need to worry about going hungry. And, by the way soldiers with swords and bows glowered at him whenever the door opened to admit the servant with the tray, he didn't need to worry about escaping, either. He wasn't going anywhere till Zgomot decided to let him out.

He didn't have a torch or a lamp. When the sun went down—which it did very early at this time of year—he sat and lay in darkness till at last it rose again.

Grimly, he made the most of the few light hours. He did pushups and situps and other calisthenics. He ran in place. He paced around and around the cell, which was about three meters square. He'd got used to short days and long nights in Russia. This wasn't as bad as that. They didn't give him a brazier, but he had plenty of blankets. And it wasn't as cold here as it had been there—nowhere close.

After he'd been in there for eight days—he thought it was eight, but it could have been seven or nine—the door opened at an unexpected time. Ice ran through him. He knew enough about being a prisoner to suspect any change in routine. Was this the day when they'd sacrifice him to the great god Mumbo-Jumbo, er, Lavtrig?

In walked the usual guards with the usual cutlery. In with them walked someone else. She couldn't have been much more than a meter and a half tall; she didn't come up to the top of Hasso's shoulder. But she carried herself like a queen. No, more like a dancer, with a straight back and long, graceful strides that made her skirt swirl around her ankles as if she belonged to a flamenco troupe.

"You are the man from a far land who took service with Bottero," she said in a clear contralto. Her accent was much better than Hasso's. It might even have been better than Lord Zgomot's; she lacked the fussy precision that informed his speech.

"That's right." Hasso nodded. "Who are you?"

"My name is Drepteaza." She made four syllables of it. She waited. Hasso repeated the name. She corrected him. He tried again. She nodded. "That's close enough," she said. "I am here to teach you to talk like a human being." That was how it came out in Lenello.

In spite of everything, Hasso smiled. "What am I doing now?"

"Talking like a western wolf," Drepteaza answered seriously. The Bucovinans loved the Lenelli no more than the Lenelli cared for them. Up till now, Hasso hadn't had to worry about that, any more than he'd worried about what Jews felt about Germans. That would only have mattered to him if he'd got captured by a band of Jewish partisans. Now, in effect, he had been. And what the natives felt about the Lenelli and about one Hasso Pemsel could literally be a matter of life and death.

He bowed to Drepteaza. "I am at your service, my lady. You are a prettier teacher than Rautat would be, that's for sure." And so she was. She was probably somewhere between twenty-five and thirty, with strong cheekbones, fine dark eyes, and an elegant blade of a nose. He would have bet she had a nice shape under that baggy tunic and skirt, though maybe her elegant gait was what made him think so.

She looked at him with as much warmth as if he'd got poured out of the slops bucket. *So much for flattery*, Hasso thought. One of the guards turned out to understand Lenello. Hefting his sword, he growled, "Watch your mouth with the holy priestess."

"Sorry," Hasso said. Maybe ninety seconds after meeting a goddess, he'd started screwing her brains out. Plainly, the Bucovinans did things differently. Hasso bowed to Drepteaza again, this time in apology. He told her, "Sorry," too, and hoped she believed he was sincere.

"I suppose you meant no harm," she said, but Murmansk winter still chilled her voice. "*To be sorry* in our language is *intristare*." She waited as she had before. He said the word. She corrected him. He tried again. The *s* was a long hiss, the *r* closer to a French than a German one, but not quite like that, either. She corrected him once more. At least she didn't expect him to get it right away. He gave it another try. She nodded, satisfied at last.

"How do you say, 'I am sorry'?" he asked.

She told him. Before he could try it, she added, "That is how a man says it. The form for a woman is—" Hasso winced, and hoped it didn't show. Somebody'd told him Polish had masculine and feminine verb forms. To him, that proved it wasn't a civilized language. *Oh, well*, he thought.

He repeated the masculine form, as well as he remembered it. This time, Drepteaza nodded right away. Hasso felt absurdly pleased with himself, as if he were a dog that had won a scrap of meat for a trick.

Then the guard said, "You better learn that one. You need it a lot, you—" He said something in Bucovinan that the priestess didn't translate. Hasso doubted it was an endearment.

She taught him a few more words. He asked, "May I have pen and parchment, please, to write them down?"

She raised a dark eyebrow. "The Lenelli taught you their letters?"

"Yes. But I have my own letters before. I probably use those. I am more used to them."

"Your own letters," Drepteaza murmured. "I had not thought of that. But you are supposed to know all sorts of curious things, aren't you? Yes, you may have parchment and pen and ink. I don't think you can use them to get away."

"Neither do I," Hasso said. "I wish I did."

The guard who spoke Lenello chuckled. Drepteaza didn't. She was a hard sell. But she did unbend enough to speak to the guards in Bucovinan. One of them touched a bent forefinger to his forehead. The salute wasn't in the least military, but was respectful. The guard hurried away.

He came back a few minutes later with writing supplies. Drepteaza taught Hasso their names in her language. He wrote them down. Drepteaza looked at the way he did it. "That is not Lenello," she said. "Is it your script?"

"*Ja*," he said absently, and then, "Yes."

"Is it easier to learn than Lenello?"

He had to think about that. "About the same, I suppose. Lenello has more characters, but that is good and bad. Each sound has its own characters with Lenello. With my writing, you need more than one letter for some sounds." He showed her some examples: *sch* and *ei* and *ch*. She caught on fast.

"Better to stick with Lenello writing," she said after some thought of her own. "Then we can still read what the blonds do."

"That make sense," Hasso agreed.

"Say the words you know. Write them, too," Drepteaza told him. She had to remind him of some he'd forgotten. He was just glad she didn't punish him for forgetting. She said, "Memorize what you know. I will come back. We will go on from there. Do we have a bargain?"

"Do I have a choice?" he asked.

As Rautat had, she said, "There is always a choice."

"Do I have a choice besides dying right away?"

"If you don't care to learn our tongue and show us some of what you know, Lord Zgomot will decide you're more trouble than you're worth. He'll probably kill you to make sure you don't go back to the Lenelli and their goddess." Was that scorn or fear in Drepteaza's voice, or maybe both at once? And did she know about him and Velona? He wouldn't have thought so ... till this moment. She resumed: "He may just break your legs so you can't escape. Is that better or worse?"

"I don't know. It's pretty bad," Hasso said.

"Yes. Learn what I teach you, then. I'll see you later." Drepteaza left the cell. So did her guards.

She didn't say what she would do to him if he didn't learn, though that warning about Zgomot's wrath certainly gave him food for thought. But he *wanted* to have something to do in his cell besides calisthenics. He would have tried to learn even if she told him not to. He smiled crookedly to himself. He might have learned better had she told him not to.

She gave him a couple of days to digest what she'd taught. Or maybe, since she was a priestess, she had enough other things to do that she couldn't bother with him for a couple of days. That crooked smile came back. *What is Hasso, that thou art mindful of him?*

She returned not long after breakfast. A growling belly wouldn't distract him, anyhow. He bowed to her. "Good day," he said in the best Bucovinan he could command.

Drepteaza and the little swarthy soldiers with her all started to laugh. She corrected his pronunciation, explaining in Lenello, "When you say it the way you did, it means 'purple day.'"

"Oh." Hasso walked to the slit window and looked out. He couldn't see much, but what he could see wasn't purple. "No, I guess not."

A couple of the guards smiled, but Drepteaza was harder to amuse. "Say it the way it should be," she said in Lenello. Then she added something in Bucovinan. She returned to Lenello: "That means the same thing in my tongue. Listen." She repeated it. "You will hear it a lot, I think."

Are you just a cool customer or a cold fish? Hasso wondered. She seemed interested in Hasso Pemsel the curiosity, Hasso Pemsel the possible font of knowledge. Hasso Pemsel the man? She might have been dealing with a talking mule.

If she had been dealing with a talking mule, before long it would have been talking in Bucovinan. She knew how to teach. "Do you teach Lenelli to speak before?" he asked. He carefully didn't say *other Lenelli*. He wanted her to think of him as something different. Whether she would or not…

She nodded now. "Yes, I've done that," she answered. "We try to learn what we can from you invaders. The more we learn, the better our chances. King Bottero is not the first to try to invade us. He won't be the last."

That struck Hasso as likely, too. "If I learn good, do you let me out of this cell?"

"Lord Zgomot will decide that. I won't." Drepteaza showed that the Bucovinans knew how to pass the buck.

"If you ask him, will he listen? If you tell him I am safe, will he believe?" Hasso trotted out future tenses in Lenello. Sooner or later, he'd have to do it in Bucovinan.

"Are you safe? Should anybody believe that?" Drepteaza asked, and then went back to the language lesson.

XV

L ittle by little, Hasso learned to speak Bucovinan. He'd started feeling at home in Lenello, which didn't work too differently from German. Bucovinan was another story. Conjugating verbs with separate masculine and feminine forms was the least of the strangenesses. Bucovinan had long vowels and short vowels. Some words had the one, some the other. None had both—except a few borrowed from Lenello, which Drepteaza called bastard words. Bucovinan didn't have real past tenses, only tenses that showed whether an action was completed or not. And Bucovinan had more trills and chirps than Lenello and German put together.

"How am I doing?" Hasso asked after a while. It probably came out more like *How I doesing is?* The only thing he was sure he had right was the *evin* at the start of the question: a little word that warned the listener it *was* a question. You could also put *evin* at the end of the sentence. Then it was still a question, but a sarcastic or rhetorical one.

"I've heard blonds speak worse." Drepteaza was relentlessly honest about such things. From everything Hasso had seen, she was relentlessly honest all the time. Maybe it was because she was a priestess. Maybe it was just because she was who she was.

Hasso bowed. "Thank you." That had a particle that went with it, too. If you put it at the start, it meant *Thank you very much*, and you meant what you were saying. If you put it at the end, it meant *Thanks a lot*, and you didn't. Hasso put it at the end.

Drepteaza smiled. "See? Many Lenelli would never know to do that. But your pronunciation is terrible."

"I am not a Lenello," Hasso said, for what seemed like the ten millionth time.

"I have seen that," Drepteaza said, or maybe it was something more like, *I am seeing that.* "You make different mistakes." The verb form she used wasn't one for completed actions: Hasso was still making those mistakes.

"Sorry," he muttered. She was a good teacher. He was trying to learn something that was difficult for him, and he wasn't having an easy time of it.

At least she understood that, and didn't get—too—angry at him for his errors.

She dropped into Lenello, which she still did sometimes when she wanted to make sure he got what she was saying: "King Bottero has asked Lord Zgomot to send you back to him. He offers a large ransom."

"Ah?" Hasso tried to keep his voice neutral. "And what does Lord Zgomot say?" He made himself ask the question in Bucovinan.

"He says no." Drepteaza's verb form meant Zgomot wasn't done saying no, and would go right on saying it. The priestess went on, "Lenelli ransom captives from one another. They hardly ever ransom them from us."

"I see." Again, Hasso did his best to sound noncommittal. The Bucovinans had to resent not being treated as equals by the Lenelli. And they had to get suspicious when a Lenello king *did* treat them that way. What did Hasso know that Bottero didn't want them to find out?

"Another message also came from Drammen." Drepteaza seemed to be working to sound neutral, too. Her voice came out as empty of everything as if it emerged from a machine's throat.

"*Evin?*" Hasso said. By itself, the particle meant *Yes?* or *What is it?*

"From the woman in whom the goddess dwells." Drepteaza said that in Lenello. And, saying it, the priestess didn't sound noncommittal any more. She couldn't come close to hiding her scorn—or her fear.

"*Evin?*" Hasso said again. How much did Drepteaza know about Velona and him? Some, certainly. Even Rautat knew some, and she would have talked to him. What did she think of what she knew? Nothing good, from all the signs.

"She wants you back, too," said the priestess of Lavtrig, a deity who didn't come to take possession of her, a deity who probably didn't do any more than all the many gods of the world from which Hasso came. A distinct curl to her lip, Drepteaza went on, "All the more reason to keep you here."

Hasso had wondered whether she and Lord Zgomot would feel that way. In Lenello, he asked, "You aren't afraid the goddess is angry if you say no?"

"Why should we be?" Drepteaza asked. "The only reason the blonds' goddess ever notices us is to hurt us. She will do that anyway. But you—you may teach us things we need to know so she can't hurt us so badly."

She was bound to be right about the goddess. About Hasso … Still using Lenello—he wanted to make sure she followed him—he said, "How can I show you anything if you keep me locked in this cursed cell all the time?"

He expected her to say no, or to say she couldn't decide anything by herself. Asking her sovereign would let her stall for a couple of days, keep Hasso's hopes up, and let him down easy when Lord Zgomot told him he had to stay locked up. But Drepteaza asked, "Will you give your parole not to try to escape?"

"You believe me if I do that?"

"Yes," she answered, switching from her tongue to Lenello to add, "You may even swear by the goddess if you like."

Hasso considered that. He needed no more than a heartbeat to decide it was a bad idea. "I will give it. If saying isn't good enough for you, why should swearing be better?" he asked, also in Lenello: he wanted to be as sure as he could of saying just what he meant.

And he judged Drepteaza—and, presumably, Lord Zgomot as well—aright. The priestess looked pleased, which didn't happen every day; most of the time, she was all business. "Well said," she told him in Bucovinan. "Come, then, if you care to."

"May I please wash first?" he asked, still in Lenello.

She nodded. "Yes, you should be fit to go out in public. We will take you to the baths."

* * *

The baths were public and mixed, partly like ancient Rome and partly like Japan. You rubbed yourself in a small hot pool with a root that smelled something like licorice; it did a pretty good job of getting rid of dirt and grease. Then you rinsed off in a larger, cooler communal pool. Perhaps a dozen little pools surrounded the big one.

Communal meant what it said: men and women bathed together. Their relaxed attitude among themselves showed the difference between nudity and nakedness. Hasso, by contrast, drew startled stares and whispers. He understood why, too—a swan couldn't have been more conspicuous at a conclave of crows.

Even the tallest natives hardly came up to the bottom of his chin. He wasn't a shrimp any more, as he had been among the Lenelli. That felt good. The hair on his body, like that on his head, was yellow, not dark or grizzled. His skin was pink rather than olive. Even his battle marks were strange. Bullets left round, puckered scars, not the long, thin traces of knife and sword wounds.

Some of his guards had stripped with him. Others wore mailshirts and helms and kept weapons. Parole or no parole, they were being careful. One of the bathing guards pointed to a bullet wound on Hasso's leg and asked, "What did this? An arrow?" He sounded as if he didn't believe it.

And it wasn't true. Shaking his head, Hasso answered, "No." They were speaking Bucovinan, so he kept things as simple as he could. He imitated the noise of the submachine gun.

He got back a blank look. The guard must not have been at the battle where he used up the last of his Schmeisser ammo. From the next pool over, Drepteaza spoke too fast for Hasso to follow. She'd also taken off her clothes and started bathing. Her figure was even sweeter and riper than Hasso had guessed. He looked at her only in glances out of the corner of his eye. He'd gone a long time without a woman, and didn't think the natives would appreciate a bathhouse hard-on.

Whatever she said, it seemed to ease the guard's mind. "So you are a warrior, then, and not a—" he said.

"Don't understand last word," Hasso said.

"A wizard," Drepteaza told him in Lenello.

"Yes, warrior," Hasso said hastily. "Not ... what is word?" The guard repeated it. Hasso added it to his vocabulary. "No, not wizard," he repeated. "Only warrior." He didn't want the Grenye to think he could work magic. That would only make what was already bad worse. And he didn't much want to think he was a wizard, either.

Did he protest too much? Was that what Drepteaza's raised eyebrow meant? Well, better a raised eyebrow than a raised … Hasso managed to walk from the warm pool to the cooler one without embarrassing himself worse than he was already.

He felt like a new man once he'd bathed. The new man was chilly. The natives heated the pools, yeah, but the building that housed them was drafty, and it was winter outside. And he wrinkled his nose when he redonned the outfit he'd been wearing since he was captured. "Can wash clothes, too?" he asked Drepteaza.

First she corrected his grammar and pronunciation. Then she put on her own clothes. He sighed—mentally—when those dark-tipped breasts vanished under her tunic. They'd given him something to think about during lessons besides grammar and pronunciation. Then she said, "Yes. Why not? You can wear ours while we wash yours."

Hasso didn't think the Bucovinans would be able to find anything to fit him. But they gave him breeches and an embroidered tunic that were, if anything, on the big side. Then he remembered they had Lenello prisoners—and also Lenello renegades. Those people had to wear something, too.

When he remarked to Drepteaza that he hadn't met any of them, she said, "No, and you won't, either, not for a while. We don't know how far we can trust you. We don't know how far we can trust all of them, either. Some we know we can't trust too far." Her face clouded. "Some Lenelli here want to rule us, not help us."

The natives were in a bind. They needed help from the Lenelli, who knew too many things they didn't. But the Lenelli, even the ones here, were imperfectly disinterested. How much were they out to help Bucovin, and how much themselves? How often had the Grenye—not just in Bucovin, but farther west, too—got burned?

Quite a few times, by Drepteaza's tone.

How do I look innocent? How do I sound innocent? Am I innocent? Hasso wondered. Those were all damn good questions. He wished he knew the answers.

***

Once the Bucovinans decided he wouldn't sprout feathers and fly away, they let him out of his cell more often. He always had an escort, though: several unsmiling soldiers—swordsmen, pikemen, and archers—and Drepteaza. The priestess went with him most of the time, anyhow. When she couldn't for whatever reason, Rautat did.

"You ought to thank me," Hasso told the veteran underofficer one day. "If not for me, you wouldn't have soft duty at the palace."

"I'd thank you more if you hadn't scragged so many of my buddies," Rautat answered: he sounded like a sergeant even speaking Lenello. Aiming a blunt forefinger at Hasso's middle, he continued, "Now go back to Bucovinan. You're supposed to be learning my language, remember?"

"Right," Hasso said … in Bucovinan. Rautat grinned. Hasso came to attention and clicked his heels.

"What's that nonsense all about?" Rautat also fell back into his own tongue.

"Shows…" Hasso had no idea how to say *respect* or anything like it. "Like this," he said, and saluted. "My people do."

"Pretty silly, if you ask me." Rautat was short—all Grenye were short next to Hasso—but he was feisty. He gestured with his thumb. "C'mon."

They actually left the palace, the first time they'd let Hasso do that since he came to Falticeni. He wore a heavy sheepskin jacket, but the cold wind still started to freeze his nose. It wasn't Leningrad or Moscow winter, but it sure as hell wasn't a holiday on the Riviera, either.

Bundled-up Bucovinans gaped at him the way he'd eyed tigers in the zoo when he was a kid: fascination mixed with dread. But he wasn't behind stout iron bars, even if he did have guards along. *See? The monster is loose!* What else were the natives going to think after everything that had happened since the Lenelli landed on their shores?

Somebody yelled something at him. He didn't understand all of it, but he heard something about his mother and something about his dog. Englishmen called somebody they didn't like a son of a bitch. Whatever this endearment was, it seemed based on the same principle.

Hasso pointed to a tavern. "A mug of beer to me, please?" he said.

"*For* me, you mean," Rautat said. He spoke to the troopers with them. A pikeman went over and stuck his head into the tavern.

"No," he said when he came back. "One of those big blond buggers is already in there swilling."

"Drepteaza would—" Rautat spook too fast for Hasso to follow. When he said so, the underofficer slowed down: "She would murder me if I let you gab with another Lenello. There. You got that?"

"Yes, but I am no Lenello," Hasso said—one more time.

Rautat looked up at him—up and up. "Close enough, buddy."

Hasso didn't find any answer for that. The Ivans wouldn't care that a man they captured from the *Wiking* SS panzer division was born in Norway rather than Germany. They'd knock the poor bastard over the head anyhow. He reminded himself again that he ought to thank God, or maybe the goddess, the Bucovinans hadn't done that to him.

"Am another tavern not far from?" he asked. "I have thirsty."

"You talk as bad as a Lenello would, too," Rautat said, laughing. But he knew where the next closest tavern stood. Hasso hadn't expected anything else. Rautat struck him as the sort who *would* know such things. Like any old soldier, the native had the knack for making himself at home wherever he went.

Ducking to get through the low door, Hasso found himself in what was plainly a soldiers' dive. A considerable silence fell when he went in. Again, Rautat talked too fast for Hasso to follow. Whatever he said, it must have worked, because the men in there didn't leap up and go for the *Wehrmacht* officer, and a good many of them had plainly wanted to do just that.

Then Rautat talked to the tapman: "Beer for him, and beer for me, too." That Hasso understood—it was important, after all.

The tapman held out his hand, palm up. Rautat crossed it with copper. Lenello coins were pretty crude, at least by the standards Hasso was used to. Bucovinan coins, being cruder imitations of crude originals … But as long as the natives didn't fuss, it wasn't his worry.

"Here." Rautat perched on a stool by an empty table. He waved Hasso to another one. A couple of the German's watchdogs also sat down. The rest hovered over him. Like the rest of the men in here, they probably would have been happier to kill him than to guard him. But they followed orders. If they intimidated him while he drank, chances were they didn't mind.

A barmaid brought the beers. She smiled at Rautat and looked at Hasso … yes, as if he were a tiger out of its cage. The rest of the guards ordered beer, too, except for one who chose mead instead. The barmaid seemed glad to get away.

"To your health," Rautat said to Hasso, raising his mug.

"To your health," Hasso echoed, returning the gesture. They both drank. The beer was better than what they'd given him in his cell, but not much. To somebody used to good German beer, what the Lenelli and the Bucovinans made mostly tasted like sour horsepiss. You could drink it if you had to, though, so he did. Drink water here, as in Russia, and you begged for dysentery.

Why didn't the damn wizards do something about that? Hasso's guess was that if they tried they'd be too busy to do anything else.

One of the soldiers already in the tavern came up to Hasso and unloaded a torrent of gibberish on him. "Sorry, not understand," he said, and then, to Rautat, "What does he say?"

"Nothing you want to hear," the underofficer answered in Lenello. "What a rotten dog you are and how he'd like to carve chunks off your liver and eat them raw."

"Tell him I'm insulted," Hasso said in the same language. "Tell him the least he could do is cook them first."

Rautat translated that. Hasso wondered whether he would get a laugh or start a fight. He outweighed the native by close to thirty kilos, so brawling didn't seem fair. But he didn't intend to let the Bucovinan pound on him without hitting back.

The soldier stared at Rautat, then stared at him. "He said *that*?" the man said; Hasso had no trouble at all following him. Then the fellow started to chuckle, and he said something the *Wehrmacht* officer didn't understand before going back to his own table.

"What was that?" Hasso asked Rautat.

In Lenello, Rautat answered, "He said you may be a big blond bastard, but you may almost be a human being, too."

"Thank you," Hasso said, deadpan, putting the polite particle at the end. Rautat broke up. Hasso took another pull at his mug of beer. The Grenye were recognizable human beings, too, even if they couldn't work magic—maybe especially because they couldn't.

***

When Rautat and the rest of the guards brought Hasso back to the palace, he got a surprise. While he was gone, the servants had cleaned up his cell and taken out the nasty straw pallet, replacing it with a wool-stuffed mattress on a wooden frame with leather lashings. They'd given him a stool and a basin and pitcher—and a brazier, to fight the freezing breezes that howled in through the window. Now it was a real room—almost.

He bowed to Rautat. "Thank you," he said again, this time with the polite particle in front to show he was sincere.

"Don't—it wasn't my idea." Rautat repeated himself till Hasso understood, then added, "If you want to thank anybody, thank the priestess. She's in charge of stuff like this." Again, he doubled back till the German got it.

"I do that," Hasso said.

He didn't get a chance till late in the afternoon. He spent some of the time in between asleep on the nice, new mattress. All too soon, it would be full of bugs, as the old one had been. He didn't like that, but after more than five years of war in Europe he didn't think it was the end of the world, either. He'd been lousy and fleabitten and bedbug-bedeviled before. You itched, you scratched, you killed what you could, and you got on with your life.

When Drepteaza came in—accompanied, as usual, by tough little Bucovinan guards—he bowed lower to her than he had to Rautat. "I thank you," he said, the polite particle properly in front, and waved to show why he was thanking her.

The native soldiers laughed at him. Drepteaza smiled, "You say, 'I thank *you*,'" she told him, using the feminine form of the pronoun. Hasso swore in German, which made him feel better and didn't offend anybody here, and thumped his forehead with the heel of his hand. Too goddamn much stuff to remember! Drepteaza went on, "And I say that you are welcome. You will be here a while. You may as well be comfortable."

He doubted he would ever be comfortable in this world. The twentieth century had too much that simply didn't exist here. Electricity, hot and cold running water, refrigeration, glazed windows, phonographs and photographs, radios, cars... But, again, he'd done without most of that stuff for years. You didn't have to have it, the way so many people thought you did. Life was nicer with it, sure, but you could manage without.

"And you'll earn these things," the priestess said. "We do expect to learn from you, you know." She repeated herself in Lenello so he could have no doubt about what she meant.

"I understand," he answered, which wasn't the same as promising to deliver. Whatever he gave the Bucovinans would hurt the Lenelli. The hope that he would give them things that would hurt the Lenelli was the only reason the natives hadn't murdered him instead of taking him prisoner.

Drepteaza eyed him shrewdly. "You understand, but you don't want to do it. Plenty of real Lenelli do, and you aren't one."

You're just as foreign there as you are here, so why not help us? That was what she meant, all right. She wasn't quite right, though. Hasso felt more at home among the Lenelli than he did here, and he doubted things would have been different had he landed here first. The Lenelli came closer to thinking the way he did. They were conquerors. They were winners. Bucovin was a land trying to figure out how not to lose. It wasn't the same.

He couldn't say that to Drepteaza without insulting her. So he said something simpler: "I swear—swore—an oath to King Bottero."

"I've heard about it." The swarthy little priestess looked at him. "How much would your oath matter if you weren't sleeping with that blond cow?"

"Velona's no cow!" Hasso exclaimed: the first thought that sprang into his head. You could call her all kinds of things, but cow? If you called her a cow, you'd never met her and you had no notion, no notion at all, what she was like.

Drepteaza gave him the native equivalent of a curtsy; it looked more like a dance step. "Excuse me," she said with wintry politeness. "That blond serpent, should I call her? That blond wolf-bitch?"

Those both came closer. Still, Hasso said, "I don't insult you or your folk."

This time, Drepteaza looked through him. "The Lenelli are not your folk. You said so yourself."

And he had, again and again. "But—" he began.

"But what?" The priestess sounded genuinely confused. Then her eyes widened. She said something in Bucovinan that he didn't get. She must have seen he didn't, for she went back to Lenello: "You really love her!" She couldn't have seemed more appalled had she accused him of breakfasting on Grenye babies.

He remembered that Velona had sounded just as horrified herself when she realized the same thing. "Well, what if I do?" he said roughly, doing his best to forget that.

"Moths fly into torch flames because they must. Do they love them when they do?" Drepteaza said—the exact figure Velona had used.

Hasso's ears heated. "I don't know. I'm not a moth," he said.

"No, you're not, which only makes it worse. You have a choice, and you choose to be a fool," Drepteaza told him.

The more she argued with him, the more she put his back up. "What am I supposed to do? Tell my heart no?" he asked.

"You would if you had any sense. If you had any sense—" Drepteaza broke off and threw her hands in the air. "Oh, what's the use? If you could show a fool his folly, he wouldn't be a fool any more." She turned and spoke to the guards in Bucovinan: "Come on. It's hopeless. *He's* hopeless."

Hasso understood that just fine. Yes, she was a good teacher. She just didn't want to teach him any more. The closing door and the thud of the bar on the outside falling back into place had a dreadfully final sound.

***

He wondered whether the Bucovinans would take away his small comforts again and remind him he was a prisoner. For that matter, he wondered whether he would find out how ingenious the local torturer was. If you told your captors things they didn't want to hear, you had to expect to pay the price.

Drepteaza really hadn't wanted to hear that he loved Velona. For that matter, neither had Velona. It would have been funny if it hadn't put his ass in a sling. Hell, it was pretty funny anyhow.

They went on feeding him, and the food stayed better than the prison slop he'd had before. Somebody—maybe Drepteaza, maybe Lord Zgomot, maybe just Rautat—was in a merciful mood, at least as far as that went. Not expecting any mercies, Hasso was grateful even for small ones.

He spent the next several days wondering whether small ones were the only ones he'd get. The natives who brought him food didn't speak to him, and didn't answer when he tried to speak to them. Neither did the ones who emptied his chamber pot.

And nobody else showed up. Drepteaza didn't come in to teach him more Bucovinan. Rautat didn't come in with guards to escort him around Falticeni. They let him stew in his own juices instead.

I'm not going to stop feeling what I feel about Velona, he thought. *I'm not going to forget my oath to Bottero.* Some more time went by. *I hope I'm not, anyway.*

He did what he'd done before: he slept as much as he could. The long, cold winter nights lent themselves to that. *To sleep, perchance to dream . . .* If he wasn't too hungry and he wasn't too cold, why not? He couldn't turn on the radio or even curl up with a good book.

At first, he didn't dream much, or didn't remember what he dreamt if he did. He'd never paid a whole lot of attention to his dreams, so that didn't worry him. And even if he had been, the clout in the head he'd taken might have scrambled his brains worse than he knew.

When he *did* start noticing what he dreamt, that was enough to make him sit up and wonder what the hell was going on. All the dreams had the same theme: somebody was looking for him, trying to talk to him. He had no idea who or why. The dreams didn't seem threatening. That was as much as he was willing to say about them, even to himself.

When, after a couple of weeks, Drepteaza did start giving him lessons again, he mentioned them to her. He tried first in his very basic, very bad Bucovinan. When that failed, he switched to Lenello. She heard him out with her usual thoughtful air. Once he finished, she said, "I will pray, and see if that does anything."

It didn't, not as far as Hasso could tell. She listened gravely when he told her so, then promised to speak to Rautat about it. The veteran underofficer came up to Hasso and winked at him. "*I* know what you need," he said.

"Do you?" Hasso said. "I don't." Rautat thought that was the funniest thing he'd ever heard.

Hasso found out why a couple of nights later, when a reasonably good-looking Bucovinan woman came into his room without any guards escorting her. "My name is Leneshul," she said in fair Lenello. "They say you have been without pleasure too long. I can give you some." As matter-of-factly as if she were going to wash dishes, she pulled her top off over her head and tugged her skirt and drawers down to the floor. "Do I suit you?" she asked, standing naked—and she *was* naked, not nude—before him. "You can have someone else if I don't."

Part of him wanted to tell her to leave and not to ask anyone else to come in her place. But he was almost painfully aware of how very long he'd gone without. It didn't have to mean anything—just relief and, as she'd said, some momentary pleasure. "You'll do," he told her, and got out of his own clothes.

He wasn't sure she enjoyed it, but he wasn't sure she didn't. She was certainly limber and uninhibited. He rode her the first time. After they finished, she sucked him hard again and straddled him. He squeezed her small, firm breasts as she bucked up and down. She threw back her head and groaned. If she came, it was right then. He knew he did a moment later.

"There," she said, leaning down to brush her lips across his. "Is that better?"

"*Oh,* yes," he said. She laughed throatily.

He slept without dreams that night. Drepteaza asked him about it at their language lesson the next morning. She seemed pleased at his answer. "Rautat was clever," she said. "More clever than I was. You may have Leneshul any night you please—or another woman, if you'd rather."

What about you? Hasso wondered. Drepteaza was cool, almost cold, as if she had no idea how pretty she was. That made the prospect of heating her all the more exciting. But she looked at him as if he were a side of beef. If he offended her, she could do anything she wanted to him. He kept his big mouth shut … about that, anyway.

"Leneshul is all right," he told her.

"Then she will come to you again," Drepteaza said briskly. And Leneshul did, two or three nights a week. On those nights, Hasso never had any of the dreams that disturbed him. He had them less often on other nights, too.

But when they did come on other nights, they seemed more urgent, as if whatever was behind them felt itself thwarted and so tried harder than ever to break through. That alarmed him; he felt pursued. He used the solace of Leneshul's compliant body as often as he could.

No matter what he did, he couldn't get it up every single night. He wished he were ten years younger; then he might have. But when he was ten years younger, the future stretched out before him with a broad and shining path. The *Führer* was turning the tiny *Reichswehr* into the *Wehrmacht*, restoring German pride, restoring German power. What could stand in the way of a proud, resurgent nation?

Well, he'd found out what could, all right. And here he was in a strange world, older and more scarred and screwing his head off not for love or even lust but out of fear.

That helped wear him out, too. One night, he fell asleep right after supper. If Leneshul came to his room that evening, she quietly left again, and he never knew it. And so … he dreamt. And whatever had chased him for so long finally caught up with him.

"Hasso!" He heard his own name echoing, as if down a long, windy corridor. "Hasso Pemsel!"

He didn't want to answer. He didn't want to acknowledge. The harder he fled, though, the more his name pursued him. Names had power. So the wizards said, and here he was a wizard—of sorts.

At last, hounded, he stood and turned at bay. "What?" he shouted back into the void.

Time passed. A minute? An hour? It was a dream—he couldn't be sure. Time: that was all he knew. Then, dimly, a face appeared in the void, a face he knew. *Aderno's face*, he realized. "By the goddess, I've had a demon of a time raising you!" the wizard said.

When he named the goddess, Hasso seemed to see the cult statue floating beside him. The German also seemed to see Velona's face instead, or perhaps as well. He had trouble being sure which, but what difference did it make? It was only a dream … wasn't it? "Well, here I am," Hasso said.

Aderno nodded. "We heard you'd lived," he said. "We weren't sure, but it seems to be true. That was why Bottero tried to ransom you."

"Yes, I'm still around. They take me to Falticeni," Hasso said. Even in a dream, he stuck to the present tense as much as he could when speaking Lenello.

"You're not—telling them anything, are you?" Aderno sounded more anxious than perhaps he thought he did. Maybe covering up was harder in a dream. Or was Aderno dreaming? So much Hasso didn't know.

"No, I don't say anything," he replied. "You are well? Bottero is well? Velona is well? Mertois is well?" He asked after people he knew. He didn't waste time asking after Orosei—he knew the master-at-arms was dead.

"Mertois has a broken leg. He will limp ever after," Aderno said. "The rest of us are well enough. Bottero and Velona are wild for revenge against the savages. The Grenye can't do that to real men and expect to get away with it."

The first few times the Ivans gave the *Wehrmacht* a good clout, German soldiers felt the same way. Poland and the West and the Balkans had been easy. Nothing came easy in Russia, not even the victories. And, as year followed year, those got harder and harder to find. *Sorry, Aderno. You don't get walkovers forever, no matter how much you wish you did.*

Or maybe you did with magic. The Lenelli sure thought so. They'd stripped themselves thin of wizards before the latest battle. What they'd had was Hasso, in fact. But nobody'd suggested that he try a spell to see if the Bucovinans were up to any funny business. Nobody'd imagined they could be. So much for understanding the enemy!

When Hasso didn't answer right away, Aderno said, "We can do it! By the goddess, outlander, we can!"

When he called on the goddess again, the cult statue grew more distinct. So did Velona's face. Were they two sides of the same coin? Hasso was no damn good at such things. The doctrine of the Trinity and the notion of transubstantiation only made his head ache. It wasn't the goddess' voice that called to him, though. It was Velona's: "Are you all right, Hasso Pemsel?"

"Hello, sweetheart. Yes, I'm doing well enough, I guess," Hasso answered. "I hope you are."

"I miss you," she said. "I didn't think I would, but I do. I want to get you back. If I have to burn down all of Bucovin to do it and kill all the stinking Grenye savages in the way, I will."

Not even the *Führer* was that blunt. Hasso didn't doubt she meant every word of it. Whatever else you said about Velona, she'd never once made the acquaintance of hypocrisy.

"Have they tried to trick you into doing things for them? Have they given you sluts to try to make you forget me?" she asked.

"I don't do anything for them. And I can never forget you. You know that." Hasso didn't answer all of the last question. He had to share Velona with the king. How could she get mad at him for somebody like Leneshul?

Maybe you couldn't keep secrets in a dream. Whether he told her or not, she knew. And she didn't like it for beans. "I am a goddess! I do what I have to do!" she cried. "You—you're only a man! How dare you take some smelly little black-haired twat? How *dare* you?"

Much too late, he remembered she hadn't wanted him sniffing around Grenye serving girls back in Drammen, either. What could he say? That he had no idea whether he'd ever get away from Falticeni? She should have been able to see it for herself. If she could, she didn't care—she was playing the woman scorned right up to the hilt.

"Aderno!" she cried. "Center my power while I smite this wretch!"

Hasso *was* a wizard of sorts. An ordinary man might well not have escaped the goddess' wrath. He could feel it building like heat lightning on a hot summer day in the southern Ukraine. How to flee? How to get away?

He screamed himself awake.

XVI

He must have done some impressive shrieking. Next thing he knew, three guards were in the room with him, each man with a sword in one hand and a torch in the other. Their shadows swooped around and behind them like something out of a scary movie. *Nobody in this whole goddamn world knows what that means,* Hasso thought miserably. *Nobody but me.*

"What happened?" the first guard asked.

"Why did you yell?" said the second.

"Did somebody try to do something to you?" asked the third.

"Don't be stupid, Elyash," the first guard said. "Nobody in here but him—and us. Anybody who wants to get at him has to come through us, right? Nobody did, right?"

It wasn't necessarily so. Hasso wished it were. "Princess Drepteaza come see me?" he asked in his rudimentary Bucovinan.

The guards looked at one another. They didn't want to bother her in the middle of the night. It wasn't quite the raw fear that would have made flunkies hesitate before disturbing Velona. That could be dangerous in all kinds of ways, including physically. Drepteaza wouldn't—couldn't—blast you where you stood. That didn't make the little swarthy men eager to wake her up.

But the second guard said, "That shriek he let out ... Maybe we'd better. We can blame it on him."

Hasso didn't think he was supposed to catch that. He held his face still. Knowing more of the language than they thought he did couldn't hurt. After a little more guttural wrangling, the trooper called Elyash went off to see if Drepteaza would come. One of the others used his torch to light a lamp for Hasso. Then they withdrew from the room, leaving him alone in the dim, flickering light.

He could have gone back to sleep ... if he'd had the nerve. How many times during the war had he heard a bullet crack past him? More than he could count—he knew that. His scars spoke of times that hadn't been misses, but he wasn't thinking about those. He was thinking he might have dodged something worse than a bullet, something on the order of a 155mm shell. And, unlike a 155, it might still be waiting for him if he lay down and closed his eyes.

Will I ever be able to sleep again? he wondered. Soldiers on the Russian front always talked about sleeping with one eye open so the Ivans couldn't sneak up and cut their throats. But what happened when somebody could sneak up on you from inside your own head? Hasso shivered. Nothing good, that was what.

"Velona," he whispered sadly. Why couldn't she understand about Leneshul, even a little bit? But the answer to that formed as fast as the question. Because she was who and what she was, that was why. She wouldn't let a native girl upstage her, even if she wasn't there to be upstaged.

What did they call using a woman to get information out of a prisoner? A honey trap. The Bucovinans could have been tearing his toenails out. They could still start any time they pleased, too. Bless them, the fools, they'd given him a woman instead. And he hadn't even told Leneshul anything. He'd just used her as a nicely rounded sleeping pill to evade bad dreams.

The door opened. In came Drepteaza, her hair all awry and her face twisted from fighting against a yawn. "More trouble in the night?" she asked in Lenello.

"*Ja*," Hasso said. She nodded; she'd come to understand that. He wished he could go on in German; even in Lenello, he couldn't speak smoothly. But German, like memories of movies, was his alone here. Lenello, then: "Those dreams in the night—now I know what makes them."

"And?" Drepteaza waited for him to tell her what she needed to know. The feeble lamplight left her eyes enormous.

"A wizard from Bottero's kingdom sends to me in my sleep," Hasso said.

Her jaw set, as if she were taking a blow she hoped she was braced for. "I wondered whether that was so," she said softly, as much to herself, Hasso judged, as to him. She made herself stand straight. "And what does the wizard want?"

"To get me back for the Lenelli." Hasso answered with the truth. That was what Aderno *had* wanted, anyway, till Velona found out Hasso was laying a Grenye woman. Now they probably both wanted him trussed and roasted and served up with an apple in his mouth like a suckling pig.

"*They* think you know things," Drepteaza remarked. Hasso kept quiet, which struck him as the safest thing he could do just then—not that anything seemed very safe at the moment. The priestess eyed him. "But these are *bad* dreams for you. Elyash said you screamed tonight: screamed like a man over hot coals, he told me."

And how did Elyash know what a man sounded like when he hung over hot coals? Better not to inquire, chances were. "This is a bad dream tonight, yes," Hasso said.

"Why?" Drepteaza asked.

Hasso wondered whether he ought to evade that question. As much as Velona didn't like native women, Drepteaza didn't like Velona. The Lenello woman had already tried to fry his brains from the inside out. What would the Bucovinan woman do? Did he want to find out?

On the other hand, what exactly did he scream when he woke up? Did the guards hear it? Did it have Velona's name in it? If he lied and Drepteaza found out, what would she do then? Again, did he want to find out?

He decided he didn't. Hell had no fury like a woman scorned? How about a woman hoodwinked? And so, carefully, he said, "Velona is—*was*—in this dream."

"Oh, really?" No, the Bucovinan priestess didn't like that, not even a little bit. She didn't like anything that had anything to do with Velona. But her frown was more one of concentration than of fury—Hasso hoped so, anyhow. "You like Velona, though. You *love* Velona." Drepteaza made it sound indescribably perverse. "Why do you say seeing her was bad? And why did she appear in the dream in the first place?"

Drepteaza might be a native woman who only came halfway up Hasso's chest. That didn't mean she was a fool. Oh, no—on the contrary. How many people in Hasso's world had come to grief by equating the two? The *Führer* had in Russia. The *Wehrmacht* officer hoped he wouldn't make the same mistake himself, not when she'd picked two vital questions.

He answered them in the opposite order from which she'd asked them: "She appears because she wants—*wanted*—to get me back to Drammen." The past tense mattered here. He kept using it: "And seeing her was bad because she … got angry because of Leneshul."

"She did, did she?" Drepteaza laughed. "That's the funniest thing I ever heard. What does she expect you to do when you're here and not with her and you won't be going back to her? Sit around and play with your dick all the time?"

Hasso didn't care for the sound of *and you won't be going back to her*. Nothing he could do about it, though. And Velona probably did expect him to do just that, or else to live in the glorious memories of her. Life didn't work that way, but he thought it was what she expected.

Maybe Drepteaza did, too, for she shook her head and exclaimed, "The nerve of that woman!" She really did sound indignant.

"Sorry to bother you," Hasso said.

"Don't worry about it. I wouldn't have missed this for the world." Drepteaza paused, just when Hasso thought she would get in her last little dig and go back to bed. Maybe it was only a trick of the dim, unreliable lamplight, but suddenly she looked much older and much more worried. In a voice that tried to stay casual but didn't quite succeed, she asked, "*You* don't have anything to do with magic, do you?"

Rautat had asked him that before, but this time the question took him by surprise. If he'd been expecting it, he could have said, *Of course not*, and that would have been that. But what came out of his mouth was, again, the exact and literal truth: "I can do a little, but I don't know much about it."

"You … can … do … a … little." He never forgot how Drepteaza spaced out the words, or how enormous her eyes seemed. That was also partly a trick of the light, yes, but it seemed somehow more. She stabbed out a finger at him. "Why didn't you say so before?"

"What good does it do you? You can't trust me. Even if you could trust me, I'm not a quarter trained. I'm not a quarter of a quarter trained. What I know is this." Hasso held his thumb and index finger close together. "What the Lenelli know is *this*." He threw his arms wide.

Drepteaza's eyes narrowed now, narrowed dangerously. She didn't believe him. "But they wouldn't care about you if you didn't know things we don't."

"Neither would you," he pointed out.

"Of course we wouldn't—are we fools?" She didn't waste time denying it. "But if they want you back so much, that means—" She broke off. Hasso could fill in the blank. *That means you're worth something after all.*

If he denied it, they'd knock him over the head. No more Leneshul. It would be toenail-tearing time. "In the world I come from, there is no magic," Hasso said. "What I know has nothing to do with magic. It has to do with, uh, arts and craft." No way to say *technology* or *engineering* in Lenello.

"So we could use it as well as the blonds?" Drepteaza said. Hasso didn't say yes or no. She went on, "You had better show us some of this."

"You know why I don't. I have an oath to King Bottero." Hasso liked the Lenelli. He felt he could almost become one of them if he stayed here long enough and got used to their ways. In Bucovin his looks, if nothing else, would leave him a stranger the rest of his life. He would be as bad off as a Jew in Germany. Maybe worse—some Jews looked like Aryans. He sure as hell didn't look like a Grenye. A good thing they took oaths more seriously here than in his own world.

"Velona tried to harm you, yes?" Drepteaza said. "The wizard tried to harm you, yes? What is your oath to their king worth to you if it's worth nothing to them? Or do you think they struck at you without his knowledge, without his let?"

"I don't know," Hasso said slowly. "I have to think about that." It was worth thinking about, too. Priestesses were supposed to have answers, weren't they? He didn't know whether Drepteaza did. She sure had some good questions, though.

"We have to think about you, too," she said. "You can't do much! Oh, Lavtrig preserve us!" She walked out of the room shaking her head.

***

When Hasso got breakfast the next morning, the serving girl who gave him his tray looked at him as if he had horns and a tail and she thought he'd start breathing fire any minute. The morning before, she'd laughed and joked with him. She'd taken him for granted. She didn't any more. He knew what that had to mean.

"Only I," he said, knowing he'd botched the Bucovinan grammar as soon as the words were out of his mouth. But Jiril didn't speak Lenello—or at least she'd never let on that she did.

She might have just found a scorpion in her sock. "Wizard!" she said, and aimed at him a pronged gesture that couldn't possibly do her any good.

He sighed. Either Drepteaza had blabbed—which didn't seem likely, but wasn't even close to impossible—or the guards had overheard and started running their mouths. It made no real difference. Any which way, the cat was out of the bag.

The Lenelli admitted that some of their renegades had used magic for the natives. The Bucovinans had said the same thing. They'd also talked about the trouble they had keeping Lenello wizards using the magic for them and not to rule them.... *Or worse*, Hasso thought. If the SS had had magic to help it clear out the ghettos in Poland and Russia, wouldn't it have used every spell it could? In a heartbeat. Hasso had no doubts about that at all.

What *could* he do? He muttered to himself. What he could do and what he might do were two different creatures. Could he run a panzer without training? Not bloody likely. So why should he expect to work magic without learning how?

But the Bucovinans probably thought he could. All they knew about magic was that they couldn't work any. That might be useful.

Or it might get him killed, if they decided it made him too dangerous to leave alive. And he couldn't do a damn thing about it. Some wizard that made him!

How Jiril looked at him wasn't the only sign that things had changed. Nobody else came in all morning. The guards didn't want to let him out, either. He was half surprised that they didn't come in and take away his furniture. The maid who brought him lunch seemed less frightened than Jiril had, but she also wasn't easy with him.

No sign of Leneshul at all, dammit.

Drepteaza didn't visit till late afternoon. When she did, a full complement of tough-looking guards came in with her. The natives hadn't bothered with that for a while. They looked ready to ventilate him if he breathed funny, too. Maybe not back to square one, but square two? It seemed that way, worse luck.

Drepteaza didn't act afraid, but she didn't act even halfway friendly any more, either. What *did* her expression mean? Something on the order of *more in sorrow than in anger*, Hasso judged. And, sure enough, the first words out of her mouth were, "What are we supposed to do with you, Hasso Pemsel?"

The way she used his full name reminded him of Velona, a sudden stab he really didn't need just then. She spoke in her own language, but he answered in Lenello: "Priestess, you should set me free and give me a big estate and servants and plenty of gold and silver to pay for them."

She blinked. Whatever she'd expected, that wasn't it. One of the guards glowered at him. Another one laughed. They knew Lenello, then. After a moment, Drepteaza said, "Maybe that would keep us safe from you. If we were sure it would, it might be worthwhile. Killing you is surer—and cheaper."

She wasn't kidding. She didn't joke very often, and he always knew when she did. Much too conscious that he was talking for his life, he said, "I am a captive for some time now. You could kill me whenever you want."

"Before, we knew you were a snake. Now we know you are a viper," Drepteaza said. "You can do more and worse to us than we thought."

"Or I can do more and better for you," Hasso said.

"Maybe you can. But you still have your famous oath to King Bottero—Bottero the invader, Bottero the robber, Bottero the murderer, Bottero the torturer." No, Drepteaza wasn't joking. "The goddess who does not care what a man is, the wizard who tries to slay his own lord's sworn man. Do they deserve your oath, Hasso Pemsel?"

That was a different way of asking what she'd asked the night before. Unhappily, Hasso said, "They're worried about what I can do, what I know. So are you, remember."

"There is a difference," Drepteaza said.

"What?" Hasso asked.

She gave him a look that said he was either disingenuous or very, very stupid. "You already helped them. That attacking column you showed them, and whatever magic you worked for Bottero…"

Not to mention rescuing Velona, Hasso thought. The Bucovinans didn't know about that, which was a good thing for him. He uncomfortably recalled the spell he'd made to find the underwater bridges. The natives didn't know about that, either, and Hasso wasn't a bit sorry they didn't.

"In my world, a prisoner only has to give his name, his rank, and his pay number to his enemies," he said. Never mind that people broke the rules all the time when they needed to squeeze something out of somebody. The rules were what they were.

"You give your soldiers numbers?" Drepteaza frowned. "Why aren't names enough?"

"We have more soldiers than we have names—many more," Hasso answered. When he told her how many men the *Wehrmacht* held, she didn't want to believe him. Neither had the Lenelli when he talked about such things.

Unlike the Lenelli, who usually thought they knew it all, Drepteaza didn't argue with him. She just said, "Well, let that be as it may," and went on, "You are not in your world now, Hasso Pemsel. You are here, and you have to live by our rules."

"Don't I know it!" he exclaimed.

"We could have killed you. We could have killed you the width of a millet grain at a time. We could have sent you to the mines—a living death. Did we do any of that? No. We treated you well. Don't you want that to go on?"

"Of course I do. But you don't do it for me. You do it for you," Hasso said.

"And Bottero helped you just because he liked you." The priestess could be formidably sarcastic. Hasso didn't know what to say, so he kept his big mouth shut. Drepteaza looked through him. "So you still need to think, do you? If you must, you can do that—for a little while, anyway." Out she went.

***

Nothing much changed for the next few days. One thing did, though: Leneshul stopped coming to him. He knew what that meant: the Bucovinans weren't going to let anything stand in the way of whatever magic Aderno and Velona aimed at him. Whose clever idea was that? Drepteaza's? Lord Zgomot's? The trouble was, it *was* clever. If the people he called his friends kept trying to kill him, how long would he, could he, stay friendly to them?

If they did kill him, not very long.

If they didn't … Hasso hoped Drepteaza was counting on his living through whatever the Lenelli aimed at him. He hoped so, yes, but he couldn't be sure.

Since he didn't have a woman, he took matters into his own hands, so to speak. But, as he'd found with Leneshul, he couldn't get it up every day. The spirit was willing, but the flesh was older than that, dammit. Had he been twenty-one… One night, he fell asleep unshielded by self-abuse. He'd seen Velona in his dreams before, but not the way he had when she and Aderno assailed him.

He'd had dreams the past few nights that made him think he would have company when he slept unwarded by pleasure of any sort: dreams that reminded him of someone knocking on a distant door.

Tonight, the door wasn't distant. Tonight, Aderno didn't bother to knock—he just walked on in. "Ah, there you are," he said, as if he and Hasso were picking up a conversation after breaking off to eat lunch.

Hasso suggested that the wizard and his unicorn enjoyed a relationship different from mount and rider. It was a male unicorn.

"Naughty, naughty," Aderno said, his voice surprisingly mild. "That was a—a misunderstanding, you might say."

"*You* might say," Hasso retorted. "The only thing that misses is, I don't end up dead." Yes, he went right on sticking to the present tense when he could.

"It was a misunderstanding, I tell you." Aderno seemed to look back over his shoulder. "Isn't that right, Velona?"

She hadn't been there before. She was now. Dreams could do some crazy things—Hasso knew that. Seeing her strongly sculpted features sent a lance of pain through his heart. "I *am* sorry," she said. "I was upset when I found out. But it makes sense, where you are." She sounded like someone having trouble getting an apology out. Hasso didn't think she sounded like someone who had to lie to get an apology out.

But, when you got right down to it, so what? She'd done her level best to kill him, and it damn near turned out to be good enough. If he weren't some sort of half-assed wizard himself, chances were he'd be holding up a lily right now.

"Thanks a lot," he told her, as sardonically as he could.

He watched Aderno's dream-projection of her blush. She got the message, all right—unless Aderno was playing with her image to fool him. The only thing Hasso was sure of was that he couldn't trust anybody. He had no one to watch his back. He had had the Lenelli, but no more. Now he was … what?

The loneliest man in the world, that was what. Lots of people said that; for him, in this world, it was literally true. No doubt it had been ever since he got here, but he hadn't wanted to look at it. For quite a while, he hadn't had to. Now he saw no other choice.

"We worried about you," Velona said. "For a while, we didn't know if you were alive or dead. Then we got word the savages had you in Falticeni. We didn't know what they were doing to you, so—"

"You decide to do it yourself, in case they don't do a good enough job," Hasso broke in.

"No!" Velona said. But, Hasso noted, she didn't say, *By the goddess, no!* She took swearing by the goddess seriously; she wouldn't do it if she didn't mean it. Since the goddess, as it were, kept a flat inside her head, that made sense. The absence of the oath saddened Hasso without much surprising him. Velona went on, "We think we can bring you out of there, bring you back to Drammen, by magic."

"Oh?" Was that hope inside Hasso, or suspicion? "Why don't you do that before, instead of trying to boil my brain?"

"I was angry," Velona said simply—the first thing Hasso heard from her he was sure he believed. "I thought the Grenye would use their sluts to seduce you away from the cause of civilization. And I wanted you all for myself. By the goddess, I still do." She meant that, then. It was flattering, no doubt about it. She was one hell of a woman. She was one hell of a hellcat, too.

"I think we can do it, Hasso," Aderno said before the *Wehrmacht* officer could answer her. "If you open your will to mine—"

"No," Hasso said at once. If he opened himself to Aderno, he left himself vulnerable to the Lenello sorcerer. He might be a half-assed wizard, but he could see that much. And if you left yourself vulnerable to somebody who'd just tried to do you in—well, how big a fool were you if you did that? *A bigger fool than I am*, Hasso thought.

"You don't trust me." Aderno sounded affronted.

"Bet your balls I don't," Hasso said. The *Führer* had got an awful lot of mileage out of making promises he didn't mean to keep. Anyone who watched him in action had to wonder about promises forever after. Words, after all, were worth their weight in gold.

"Would you trust *me*, sweetheart?" Velona's dream-image looked almost, or maybe not just almost, supernaturally beautiful. Was she calling the goddess into herself to overwhelm his senses? But for what she'd done a few nights earlier, it likely would have worked. Now … He was inoculated against such things.

"I don't trust anybody any more," he said. "How can I?"

Even in the dream, he saw he startled her. Would anybody from this world have been able to resist her when she did something like that? He wouldn't have been surprised if the answer was no. But he wasn't from here. He knew there was something to the goddess—he'd seen as much—but he didn't automatically accept her as his deity.

After Velona's amazement, anger came back. And it wasn't just hers: it was also the goddess'. "Would you turn your face against *me*, Hasso Pemsel?" Velona asked, only something more rang in her voice.

"I don't want to turn against anybody," he said. "I just want people to leave me alone for a while."

He might as well not have spoken. "You will pay," Velona intoned—or rather, the goddess intoned through her. "You will pay, and Bucovin will pay for harboring you. Do you think you can thwart *my* will?"

"Well, the Bucovinans are still doing it," Hasso said. If anyone had talked to Hitler that way after Operation Barbarossa failed, the *Führer* would have handed him his head. But it might have done the *Reich* some good.

Velona didn't want to listen, any more than Hitler would have. Hasso might have known—hell, he had known—she wouldn't. People obviously weren't in the habit of telling the goddess no. "Insolent mortal! If you would sooner live among swine than men, you deserve the choice you made."

She hit him with something that made what Aderno and Velona did the last time seem a love tap by comparison. It wasn't quite enough to do him in, though, because he woke up screaming again.

***

Drepteaza eyed Hasso, God only knew what in her eyes. "This could grow tedious," she said in stern Lenello, and then yawned.

"I don't like it any better than you do," the *Wehrmacht* officer mumbled. "Less, I bet."

He'd already summarized his latest encounter with Velona and Aderno. The Bucovinan priestess sighed. "Well, Leneshul can come back to your bed, if that makes you any happier. She may do you some good, anyhow."

Hasso inclined his head. "I thank you," he said in Bucovinan, thinking, *I'd rather go to bed with you.* Not for the first time, he wondered how smart—no, how dumb—he was. His goddess-filled lover had just tried to do him in twice, so now he wanted to sleep with a priestess instead. Maybe he ought to have his head examined to see if it held any working parts.

Drepteaza nodded absently. "I do this more for us than for you," she said. "Whatever you know, the Lenelli don't want you showing it to us. That seems plain enough, doesn't it?"

"I suppose so." Hasso figured that was part of it, too. But he would have bet marks against mud pies that Velona's rage weighed more in the scales.

"But, of course, you don't want to show it to us, either, whatever it is," Drepteaza said. "You have sworn an oath to the people who want to kill you, and it counts for more than anything else."

That was irony honed to a point sharp enough to slip between the ribs, pierce the heart, and leave behind hardly a drop of blood. Hasso's ears heated. "I try to be loyal," he said.

"Loyalty is a wonderful thing. It is also a road people travel in both directions— or it should be," Drepteaza said. "If you are loyal and your lord is not…"

What had Bottero promised when Hasso swore homage to him? He'd vowed he would do nothing that made him not deserve it. Had he kept his half of the oath? When you got right down to it, no.

He's forsworn, all right. I can do whatever I want, and do it with a clear conscience.

The thought made Hasso no happier. He didn't want to take service with the Grenye, to pledge allegiance to Lord Zgomot of Bucovin. It reminded him too much of *Wehrmacht* men joining the Red Army and going to war against their old comrades. Some few had done it, he knew. And great swarms of Russians fought for the swastika and against the hammer and sickle.

Yes, they did. And Hasso knew what he thought of them. "You can use a turn-coat," he said miserably. "You can use him, but you can never like him or trust him or respect him."

"You do have honor." Drepteaza sounded surprised when she said it. Somehow, that seemed the most unkindest cut of all. After a moment, she went on, "Tell me this, Hasso Pemsel: do the Lenelli like you or trust you or respect you?"

"They ... did." Hasso made himself pause and use the past tense. The present wasn't true, however much he wished it were.

"They did, yes, when you were useful to them. Then they threw you away like a bone with the meat gnawed off it," Drepteaza said. "So why hold back now? Don't you want your revenge? Don't you deserve it?"

Hasso didn't answer right away. He had to look inside himself to find where the truth lay. When he did, it only made him even more uneasy, and here he hadn't thought he could be. Joining Bucovin, joining the Grenye, wasn't like going over to the Slavic *Untermenschen*. No, it was worse than that. Every time he looked at them, he thought of Jews, a whole great country full of grasping, swarthy Jews.

And he slept with Leneshul. And he wanted to sleep with Drepteaza. But that was *his* sport. Helping this folk against the Aryan-seeming warriors from across the sea...

"I don't know," he whispered. "I just don't know."

"Well, you had better make up your mind, Hasso Pemsel." Drepteaza didn't know what was bothering him. He didn't think he could explain it, either, not so it made sense to her. "You'd better make up your mind," she repeated. "And you'd better hurry up about it, too. You don't have much time left." And away she went, taking with her the captor's privilege of the last word.

***

Somebody pounded on Hasso's door, much too early in the morning. Next to the *Wehrmacht* officer, Leneshul groaned. "Who's that?" she muttered. "Why doesn't he go away?"

"Shall I find out?" Hasso asked. Leneshul only shrugged and pulled the blankets over her head, not that that did any good against the racket. Whoever was out there was bound and determined to come in.

Yawning and cursing in German, Hasso pulled on his trousers and walked to the door. He threw it open, then stopped in surprise. That wasn't a dark little Bucovinan out there, but a blond taller than himself. And, he realized a heartbeat later, someone he knew, too.

"Scanno!" he exclaimed. "What the demon are you doing here?"

"I could ask you the same question, buddy," the Lenello from Drammen answered. "They wanted me to come here and talk some sense into your pointed head, that's why I'm here. Nechemat's cursed glad to get away from all the Lenelli, too."

Nechemat, Hasso gathered, was Scanno's Grenye wife or lover. The German had seen her but never met her. "But you're a Lenello," he pointed out.

"On the outside, sure." Scanno breathed beer fumes into Hasso's face. Whether in Drammen or Falticeni, he liked to drink. He liked to talk, too. "I don't act like those dumb buggers, though. You think Grenye aren't people just on account of they're mindblind? Shit, *I'm* mindblind. Most Lenelli are. What's the big deal?" He eyed Hasso with more shrewdness than the *Wehrmacht* officer would have thought he owned. "I hear you're not. *That* could be a big deal. And you know other stuff, whatever the demon it is. So could that."

"They tell you everything?" Hasso asked. "Back in Drammen, they tell you everything?"

"All kinds of crap goes on under Bottero's big, pointy beak," said Scanno, who had a big, pointy beak himself. "A little harder to slip away than it used to be—I bet that's your fault, huh?"

"I suppose so." Hasso hadn't had time to do a really good job of training the Lenelli in security and counterespionage. If the likes of Scanno could beat his setup ... He knew what that meant. Bottero's men hadn't had time to figure it all out and make it their own yet. They were doing it because he'd told them to, not because they saw all the benefits and ins and outs for themselves. Hasso made himself ask, "How is the king?"

Scanno laughed, a big, booming laugh that made the Bucovinan guards stare. "Well, it's not like he invites me to the palace for roast duck and wine with sugar in it," the Lenello renegade said. "If he knows who I am at all, he figures I'm that drunken stumblebum who'd sooner slum it with the Grenye than stick to my own kind. And he's right, too."

He said that even as the same thought formed in Hasso's mind. If Scanno could see himself so clearly, the rest of what he said carried more weight.

"But anyway, Bottero's not happy right now. I don't need to eat his duck and drink his sugarwine to know that," Scanno went on. "Any time one of the kings loses to Bucovin, he's ready to spit nails. It's *embarrassing*, that's what it is. And he's got to worry that his loving neighbors will jump on his back. He took a real licking this time. *You* took a licking. What's this strike column I heard about?" Briefly, Hasso explained. Scanno grunted. "That's pretty sly, all right. But it didn't work this time."

"No, it didn't," Hasso agreed. "So why do you throw in with the Grenye and not your own folk?"

"I like 'em better," Scanno answered. "I mean, pussy's pussy—who cares if the hair on it's yellow or brown? And the Grenye, they don't brag and strut and carry on all the stinking time. They're people you can get along with. Besides, isn't it about time somebody gave the poor sorry cocksuckers a fair shake?"

Scanno bragged and strutted and carried on as much as any Lenello Hasso had ever known. Maybe he didn't know himself so well as the German had thought he did. Or maybe his size and his noise—and his yellow hair—made him stand out more among the natives than he ever would among his own people. Maybe he liked that. If he did, well, so what? What did it mean? That he was human. Who wasn't?

But that question had another answer, one it wouldn't have had in Hasso's old world. Scanno, plainly, had never gone to bed with Velona or anybody like her. True, the difference wasn't that she was a blonde, not a brunette. The difference was the goddess.

Yes, and the other difference is that she wants you dead now, Hasso reminded himself. *Details, details.*

"Here—I've got another question for you," Scanno said. "Were you at that place called—what the demon was the name of it? Muresh, that was it. The one where Bottero's boys went hog wild?"

"Yes, I was there."

"Did you play their games?"

"No." Hasso didn't say he'd seen such things before in Russia. He'd played those games then—the Ivans were enemies he hated, unlike the Bucovinans, who were foes merely in a professional sense. And the Russians had taken their revenge once the Red Army crossed the *Reich's* borders. Oh, hadn't they just?

Scanno grunted again. "Didn't think so. Bucovin doesn't massacre for the fun of it, either." *Bucovin isn't strong enough to,* Hasso thought. *The guys chasing Velona sure weren't out to play skat with her.* Scanno went on, "Why *don't* you throw in with the Bucovinans? They're a better mob than the ones out west." He jerked a thumb in the direction of Drammen.

That … might or might not be true. Hasso sighed. He really didn't have an answer, not one Scanno would get. *They look like a bunch of filthy kikes, dammit.* He sighed again. "I don't know. Why don't I?"

XVII

Scanno seemed to be an important fellow in Falticeni. The Bucovinans respected him even if his own folk didn't. When he told Lord Zgomot that Hasso might play along, Zgomot summoned the *Wehrmacht* officer in nothing flat.

Hasso bowed to the dark little man. From some things the natives had said, a lot of Lenelli, even renegades, had trouble bringing themselves to do that. Hasso didn't—why should he? Hitler was a dark little man, too, even if he did have blue eyes. And plenty of Germans these days were bowing down before Stalin, who by all accounts was even smaller and darker than Zgomot.

Among the Lord of Bucovin's courtiers stood Scanno and Drepteaza and Rautat. They all looked expectant. Scanno also looked almost indecently pleased with himself. He was a rogue—no doubt about it. But he likely did Bucovin more good than half a dozen more staid fellows would have.

Zgomot came straight to the point, asking in Lenello, "So you will show us what you know?"

"I try to show you some of it, yes, Lord." Hasso picked his words with care. He wasn't sure he could make gunpowder. Even if he could, he wasn't sure it would work in this world. And even if it did, he was a long way from sure he wanted it to work for the Bucovinans.

"If you do what we hope you can do, you will not lack for anything we can give you," Zgomot said. "If things turn out otherwise ... If things turn out otherwise, we will treat you the way you deserve. Do you understand me?"

"I do, Lord," Hasso answered. If he performed, he would get anything he wanted—except Velona. If he didn't, he would get the chopper. That seemed fair enough ... to someone whose neck wasn't on the line. Hasso had to fight the impulse to rub at his nape.

Zgomot's eyes might be dark and pouchy, but they were also uncommonly shrewd. "I understand that you do not love us, Hasso Pemsel. This is not a bargain about love. We have treated you well when we did not need to. We hope you will repay us for our kindness."

"I hope you do, too, Lord." Hasso had to fight even harder to keep that hand away from the back of his neck.

He hoped this would be it, and he could see if he could get his hands on salt-peter and charcoal and sulfur. If he couldn't, he was, not to put too fine a point on it, screwed. But the Lord of Bucovin wasn't quite done with him yet. "The holy priestess" —he pointed toward Drepteaza with his chin— "tells me you have somewhat of the wizards' blood in you."

Hasso nodded to Zgomot. "So it would seem, Lord, though I am not trained in magic."

"I will give you a piece of advice some Lenelli" —Zgomot didn't say *some other Lenelli*, which was a kindness of sorts— "would have done well to heed. We have no magic. You know that. But if you use it against us here in Falticeni, it will do you less good than you think. Do you hear me?"

"Some Lenelli tell me the same thing, Lord," Hasso answered. Even Velona's goddess-given powers had weakened, though they hadn't failed, as she neared the capital of Bucovin. She didn't know why but she knew it was so.

"The Lenelli don't like it when we have a wizard in our midst. They think he makes us more dangerous to them," Zgomot said. "But we don't always like it, either, because a wizard in our midst is dangerous to us. So far, though, no Lenello wizard has managed to hold on to Bucovin longer than a month or so. Even wizards, we find, can't watch everyone all the time."

He was small and swarthy and dumpy. He was also clever and cynical, and probably made a damn good king. If he was considerate enough to warn Hasso, the German decided he ought to take that as a compliment. Bowing, he said, "I understand, Lord. I never want to be a king—or even a lord—myself."

"Few men do—at the beginning. They find the ambition grows on them after a while, though." Zgomot had a formidable deadpan. Hasso wouldn't have cared to play cards against him. He went on, "It's sad, but most of those men don't come to a good end. You wouldn't want to see that happen to yourself, would you?"

"Now that you mention it, no." Hasso tried to match dry for dry.

He must have succeeded, because one corner of Zgomot's mouth twitched upward before the Lord of Bucovin could pull his face straight again. "All right," the native said. "Do what you can do, and we will see what it is." With that less than ringing endorsement, he dismissed Hasso from his presence.

***

Charcoal was easy. Sulfur was manageable, anyhow. Hasso didn't know the Lenello name for it, but he described it well enough to let Drepteaza recognize it. "We use it in medicine, and we burn it to fumigate," she said. "It stinks."

"It sure does," Hasso agreed. "How do you say *fumigate* in Bucovinan?" They still used Lenello most of the time. He was more fluent in it, and he needed to be as precise as he could here. For that matter, he hadn't known how to say *fumigate* in Lenello till she told him, but context was clear there.

She told him. Literally, the word meant something like *burn-to-stink-out-pests*. German could paste small words together to make big ones. Bucovinan did it all the time. It also pasted on particles that weren't words in themselves, but that changed statements to questions or commands; showed past, present, or future; showed complete or incomplete action; and did lots of other things German would have handled with cases and verb endings. The language struck Hasso as clumsy, but it got the job done. He preferred Lenello not only because he knew it better—it also worked more like German.

Even in Lenello, he had a devil of a time getting across the idea of saltpeter. In the old days, in Europe, it had been a medicine to keep young men from getting horny. It probably worked as badly as any other medicine from the old days, but that was what people used it for before they found out about gunpowder… and afterwards, too.

In Europe. Neither the Lenelli nor the Bucovinans seemed to know about that. And Hasso didn't know what the stuff looked like in the wild, so to speak. He got frustrated. So did Drepteaza. "If you don't know how it looks or where to find it, how do you expect me to?" she asked pointedly.

"*Scheisse*," Hasso muttered. Swearing in German still gave him far more relief than either Lenello or Bucovinan. But saying *shit* made him remember one of the few things he *did* know about saltpeter. "Dungheaps! You find it in dungheaps! You know the crystals you find at the bottom of them sometimes? That's saltpeter." He had to cast about several times before he got Drepteaza to understand *crystals*, too.

When she did, though, she nodded. "All right. Now, at least, I know what you're talking about. I don't know how to say it in Lenello. In my language, it's—" The Bucovinan word meant *shitflowers*.

Hasso grinned and nodded. "I remember that one—I promise," he said. "Do you have any of it?"

"I don't think so," she answered. "It isn't good for anything." She paused. "Not for anything we know, anyway."

"Can you get me some?" he asked.

"I suppose so. Some temple servant will think I've gone mad when I tell him to fork up a dunghill, but I suppose so. How much do you need?"

If he remembered right, black powder was three-quarters saltpeter, a tenth sulfur, and the rest charcoal. If he didn't remember right, or somewhere close to right, he was dead meat. "If this works, as much as I can get. To show it works … Say, this much." He put both fists close together.

"You'll have it." Drepteaza looked bemused—and amused, too. "Who would have thought anybody wanted shitflowers? What else will you need?"

"A good balance, to weigh things on. And grinders—stone or wood, not metal."

"Why not metal?"

"If I strike a spark … Well, I don't want to strike a spark." If he was going into the gunpowder business in a big way, he wouldn't be able to do it all himself. He would have to make sure the natives didn't do anything stupid or careless, or they'd go sky-high. Even in modern Europe, munitions plants blew up every once in a while. But he'd finally found one good thing about the absence of tobacco, anyhow. Nobody'd drop a smoldering cigar butt into a powder barrel.

Then he had a really scary thought. Could a Lenello wizard touch off gunpowder from a distance? Would he have to figure out a spell to keep that from happening? If he did, if he could, would he be able to take the spell off again to use the powder on the battlefield?

His head started to hurt. This was all a hell of a lot more complicated than it would have been in Germany in, say, 1250.

What he was thinking must have shown on his face. "Is something wrong?" Drepteaza asked.

"I hope not," Hasso answered. For a while, Lenello wizards wouldn't be able to figure out what he was doing. He hadn't gone into any great detail about gunpowder back in Bottero's kingdom. One of the people he *had* talked with was Orosei, and the master-at-arms was too dead to give much away now.

"Is it something to do with magic?" she asked.

Hasso jumped. He couldn't help it. "How do you know that?" His poker face wasn't as good as Lord Zgomot's, but he didn't like to think anybody—let alone a native—could read him so well.

Drepteaza's smile lifted only one corner of her mouth. "When we worry about things going wrong, we worry about magic. Why should you be any different?" It always worked against her folk. The Lenelli didn't look at things the same way. But then, magic worked for them.

"Maybe I should teach you fighting tricks you can use right away, and not this," Hasso said. "This takes some time before it turns into anything."

"When it does, it will be important, won't it?"

"I hope so," Hasso answered, trying not to think about wizards wreaking havoc on gunpowder once he'd made it.

"Then do this," Drepteaza said firmly. "Do the other, too, but do this. I don't know what it will be, but I want to find out."

"I have the charcoal. I have the sulfur. I am just waiting for the shitflowers." Hasso enjoyed the word.

Drepteaza took it for granted. Both the Lenelli and the Bucovinans were earthier folk than Germans. They didn't flush bodily wastes down the drain—they had to deal with them. In the field, so did Hasso. He'd covered up like a cat when he could and just left things where they were when he couldn't. But a city full of people couldn't very well do that, not unless it wanted to get buried in waste.

He supposed the crystals the natives gave him were saltpeter. They certainly stank of the dungheap. But if the locals gave him something else by mistake or to test him, he wouldn't have known the difference. He washed the crystals and got rid of the filthy, scummy stuff that floated on top of the water.

But he also discovered he was getting rid of a lot of the saltpeter, because it dissolved in water. So he couldn't just pour out the water. He had to skim off the scum and then boil the water to get back what had gone away. Drepteaza watched in fascination as he worked. "Were you ever an apothecary?" she asked.

"You have the touch."

Hasso shook his head. "It would be nice. Then I would have a better idea of what I'm doing."

"If you don't know, no one does."

"That's what I'm afraid of," he answered.

He ground a little of the saltpeter, the charcoal, and the sulfur very fine and mixed them together, then touched them off with a flame. They burned enthusiastically, but not so well as he'd hoped. He mixed up another small batch, wet it, and kneaded the mixture into a paste. Then he let it dry and ground it again, being very careful not to do anything that could make a spark.

Once he finished, he had enough powder to fill a fat firecracker. The only problem was, the natives didn't have cardboard to make a firecracker casing. (Neither did the Lenelli.) After some thought, Hasso asked for thin leather. Drepteaza had trouble containing her amusement as she watched him struggle to put together the case. "You may make a good apothecary, but you were never a glover or anything like that."

Shakespeare's father was a glover. Hasso didn't know how he knew that, but he did. Knowing it was useless back in his old world, and worse than useless here. He gave Drepteaza an irritated look. "And so?"

"And so you ought to have someone else do the work instead of trying to do it all yourself," she answered. "You know what you want to do. Let other people do what they know how to do."

He was flabbergasted, not least because she was so obviously right. He knew lots of things the Bucovinans didn't. He'd let that blind him to an obvious truth: they knew lots of things he didn't, too. One of their artisans would have taken twenty minutes to deal with what was costing him a day's worth of work and turning out crappy.

Maybe Drepteaza knew a fine leatherworker herself. Maybe she asked one of Lord Zgomot's servants for a name. However she did it, she found a Grenye with a nearsighted squint who was miraculously capable with a knife and a needle. Drepteaza translated for Hasso, explaining exactly what he wanted.

"I'll do it," the glover said. Hasso understood that bit of Bucovinan just fine. It took the man longer than twenty minutes, but not much. His stitches were as tiny and as close together and as perfectly matched as a sewing machine's might have been.

The glover watched with interest as Hasso used a clay funnel from the kitchens to fill the case with powder. After the *Wehrmacht* officer had done that, he told Drepteaza, "Now he can sew up almost all of the opening at the top."

"Why not all of it?" the glover asked. Then he brightened, finding an answer of his own: "Is this thing a suppository?" Drepteaza translated the question with a straight face.

If you stuck it up there and touched it off, it would get rid of your hemorrhoids, all right—assuming it worked. Imagining that, Hasso started to giggle. He couldn't explain why. None of the natives had seen gunpowder in action.

"Just tell him no," he replied, as matter-of-factly as he could.

"How will you make it do whatever it does without hurting yourself?" Drepteaza asked after she told the glover no. She might not have seen gunpowder, but she had a good eye for the possibilities.

"I need to make a *fuse*," Hasso said. The key word necessarily came out in German. If gunpowder caught on here—*and if I live long enough*, he thought—the technical terms would be in a very foreign language.

In the *Wehrmacht*, fuses came in two flavors—timed, which burned at about a meter a minute, and instantaneous, which burned at about forty meters a second. You could improvise a fuse with powder and cord, but it would burn pretty damn quick. Hasso didn't know how to make timed fuse. He didn't think the Bucovinans would let him spend very long experimenting, either. He wouldn't have if he were Lord Zgomot.

And so he did some more improvising. He rubbed gunpowder into about a meter of cord, and put the end of that into the leather case holding the rest of his charge. Then he attached the other end to a length of candle wick, which would have to do duty for timed fuse.

He borrowed a toy wagon and a couple of little wooden soldiers and set them near the charge. Everything sat on the bare rammed-earth floor of a palace storeroom. Lord Zgomot, Drepteaza, and Rautat were the only witnesses when Hasso lit the wick and hastily stepped out of the room.

"It makes a loud bang—don't be afraid," he said. *I hope like hell it does. They'll hang me up by the balls if it doesn't.*

Rautat nodded. "You can say that again. If it's like your thunder weapon, it'll go *blam! blam! blam!*"

"Only once," Hasso said. "Thunder weapon is all used up. Can't make anything like that—too hard. Too hard for Lenelli, too. They—"

Boom! The explosion interrupted him. Rautat flinched. Lord Zgomot jumped. Drepteaza opened her mouth, but she didn't let out a squeak. Neither did the two men. The Bucovinans had nerve, all right.

"Let's see what it does," Hasso said.

Before they could, several servants came running up to find out what the demon had happened. They'd never heard a boom like that before. Lord Zgomot sent them away. Hasso couldn't follow most of what he said, but it sounded reassuring. He seemed to have a knack for giving people what they needed.

After the servants went away, Hasso and his comrades walked into the storeroom. Rautat wrinkled his nose. "Smells like devils," he said. Hasso thought the brimstone reek smelled like fireworks. It didn't smell like war to him; the odor of smokeless powder was different, sharper.

The toy wagon lay on its side near one wall. One of the wooden dolls wasn't far away. The other one was in pieces on the other side of the room. Only a couple of tattered scraps were left of the leather sack that had held the gunpowder.

"A pot full of this could smash real people and real wagons the same way, yes?" Lord Zgomot asked.

"Yes, Lord. That's the idea," Hasso said. That was one of the ideas, anyway. The Bucovinans had catapults—they'd borrowed the idea from the Lenelli. Catapults could fling pots full of gunpowder at charging Lenello knights. The big blonds wouldn't like that. Neither would their horses, or their wizards' unicorns.

Wizards ... Wizards went on worrying Hasso. What could they do to gunpowder? How soon would they figure it out?

And how soon would he have to go into the cannon-founding business? Cannon could easily outrange catapults. But he didn't know how to make them. Oh, he had an idea. You needed a hollow tube with a touch-hole at the end opposite the muzzle. But how thick did it have to be? If it blew up instead of sending a cannonball at the enemy, he wouldn't make himself popular in Bucovin. What kind of carriage should it have? Sure, one with wheels. That covered a lot of ground, though, ground he knew nothing about. One firecracker was a tiny start, no more.

No, this wouldn't be easy. Lord Zgomot wanted weapons to sweep away the Lenelli. Who could blame him? Hasso couldn't give him those weapons with a snap of the fingers. It wasn't that easy. *And who'll blame me because I can't?*

He knew the answer to that. *Everybody.*

***

Hasso didn't trust the Bucovinans to make gunpowder, not yet. They didn't know enough to be careful. After they watched him for a while, they probably would—after they watched him and after they saw some explosions. You had to respect the stuff or you had no business working with it.

At Drepteaza's suggestion, Rautat started learning the craft from him. The veteran underofficer had seen what firearms could do. If he didn't respect gunpowder, what Bucovinan would?

Hasso needed a while to realize that question had two possible answers. The one he wanted was that the Bucovinans would do fine after they got the hang of things. But the other one was also there. Maybe they wouldn't get the hang of it at all. Maybe they were too primitive. The Lenelli were somewhere close to the level where Europeans had been when they started making guns. The Bucovinans...

The Bucovinans were trying to pull themselves up to that level by their own bootstraps. How far below it had their several-times-great-grandparents been when the Lenelli first landed on these shores? A thousand years below? Two thousand years? Something like that. They'd started working iron, and they'd had kingdoms of sorts. The Lenelli had smashed a lot of them to confetti.

Bucovin survived. Because it lay farther east, it had had more time to absorb what the Lenelli brought with them before they actually bumped up against its borders. And, for whatever reason, magic didn't work so well near Falticeni. Hasso scratched his head. He wondered why that was so.

But he had more urgent things to worry about. "This isn't just like the thunder weapon you had before," Rautat remarked.

"It sure isn't," Hasso agreed. With a couple of dozen Schmeissers and enough ammo, he could have gone through all the Lenello kingdoms and Bucovin without breaking a sweat. But he didn't have them, so no point getting wistful about it.

"I know you say you can't make anything like that," Rautat said. Hasso nodded. The Bucovinan went on, "Well, how close can you come?"

"Not very." With a lot of work, Hasso figured he could eventually make a smoothbore matchlock musket. That wouldn't happen soon. It also wouldn't be that much more deadly than a bow and arrow, though it would be a lot easier to learn.

"Too bad," the underofficer said, and then, "You'd better not be holding out on us."

"I'm not, curse it!" Hasso said. "Why would I show you this much and not the rest, if I could do the rest? It makes no sense."

Rautat fingered the graying tendrils of his beard. "I guess so," he said, but he didn't sound a hundred percent convinced.

Wonderful. Just what I need, Hasso thought. *Even the guys who work closest with me don't trust me.* But he'd had that unhappy thought before. Nobody trusted someone who changed sides. You got what you could from a turncoat, but trust him? He'd already thrown away one loyalty. Why would he worry about another?

And Hasso knew he would go back to Bottero's kingdom in a flash if he got the chance. The Bucovinans had to know it, too, because they made sure he never got a chance. They didn't go into the garderobe with him when he needed to take a leak—not usually, anyhow—but that was about the only time he wasn't watched except when he was alone in his room. Lord Zgomot didn't get watched over the way Hasso did.

Well, why should he? Zgomot had no reason to light out for the tall timber. Hasso damn well did.

Would Velona take him back? He could hope so, anyhow. And even if she decided he was a racial traitor, Bottero would still think he was useful, wouldn't he? Sure he would.

Hasso found himself grinding his teeth, which wasn't the smartest thing he could do in a country where the dentists had never heard of laughing gas. Yeah, Bottero would think he was useful. But the Lenello king wouldn't fully trust him any more, either. He'd worked for Bucovin, for the contemptible Grenye.

He was screwed any way you looked at it.

✳✳✳

A couple of evenings later, he told Leneshul not to bother coming back any more. "All right," she said, and left with no more ceremony than that. She'd given him what he wanted, but she hadn't wanted anything from him. To her, he was just a job. Now she could go do something else.

The next morning, Drepteaza said, "Shall I find another woman for you?"

"In a while, maybe. Not right now," Hasso answered.

She frowned. "Even if you get no more bad dreams, it's not healthy for a man to go without a woman too long. You'll get grumpy and grouchy."

"If I have a woman I don't care about, it's not much better than no woman at all," Hasso said.

"I'm sorry Leneshul didn't please you as much as I hoped she would," Drepteaza said. "But I don't know what to do about that."

"You could—" Hasso broke off.

"What?"

"Nothing. It's nothing." Hasso buried his nose in a mug of beer. *Me and my goddamn big mouth*, he thought.

"What is it?" Drepteaza persisted. "If it is anything reasonable, we will do it for you. You do seem to be helping us. We pay our debts."

Reasonable? That was funny, or would have been if only he were laughing. He took another pull at the beer. Even in wartime Germany, it would have been pretty bad. By local standards, it was pretty good. *If only I knew something about brewing. If only I knew something about anything.* "Nothing," Hasso said again.

Drepteaza looked severe. "You say it is nothing. Then you will get angry because we can't guess what it is and deliver it to you without being asked. We know how these things go—we've seen them before."

She wasn't going to leave him alone. He could see that coming like a rash—or like a salvo of *Katyusha* rockets from a Stalin Organ. Well, maybe the truth would shut her up. She couldn't get *too* mad—he hoped—not when she'd asked for it. "If I wanted any woman in my bed, it would be you." *Any Bucovinan woman.* Yes, he had to make the reservation even after Velona tried to kill him. If that didn't say he had it bad, what would?

He didn't shock the priestess. To his immense relief, he saw that right away. He saw no answering spark flash, though. *Damn!* "It is a compliment. I ought to thank you for it. I *do* thank you for it," she said slowly.

"But." Hasso packed a world—two worlds—of bitterness into one word.

"Yes. But." Drepteaza did him the courtesy of not misunderstanding, and of not beating around the bush the way he had. "I am very sorry, Hasso Pemsel, but when I look at you I see a Lenello. I don't know what else to say. I don't think anything else needs saying—do you?"

The Lenelli looked down their noses at Grenye. That the Grenye might look up their noses at the Lenelli—they weren't tall enough to look down them—hadn't crossed Hasso's mind. The Lenelli, after all, looked like Aryans. Of course they were better than these little swarthy people ... weren't they?

Didn't he himself want to sleep with Drepteaza more in spite of her looks than because of them? Well, yes and no. Yes, she was small and dark. But she was also very pretty and, as he knew from the baths, made just the way a woman ought to be. Maybe she was built no better than Leneshul. Even so, she was a hundred times as interesting—which had nothing to do with looks.

"You don't say anything," Drepteaza remarked.

"What am I supposed to say? I already say too much," Hasso answered.

She sent him a wry smile. "You're no Lenello, regardless of how you look. If you were, you would be telling me how wonderful you were and what an honor it would be for me to open my legs for you."

Hasso's ears felt on fire. Well-bred women in Germany didn't talk about opening their legs even after you propositioned them. They might do it, but they didn't talk about it so baldly. He tried to match her tone: "If you don't already know I am wonderful, what can I say to make you believe it?"

"Probably nothing." Few German women had Drepteaza's devastating honesty, either. She went on, "I look at you, and I see things like Muresh. I see a countryside full of massacres like that, from here all the way west to the seacoast. And I should be *honored* to sleep with you?" She shuddered.

She might as well be a Jew looking at an SS man, Hasso thought. He did some shuddering of his own. The SS was bound to be out of business now. The Jews who were left in Europe, and the Jews from America and Russia, were having their turn. Hasso didn't—couldn't—know what was going on in the *Reich* now in the aftermath of a lost war, but he wasn't sorry not to be there to see it. Hard times: he was sure of that.

And if the Jews were taking revenge, could the Grenye of Bucovin do the same? The Jews hadn't had to worry about magic. Oh, some of the Nazi bigwigs dabbled in the occult, but it sure didn't do them a pfennig's worth of good. It was real here, though—no doubt about it. *And I'm helping these dark little mindblind...?*

If I want to keep on living, I am.

Besides ... "No matter what I look like, I am not a Lenello," Hasso said carefully.

"Yes, so you keep insisting, and it seems to be true. But you still look like one, so it helps you less than you think even if it is." The skin at the corners of Drepteaza's eyes crinkled; the ends of her mouth turned up the tiniest bit. "And we both know a man will say anything at all to coax a woman into bed with him."

"What?" Hasso did his best to look comically astonished.

It must have worked—Drepteaza burst out laughing, which didn't happen every day, or every week, either. She wagged a finger at him. "You are a wicked man. Wicked, I tell you."

Most of her was kidding; she made that plain enough. But down underneath, at some level, she had to mean it. And so Hasso couldn't just go on with the joke and say something like, *At your service.* Instead, he said, "Well, the Lenelli think so, too."

"Yes." The priestess sent him a hooded look. "And it could be, couldn't it, that all of us are right?"

***

A blizzard roared in that afternoon. If anything, it came as a relief to Hasso. It took his mind off the foot he'd stuck in his mouth, anyway. Listening to the wind wail, watching it blow snow past almost horizontally, reminded him there were bigger things in the world than his own foolishness. For a while that morning, he hadn't been so sure.

Then his nose started to freeze, so he quit watching the blowing snow. It wasn't anything he hadn't seen before—that was for damn sure. Next to some of the blizzards he'd seen in Russia and Poland, this one was no more than a plucky amateur.

He wondered how soon he'd regret telling Leneshul to get lost. Then he didn't wonder any more: he'd regret it as soon as he got horny again. That was as plain as the—chilly—nose on his face.

But, dammit, she wasn't what he wanted. Yeah, any pussy was better than none, but he missed Velona. There was a woman and a half—well, more than a woman and a half, when you got right down to it. A woman and a goddess.

Drepteaza wasn't a woman and a half. She was so short, she hardly seemed one whole woman. But she was, and then some. And so? So *she* didn't want *him*.

"I can't win," he muttered. Maybe she was a lousy lay. Maybe she'd think *he* was a lousy lay. Maybe they just wouldn't work. *Maybe I'm trying to tell myself the grapes are sour because I don't get to taste them.* Aesop was no dummy. He knew how things worked, all right.

A Lenello woman came in with his supper. Mutton stew, it smelled like, and heavy on the garlic. He didn't much care for garlic, but the Bucovinans put it in everything this side of beer. The pitcher of beer wouldn't be anything to write home about, either—as if he could write home from here. Then again, the natives could have boiled him in beer and shoved garlic cloves up his ass, so how could he complain?

"Good day," the serving girl said in Lenello.

"Good day," Hasso answered in his bad Bucovinan.

"You have heard about the trouble?" she asked. Most of the people who dealt with him here knew more Lenello than he did. Back when the German tribes bumped up against Rome, how many Goths and Franks would have spoken Latin? Quite a few, probably.

"No. What trouble?" Hasso stuck to Bucovinan—he needed the practice. He was also out of the gossip loop. No surprise—he was a foreigner who didn't speak any known language very well.

Still in Lenello, the serving woman said, "Your people attack our border villages again. Much burning. Much killing."

"My people? I have no people here," Hasso said.

She looked at him as if he were an idiot. That had to be what she was thinking, too. "King Bottero's people," she said, speaking slowly and plainly. "You are from King Bottero's kingdom, yes?"

Hasso couldn't even say no. That had been his local address till the Bucovinans captured him. Even so, he told the serving woman the same thing he'd told Drepteaza: "I am not a Lenello."

Drepteaza listened to him. Drepteaza appreciated subtleties. Even Rautat recognized the possibility that he might be different from the rest of Bottero's men. The serving woman just sniffed. "You look like a Lenello. You come from Bottero's kingdom. What are you supposed to be, a parsnip?" She walked out of the room without giving him a chance to answer.

"*Ja.* A goddamn parsnip," he said in German. "What am I supposed to be? God, I wish I knew." He poured beer from the pitcher into a mug. She hadn't given him enough to get drunk on. The Grenye of Bucovin didn't get smashed every chance they could, the way so many Grenye in the Lenello kingdoms seemed to. These natives didn't have to measure themselves against the big, blond, magic-using invaders every hour of the day, every day of the week. They still kept some sense of their own worth.

He ate the stew. Damned if it didn't have parsnips in it. So now he was part parsnip, anyhow. He put more charcoal on the brazier, crawled under his furs and blankets, and went to bed. What else did he have to do when he wasn't making gunpowder? He hadn't taken a woman: not Leneshul, not Drepteaza, not even this snippy servant. He hoped Aderno and Velona wouldn't hound him in his dreams. After everything else today, that would have been too much, even if he lived through it.

They didn't. He got a full night's sleep—or most of one, anyway. Somebody banged on his door before the sun came up the next morning. When he opened it, Rautat stood in the hallway. "Can you use your gunpowder against the Lenelli?" he asked. The German word sounded odd in his mouth. "Have you got enough?"

"Do I have a choice?" Hasso said. "If I do, I'd rather not."

Rautat scowled. "You better talk to Lord Zgomot. He sent me."

XVIII

People who ran stuff didn't like you to tell them no. It didn't matter whether you called them lord or king or *Führer*—they still didn't like it for beans. Stories about Hitler's tantrums—even his carpet-chewing—made the whispered rounds in Germany. When you said no to Bottero, he could look as if he wanted to pinch your head off.

And as for Lord Zgomot ... well, he just looked mournful. "We have some of this thing. It is, for once, a thing the Lenelli have not got. Why not use it against them, then?"

"Lord, if you order, I use it," Hasso said—he didn't want to push his luck too far. "But this is not the best time."

"They are on our land again," Zgomot said. "They are killing and raping and robbing, the way they do. Why is this a bad time?" His tone said Hasso had better have himself some goddamn good reasons.

And Hasso thought he did. He ticked them off on his fingers as he spoke: "First, Lord, not much gunpowder yet. We have more later." The Lord of Bucovin nodded impatiently—he knew that. Hasso went on, "Second thing is, better not to let Lenelli know what you have too soon, yes? These are raids, yes? Better to use gunpowder in big fight, get big win, not let them see what it does till too late."

He wished he could talk better. Even in Lenello, he sounded like a jerk to himself. Why should Zgomot take him seriously if he sounded like a jerk? And it was a good thing he didn't have to try to speak Bucovinan. He was better at it than he had been when he got to Falticeni, which meant—dismayingly little, when you came right down to it. He still needed to go some to get to sound like a jerk in Bucovinan.

Lord Zgomot sat lonely on his throne, thinking things over. Torches crackled as they burned in their sconces. Fat candles glowed to either side of the high seat. All the same, in the predawn stillness the throne room was a cold, dark, drafty place. Torches and candles couldn't push darkness back the way lightbulbs did.

At last, the Lord of Bucovin sighed. It was cold enough in there to let Hasso see his breath smoke. "You make more sense than I wish you did," he said, speaking slowly and carefully—Hasso remembered Lenello was a foreign language for him, too. "Let it be as you say. I will move against the bandits with ordinary soldiers, as we have already begun to do."

Hasso bowed. "You are wise, Lord."

"Am I?" Zgomot's tone was as bleak and wintry as the air inside the throne room. "You know I do not trust you completely, or even very far. You know I wonder if you do not want to use the gunpowder because you fear it will hurt the Lenelli and you are still loyal to them in your heart."

He was uncommonly blunt—scarily blunt, in fact. The dagger of ice that went up Hasso's back had nothing to do with the cold in here. "It is not so," the *Wehrmacht* officer insisted. "I want to hurt them more. I am sorry it needs to be later. This is not a big enough field to do it the good way, the, uh, right way."

"So you say." Zgomot leaned forward a little to eye him more closely. "So you say, when you lay with the Lenello goddess and our priestess does not care to lie with you. Never mind that you are tall and fair and they are tall and fair and we are not so tall and not so fair. Woman trouble will turn a man towards one side and against the other as easily as anything else. More easily than a lot of things."

Hasso thought of Helen of Troy, and of Brunhilde. Zgomot wasn't wrong, not speaking generally. And Hasso longed for Velona the way the tongue longs for a tooth after it got pulled. Never mind that it was hurting you. The tongue still wanted it to be there, wanted things to go on as they always had. *It won't happen, tongue*, Hasso thought.

"Velona tries to kill me now twice in my dreams," he told the Lord of Bucovin. "So you say."

"Yes, Lord. So I say. If I am a liar about this, I am a liar about everything."

"That thought has also crossed my mind." Zgomot's voice grew more wintry than ever. "And what about Drepteaza, Hasso Pemsel?"

"Why ask me? Why not ask her?" Hasso spread his hands. "A woman who does it but doesn't want to ... Not much fun in that. I think it's a shame—that is no lie. But what can I do?"

"No, you are not a Lenello," Zgomot said, as several Bucovinans had before him. Hasso waited to find out why the sovereign didn't think so. He didn't have to wait long. Zgomot continued, "Most of the big blond bastards—excuse me—force our women for the fun of it. We have seen that. I daresay you have seen it, too."

"Yes, I see that." Hasso admitted what he could scarcely deny. He might have argued that it wasn't true of *most* Lenelli, but he knew it was true of enough to make Zgomot's point for him.

"Maybe, in this snow, we can ambush a raiding party...." Careful and methodical, the Lord of Bucovin started making plans to deal with the enemy even if he couldn't do it the way he'd wanted.

The Lenelli didn't understand why they had trouble beating Bucovin when so many other Grenye kingdoms fell at the first shove. Hasso wondered whether Zgomot's father and grandfather were as clever as he was. That might go a long way towards explaining things.

And why *did* magic have more trouble the closer you got to Falticeni? Hasso didn't know. Neither did the Lenelli. Obviously, neither did the Bucovinans. There had to be a reason. How would you go about finding out? A real wizard might know. Hasso hadn't the faintest idea.

Maybe he was lucky such things didn't work so well here. Maybe that had helped keep Velona and Aderno from cooking his brains in his dream. He had no idea how to go about learning whether that was so, either.

Lord Zgomot seemed to remember he was there. "You may go, Hasso Pemsel. For better or worse, you persuaded me. You persuaded me you aren't deliberately lying to help Bottero's men, anyhow. I am not sure you are right, but I am not sure you are wrong, either, so I will take your advice."

King Bottero might or might not have listened to him. Whether he did or not, he wouldn't have analyzed things so carefully. Hitler ... Telling Hitler no wasn't a good idea. Of course, telling him yes might not be a good idea, either, because he often demanded the impossible.

Hasso got out of the throne room as inconspicuously as he could. When you were a big blond in a land full of squat brunets, that wasn't very. Lord Zgomot's guards and his courtiers all followed him with their eyes till he was gone.

One thing Zgomot hadn't asked him to do once gunpowder was out of the picture: he hadn't asked him to go to Bucovin's western marches and either fight against the Lenelli or use his magic against them. Why not? An obvious question with an only too obvious answer. *He doesn't trust me that far. He said so himself.*

He almost turned back and volunteered to go fight the Lenelli, with bare hands if need be. But he knew Zgomot would turn him down, and for reasons other than mistrust. The *Wehrmacht* wouldn't have handed a top panzer engineer a Schmeisser and sent him out against the Ivans. He was more useful making better panzers, and no corporal plucked from the ranks could replace him at that. Here, Hasso might be able to stand in for a Bucovinan horseman, but no native could stand in for him.

No Lenello wizard could stand in for him, either. *I'm unique,* he thought. If he'd known he would be so alone after he sat down on the Omphalos ... he would have damn well done it anyway. Whatever his troubles were in this new world, they beat the hell out of getting shot in Berlin or enduring the Red Army's not so tender mercies. Whenever he felt bad about the way things were going, he needed to remember that. And he needed to remember that the difference between bad and worse was a lot bigger than the difference between good and better.

Rautat ran into him in the hallway, surely not by accident. "Well?" the underofficer asked. "Did you talk the lord out of using gunpowder?"

"Yes, I do that. *Did* that," Hasso answered. His Lenello wouldn't get any better in Falticeni. Pretty soon he'd have a Bucovinan accent to go with the German accent he'd never be able to help. Then he'd sound really funny to somebody from Drammen.

"Well, well!" Rautat didn't even try to hide his surprise. "You don't change

Zgomot's mind every day." He laughed at himself. "I never change his mind. If not for you, he wouldn't know who the demon I am. Life would be easier that way, too."

"Life is never easy. It has teeth." Hasso pointed to the dragon's fang that had been here since before the Lenelli crossed the ocean and found this new land for themselves.

Rautat eyed the formidable fang. "Most of the time, I hope, not such sharp ones."

Hasso wouldn't have wanted anything with teeth like that crunching down on him, either. "Dragons live in the north?" he asked, pointing in that direction.

"Yes, of course. Everybody knows that." Rautat caught himself. "Everybody but you, I guess. No dragons in the place you come from?"

"Only mothers-in-law," Hasso answered.

It wasn't much of a joke—he didn't think so, anyhow. Rautat blushed like a scandalized schoolgirl, though, and giggled like one, too. "We ... don't usually talk about those people," he said. "You startled me when you did. Like dragons? Oh, my!" He started giggling again.

He not only didn't like to talk about mothers-in-law, he wouldn't even name them. Hasso wondered how big a taboo he'd just violated. Not a small one, not by Rautat's reaction.

"How often do dragons come down here?" Hasso asked. Maybe he could find out more about the mother-in-law business from Drepteaza. It might give him something to talk about with her that wasn't too dangerously intimate, anyhow. "Can you make them go one way or another?" he persisted. Vague thoughts of siccing a dragon on the Lenelli flitted through his mind.

"Dragons come when they want to come. You can't do anything about it. We were lucky to kill even one," Rautat said. "We thought it was a miracle. We thought we were wonderful. Then the big blonds came out of the west, and we found out we weren't so wonderful as we thought."

The way his eyes traveled Hasso's long frame said the German was still about ninety-eight percent Lenello to him, too—maybe ninety-nine percent. Since he felt much more Lenello than Grenye here himself, and since those were the only choices he had in this world, how could he blame Rautat—or Drepteaza—for seeing him that way?

***

Lord Zgomot gave whatever orders he gave. Hasso stayed in the palace in Falticeni. Eventually, he supposed, after everyone else did, he would find out what happened. In the meantime, he could keep on fiddling on with gunpowder, getting ready for the real war he and Zgomot and the rest of Bucovin knew was coming.

He wondered how big a fool he was. Should he have promised the Lord of Bucovin the sun and moon and little stars, gone off toward the western border, and tried to get back to the Lenelli, back to Bottero's kingdom? Magic worked better in the west. He might have put one over on the natives and slipped away without their being the wiser.

Yes? And then what? he asked himself. Would Bottero welcome him back with open arms after he'd given Bucovin the secret of gunpowder? He hadn't even given that to the Lenelli—when was there time? Besides, after rescuing Velona he wasn't in such desperate need of another trick to keep himself alive among them.

And they were more willing to take him at face value. Unhappily, he nodded to himself. That was the phrase, all right. The Lenelli *wanted* to accept him, because he looked like them. The Grenye didn't, because to them he was guilty of being a Lenello till proved innocent—and probably after that, too.

His thoughts drifted back to the escape he hadn't made, hadn't even tried. What about Velona? Would she welcome him back with open arms? Even more to the point, would she welcome him back with open legs? Not by what he'd seen in his dreams. He hadn't just betrayed the Lenelli, not to the goddess on earth. He'd betrayed her personally when he lay down with Leneshul. That was how she saw it, anyway. She was good at an awful lot of things. Was she good at forgiving? Hasso didn't think so.

"God damn it to hell," he muttered, there in the loneliness of his room. "I am fucked. I am really fucked."

When he came out into the wider loneliness of the palace, he felt the same way. How could he help it? He had trouble getting excited about working on the gunpowder. He stayed careful and attentive with that, because he didn't want to blow himself up. With less urgent items like language lessons, he had trouble meeting even a lesser standard.

Drepteaza noticed right away. "Shall I find you another tutor?" she asked. "Are you so angry that I don't want to go to bed with you that you don't want anything else to do with me any more? I can understand how you might be. It seems petty to me, but maybe it doesn't to you."

"No. It is not you." To emphasize that, Hasso spoke in Bucovinan as best he could. "It is—everything." His wave took in not only the room, not only the palace, not only Falticeni or Bucovin, but the whole world. "I do not belong here. I never belong here. Never."

"I think you are wrong. I think you must be wrong," the priestess said seriously. "You told me how you came here, how you sat on the stone in your world and then suddenly you found yourself in this one."

"Yes? And so?" Hasso said. *The first thing I did when I got here was shoot myself some Grenye. The next thing I did was screw the Lenello goddess on earth.* Once upon a time, he'd thought that meant something important. Now? Now he had to do some new thinking.

But Drepteaza insisted, "It must mean something, Hasso Pemsel. Things don't just happen. They happen for a reason."

"What about the Lenelli?" Hasso asked.

She winced, but she had the courage of her convictions. "Even the Lenelli came here for a reason," she said. Then her mouth quirked in one of her wry grins. "To rob, to kill, to rape, to enslave…" But she shook her head. "That is not what I mean. They are part of the larger purpose, too."

"Whose purpose?" Hasso asked. "The purpose of your gods? The purpose of the Lenello goddess?" He didn't bother naming the God he'd left behind in the ruins of Berlin. Once upon a time, he'd been a believing Christian. How you could go on being a believing Christian after five and a half years of war … Well, he hadn't, so what point worrying about that? And they already had plenty of deities running around loose here. What did they need with another one imported by the only man who'd once believed in Him?

"I don't know," Drepteaza answered with another of those disarming grins. "The goddess is real—that is plain. We believe Lavtrig and our other gods are real, too, though they are quieter in the way they poke the world with their fingers. Whether something larger lies behind all that—well, who can say? But the wicked do not triumph forever. Nothing can make me believe that."

Then why did the Reds beat Germany? Hasso wondered. *Why wouldn't the USA and England see that Stalin was more dangerous than Hitler ever could be?*

Maybe God was out having a few drinks with the Lenello goddess and the Bucovinan gods. That made as much, or as little, sense to Hasso as anything else. He spread his hands. "I have no answers, priestess."

"You would scare me if you said you did," Drepteaza said. "You would scare me worse if you made me believe you." She eyed him. "More than most people, you would make me wonder if you did say something like that."

"Me? All I'm trying to do here is stay alive," Hasso said.

"You've seen another world. You must have had a god—or maybe gods—of your own there."

"*Ja.* I was just thinking about Him, in fact. He doesn't answer."

"Then why are you here now?"

He shrugged. It was a damn good question. But, again … "I don't know." Did the Omphalos have anything to do with the God Who was also Father, Son, and Holy Spirit? The ancient Greeks wouldn't have said so. Whether they were right—again, Hasso didn't know.

Drepteaza didn't want to leave it alone. "And," she continued, "you spent all that time with the goddess on earth. If you don't know more about such things than most people, who does?"

"I know a good bit about Velona—what a lover can know in the time we were together. A lover who has to learn a language first, I mean." Hasso corrected himself. "About the goddess … All I know about the goddess is that she frightens me. She's … bigger than I am."

"Well, yes," Drepteaza said. "Of course. That's what makes her a goddess. Whether she's big enough to eat Bucovin … She thinks she is. So far, she's proved wrong, but she keeps trying."

Thinking you were bigger than you really were was one of the worst mistakes you could make. Not even Hitler could argue with that, not any more. If you got into a war with the two biggest countries with the two strongest economies in the world—mm, chances were you wouldn't be happy with the way things turned out. And chances were Hitler wasn't, if he was still alive.

"Is that all you need to be a god?" Hasso asked. "To be strong?" He hadn't thought about it in those terms before. Back in his own world, he'd taken for granted the answers other people gave him. He had more trouble doing that here, because he was hearing different things from different people.

Maybe they're all wrong, he thought. *But how can I know? How do I make up my mind?* He'd never imagined there could be such a thing as too much freedom, but maybe there was.

And Drepteaza looked at him in surprise. "What else is there, Hasso Pemsel?"

Another alarmingly keen question. Hitler and Stalin ruled their countries as virtual gods because they were strong. Some people would say one of them was good and some the other, but who would say they both were? Nobody. Maybe it was true for beings genuinely supernatural, too. Why wouldn't it be?

One reason occurred to him. "A god should be good, too, yes?" That, to him, needed to count more for real gods than for the self-made variety.

"What *is* good?" Drepteaza asked, and, like Pilate asking about truth, she didn't wait around for the answer.

***

Reports about the Lenello raiders came back from the west. They plundered and killed, and then they withdrew. How much Bucovinan harassment had to do with that, Hasso couldn't tell. He couldn't tell how much good his gunpowder would have done, either.

He took another lover, a woman named Gishte. He didn't think she was any more excited about him than Leneshul was, but she was more polite about it. That would do—for a while, anyhow.

He made damn sure he never took another bath with Drepteaza. It wouldn't have meant anything to her. That wasn't the point. It would have meant much too much to him. As things were, he played back memories of her nakedness as if he'd been a frontline *Signal* cameraman filming it on the spot.

All sorts of crazy thoughts went through his head. What would happen if he got enough gunpowder to blow up the castle here? Falticeni and Bucovin would never be the same. Of course, he would also blow himself up, and he didn't want to do that. If he were suicidal, he never would have sat on the Omphalos. He would have fought on till he got killed. It probably wouldn't have taken long.

Rautat made sure he had plenty of beer and mead and even wine. Gishte liked that; she got lit up whenever she saw the chance. That told Hasso some of what she really thought of him, though she didn't slip even when she was drunk.

"What good does drunk do you?" he asked her one morning before she started drinking hard.

"What good does sober do me?" Gishte returned, a counterquestion for which, like so many here, he had no good answer. He did hope she wasn't drinking because she was going to bed with a Lenello—or somebody who looked like one. When he came right out and asked her about that, she shook her head. "No, you're not so bad, and the priestess told me I didn't have to screw you if I didn't care to. I just like to get drunk, that's all."

What was he supposed to say to that? Plenty of Lenelli liked to get drunk, too—Scanno came to mind. So did plenty of Germans. As for the Russians, the less said about that, the better. It didn't stop them from beating the snot out of the *Wehrmacht*. Sometimes it even helped. Waiting in the trenches, you'd hear them getting plowed and yelling and shouting and carrying on, and then they'd come at you not caring if they lived or died. An awful lot of them *did* die, which too often didn't stop the rest from overrunning your position.

He'd seen so many drunken Grenye in Drammen, he'd figured all drunken Grenye drank to avoid comparing themselves to Lenelli. Didn't Indians do that kind of thing in the United States? Drinking because you liked to get drunk seemed too … ordinary to fit in with being a native.

Maybe I have to start thinking of them as people, Hasso thought. *Short, squat, dark, mostly homely people who don't look like me.*

Gishte wasn't homely, though she was a long way from gorgeous. He'd bedded gorgeous—he knew about that. The thought of Velona, and of losing Velona, stabbed at him again.

Next to Velona, Drepteaza wasn't gorgeous, either. Well, who was, dammit? Velona turned movie stars plain. With Drepteaza, it didn't seem to matter so much. That was partly because Drepteaza had one hell of a shape of her own, as Hasso had every reason to know.

And it was partly because Drepteaza was *interesting*. She didn't have the live-wire aura that Velona wore like a second skin, but who did? She also didn't go off like nitroglycerine if she got angry. She was … good people.

Yeah, she's good people, Hasso jeered at himself. *And she doesn't want thing one to do with you, not that way, even if you have seen her naked.*

"Hey, don't pour down all of that by yourself," he told Gishte, and he got drunk, too. Why the hell not? He couldn't think of a single reason. Making love with Gishte when they were both smashed was fun, too. He thought so at the time, anyway. And, when you were smashed, you didn't give a rat's ass about anything but right then.

***

The bad news about a bender was, you had to come down from it. Drepteaza eyed Hasso as if he were something the cat was trying to cover up. "Have a good time yesterday?" she asked at breakfast the next morning.

"Gnurf," he answered, squinting at her through eyes as narrow as he could make them. Wan winter sunlight and torches he usually wouldn't have tried to read by seemed much too bright today.

"You need something better than porridge," she said, and spoke in Bucovinan to a serving woman. The woman came back with a bowl of strong-smelling soup.

"What is it?" Hasso asked suspiciously.

"Tripe and spices," Drepteaza told him. "It takes the edge off things."

Feeling like a man defusing a bomb, he tried it. But the bomb had already gone off, inside his head. The soup did help calm his sour stomach. He thought the mug of beer he downed with it went further toward reconciling him to being alive. To his own surprise, he did get to the bottom of the bowl of soup. "Thanks," he said to Drepteaza in Bucovinan. "Better."

She looked at him like a *Feldwebel* eyeing a private fresh from the Russian front who'd just painted Paris red ... before Paris fell again. "You're not going to be worth much the rest of the day, are you?" She sounded more resigned than critical.

"Sorry." Hasso was sorry about how he felt—that was for sure.

She startled him with a smile. "It happens," she said. "You're a human being, too."

That was how Hasso turned the word into German in his mind, anyhow. The literal meaning of the Bucovinan was *somebody who speaks our language*. The ancient Greeks had called foreigners *barbaroi*—people who made *bar-bar* noises instead of words that meant something. *Nemtsi*, the Russian name for Germans, meant *tongue-tied ones* or *mutes*. Considering how little Bucovinan Hasso actually spoke, Drepteaza either stretched a point or paid him a considerable compliment.

He stood up. He seldom cared to do that around her; it reminded her how different from her folk he was. But right now that was exactly the point. Bowing, he said, "Not a cursed Lenello, eh?"

She bit her lip. Did she turn red? She was too dark and the lighting too gloomy to let Hasso be sure. "You can't help the way you look, Hasso Pemsel," she said. "And I can't help looking at you and seeing ... what you look like."

Rumors ran through the *Wehrmacht* that Hitler didn't trust Field Marshal Manstein because he thought the officer had Jewish blood. Manstein's impressive sickle of a nose no doubt had a lot to do with those rumors. What was this but more of the same?

Hasso sighed. "You see what you want to see, whether it is there or not." To make matters worse, he had to say that in Lenello; it was too complicated to let him turn it into Bucovinan.

"Maybe I do. Probably I do, in fact," Drepteaza said, also in Lenello. "And what do King Bottero and his men see when they look at us? What does Velona see when she looks at us?" Did her voice take on a certain edge when she named the goddess on earth? Hasso thought so.

Before he answered, he sat down again. Looming over her if he wasn't making a point was just plain rude. Besides, his head hurt less when he got off his feet. "You know what they think," he said uncomfortably. And he'd thought the same thing till he came to Falticeni as a captive. How could he help it?

"Oh, yes. I know." Drepteaza's nod was a ripple atop an ocean of hard-restrained bitterness. "I know too well. We are small and swart and ugly. And the Lenelli can work magic and we can't. To the Lenelli, that turns us into something not much more than beasts. But only a handful of them are wizards. The rest are as mindblind as we are. Does that turn them into beasts, too?"

Scanno had pointed out the same thing. When Hasso stayed in Drammen, he'd never once asked about it. He wondered why not. King Bottero could no more cast a spell than Drepteaza. But Bottero, wizard or not, was tall and fair and blue-eyed. To the Lenelli, that put him several steps up on the natives.

Didn't German propaganda go on and on about Jewish mouths and noses? Didn't the Aryans of the *Reich* look down their straight noses at Italians because they were small and dark and excitable? Negroes? The less said about Negroes, the better. The *Führer* hadn't wanted to shake that colored sprinter and jumper's hand even after he won all those gold medals at the Berlin Olympics.

And, coming back to this world, the Bucovinan priestess was dead right. Most Lenelli *were* as mindblind as her own folk. That didn't turn them into *Untermenschen* in the eyes of their countrymen.

All that talk was ... talk. The Lenelli didn't like the Grenye because they looked different, they talked different, and they were in the way. Those were all common enough reasons for two folk not to like each other: Germans and Frenchmen sprang to mind. But the mindblindness gave the Lenelli an extra excuse to use the natives any way they pleased.

It all seemed as plain as a punch in the jaw to Hasso, who looked at the way things were here from the outside. Suddenly, out of the blue, he wondered what a Lenello dropped into his world would think of the *Reich*'s racial notions. Would they look as foolish to him as Bottero's ideas did to Hasso?

He was damned if he could see why not.

Hell, some of those policies looked foolish even to a lot of Germans. If they'd used all the people in the USSR who hated Communism and Stalin instead of jumping on them with both feet and driving them back into the Red fold, they could hardly have done worse on the Eastern Front. And there were times when soldiers didn't move because trains were busy hauling Jews around behind the lines. If you were going to deal with the Jews like that, wouldn't after the war have been a better time?

Why didn't I pay more attention to this while I was there? Hasso wondered. He hadn't seen any need to: that was why. Everybody set above him, everybody beside him, and everybody below him seemed to have pretty much the same ideas.

"My God! We threw the stupid war away, and we didn't even know it!"

"What?" Only when Drepteaza asked did he realize he'd spoken German.

"Nothing. Nothing I can do anything about now, anyway," Hasso answered sheepishly. "Something from back in the world I come from."

"Oh." Drepteaza sent him a shrewd look. "Something that has to do with a woman there?"

She might be shrewd, but that didn't make her right. He shook his head. "No, not with a woman. With my kingdom, and with its affairs." The *Reich* wasn't a kingdom, of course, but explaining what it was was beyond him in either Lenello or Bucovinan. It might have been beyond him in German, too.

Drepteaza didn't press him, which was something of a relief. She just said, "I hope you'll remember you're here now."

He nodded. "I'm not likely to forget it," he said.

***

"Ha!" Scanno called when Hasso came down to the soldiers' buttery a couple of days later. The renegade set down his spoon—he was eating tripe soup that morning. He went on, "They do let you out every now and again."

"Yes, every now and again." Hasso didn't feel like talking to him—and then, all of a sudden, he did. "Can I ask you a question?"

Scanno spooned up another mouthful of soup. Then he said, "You can always ask. If I don't like it, maybe I'll kick you into the middle of next week."

"You can always try," Hasso said politely—too politely. He wasn't afraid of Scanno, not even a little bit. The renegade scowled at him: Scanno was as arrogant and full of himself as any other Lenello. Hasso didn't care. He asked, "When Aderno tries to put a spell on you in Drammen, how do you know he can't?"

"Oh. That!" Scanno laughed. "On account of I've had other wizards try to ensorcel me, and not a one of 'em could do it. Not since I was a kid, matter of fact."

"Really?" Hasso said.

"Sure. Why the demon would I waste my time lying to you?" Scanno returned to his tripe soup, which seemed more interesting to him than Hasso was. "Makes your insides hurt not quite so bad, anyway," he remarked.

"Yes, I know," Hasso said, at which the renegade laughed. "Have you got any idea why this is so?" Hasso persisted.

Scanno started to shake his head, then thought better of it. Hung over, Hasso had made that same quick choice more than once. Just talking hurt less, and Scanno did: "Never even worried about it. It's something about me, that's all, like I'll spend the night farting if I eat leeks for supper."

"Right," Hasso said—sometimes you could find out more about somebody than you really wanted to know. He tried a different angle: "Do you remember when this starts? Not when you are a child?"

"No, after that, like I told you." Scanno frowned, trying to remember. "If you're smart, you don't *want* wizards trying to mess with you," he observed. Hasso didn't say anything. He'd already seen that Scanno wasn't smart that way. And, sure as hell, the renegade continued, "Must've been about fifteen years ago. I called some high and mighty wizard a cocksucking son of a whore, and he told me he'd turn me into a pig for that. And the bastard tried, and he couldn't."

"And what do you do—what *did* you do—afterwards?" Hasso asked.

"I pitched his sorry arse into a hog wallow, and better than he deserved, too," Scanno answered. "I've had a couple of other run-ins with those walking chamber pots since, and they've never been able to bother me."

"I see." Actually, Hasso wished he did. He'd taken Scanno's immunity to magic as part and parcel of what made spells falter near Falticeni. Maybe he was wrong. Maybe it was personal. Well, that could be interesting, too. "How do you suppose this happened? Spells work on most Lenelli, yes?"

"Sure," Scanno said. "I always figured it was because I was such a tough bastard." He would have seemed tougher if his hands didn't shake and if his eyes didn't look like a couple of pissholes in the snow.

Instead of pointing that out, Hasso said, "If you ever see why, talk to me. Talk to Drepteaza. Talk to Lord Zgomot. The Bucovinans want to know—they need to know—how to keep magic from biting on them when they get far from Falticeni."

"Tell me about it, the poor, sorry bastards." Scanno laughed. "Can you see Bottero's face if it *didn't* bite?" That made Hasso laugh, too, because he could. Then Scanno said, "Boy, wouldn't it make the goddess on earth pee in her drawers?"

Hasso didn't deck him. That only proved he had even more discipline than he'd ever imagined. He did make a growling noise down deep in his throat—he couldn't help it. The worst of it was knowing Scanno was right. If magic did fail against Bucovin, Velona would be incandescent.

She was gone, lost. She wanted him dead. He wanted her back. The Grenye in Drammen had plenty of reasons to get drunk. So did Hasso, in Falticeni.

XIX

Lenello raiders went on harrying Bucovin's western villages all through the winter. They kept some of the towns they seized. That bothered Lord Zgomot, who said, "They are going to jump off from those places when they really pick up the war again come spring."

"Well, of course," Hasso said when word of the Lord of Bucovin's comment got to him through Drepteaza. He heard everything second- and third- and fifth-hand, when he heard of it at all.

"This is not what the Lenelli usually do," she said.

"I wonder why not," Hasso said. "Are they really so stupid? I did not think so when I was with them."

That got him summoned before Zgomot. "Did you give the blonds the idea of biting and holding on instead of biting and letting go?" the Lord of Zgomot demanded.

"I don't know, Lord," Hasso answered. "I don't think so. I don't remember talking about it with them, not like that. King Bottero just thinks one fast campaign will break Bucovin." Hasso had thought the same thing. Why not? He hadn't known any better. Hitler had thought the same thing about the Russians. Well, so much for that. So much for this, too.

"Maybe you made them think about the way wars are supposed to work," Lord Zgomot said. "Lavtrig knows you've done that with us. We don't see things the way we did before we caught you—all the gods know that's so."

Was that praise? Hasso supposed it was, though he suspected the Lord of Bucovin wasn't sure, either. "You were going to send out raiders, Lord," the German remembered. "Any luck with them?"

"Not much," Zgomot answered. "The border is … the border. Magic works there—it works just fine. We could not gain surprise."

"Ah." Hasso wondered whether this clever little Grenye would ask him to give the raiders some kind of sorcerous smoke screen. He thought he might be able to figure out how to do that. He wasn't a trained wizard, but he'd seen that he could make magic work.

But Zgomot asked him nothing of the sort. Hasso remembered what he'd heard about the natives and sorcery. A wizard who'd work magic for them would decide

217

that, as the seeing man in the country of the blind, he ought to show them which way they should go. And, if they didn't feel like going that way, he would try to make them do it. No, their experience with sorcery was far from happy.

Instead, the Lord of Bucovin said, "Will we have enough gunpowder to fight the big blond bastards—excuse me, Hasso Pemsel: the big blond *Lenello* bastards—when they invade us this spring? Because they will—or do you doubt it?"

"No, Lord, I don't," Hasso answered. For a long time, Hitler had disguised his aggressive plans. Bottero didn't waste any time trying. The Lenelli were very direct in their dealings with Grenye. *You have it. I want it. I'm going to take it.*

"The gunpowder?" Zgomot prompted.

"Sorry, Lord. My thoughts go somewhere else. Yes, we should have enough. If their wizards figure out how to set it off at a distance, though … What we have then is trouble."

Lord Zgomot took that in stride. "When did Grenye have anything but trouble since the big blond bastards first washed ashore here? Never once. And there are all kinds of trouble, too. You know King Bottero is married to old King Iesi's daughter?"

Hasso knew Queen Pola came from the Lenello realm just north of Bottero's. He'd forgotten Iesi's name, if he ever knew it. But he could say, "Yes, Lord," without stretching things too far.

"Well, I hear Iesi may move east, too," the Lord of Bucovin said. "I don't know whether his army will come separately under his command or march along with King Bottero's in one big host. But they may move."

"If they come by themselves, we should hit them first," Hasso said.

"Oh? Why?"

"Because Bottero already knows some of my tricks," the German replied. "We can surprise Iesi and his men—or I hope we can, anyhow. If we drive him back, then we deal with Bottero." *Try to deal with Bottero.* But he kept that to himself.

"You don't think Bottero will have told Iesi about the kinds of things you do?" That *will have told* perplexed Hasso for a moment; he didn't hear a future perfect every day. Before he could answer, Zgomot took care of it for him: "No, of course he won't. If he ever had to fight Iesi or one of the other blond kings, he would want to be able to give him a surprise. Fair enough. If Iesi comes by himself, we try to hit him first and knock him out of the fight."

He might be mindblind, but he was nobody's fool. Neither was Bottero, come to that. If you were going to make a halfway decent king, brains were an asset.

"Do you let me fight your enemies, Lord?" Hasso shook his head in exasperation. He felt mindblind himself, fighting with languages he didn't speak well enough. "*Will* you let me fight your enemies, Lord?"

Zgomot looked pained. Hasso knew things he didn't and could do things he couldn't. That made the *Wehrmacht* officer valuable. It made using him necessary and losing him unfortunate. It also made him dangerous. As if that weren't obvious enough anyway, Hasso came in a large, blond package.

"I do not want you hurt." The Lord of Bucovin picked his words with care. You didn't want to offend the captive genie, lest it turn on you. After gnawing at the inside of his lower lip for a moment, Zgomot added, "I do not want to take the chance that you will desert to the Lenelli again, either."

He must have decided that Hasso could see that he could see the possibility. It was, in the mildest possible way, a compliment. It was one Hasso could have done without. "If you don't trust me to fight, why do you trust me to make gunpowder for you?" he asked. "Maybe I blow the palace to the sky." He'd thought about it.

"Maybe you will," Zgomot said steadily. "My thinking is, you are less likely to do that if you stay inside the palace yourself."

Hasso gave him a crooked grin. "My thinking is, you're right." He remembered Russians who'd killed without caring for their own lives. Before things really fell to pieces in the *Reich*, the papers had stories about Japanese pilots who flew their airplanes into American warships. Hasso admired their courage without wanting to emulate it. He liked living. Dying at the age of 103, shot by an outraged husband, struck him as a good way to go.

"This also strikes me as one more reason to keep you where you are," Zgomot said.

Damn! Hasso thought. He could see why it would strike the Lord of Bucovin that way. "How do I persuade you that you can trust me?" he asked.

Zgomot gave him the courtesy of taking the question seriously. He didn't answer right away, but plucked at his beard as he thought things over. "If you fight well against Bottero's men," he said at last, "that may convince me."

"If you don't let me fight against Bottero's men, how am I supposed to fight well?" Hasso inquired, less acidulously than he might have.

Zgomot stroked his chin again. His eyes twinkled—or maybe it was just a trick of the light. "It is," he admitted, "a puzzlement."

***

Iesi didn't move. Bottero kept moving. He worked more methodically than he had during the autumn. That invasion had been a blow aimed at Bucovin's heart. When it failed to reach Falticeni—when it failed, period—the Lenelli pulled back to their own border.

Now Bottero was trying something different. He was taking one town, making sure he had it, and then going on to the next. Making sure he had a town involved either massacring the local Grenye or chasing them off to the east with no more than the clothes on their backs. Some of the women didn't even get those.

As news of what the Lenelli were doing and how they were doing it came to Falticeni, Lord Zgomot's face got longer and longer. His own people had to be screaming at him to do something. How long would he stay Lord of Bucovin if he didn't?

What'll happen to me if Bucovin gets a new lord? Hasso wondered. He feared it wouldn't be good. He also feared Zgomot would order him to use gunpowder against the Lenelli, and he didn't think the time was ripe.

If you have trouble, attack from an unexpected direction. That maxim had served the Germans—especially Manstein—well in Russia.

So Hasso decided he'd better take the initiative with Zgomot before Zgomot took it with him. "Lord, you are in touch with a lot of Grenye inside Bottero's kingdom, is it not so?" he asked.

"Yes, of course it is so," Zgomot answered impatiently—his temper was fraying round the edges, something Hasso hadn't seen from him before. "You ought to know it is so, outlander. If what you told me is true, you did your best to keep them from doing Bucovin any good, and your best was better than I wish it were. So why do you want to know now?"

"Can you touch them off?" Now that Hasso had gunpowder, he could use figures of speech based on it. He hadn't realized how many of those there were till he had to do without them. "If the peasants blow up behind Bottero's line, he'll need to leave Bucovin alone to deal with them."

"Gods help them when he does," Zgomot said. Hasso only shrugged. The Lord of Bucovin sent him a measuring stare. "You're as cold-blooded as a serpent, aren't you, Hasso Pemsel?"

With another shrug, Hasso said, "If I serve Bucovin, I have to think of Bucovin first, yes?"

"Yes … if you serve Bucovin." Zgomot didn't mean it the same way Hasso had.

Well, he had his reasons for doubting the German. His biggest reason likely was that Hasso looked like a Lenello. Besides, Hasso was fighting on King Bottero's side when the Bucovinans captured him. The Lord of Bucovin wouldn't forget it, or that Hasso had been boffing the goddess on earth. None of that would inspire confidence, not from Zgomot's point of view. *All right, maybe my looks aren't the biggest reason*, Hasso thought. *But they sure aren't the smallest one, either.*

Back to business now. "What I tell you to do probably does hurt King Bottero," Hasso said. "I don't see how it can hurt Bucovin. A lot of Grenye in Bottero's kingdom aren't even Bucovinans."

"I should hope not. They belong to the small tribes, the weak tribes," Zgomot said. Bucovinans had almost as much scorn for the Grenye who'd quickly succumbed to the invaders from overseas as Lenelli did for Grenye in general. But the Lord of Bucovin continued, "Even if they are ruined men, I hate to throw them into the fire. They are still of our blood, of our flesh."

"What good does it do them if Bucovin falls?" Hasso asked.

Zgomot grunted. "A point, no doubt. I do not know how much good an uprising will do us, but I do not suppose it can hurt. And you are right, of course—we have ways of making one happen."

If the border was as tightly held as Hasso had tried to arrange, it wouldn't be so easy to sneak into Bottero's realm. He'd tried to make it hard for Grenye to sneak out of the Lenello kingdom, though; he hadn't worried about any of them sneaking in. He thought he would have, sooner or later, but he hadn't yet. So many different things going on...

And how much attention would Bottero's marshals and wizards pay to his advice now that he wasn't in Drammen any more? How much attention would they pay now that he'd gone over to the other side? They would probably do the opposite of anything he'd ever proposed, just on general principles.

If he aimed to return to the Lenelli's good graces, he'd find some magical way to get in touch with Aderno and warn him the uprising was coming. Could he manage to touch the wizard in his dreams? Maybe he could. He whistled softly. Talk about playing both ends against the middle!

Next question was, did he want to try anything like that? He fit in better in Drammen than he did in Falticeni, no doubt about it. But fitting in better wasn't the same as fitting in well—no doubt about that, either. And Aderno and Velona had both done their level best to kill him, which didn't encourage him to try to do anything nice for them.

If I could get Velona back again ... Any man would do almost anything to have a woman like that. But it wouldn't be the same as it was. He could see as much, however much he wished he couldn't. And, except for Velona, he had no overwhelming reasons to prefer the Lenelli to the Grenye.

I look right among the Lenelli. There was the other side of Zgomot's worrying about his loyalty because he was big and blond. It did matter, but only so much. He was a foreigner in Bottero's kingdom, too, even if a less obvious foreigner.

Grenye women are homely. Much of that went back to Velona again. Velona would have been a knockout—a knockout and a half—anywhere. Next to her, most Lenello women were homely, too; Hasso wouldn't have wanted to end up in bed with Queen Pola for all the tea in China. He did think the average Lenello woman was prettier than the average Grenye.

Drepteaza ... He muttered to himself. No matter what he thought of Drepteaza, she didn't think much of him. She thought he looked like a goddamn Lenello, was what she thought. And there he was, banging head-on into looks again.

"You're thinking hard." Zgomot startled him out of his none too happy reverie.

"Yes, Lord." Hasso couldn't very well deny it.

"You don't say much," the Lord of Bucovin remarked.

"My head is full of mud," Hasso answered. "I don't have much worth saying."

"No, eh?" Zgomot didn't believe him, but seemed too polite to push about it. Since Hasso hadn't told the whole truth, that was just as well. Zgomot lifted an imaginary mug. "May you bring as much confusion to our enemies."

"May it be so." Did Hasso mean it? He decided he didn't want to try to reach Aderno in his dreams, so maybe he did.

***

When Scanno was sober, he remembered he was a fighting man. He liked to practice with Hasso. "Now I can pick on somebody my own size," he said. He was bigger than the German, too, but only a little. When they used wooden practice swords, he did pick on Hasso. Even half-drunk, which he was a lot of the time, he was better with a blade than the *Wehrmacht* officer ever would be.

"How old were you the first time you picked up a sword?" Hasso asked, rubbing his ribcage where one of Scanno's strokes had got through. He would have an ugly bruise there tonight.

The renegade shrugged. "*I* don't know," he said. "Two, three, maybe four. If you're going to be a warrior, you need to *be* a warrior. You start learning how as soon as you can."

That was true among the Prussian *Junkers*, too, but not to the same degree. Learning to shoot a rifle—especially a modern one, with a flat trajectory and good sights—was a lot easier than learning to fence and ride. Hand-to-hand combat in Hasso's world was nice to know, but you needed it a lot less than you did here.

"Let's try spears," Hasso said. The Bucovinans used shafts with rags padding the end, the same as the Lenelli did. Had they come up with the idea on their own or borrowed it from the blonds? Hasso wondered whether even the locals knew any more.

He could hold his own with spears. That made him feel better about himself and his place here. *Moral—don't get caught with just a sword*, he thought. Though the day was chilly, he and Scanno worked up a good sweat thrusting and parrying.

Scanno swigged from a big mug of beer. "Can't sweat all the good stuff out of me," he said, wiping his forehead on his sleeve. He took another pull at the mug. "Now I suppose you'll want to thump my sorry ass."

"You give me fencing lessons. Shouldn't I give you wrestling lessons?" Hasso hoped he sounded more innocent than he felt—he did want some of his own back. "If you're going to be a warrior, you need to *be* a warrior. Who says—said—that? Somebody who looks a lot like you."

"Me and my big mouth." Scanno gave a crooked—and rather slack-lipped—grin. "All right. Let's get it over with. You can throw me around like a sack of beans."

Hasso did, too. He also got thrown around some himself, even if Scanno wasn't so quick learning the new moves as Orosei had been. But then, Orosei was the king's master-at-arms, and Scanno never more than middling good. He might have learned faster had he stayed sober more, but he might have done all kinds of things had he stayed sober more.

At one point in the proceedings, he landed on his head. He didn't move for close to a minute afterwards. Hasso eyed him in some alarm—he hadn't intended to throw him that hard. You didn't want to hurt anybody while you trained, but accidents happened every now and then.

Just when the German was about to see whether artificial respiration would do any good, Scanno rolled over, sat up, shook his head, and winced. "Got to make my eyes uncross there," he said.

"Sorry," Hasso told him. "I didn't mean to do that."

"Shit happens." Scanno shrugged, then winced again. "Don't think I got hit so hard since I ran into a dragon's skull."

"Right," Hasso said. Scanno was full of figures of speech for a hangover. He hadn't heard that one before, but he liked it.

"Wait. Wait." Scanno shook his head once more, despite the horrible face he pulled as soon as he did it. "You think I'm talking about being drunk, don't you? I really *did* run into a dragon's skull. Came cursed close to killing myself doing it, too." He got to his feet. It took some effort, but he managed.

Hasso steadied him. "Well, all right. That sounds like a story worth hearing."

"I know what you mean. You mean you won't believe a bloody word of it," the renegade said. That was exactly what Hasso meant, but he didn't feel like admitting it. Scanno went over to his mug of beer and upended it. Hasso didn't think he could have drunk so much at a single draught, but he hadn't had Scanno's practice. "This was probably about twenty years ago, you understand."

"Sure," Hasso said. A lot of things could change in twenty years. Twenty years ago, Hitler was probably just about getting out of jail and publishing *Mein Kampf*. The Weimar Republic still ruled Germany, whose army was just big enough to blow its own nose, and maybe to sneeze if it got permission from France and Poland first. The shackles of the Treaty of Versailles still held the country down. Hitler'd thrown them off, all right, just the way he promised he would ... and started down the path that would wreck the *Reich* far more completely than Versailles did.

"I was hunting deer in a noble's forest—you know how it is," Scanno said.

"Poaching." Hasso knew just how it was.

"Yeah. You better believe it, buddy." Scanno's grin was utterly without self-consciousness—or guilt. "I needed the venison a demon of a lot more than that rich bastard did, too. My backbone was rubbing against my belly, and there aren't many feelings worse'n that one."

"Tell me about it." Hasso had been hungry more than he cared to remember on the Eastern Front. Who hadn't?

"Uh-huh." Scanno took hunger for granted, too. In this world, one bad harvest meant people went hungry. Two bad harvests in a row meant famine. Scanno continued, "So there I was, where the law said I wasn't supposed to be. Right at the beginning of summer, you know, when everything's all green and grown and luscious—me and my bow, sneaking through the woods." He grinned again, relishing the memory.

"So you run into a dragon then?" Hasso said. "I hear about one in King Cherso's realm—what was it, three years gone by now?"

"I heard about that one, too. Never saw it, 'cause it never came this far south, goddess be praised." Scanno still swore by the Lenello divinity, then. That was interesting, or might be. "Yeah, I ran into a dragon, all right, only not quite the way you think."

"Tell me more," Hasso urged. Scanno could spin a yarn, all right. How much of it to believe … Well, you could always figure that out later.

Before going on, Scanno refilled the mug from a pitcher. "Can't hardly talk with a dry throat," he remarked, and poured down another good draught. After what he'd drunk, Hasso wouldn't have been able to walk, but the Lenello seemed to need more even to feel a buzz. "Where was I?"

"In the woods, running into a dragon."

"Oh, yeah. I spotted this buck—a big old fat buck. Nice antlers on him, too, if you care about that kind of crap. Me, I was after meat. He was upwind of me, so my scent didn't give me away. I did the best sneak ever—I mean *ever*—till I got close enough to draw and let fly. Hit the bastard, too." He quaffed again.

"Then what happened?" Yes, Hasso was hooked in spite of himself.

"You know how it is. Only way you can kill clean is through the eye or maybe through the heart if you're lucky. I got him maybe a palm's breadth back of the heart. He was gonna die, and die pretty cursed quick, but not right there, worse luck. He took off running, and I took off running after him. I didn't want to lose him. You better believe I didn't—he would've kept me eating for days and days."

"How did you run into the dragon, then?" Hasso asked.

"How? With my head, that's how. I was crashing through the bushes after the stag, and I tried crashing through one and crashed into the dragon's skull instead. The bushes had grown up so you couldn't see the bones—I guess all that dead dragon made good manure for them. I went *wham!* Next thing I knew, I was lying on the ground, and quite a while had gone by."

"How could you…? Oh. The sun." Hasso felt foolish. He was used to wrist-watches and clocks and always knowing just what time it was. Getting accustomed to slower, more approximate timekeeping hadn't been easy.

Scanno nodded. "That's right. I woke up with a demon of a headache, and with a goose's egg right between my eyes. If I was going a little bit faster, I bet I would've broken my stupid head. I got up—that took some doing, too—and I found what I'd run into."

"What about the buck?" Hasso asked.

"Gone," Scanno said mournfully. "I lost the blood trail the other side of those bushes hiding the skeleton. The headache I had, I lost my appetite, too, but I knew that would come back sooner or later. I didn't quite starve, or I wouldn't be here now, right?"

"Right," Hasso said. "It's a good story."

"But you don't believe a word of it."

"I didn't say that."

"Like you needed to." Scanno drew out something on a thong from under his tunic. Lots of Lenelli and Grenye wore amulets of one kind or another. Scanno's was plainer than most: a fragment of what looked like bone, drilled through so it would take the leather thong. "This is dragon skull. I worried it off with my knife. Hard like anything—I had to hone the blade afterwards."

"All right." For all Hasso knew, the bit of bone came from a donkey. He didn't want to argue with Scanno, though. What was the use? He couldn't prove the Lenello renegade was lying.

Or maybe he could, if he could master the truth spell Aderno had used. Would it work here in Falticeni? Most magic seemed to falter here. And Aderno's spell, for that matter, had faltered against Scanno back in Drammen.

Instead of experimenting with sorcery, Hasso asked, "Do you want to throw me around for a while?"

"Sure!" Scanno said eagerly, and he did.

***

Hasso used the baths in the palace almost every day. Scanno laughed at him for that; the Lenelli were a less cleanly folk than the Bucovinans. Hasso took the ribbing and ignored it. He'd been clean and he'd been dirty, and he liked clean better. Besides, even with the drafts, the bathhouse had to be the warmest room in the palace.

Rautat noticed his habits, too. "One more thing that says you really aren't one of those people, even if you look like them," the veteran underofficer remarked as he scrubbed in a hot pool of an afternoon. His scars weren't puckered craters like Hasso's; they were long, pale lines on his dark skin.

"I'm me, that's all," Hasso answered. They were both using Bucovinan. Hasso had got to the point where he could follow it pretty well. He spoke more hesitantly.

"Yeah, well, you aren't so bad." Rautat ducked his head under the water and came up blowing like a porpoise.

"Thanks." Hasso submerged, too.

When he came up, a couple of women were walking past, heading for another pool. They chatted idly, paying Rautat no attention and Hasso hardly any; people in the palace were used to him by now. Neither of them wore any more than she'd been born with. The Bucovinans were easy in their skins, easier than the Lenelli and much easier than any Germans except a few resolute naturists.

Back in Germany, Hasso had always thought those people were nuts. When he landed in a country where everybody took nudity in stride, he had to think again. He'd been doing nothing but thinking again since he landed in this world. What was one more time?

He did notice that, just as he tried not to bathe while Drepteaza was in there, she also found ways not to come in while he was. If she was already washing when he came in, she hurried to get out. If he got there before her, she would wait till he finished.

She didn't seem angry at him, not when they met for language lessons or to talk about gunpowder and other things he knew and the natives didn't. Maybe she thought he wasn't just seeing her nude—he was seeing her naked. If that was what was going on—he didn't want to come right out and ask her—he admired her tact. He also admired her for understanding that foreigners had different ways of looking at things, whether literally or metaphorically.

And, if that was what she thought, she was dead right.

He wished she were interested. Laying Grenye women who gave themselves to him because they were supposed to was better than not laying anybody. But he remembered Velona too well. After going to bed with her, the natives didn't seem like anything special. And, except as convenient bodies, he didn't care much about Leneshul or Gishte.

Drepteaza would be different—he was sure of that. It wasn't just that she was prettier than they were. She was smarter and livelier and....

And she wasn't interested in him.

You can't have too much of what you don't want. Somebody'd said that where Hasso could hear it, and he thought it was true. Screwing the Grenye women gave him physical relief, yes indeed. But it wasn't what he wanted, so every time he did it he felt emptier inside.

Yeah, Drepteaza would be different. He was sure she would ... except he was what she didn't want. He wasn't a Lenello. No matter what he was, he looked like one. For the priestess, the way he looked was plenty.

Not wanting somebody because of how he looked—wasn't that surprising, not really. Hasso had judged plenty of people by their looks—Frenchmen (and -women), Jews, Ivans, Poles. It was much less enjoyable when other people judged him.

"You worked in Drammen, you say," he said to Rautat, there in the baths. Anything was better than brooding about all the reasons Drepteaza wanted nothing to do with him.

"That's right." Rautat nodded, water dripping off his chin and the end of his nose. "Wanted to pick up the lingo, wanted to learn things the Lenelli know and we don't. Did it, too, and came home."

"What do you think of Lenelli, then?" Hasso asked.

"Bunch of big blond pricks," Rautat said promptly. "No offense."

"Yeah, sure," Hasso said. They both grinned.

"Well, it's the truth. They treat Grenye like donkey turds in the street," Rautat said. "And the Grenye there, some of them are so beaten down, they feel like they deserve to get treated that way, poor sorry bastards. If they try to stand up, they get knocked down. Is it any wonder so many of 'em stay plastered all the time? I guess it doesn't get to you so much that way."

"What about Lenello women?" No, Hasso couldn't stay away from the sore spot.

"Big blond cows," Rautat replied. "Who wants a gal taller than he is?"

Velona was damn near as tall as Hasso. He thought he would have wanted her if she were three meters tall. Whether she would have wanted him then, of course, was a different story. And Queen Pola was almost as tall as he was, too, and he didn't want her for beans. If she were fifteen or twenty centimeters taller than he was, she would have made him want to run away.

"Maybe you have something there," he said.

"You better believe it." Like any good underofficer, Rautat was sure of himself. "I guess Lenello women are all right for you, 'cause you're a big blond guy yourself." He didn't say *big blond prick* again, which was something. "But me, I pick on somebody my own size." Hasso thought that was what the idiom meant, anyhow; it might have been bawdier.

He didn't want to leave the baths. Before long, it would be spring, and then summer. Bucovin would warm up. But it wasn't warm now, even if Velona had been right: it didn't get as cold as Russia.

Dammit, he couldn't get her out of his head. He didn't want to be one of those men who spent years mooning after a lost lover and never did get on with their lives. He didn't want to, no, but he didn't know what he could do about it. He'd really and truly fallen in love with her.

She'd warned him not to. How were you supposed to listen to a warning like that, though? If you were a male human being, how could you help falling hard for a gorgeous, sexy woman who screwed like there was no tomorrow?

Velona had warned of worse than a broken heart, but that was bad enough. But not many women—none he knew of except her—could have come so close to frying his potatoes for him when she was in Drammen and he was in Falticeni. And yet…

If I got back to Bottero's kingdom and Velona took me back, would I be happy? Would I want to pick up where we left off? As soon as he asked the question, he saw the answer. *Bet your ass I would.*

It wouldn't be the same, though. Oh, maybe for her it would. She wouldn't have changed any—well, a little, or she wouldn't take him back no matter what. But he'd spent as much time by now in Bucovin as he had in Bottero's realm. He'd seen the other side of the hill. And, like Scanno, he'd seen things weren't quite so simple as most Lenelli thought.

Velona and Bottero and the rest of the colonists from across the sea thought Grenye were little and ugly and stupid and mindblind—the last two weren't the same, but each amplified the other. And they thought that, because of all those things, they could push the Grenye aside like so many animals, domesticating some and killing the rest and using the land they took any way they pleased.

Well, the Grenye *were* little. No matter what Rautat thought, Hasso liked Lenello looks better. As far as he knew, the natives *were* mindblind … but so were almost all of the big blonds.

Dammit, the Grenye were *people*. Some of them were stupid, but so were some Lenelli. Lord Zgomot and Drepteaza were as smart as anybody he'd run into in Drammen. Did they deserve to get pushed to the wall?

Hasso wondered why he hadn't wondered about any of that stuff when he rolled into Russia in a halftrack on 22 June 1941. The Ivans turned out to be as smart as anybody else, too. Did they ever! Hitler should have spent more time wondering about that stuff, too.

"The other side of the hill…" Hasso muttered.

"What's that? More of your language?" Rautat asked, which made him realize he'd slipped into German. "What does it mean?" the Bucovinan went on.

"It means I see Drammen, and I see Falticeni, too," Hasso answered. "I get to know Drammen and Falticeni both."

"Well, so have I," Rautat said. "So have lots of Bucovinans. Not so many Lenelli here—some like Scanno, and some traders, and some spies. Most of them just want to get as much from us as they can. They don't give a turd what we want." He cocked his head to one side, as he had a way of doing. "I used to figure you were like that. Now I'm not so sure. Sometimes you act like a human being."

There it was again—*somebody who speaks our language.* And they *were* still speaking Bucovinan. Hasso managed a wry smile. "Well, I try."

"Yeah, I know," Rautat said seriously. "Not a fart of a lot of big blond pricks who do." He gave back a smile that matched the German's. "Like I always say, no offense."

"Tell me another one, you little prick," Hasso retorted—*little dark prick* just didn't sound right. Rautat splashed him. He splashed back. They ducked each other and raised hell like a couple of six-year-olds. Hasso had never imagined having fun in Falticeni, but this sure felt like it.

XX

When spring came, King Bottero's men stopped harrying Bucovin—for a while, anyhow. Hasso wasn't surprised. Like fall, spring was the mud time. *Rasputitsa*, the Ivans called it. They needed a word for it, because they had a godawful one. All of winter's snow melted there, and for six weeks nothing moved. It wasn't so bad here, but it wasn't good.

And reports came back from the west that the Grenye peasants in Bottero's realms were kicking up their heels. Hasso felt good and bad about that at the same time. It took some of the pressure off Bucovin, which was why he'd proposed it to Lord Zgomot. But the Lenelli were bound to give the rebellious natives a hard time.

"We have to take care of ourselves first," Zgomot observed. "And those Grenye aren't Bucovinans anyway—I've said so before."

"Yes, but they're people," Hasso answered.

Zgomot gave him an odd look. "That is the last thing I would expect to hear from a Lenello." He held up a hand before Hasso could reply. "I know you are not a Lenello. By Lavtrig, Hasso Pemsel, I do. You look like one, though, and you cannot say you do not. And so I naturally think—"

"I understand, your Lordship. It's an easy mistake to make. Lots of people here do it."

Hasso had made plenty of mistakes along those lines himself. He thought he kept his tone smooth here. He must not have done such a good job, though, for Zgomot's gaze sharpened. "You wish some of those people looked at you in a different way. One person in particular, perhaps."

"Perhaps," Hasso agreed tonelessly. How much had Drepteaza told the Lord of Bucovin about that? What did Zgomot think of it? Whatever it was, it didn't show on his face. Hasso went on, "Nothing I can do about it. I look the way I look, not any other way."

"Most of us are guilty of something like that," Zgomot said. Hasso chuckled in spite of himself; the Lord of Bucovin had a refreshingly cynical view of the world. He added, "After a while, other people might even forgive you for it. One person in particular, again, might."

"Really?" Again, Hasso did his best not to show too much with that—he hoped—casual-sounding question. Zgomot nodded. Did one corner of his mouth quirk up, just a little? Hasso thought so, but wouldn't have sworn to it. He decided he needed to know more. "Did she tell you that?" he asked.

"Not in so many words. Women do not like to put things in so many words," the Lord of Bucovin replied. "But you listen to what they do not say, and you watch them, and after a while maybe you start to know what is going on." Now he *was* smiling, and smiling crookedly. "And sometimes you are right, and sometimes you are wrong, and that is what makes women women."

"*Ja*," Hasso said. "You can't live with 'em and you can't live without 'em."

"They say the same kinds of things about us," Zgomot said. "It would not surprise me if they were right, too."

"No, wouldn't surprise me, either," Hasso agreed. "If you would excuse me, Lord...?"

"Where are you going?" A moment later, Zgomot waved aside his own question. "Never mind. I think I can guess. You will likely find her in the temple at this time of day."

"Thank you, Lord." The palace had its own temple. The palace had enough of its own things to be almost a city of its own within Falticeni. With its smithy and bakeries and storehouses and chapel (which Hasso recalled only too vividly), King Bottero's palace was the same way. Were the Grenye imitating the Lenelli again, or was that just the nature of working palaces? Plenty of the ones back in Europe were cluttered places, too.

Paintings and statues—some in wood, others in stone—of Lavtrig and the other Bucovinan gods ornamented the temple. They weren't a handsome pantheon like the gods of Greece and Rome, or even an impressively grim one like those of Scandinavia. Some of them looked like the forces of nature they were supposed to represent. Others were monstrous in one way or another. The god of death had a corpse-pale face and fangs like a viper. They got more macabre from there.

Drepteaza was lighting a taper in front of a god—or perhaps goddess—whose earthly representation was a lump of brownish sandstone. After murmuring a prayer, she nodded. "Good day, Hasso Pemsel."

"Good day," Hasso answered. "What is that deity? What does he—she?—do?"

"Jigan endures," Drepteaza told him. "Enduring is a useful thing for Grenye to be able to do these days, don't you think?"

"Useful for anyone," Hasso said. "Do you—will you—talk to me?" He tried to do his talking in Bucovinan. He still felt more fluent in Lenello, but he wanted his accent, which was not like the one the Lenelli had, to remind her he differed from them.

"I will talk with you," she said. "What do you want to talk about?"

"Us," Hasso said.

Drepteaza frowned. "I'm not sure there's anything to talk about. Should there be anything to talk about?"

"I … hope so." Hasso started to say, *I think so,* but changed his mind halfway through. He didn't want to sound like someone who was insisting. He was in no position to insist. If Drepteaza wanted him dead, all she had to do was speak to Lord Zgomot, and he would die—slowly, if she felt like it.

"No harm in talk," she said now. "Shall we go out to the garden? No one will bother us there—or if anyone tries, we can send him away with a flea in his ear." That was how Hasso translated the Bucovinan phrase, anyhow; the literal meaning was *a flea on his ass.* Bucovinan was an earthy language.

Gardens were not an idea the natives had had for themselves. Along with so much else, they'd borrowed the notion from the Lenelli. Several nobles in Drammen had formal gardens behind their homes. Lord Zgomot had one on the palace grounds as much to show he was somebody as to admire the flowers.

A gardener trimming bushes took one look at the priestess and the tall foreigner and decided to find something to do in a different part of the palace. He was no fool; in his muddy sandals, Hasso would have done the same thing. Or maybe the fellow was—had he hung around, Hasso would have paid him to go away.

Hasso didn't recognize many flowers. Big stretches of the garden weren't blooming yet; not everything was even green. Drepteaza sat down on a bench of some hard, smooth reddish wood. After a moment, Hasso sat down beside her. She didn't move away on the bench, which was—or at least might have been—reassuring.

She seemed as self-possessed—to say nothing of self-assured—as usual. "Well, Hasso Pemsel, what do you want to say?" she asked.

Now that he had to talk, he felt tongue-tied. How long had it been since he really talked to a woman? *The last time you did with Velona,* he answered himself. But that wasn't the same thing: they'd been lovers before they could talk to each other at all.

It had to be back before the war, then. After the fighting started, he'd sweet-talked French shopgirls and Russian peasants into bed with him, but that wasn't the same, either. With them, as with the Grenye women here, he wasn't doing anything but screwing. Life got complicated when you wanted more than that.

Well, if he chickened out now, he'd probably never get another chance with Drepteaza. Hell, if he chickened out now, he wouldn't deserve another chance. *Faint heart never won fair lady.* The worst that could happen if she told him to get lost was … he'd feel even more miserable than he already did.

He jabbed a thumb at his own chest. "I am no Lenello," he declared. Was he getting it out in the open or just being clumsy? Damned if he knew.

"Yes, I've seen that," Drepteaza agreed gravely. "When you first got here, I wasn't sure what you were. Now I think you are what you say you are: a man from another world who joined the Lenelli because you found yourself among them—and because you looked like them."

Hasso could have done without that last. But, when he saw three little dark men chasing one tall blond woman, what was he supposed to think? Had he seen three Lenelli chasing one Grenye woman—well, who could say what he would have done? Life wasn't in the habit of letting you take it over.

He made himself nod. "Yes, I look like. But am not." He pointed at himself again.

"I told you, I know that," Drepteaza replied. "It matters less than you think, I'm afraid. You still do look like one. I don't see how I could want someone who looks like that."

There it was, plain as a wet fish in the face. "You look like a Grenye," Hasso said. "Doesn't bother me."

That surprised her—he could see as much. Her answering smile was sweet and sad. "Plenty of Lenelli have lain with Grenye women. Most men are less choosy than most women. When they want, they take whatever they can find."

"For screwing, sure." Speaking Bucovinan, Hasso had to be blunt, too. "If screwing all I want, I be happy with Leneshul and Gishte. More to life than just screwing, I think. Yes? No? Maybe?"

"Yes—sometimes," Drepteaza said. "You flatter me, you know?" She had to explain what *flatter* meant. When Hasso nodded, she went on, "I don't think a Lenello would waste his time talking like this. He would think I was his because he was a Lenello and I wasn't."

"Not a Lenello," Hasso said one more time. He slipped an arm around her, drew her close to him, and kissed her.

She didn't scream or beat him over the head or even try to get away. She just… didn't kiss him back. If a one-sided kiss wasn't the most useless thing in the world, Hasso had no idea what would be. He broke it off in a hurry.

"I'm sorry," Drepteaza said, his hand still dead on her shoulder. "It isn't there. I almost wish it were—things might be simpler. But I won't lie to you. Do you want me to leave you alone and have nothing to do with you from now on? Would that be easier for you? I'll do it if you want."

She would do almost anything if he wanted her to—except what he really wanted her to do. Lord Zgomot, dammit, wasn't as smart as he thought he was. Hasso shook his head. "What difference does it make?" he said dully. As if in afterthought, he lifted his hand.

Drepteaza didn't slide across the bench to put some distance between them. She sat where she was, confident he wouldn't do anything more than he'd already done. He had no idea where to go from there. He didn't see anything he could do or say that would make any difference. Muttering, he heaved himself to his feet and strode off.

"Hasso!" she called after him. "Hasso Pemsel!"

He kept walking. She said something no well-brought-up German woman would have imagined, let alone said. Was it aimed at him or at herself or at both of them at once? He didn't know, and he told himself he didn't care.

When he went back into the palace, he ran into Gishte—almost literally. She was carrying an armload of clean linens up a corridor. "Come with me," he said.

"Right now?" She sounded surprised, and maybe a little annoyed, too—couldn't he see she had other things to take care of?

But he nodded. "Right now."

She sighed. "Men!" She went with him, though.

Back in his chamber, he did what he chose to do. When it was over, she got up and squatted over the chamber pot to free herself of as much of his seed as she could, put on her clothes, picked up the linens, and left. He lay there, no happier than he had been before he went into her.

You can't get too much of what you don't want.

Now he knew exactly how true that was. He sure as hell did. And what good did knowing do him? No good at all. He couldn't think of one goddamn thing that did him any good at all.

***

"I think it is time for us to show the Lenelli what we have, time to show them they would do better to leave us alone," Zgomot said.

"Whatever you want, Lord," Hasso answered. Two days after Drepteaza turned him down, he still had trouble giving a damn about anything.

"All right, then." By the Lord of Bucovin's tone, he hoped it was all right, but he wasn't a hundred percent sure. Also by his tone, he hoped Hasso wouldn't notice. What he said next explained why: "I shall send you to the west, Hasso Pemsel. This gunpowder is your ... stuff. You know more about it than we do. You will use it best against the enemy."

"I do that," Hasso agreed. *Will I do that? Or will I see whether Bottero and Velona—oh, Velona!—will take me back after all?* Lying in Velona's arms, he would forget about Drepteaza. Lying in Velona's arms could make you forget your own name—but you'd sure be happy while you were forgetting.

"Rautat and some of the others who have worked with you will go along," Zgomot said. "They will learn from you and see how you do what you do. Then they will be able to do it for themselves."

Did that mean, *Then we won't need you any more?* Maybe. Or maybe Lord Zgomot suspected Hasso knew more than he was telling. Hasso did, and he wouldn't have been surprised if Zgomot suspected—the native was one sharp cookie. The German was damn sure Zgomot meant, *Rautat and the others will keep an eye on you.* It made sense from the Lord of Bucovin's point of view. Hasso could be dangerous for Bucovin, or he could be dangerous to Bucovin.

He nodded now, as if blissfully unaware of everything Zgomot had to be worrying about. "Whatever you want, Lord," he repeated. He wasn't about to argue, not when Zgomot was letting him leave the palace, leave Falticeni, and get somewhere near the Lenelli once more.

The roads dried out enough for him to move with a wagon a few days later. The wagon carried jars full of gunpowder. He finally had fuses that worked well enough. Considerable experiment had shown that cord soaked in limewater and gunpowder did the job—better than anything else he'd found, anyhow.

"I want to see the Lenelli when things start going boom," Rautat said as they left Falticeni. He and Hasso rode horses; Hasso wasn't about to try to drive the wagon, an art about which he knew less than he did about Egyptian hieroglyphics. Rautat went on, "The noise will be plenty to scare them all by itself."

"Once, maybe. Maybe even twice. After that? No," Hasso said.

Catapults. His thoughts came back to them again. The Lenelli—and the Bucovinans, imitating them as usual—used them as siege engines, but not as field artillery. He wondered whether the natives or the renegades in Falticeni could flange up something that could travel with an army and would let him fling jars of gunpowder two or three hundred meters. Load them with scrap metal and rocks along with the powder, the way he had with these, and they'd make pretty fair bombs. In the meantime...

In the meantime, he'd have to lay mines and set them off with fuses. He whistled tunelessly. That might not be a whole lot of fun. How was he supposed to get away again afterwards?

Why didn't you think of these things sooner? he asked himself.

One obvious way around the problem was to use an expendable Bucovinan to touch off the fuses. The poor son of a bitch would probably even think it was an honor. The natives hated the Lenelli the way ... Hasso didn't like completing the thought, but he did: *the way the Russians hated us.*

After Muresh and the calculated frightfulness of the winter attacks—and after years of similar things—the Bucovinans had their reasons for hate like that. And the Germans had given the Russians plenty of reasons of that sort, too. Looking back, Hasso could see it plain enough. Well, the Ivans got their revenge when the pendulum of war swung back toward the west.

Why am I helping this folk against that one, when I'm more at home over there? Hasso wondered. Was that why the Omphalos stone brought him to this world? He had trouble seeing how it could be.

Then the landscape started looking more familiar. "Somewhere not far from here, you catch me," he said to Rautat.

"That's right." The Bucovinan nodded. "We're only a little ways away from the battlefield. If you know how hard we worked to open up a gap in our line to make you aim your horses there without having it look like we wanted you to..."

"Nicely done," Hasso said. "You fool the Lenelli. You fool me, too."

Rautat grinned as if the idea were all his. But he said, "Lord Zgomot is a clever man. Better to use your own strength against you, he said."

Hasso nodded. It was good strategy—if you could bring it off. Manstein had, when the Red Army charged west after Stalingrad and then got an unpleasant surprise. And the Russians had at Kursk the next summer, letting the *Wehrmacht* bleed itself white trying to bang through defenses tens of kilometers deep. Nobody in the other world would ever hear about Lord Zgomot's ploy. Maybe nobody in this world would, either, not in any lasting way. The Lenelli did most of the writing here, and they were no fonder than anyone else of chronicling their own defeats.

But Hasso knew full well what Zgomot had done. *He messed up my life along with Bottero's campaign*, the German thought.

They came over the top of a low rise and started down the other side. Hasso started to laugh—it was that or pound his head against something. "You waited for us here," he said.

A few heads—skulls, now, pretty much—sat on poles, Lenello helmets atop them, as a memorial to the battle. The pits the Bucovinans had dug still yawned, unconcealed now. But the field had been efficiently plundered. Even the horses' skeletons were gone. What had the natives done with them? Burned them and smashed them to powder for fertilizer, he supposed.

"Yes, we did," Rautat said. "We were scared shitless. Blond bastards are bad enough anyway, and we didn't know if the thunder thing would hit us again."

"But you stood." Hasso had to respect that.

The Bucovinan underofficer shrugged. "Can't run all the time. Have to stand somewhere, or we lose."

Sometimes you stood and you lost anyway. Hasso knew all about that, the hard way. So, no doubt, did Rautat. They rode on.

***

Bucovinans had reoccupied the keeps on both sides of the bridge over the Oltet. They'd torn out the makeshift planking the Lenelli put down to force the crossing and replaced it with new, stronger timbers. As the wagon jounced and rattled and banged across, Hasso was glad. If it went into the river, he would have to start over.

Or would that be so bad? It would give me the perfect excuse not to fight the Lenelli.

Then he got over onto the west bank of the Oltet, and into what was left of Muresh. New shanties had gone up since Bottero's men sacked and plundered and raped and killed there, but plenty of devastation remained. The people stared without a word as a big blond rode through the place in the company of Bucovinans. Nobody threw anything at him, which was good.

But Hasso remembered what had happened the autumn before. Maybe there were reasons to fight the Lenelli after all.

Once they'd ridden out of Muresh, Hasso asked, "How far ahead are King Bottero's men?" In Bucovinan, the question needed only two words. German often made compound words. Bucovinan revolved around them.

"We still have a ways to go," Rautat answered—another two words. "They aren't even where we fought the first battle last fall. Not a strike at the heart this time. More like taking away a hand and half an arm."

Hasso nodded; he had the same impression of Bottero's strategy. The Lenelli had got themselves a bloody nose when they charged ahead too fast. Now Bottero seemed to want a digestible piece of Bucovin. Once he had it, he'd go and take another bite, and then, no doubt, one more.

That wasn't how Hasso would have gone about things, which wasn't the same as saying it wouldn't work. The rule here seemed to be that the Lenelli moved forward and the Grenye gave ground before them. Sometimes they didn't move forward very fast—sometimes the frontier stood still for years at a time. But they never seemed to move back.

Maybe I'll fix that, Hasso thought. *Yeah, maybe I will. And maybe I'll do something else instead. Who knows what the hell I can do if I set my mind to it?*

He himself had no idea. That should have alarmed him. Sometimes it did. Sometimes he thought it was blackly funny.

When he came to the first battlefield, he wondered whether he ought to comb the ground for the cartridges his machine pistol spat out. Could wizards do something nefarious if they found one? For the life of him, he couldn't see how, not when the Schmeisser would never work again.

"Do you know—did you know—a fellow named Berbec?" he asked suddenly. Rautat shook his head. Hasso asked the rest of the Bucovinans with him, but they didn't know Berbec, either.

"Who is he?" Rautat asked. "Sounds like one of our names."

"It is." Hasso explained how he'd acquired the native on the field here. "I don't know what happens to him after I get caught. Maybe he belongs to Velona now. I hope she treats him well."

"Velona?" one of the Bucovinans asked.

"She was my woman." Hasso would have left it there. Rautat, who knew more, shared the gossip with his countrymen. They all muttered back and forth, too low for Hasso to make out what they were saying.

Finally, the driver of the powder wagon, a stocky fellow named Dumnez, said, "The big blonds' goddess is strong."

"Yes," Hasso said. Nobody who'd ever come within a kilometer and a half of Velona would have dreamt of saying no.

"That woman the goddess lives in is strong, too," Rautat said, so maybe Dumnez hadn't been talking about Velona after all. Rautat went on, "I saw her in both battles last fall. I'm glad I didn't get within reach of her sword."

One of the other Bucovinans pointed at Hasso. "He must be pretty strong, too, then, if she was his woman."

"He is pretty strong—not the best swordsman, but pretty strong," Rautat said. "Pretty tricky, too. Lord Zgomot thinks well of him."

He does? Hasso almost blurted it out in surprise. If the Lord of Bucovin did think well of him, he kept it to himself mighty well. But if Zgomot didn't think well of Hasso, all he had to do was say the word and the German was a dead man.

The native who'd pointed said, "The priestess likes him pretty well, too, even if he is a blond."

Hasso stiffened. Rautat hissed like a snake. The other Bucovinan winced, though plainly he wasn't sure how he'd stuck his foot in it. Hasso was, worse luck. Maybe Drepteaza did like him, but she didn't like him enough, or didn't like him the right way. Rautat obviously knew as much. If the other fellow didn't, he had to be out of the loop.

Sure enough, Rautat said, "Don't pay any attention of Peretsh. He doesn't know what the demon he's talking about."

"I can see that for myself," Hasso said.

They traveled west in silence for some little while.

When they started running into parties of Bucovinan soldiers, Hasso knew they had to be getting close to the marchlands Bottero's men were trying to occupy. Lord Zgomot wasn't going to give up his territory without a fight. In a way, seeing the soldiers made Hasso feel better—he wasn't out here by himself against everything the Lenelli could throw at Bucovin.

In another way…

Well, my life gets more complicated, he thought. He hadn't expected things to be simple. Every so often, he caught Rautat watching him when there was no earthly need for it. The underofficer always looked away in a hurry when he noticed Hasso's eye on him, but Hasso had a pretty good idea of what was going on in his head. The native had to be wondering what the big blond would do when it came time to fight the folk who looked so much like him.

Who could blame Rautat for wondering that? Who could blame him, especially when Hasso was wondering the same thing himself?

***

Hasso stared into the setting sun, shielding his eyes from the glare with the palm of his hand. The village in the distance was only blackened ruins. He didn't see any Lenelli moving around there, but they wouldn't be far off. He wished he'd had a pair of field glasses around his neck when he splashed down into the swamp. He knew something about gunpowder, but he'd never worried his head about optics.

The Lenelli up ahead—whether he could see them or not, they were there—couldn't see him. He and Rautat crouched side by side in thick bushes. The rest of the Bucovinan escort and the powder wagon waited behind the crest of a rise half a kilometer farther east.

"Somewhere around here, you'll start planting them, right?" Rautat said.

"*Ja,*" Hasso answered absently. The Bucovinan accepted it; that was one word of German he'd learned. Hasso went on, "Run a fuse from here over to the road, wait, and watch for Bottero's men to ride forward …"

Rautat laughed in eager anticipation. "Then they'll find out they aren't so cursed smart!"

"*Ja,*" Hasso said again, and then, "Let's go back. Plenty to do before we start to dig and to hide."

"Like eat, for instance." Rautat rubbed his belly. As if on cue, it growled like an angry dog. The Bucovinan laughed. So did Hasso.

They scooted back through the bushes. Hasso had learned his forest-fighting techniques in Russia, where any mistake was worth your life. Rautat was as good at moving silently as he was, maybe better. Of course, Rautat had been hunting in the woods since he got big enough to carry a bow. He'd had more practice than Hasso had.

A tiny, almost smokeless fire crackled ten meters or so away from the wagon with the jars of gunpowder. The Bucovinans understood that they couldn't get careless with fire around it. Hasso hadn't let anybody who didn't understand that come along with him. Dumnez was toasting a hare above the flames. Three more lay by the fire, already gutted and skinned and ready to cook. Yes, the Bucovinans could hunt, all right.

Hasso got his share of the tender meat. You couldn't keep going forever on hare and rabbit—not enough fat in them. But they made a good supper every so often.

As the sun set and darkness deepened, Hasso looked westward again. He didn't think the Lenelli would be able to spot the fire's glare over the rise ahead. Even if they did, odds were they wouldn't make much of it. They had to know the Bucovinans were keeping an eye on them. That wouldn't impress them, not for beans. Nothing the Bucovinans did impressed them. Bucovinans were only Grenye, after all.

Softly, Hasso began to chant. Some of the charm was in German, some in Lenello. He faced away from Rautat and the rest. They wouldn't hear his spell, or make anything of it if they did. He snorted—in rhythm with the spell. He wasn't sure there would be anything to make of it if they did. For one thing, he was an altogether untrained wizard. For another, he was still in Bucovin, even if he'd come back close to the border with Bottero's kingdom. If it didn't work … then it didn't, that was all. He would take a different tack in that case.

But it worked, all right. When he turned around, Rautat and Dumnez and Peretsh and the rest lay sprawled close to the little fire, all of them snoring softly. *I really* can *do this!* he thought, excitement surging in him. Along with the excitement went a little bit of shame. Bucovinans *were* only Grenye, after all—they couldn't work magic, and had no defense against it.

His knees clicked when he got to his feet. He wondered if he ought to cut the natives' throats before he went west. He couldn't make himself do it. They could have killed him, but they hadn't. He also wondered whether to take the powder wagon with him. They'd already unhitched the horses, though. He doubted he could harness them by dim firelight. He also feared that the noise would wake the Bucovinans, spell or no spell.

"By myself," he murmured in German. And wasn't that the sad and sorry truth? Wherever he went in this world, he was irrevocably by himself. Joining with Velona the way he had disguised the truth for a while, but it was there. Still and all, he came closer and closer to fitting in among the Lenelli than with the Bucovinans. And so … "*Auf wiedersehen.*" He started west—by himself

He went up the road till he got close to the crest of that rise—no point making things hard on himself. Then he ducked into the undergrowth, for he didn't want any Lenello sentries to spot him coming up to the top of the high ground. Back in Russia, a sniper would make you pay if you did something stupid like that. The Lenelli didn't have scope-sighted rifles or machine guns, but he didn't want them thinking somebody was sneaking up on them in the dark. They could lay a trap for him before they realized he wasn't a Bucovinan.

He leaned against the trunk of a scrubby oak. *Just for a second*, he told himself. *Or maybe a little longer—why not?* He didn't want to sneak through the bushes toward King Bottero's men in pitch darkness. Maybe an Indian could do that in a movie and not make a godawful racket. Or maybe a Bucovinan hunter—or a Lenello poacher—could do it for real. Hasso knew damn well he couldn't.

And he didn't just want to tramp up the road in the dark, either. That was asking to get killed. And so … He yawned. He slumped down against that tree trunk. As he yawned again, he wondered if he was getting caught in the backwash of his own sorcery. He also wondered if he could do anything about it. As his eyes slid shut, he was—sleepily—doubting it.

The next thing he knew, it wasn't altogether dark. And the light filtering through the bushes was coming from the east, from behind him. "Christ!" he said. He was awake now, awake and sweating bullets. If Rautat and the rest had come after him, they could have gutted him like a trout.

Were they still sleeping? Hasso nodded to himself. They just about had to be. Otherwise, they damn well *would* have come after him, and he would have woke up with his innards ventilated one way or another. So his magic still had to be holding back there.

"Oh, yeah, I'm one hell of a wizard, I am," he muttered as he got to his feet. "I'm so good, I put a goddamn spell on *me*."

It might work out for the best, he thought, and tried to make himself believe it. Now he could approach the Lenelli in broad daylight. They would see he was no dark little Grenye. That would let him get close enough to explain what he was and who he was and how he'd escaped the barbarians. From then on, everything ought to go smooth as motor oil on a camshaft.

His stomach rumbled, almost as loud as Rautat's had the day before. He had a length of garlicky pork sausage in a belt pouch. The Lenelli would know he was coming out of Bucovin just by the smell. They ate onions, but to them garlic was fit only for Grenye. Hasso wasn't wild about it himself, but eating it made him feel like an Italian, not a savage.

He worked his way forward through the woods for a while, then stepped out into the road. He hadn't gone more than about a hundred meters before a Lenello stepped out from behind some thick bushes, sword in hand. Hasso's right hand fell automatically to the hilt of his own blade. He stopped where he was, perhaps twenty meters from the blond, who overtopped him by five or six centimeters.

"Who the demon are you? Where'd you sprout from?" the Lenello demanded.

"My name's Hasso Pemsel. I just escape—escaped—from the Bucovinans."

Hasso hadn't spoken much Lenello lately. It felt awkward on his tongue. Well, so did Bucovinan.

"Funny handle you've got. You talk weird, too," the big blond said. "Where are you from, anyway?"

"Another world," Hasso answered. "I am the fellow who comes—uh, came— here by magic. I am the goddess' lover for a while." *And I want to be again, too. Whether Velona wants me to ... Well, I'll just have to see, that's all.*

The Lenello picket's eyes almost bugged out of his head. "It's the traitor! It's the goddess-cursed renegade!" he yelled at the top of his lungs. Then he swung up his sword and charged Hasso.

For a second, the German just stood there like an idiot. A millimeter from too late, he drew his own sword. He managed to turn a stroke that would have cut him in half from crown to crotch. Then he dropped the sword. The Lenello was still caught in his aborted follow-through. Hasso jumped in close. He grabbed the big blond's wrist and twisted. The Lenello dropped the blade.

"You can't do that!" he gasped.

"Says who?" Hasso twisted once more, cruelly this time. The Lenello gasped again, on a different note, above the sound of breaking bone. As he went white, Hasso brought a knee up into his crotch. He folded up on himself like a straight razor. Hasso kicked him in the face while he was falling. If you got into a fight like this, you didn't dick around.

Shouts came from the west. So did the thumps of men running in heavy boots. Hasso didn't wait to find out whether they had crossbows. Wherever he was going, it wasn't back to Bottero's kingdom. He grabbed his sword, dashed for the bushes, and did his unmagical best to vanish.

XXI

They did have crossbows, the bastards. Quarrels rustled through the leaves and branches and thudded into— sometimes right through—trunks. The Lenelli wanted to put them right through Hasso. He couldn't go as quietly as he wanted because they were pushing hard after him. The more noise he made, the more foliage he disturbed, the better the target he handed the archers.

He had to give the Lenelli something to think about, or they'd catch him and kill him. He picked up a rock and flung it off to one side. Luck was with him—it crashed off a trunk or a thick branch.

"There he goes!" Bottero's men yelled to one another. "After him! Don't let him get away!"

They crashed toward whatever the rock had hit. Hasso moved that way, too. Now he was trying to be quiet. The Lenello behind whom he suddenly appeared had no idea he was there till a callused hand covered his mouth and jerked his head back. The blond did no more than gurgle as a knife sliced across his throat.

Hasso slipped off. The other Lenelli took longer than they should have to realize they were following a trail that led nowhere. "Sondrio!" one of them called as they regathered. "Where'd you go, Sondrio?"

If Sondrio was who Hasso thought he was, he wouldn't answer till Judgment Day. The Lenelli all started calling for him. "He was over this way, wasn't he?" somebody said.

By then, Hasso wasn't over that way any more. Now he'd gained a little separation from his pursuers, and he could use all the skill at skulking he had. If they were going to catch him, they would have to earn it. They weren't such hot stuff in the woods themselves. He was glad he wasn't up against the trackers and poachers Orosei had given him by the Aryesh.

At last, one of these guys stumbled over Sondrio, perhaps literally. "Dead!" the Lenello yelled, horror in his voice. "He's dead! Bled like a goddess-cursed hog!"

All the soldiers started shouting and carrying on then, which was just what Hasso had hoped for. "He must have Grenye in the woods with him," one of them said. "Sondrio ran across them, and look what they did to him!" They

241

didn't imagine that Hasso might have doubled back. That must have seemed too crazy even to contemplate. Maybe it was, too. Hasso wondered how dumb he'd been.

Dumb or not, he got what he wanted—they quit chasing him. If they thought the undergrowth was full of lurking little swarthy men with knives ... well, they could do that. They could do whatever they damn well wanted, as long as they didn't mess with him.

He didn't breathe easy till he got back over the rise that shielded the Bucovinan encampment. No, he didn't feel easy then, either. If Rautat and the rest of Lord Zgomot's merry men were waiting for him with blood in their eye ... Well, what happened then? If both sides wanted to kill him, he was dead meat. *Why didn't you think of that sooner, you dumb asshole?*

But he knew why. Down below his belly, down in his balls and his dick, he didn't want to believe Velona didn't want him any more, didn't love him any more, didn't want to lay him any more. However you put it, he didn't want to believe it, even if it was true. No. Especially if it was true.

Want to or not, he didn't see that he had much choice any more. With Aderno's help, she'd tried to fry him twice at long range. Even that hadn't convinced him, which only proved he was a jerk or he was thinking with his cock—assuming those two weren't one and the same. No way in hell, though, that Bottero's soldiers would have done their best to massacre him unless their goddess told them it was all right. Since they had, she must have. Damn!

He looked back over his shoulder. He stopped so he could listen. Nothing either way. He breathed a sigh of relief, which differed only in his own mind from the panting he was also doing. The Lenelli behind had given up chasing him. Now—what was going on with the Bucovinans ahead?

However much he didn't want to, he had to find out. He couldn't very well stay right here and carve out a one-man realm sandwiched between Bottero's and Zgomot's. Since the Lenelli wanted him dead for sure, he had to hope the Bucovinans didn't. How much fancy talking would he need to do?

The answer turned out to be—none. When he got back to the camp, he found Rautat and the rest of the natives still sawing wood. They'd hardly moved from where they were lying when he slipped away. He hadn't expected his magic to work that well. Of course, he hadn't expected it to clobber him, either.

Next interesting question was, could he wake them up again? If he couldn't, he would have to throw them into the wagon and get out of there as best he could. But Rautat's eyes opened when Hasso shook him.

"What's going on?" the Bucovinan said, and then, seeing how light the sky was, "Lavtrig! Is it daytime? I was supposed to take a watch in the night, wasn't I?"

"I don't know. I don't keep track of that," Hasso said. They didn't give him night watches. They didn't trust him not to desert to the Lenelli—and they had reason not to. Fortunately, they didn't know for sure what good reason they had.

Rautat scrambled to his feet. "Did *anybody* keep watch in the night? Doesn't look like it. We're all asleep!" He started shaking his countrymen. As he did, he went on, "Did the Lenello doglegs use a spell on us? You could've just walked off, and we never would've known the difference. Or were you asleep, too?"

"Till a little while ago," Hasso answered. The spell *had* got him, too. That it was his own spell hadn't occurred to Rautat. *Damn good thing, too*, the German thought.

The other Bucovinans woke up as readily as Rautat had. But how long would they have gone on sleeping if Hasso hadn't got Rautat moving? He had no idea. "Where are the Lenelli, anyway?" Dumnez asked as he ambled off to take a leak behind a tree.

"Somewhere over that rise," Hasso and Rautat answered together.

"Then we don't have to worry about them right away," Peretsh said. "Let's eat breakfast." That was such a good idea, nobody said a word against it. Hasso ate hard bread and an onion—a funny breakfast, but any food was better than none, as he'd found out too often in Russia. He washed it down with lousy Bucovinan beer. If he knew anything at all about brewing, he could have made a fortune among the Lenelli or a bigger fortune in Bucovin.

He started digging holes in the road, filling them in, and running lengths of fuse off to the side. Yeah, he'd tried to desert, but his magic seemed to have covered his tracks. The other side didn't want him. This side did. Even if he didn't much want it, it looked like his best bet—his only bet—right now.

"What are you doing?" Rautat asked. "You aren't putting any gunpowder in those holes."

"I know." Hasso started digging another one.

"A hole in the ground won't hurt anybody, even with a fuse running off from it."

"I know," Hasso said again.

"I should have cut your throat in the pit and saved myself the aggravation," Rautat opined. "Do you have some kind of reason for doing this the way you are?"

"*Ja.*" Hasso went on digging without another word.

The air Rautat blew out through his lips made a whuffling noise. "Will you tell a poor dumb Grenye savage what your brilliant reason is?"

Hasso realized he'd pushed it as far as he could. When Bucovinans talked like that, they were only half kidding. The other half was all pain and rage. They didn't want to think they were as stupid and backward as the Lenelli made them out to be. They didn't want to, but they had trouble thinking anything else. When they made those jokes about themselves, you'd better not agree, not if you were big and blond.

So Hasso said, "You aren't dumb. But the Lenelli think Grenye are. You know that. I saw that." He wanted to remind Rautat he wasn't what he looked like.

"Well, sure," the underofficer said. "But what's the point of the holes?"

"I want the Lenelli to see dug-up places in the road. I want them to see fuses, even burning fuses," Hasso answered. "I want them to see that none of that does anything. Then they forget about it. They think, *Stupid Grenye try to make magic, and of course it doesn't work.* Then they don't worry about dug-up places or fuses any more. You follow?"

He wasn't just kissing Rautat's ass—the Bucovinan was plenty smart. And, after frowning for a few seconds, Rautat started to laugh. "Yeah, I get it! Bugger me blind if I don't! One of these times, they won't be just dug-up places. They'll be jars of gunpowder. And the Lenelli won't even care—till too late!"

"That's it," Hasso agreed.

Rautat came over to him, pulled him down so their faces were on a level, and kissed him on both cheeks like a Frenchman. Rautat had been eating onions, too, and hadn't cleaned his teeth any more recently than Hasso had. They were odorous kisses. Hasso didn't care. He was glad to get them. But if he'd kissed the Bucovinan, he would have felt like Judas.

"So we don't drive forward, then?" Dumnez had the wagon ready to go. "We drive back instead?"

"That's right," Hasso said.

"They'll think we were scouts or something, or maybe a crazy merchant because of the wagon," Rautat said.

One of the other Bucovinans pointed west, toward the rise. "Here come some of the bastards!" he called.

"Let's get out of here!" Rautat said.

That was a wonderful order. Hasso was sure he couldn't have put it better himself. "When we get over the next rise, we can make some more fake holes," he said. "Someone ought to stay behind to light fuses for them. I do it if you want—there are bushes to hide in."

"No, I'll let Gunoiul take care of it." Rautat pointed to one of the Bucovinan escorts. "We can't afford to lose you if anything goes wrong."

We can't afford to have you go back to the Lenelli, either. Rautat didn't say that. Hasso thought he heard it even so. Rautat was right to worry, too; Hasso would have gone back to Bottero's men if only they would have taken him. Since they wouldn't, he was stuck on this side.

He was, he feared, stuck on the losing side. No matter what he showed the Bucovinans, there was only one of him. All the Lenelli had several hundred years' worth of technology the natives didn't—no matter how hard they were working to get it.

And the Lenelli had magic, and the Grenye couldn't match that no matter what they did. So the big blonds insisted, and Hasso hadn't seen anything to make him think they were wrong.

"Well? So what?" he muttered in German. Rautat gave him a quizzical look. He pretended he didn't notice. It wasn't as if he hadn't fought in a losing war before. Any German who'd been on the Eastern Front knew all about a losing war: knew more about it than anybody in this world was likely to. Hell, any German who'd lived under a rain of Allied bombs that only got worse and worse knew all about a losing war.

Maybe the Bucovinans were doomed to go under. The *Reich* had turned out to be. But, like the *Reich*, they could sure make their foes remember they'd been in a fight.

***

All of his escorts joined him in digging holes in the road east of the next rise. They had fun running lengths of fuse into the undergrowth off to either side of the dirt track. Gunoiul grinned because he was the one who got to stay behind and light some of those fuses.

"Don't let 'em catch you, now," Rautat warned him. "We don't want them knowing what we know." Hasso beamed at him in pleased surprise. Somebody who understood what security was all about!

"Don't worry about me," Gunoiul said. "I don't want those whoresons nabbing me, either—and they won't. I'll catch up with you tonight if I can't do it any quicker than that."

The wagon and the riders with it retreated farther east still. Hasso kept looking back over his shoulder. His companions and he were moving faster than the Lenelli. The filled in holes in the road and the lengths of cord that ran from them confused the invaders out of the west, anyhow. Maybe they made them wary. Hasso could hope so. He and the natives had done all that digging to give the Lenelli the willies.

To give them the willies for a little while, anyhow. Then the big blonds would decide it was all a big bluff, one more weird, useless thing the barbarians did to try to scare them. And they would stop paying attention to filled-in holes and to cords that ran from them, even if the cords sizzled and smoked. Once they stopped paying attention—well, that was the time to show them they shouldn't have.

And once a bunch of Lenelli went sky-high, they would never be able to trust any filled-in hole in the ground with a cord again. They would have to treat all of them as real, even if most of them wouldn't be. Dummy minefields served the same purpose in Hasso's world. A few lying signs could slow down a whole armored division. He'd seen it happen.

"Grenye peasants back in the Lenello kingdoms can make these holes, too," he remarked to Rautat. "The Lenelli cannot—will not—trust their own roads."

Rautat laughed. "You're full of evil notions, aren't you?"

"I try," Hasso said modestly.

"Yes, you do." Rautat eyed him again. "If you aren't careful, you know, you'll have us trusting you in spite of everything."

"No! You wouldn't do that!" Hasso exclaimed, as if it were the worst thing he could think of. All the Bucovinans thought he was a funny fellow. How much would they be laughing if they knew he'd tried to bail out the night before? Not so very much, he feared.

Rautat ordered a halt after they made it over the next low swell of ground. "If the blonds come after us, we'll go on," he said. "But if they don't, we'll wait here for Gunoiul."

None of the Bucovinans argued. "Sounds good," Hasso said. Rautat gave him a hooded look that he understood too late. His position in the chain of command was ambiguous, to put it mildly. What kind of rank badge did an important collaborator wear? When it came to gunpowder, Rautat had to listen to him—he was the expert. When it came to tactics, the way it did here, the native could choose for himself. He didn't need Hasso butting in.

They waited. No Lenelli came over the crest of the hill to the west. After an hour or so, Gunoiul popped out of the bushes. The little dark man was grinning from ear to ear. "You should have heard them! You should have seen them!" he said.

"Well? Tell us the story," Rautat urged, as he must have known he was supposed to.

"The big blond bastards just kind of poked at the holes at first—made sure they weren't horse traps, you know," Gunoiul said. "Then I started lighting the, uh, fuses." He glanced toward Hasso, who'd given him his technical vocabulary. "The Lenelli saw the fire and smoke going through the grass, and they started having puppies. It was the funniest thing you ever saw. They were yelling and pointing and carrying on like you wouldn't believe."

All the Bucovinans laughed. Nothing they liked better than discomfited Lenelli. "Did they send soldiers after you?" Dumnez asked.

"They sure did," Gunoiul said. "I could have shot a couple of them, too, easy as you please. But I made a scary noise instead" —he went *Woooo!* on a high, wailing note— "and got out of there."

"Good!" Hasso punched him in the shoulder, the way he would have with a soldier on the Eastern Front who'd done something unexpected and clever. They wanted to spook the Lenelli here, and Gunoiul had found a new way to do it.

"Well, after that they didn't want to go very fast, let me tell you," the Bucovinan continued. "I didn't have any trouble staying ahead of them and lighting more fuses."

"That's what we wanted, by Lavtrig's curly beard," Rautat said. "And now that you're back, we want to get out of here in case you stirred up an even bigger hornets' nest than you think."

Hasso would have said that if Rautat hadn't. The *Wehrmacht* officer figured there was a pretty good chance the Lenelli were well and truly stirred. He also figured the filled-in holes and smoking, crackling fuses had only so much to do with it. Bottero's men knew he was around, even if Rautat didn't know they knew. And the Lenelli wanted him ... no, not dead or alive. They wanted him dead or dead.

As he rode off toward the northeast, he wondered whether he could escape to some other Lenello kingdom than Bottero's. That way, he would have a chance to live among folk who looked like him and who thought more like him than the Bucovinans did. But when would he get that kind of chance? And even if he did, weren't all the Lenelli likely to reckon him a renegade now?

Besides, some other Lenello kingdom wouldn't have Velona in it. There was only one of her. That there *was* one of her seemed more than miracle enough.

If he couldn't have Velona, how much difference did it make whether he lived among Lenelli or Grenye? And so…

"I think maybe you truly are Lord Zgomot's man," Rautat said out of the blue. Hasso started to laugh—who said the small, swarthy men couldn't work magic? Rautat, not surprisingly, didn't get it. "What's so funny?" he demanded.

"Nothing," Hasso said—nothing he wanted to talk about, anyhow. "I think I am truly Lord Zgomot's man, too." *Dammit*, he added, but only to himself.

***

The dreams came back two nights later. He'd been free of them for months, and thought they were gone for good. No such luck. As he lay asleep, wrapped in a blanket by a fire that had guttered down to crimson embers, he felt someone stalking him through the inside of his own head. *I ought to work out a spell to put a stop to this*, he thought, which would have been wonderful one of these days—but not now.

Patient as a wolf chasing an elk, the Lenello wizard pursued him through slumber and finally caught him. Hasso was anything but surprised to find it was Aderno. "What do you want?" the German asked.

"What are you up to?" Aderno returned.

"None of your business, not after you try to kill me twice," Hasso said.

"It's my king's business, by the goddess." When Aderno named her, Hasso saw Velona behind him. "It's my folk's business."

"I am no part of your folk. You make that plain enough. When I come to you, all you want to do is murder me."

"What are we supposed to do with you?" Yes, that was Velona. Seeing her, hearing her even in dreams tore at Hasso from the inside out. "You're up to something with the cursed Grenye."

"You Lenelli don't want me any more." Hasso didn't waste time denying it.

"King Bottero tried to ransom you. The savage who runs Bucovin wouldn't take his money," Velona replied.

What she said was true—and also missed the point. Lord Zgomot was a decent, capable, worried, rather gray little man doing the best job he knew how in a predicament Hasso wouldn't have wished on his worst enemy. To the Lenelli, he was only a Grenye. He would have been only a Grenye to Hasso, too, but for the fortunes—and misfortunes—of war.

"Sorry. I can't do anything about it," Hasso said. "Then you try to kill me. Should I love you after that?" He started bleeding inside again. He still wanted to love Velona, and wanted her to love him.

"We were denying you to the enemy," Aderno said.

He made perfect military sense. He also made Hasso want to wring his neck. The combination reminded the German of some of his own country's less clever policies during the war. He said, "When you try to kill me you turn me into an enemy."

"If you're a dead enemy, it doesn't matter," the wizard said.

If the *Reich* had knocked the Russians out in six weeks, nothing else would have mattered. Since they hadn't, they had to try to deal with the consequences of that failure—only to discover they couldn't. Now Aderno and Velona were trying to deal with the consequences of failing to kill Hasso. They could try again—and they might succeed if they did.

"You *are* up to something with the Grenye." Velona made that sound even more disgusting and outrageous than sleeping with a little swarthy woman.

"They could kill me, and they don't," Hasso answered stolidly. "More than I can say for some people."

"Killing is better than renegades deserve. Killing is *much* better than renegade wizards deserve." Velona was as implacable as an earthquake. Her dream-self turned to Aderno. "*Now!*"

Hasso had thought his own modest sorcerous abilities were what had kept him from harm when the two of them struck at him in Falticeni. Maybe those abilities helped, but he'd forgotten Falticeni lay at the heart of Bucovin: the place where, for whatever reason, Lenello magic was weakest. Here near the western border…

He didn't just scream himself awake, as he had in Lord Zgomot's palace. He puked his guts out, as if he'd eaten bad fish. He shat himself, too. He thought his ears were bleeding, but he was in too much more immediate torment to stick a finger in one of them and find out. When he had to piss, he pissed dark. What had they done to him? Everything but kill him, plainly. While the fit was going on, he almost wished they had.

Rautat and the other Bucovinans stared at him while he writhed and heaved. "I'd heard about this at the palace," the underofficer said to his comrades—Hasso heard his voice as if from a million kilometers away. "It wasn't so bad there." He was right. Nothing could have been as bad as this. Hasso would rather have stood out in the open during a volley of *Katyushas* than go through this—and if that didn't say everything that needed saying, what could?

The only good thing about the fit was that it didn't last long. Once it passed, Hasso lay on the ground, spent and gasping like a fish out of water. "Give me a little beer," he choked out. Dumnez poured him some. He didn't swallow it, but used it to rinse his mouth. It couldn't get rid of all the foul taste; some of his vomit had gone up his nose. "Where is a stream?" he asked. "Need to wash."

"Back over there." Rautat pointed. "Will anything more happen to you?"

"I hope not," Hasso said.

His drawers were ruined beyond hope. He used them to wipe himself as clean as he could, then threw them away. From now on, he would be bare-assed under his trousers. Well, the world wouldn't end. He was battered but almost unbowed when he came back to the embers of the fire.

"Look at the moon. It's still the middle of the night," Rautat said. "We're going back to sleep. Can you do the same?"

"I don't know. I find out," Hasso answered grimly. Aderno and Velona hadn't attacked him twice in one night. Did that mean they couldn't? He could only hope so.

In what was plainly meant for consolation, Rautat said, "Soon, now, you'll give the Lenelli worse than they just gave you."

And it *did* console, where it wouldn't have before. That only went to show how badly abused Hasso was. "I will," he said, and he really meant it for the first time since his capture.

***

"Get moving, you fools!" a soldier shouted. The word for *fools* literally meant *donkeyheads*; Bucovinan was not without its charms. The small, swarthy warrior went on, "The accursed Lenelli are on their way—lots of them!"

"How about that?" Rautat said, and then, to Hasso, "If lots of those big blond bastards are coming, this is the time to use the gunpowder for real, yes?"

"Yes," Hasso answered. He hadn't exactly chosen Bucovin. He'd had the choice made for him. Bottero's followers wanted him dead. Well, if they thought that was what they wanted *now*, he was going to give them some real reasons to feel that way. "We dig real holes. We put jars of gunpowder into them. We light the fuses."

"Boom!" Rautat said. Hasso nodded. Rautat continued, "And they won't be expecting it. They think it's all a bunch of Grenye crap." He laughed. "We'll show them what's crap, all right."

"One thing," Hasso said. Rautat raised a questioning eyebrow. Hasso pointed at himself. "*I* light the fuses this time."

He waited for Rautat to swell up and turn purple. He waited for the Bucovinan to say he was too valuable to do something like that—which meant he couldn't be trusted to do it. He had all his arguments ready. He was braced to threaten to put a spell on the powder so it wouldn't go off unless he lit it himself. If they provoked him enough, he was ready to try to cast that spell.

But Rautat only nodded. "You've earned the right. We'll find a good spot, with thick growth by the side of the road. That way, you'll have an easy time getting away, same as Gunoiul did."

"You really aim to let me do this?" Hasso couldn't hide his surprise.

Rautat nodded again. "I really do. If you aren't loyal to us now, you never will be. Either way, it's about time we found out." He turned to the rest of the Bucovinans who'd traveled west from Falticeni. "Come on, you lazy lugs! This is what we came here for. We've played all the games. Now we give it to the Lenelli, the way we've wanted to give it to them ever since they got here. So *dig*, curse you!"

They dug like moles. If he'd told them to dig to China, or whatever lay on the other side of this world, Hasso thought they would have done that. The hope of getting their own back against the Lenelli fired them like burning gasoline.

Was this how the Russians felt when they started winning after the *Wehrmacht* pushed them back more than a thousand kilometers across their own country?

Maybe this was even fiercer, because the Grenye had been retreating not for a year and a half but for generations. They must have wondered if they would ever get the chance to go forward. But here it was … if the gunpowder worked.

Rautat talked to the soldier who warned of the advancing Lenelli. Not too much later, he talked to another Bucovinan, this one an officer sweating in a helmet and mailshirt. Rautat pointed toward Hasso several times. He pounded his fist into his palm once. He might be only a *Feldwebel*, but he acted like a general.

He got away with it, too—damned if he didn't. The Bucovinan officer nodded, sketched a salute, and hurried away. Rautat grinned till the top of his head threatened to fall off. He also nodded to Hasso. If he hadn't been the Official Bucovinan in Charge of the Dangerous and Important Blond Person, he never could have pulled that one off, and he knew it.

Hasso placed the fuses in the jars. Next time, he would come with jars already fused. You couldn't think of everything at once, not when you were reinventing a whole art all by yourself. The Bucovinans watched him intently. If they got away and he didn't, they would at least be able to go on with what he'd already shown them. Whether they'd be able to do anything more … wouldn't be his worry, not in that case.

He hid in some bushes off to the side of the road. A lot of the fuses ran toward those bushes, but he wasn't too worried about that. For one thing, there were some dummies that went other places. And, for another, by now the Lenelli ought to think all the fuses were nothing but a big bluff. They wouldn't pay any attention to them—till too late.

Rautat left him some hard bread and dried meat, a jar of beer, and, most important of all, a couple of sticks of something a lot like punk. It glowed red and slowly smoldered without burning away in nothing flat. "Good luck," the Bucovinan said, and then, "Want me to hang around with you?"

"Whatever you want." After what had happened while they slept, Hasso didn't have any trouble sounding casual when he answered the question. "I'm not running back to the Lenelli." No matter how much he might regret it, he was telling the truth there, too.

Rautat plucked a hair from his beard, considering. At last, he said, "Maybe I'd better. *I* don't think you're any trouble, but if it turns out I'm wrong I don't want to have to explain to Drepteaza and Lord Zgomot how I left you all by yourself."

"Fair enough," Hasso said. From the underofficer's perspective, it was. You *did* need to be careful about relying on a turncoat. The German felt he had to ask, "Can you stay down and keep quiet?" Those talents were more useful in warfare in his world than they were here. Most fighting in this world was right out in the open. How long would that last if gunpowder caught on?

"I'll do it. I already thought about that," Rautat said.

"Good. Start now, because here they come," Hasso said, and hunkered down in the bushes. The first Lenello scouts had just topped the swell of ground to the west. Rautat got as flat as if a Stalin panzer had run over him. He didn't let out a peep. He barely even breathed.

Hasso didn't get quite so low as that: he needed to see out. One of the blond outriders stared at a dummy hole with a dummy fuse running from it. Another one said something to him. They both laughed and rode on. They were convinced it was just the Grenye savages trying to play games with their minds. Hasso wished he'd left somebody to light some of the dummy fuses. Too late to worry about it now.

Much too late—here came Bottero's main body, red flags flying. This had to be a bigger force than the one that was plundering Bucovinan villages. Hasso wondered why, but he didn't wonder for long. *They're after me*, he thought. It was a compliment of sorts, but one he would gladly have done without.

On rode the Lenelli: big fair men in mail and surcoats on horses big enough to bear their weight. Soon Hasso could hear the thud of hoofbeats, the jingle of harness and armor, and even the odd snatch of conversation: "Oh, that? Don't worry about it. Just the Bucovinans, trying to make us jumpy."

"Dumbass barbarians," another Lenello said.

"When?" Rautat's question was a tiny thread of whisper, inaudible from more than a couple of meters away.

"Soon," Hasso whispered back. He wanted about a third of the enemy army to pass over the real gunpowder pots before he lit the fuses. His guess was that that would cause the most confusion—and the most casualties.

He swung a stick of punk through the air to get it to glow red. Then he touched it to the fuses, one after another. From the ground beside him, Rautat grinned wolfishly. Trails of smoke streaked toward the burning pots.

A couple of Lenelli pointed to them. Others snickered and shook their heads, as if to say those didn't mean anything, either. Up till today, they would have been right. The pots buried in the road blew up, one after another.

They didn't just hold gunpowder. They had rocks and sharp bits of metal in there, too—homemade shrapnel. They gutted horses and flayed knights' lightly armored legs. Some fragments hit men in the face. Some managed to punch right through mail.

And the noise was like the end of the world, especially to men and beasts who'd never heard the like and weren't expecting it. Hasso was closer than he might have been, but still used to much worse. But even Rautat, who'd heard gunpowder go off before, let out an involuntary yip of alarm. The Lenelli and their horses screamed as if damned.

The big blonds in back of the explosions wheeled their mounts and rode off to the west as fast as they could go. The ones in front ... *They don't know whether to shit or go blind*, Hasso thought happily. They milled about, afraid to advance and even more afraid to retreat.

Then Bucovinans started sliding forward and shooting at them. Normally, Bottero's men would have driven off the archers annoying them without even breaking a sweat. Here, the bowmen were just enough to tip the Lenelli into panic.

"Magic!" somebody screamed. "The goddess-cursed Grenye *do* have magic!"

They fled then, with no shame and in no order at all. Had more Bucovinans and better-mounted Bucovinans pursued, they might have bagged most of that leading detachment of the army. *Next time*, Hasso thought. No matter how much you wanted to, you couldn't do everything perfectly the first time around.

But he'd done plenty. The way Rautat sprang up and kissed him on both cheeks proved that. So did the way the Lenelli ran. From now on, they'd piss themselves whenever they saw a cord running to some freshly turned earth. Professionally, Hasso was happy. Personally … He'd worry about that later. When he had time. If he ever did.

XXII

Things in western Bucovin were going to be different for a while—maybe for quite a while. Hasso could already see that. The natives had their peckers up. And the Lenelli ... The Lenelli had to be wondering what the devil had hit them. They sure would start to sweat whenever they saw string running to what looked like holes in the ground. And they would have to be ten times more worried about bushwhackers than they ever had before.

And all because of black powder, Hasso thought. *If I knew how to make nitroglycerine ...* After a little pondering, he realized he might. Medieval alchemists had used nitric acid, so maybe the Bucovinans knew about it. And you got glycerine from animal fat some kind of way.

Then he shook his head. To make nitro safe to handle, you had to turn it into dynamite, and he knew he didn't know how to do that. Turning out gunpowder was dangerous. You had to be careful as hell. Turning out nitroglycerine? No, he didn't even want to try. And he *really* didn't want untrained Bucovinans trying. That wasn't a disaster waiting to happen—it was a goddamn catastrophe.

Rautat nudged him. "Let's get out of here."

Plain good sense ended his woolgathering in a hurry. "Right," he said. Getting away wasn't hard. King Bottero's men had either fled back to the west or were hotly engaged with Lord Zgomot's soldiers. They didn't have time to worry about a couple of men heading the other way.

Not getting scragged by the Bucovinans was more interesting. Hasso was glad he had Rautat along. The underofficer was able to convince his countrymen that the big blond beside him wasn't a Lenello and was a friend. Hasso might not have had an easy time doing that on his own.

He felt better when he and Rautat caught up with the wagon that held the rest of the gunpowder jars. Dumnez and Peretsh and Gunoiul and the other Bucovinans on his crew were beside themselves with excitement. "It worked!" they shouted, and, "We heard it blow up!" and other things besides. Once they'd said those first two, though, they'd said everything that mattered.

"What now?" Hasso asked

"Now we go back to Falticeni and find out what new orders Lord Zgomot has for us," Rautat answered.

"We ought to leave the wagon somewhere closer to the front, so even without us it can go into action fast if it has to," Hasso said.

"Not too close," Rautat said. "Can't let it get captured no matter what."

He would have been right about that in medieval Europe. He was righter here. Hasso still worried about magic. The longer till Aderno and the other Lenello wizards figured out what gunpowder was and how it worked, the better. How much of a spell would you need to ignite it from a distance? "Where do you want to leave it, then?" the *Wehrmacht* officer asked.

"How about Muresh?" Rautat said. "Even if the big blond bastards do come that far, it can always go back over the Oltet."

Hasso found himself nodding. "Muresh should do." He liked the idea of putting such a potent weapon in a town the enemy had ravaged only the autumn before.

In fact, he needed a moment to remember that he'd been part of the army that ravaged Muresh. It seemed a long time ago—and that despite his trying to rejoin that army only a few days before. King Bottero didn't want him back? Well, long live Lord Zgomot, then!

He really had turned his coat. He shook his head. No, he'd had it turned for him. If the Lenelli wanted him dead—and they damn well did—how could he think he owed them anything but a good kick in the nuts the first chance he got?

It all made good logical sense. Which proved … what, exactly? If Jews had a country of their own, would Germans feel easy about fighting for it? He had a hard time seeing how. Why would Jews want Germans on their side, anyway?

But that one had an answer. Whatever else you said about Germans, they were better at war than damn near anybody else. They'd shown twice now that they weren't as good as everybody else put together, but that wasn't the same thing.

So here I am. I'm good at war, by God. I'm even better here than I would be back home. And I'm fighting for the side that looks like a bunch of fucking Jews. And if that ain't a kick in the ass, what is?

"Why are you laughing?" Rautat asked.

"Am I?" Hasso said. "Maybe because I am starting to pay the Lenelli back for trying to kill me." *And maybe for other reasons, too.*

The one he named satisfied Rautat. "Revenge is good," the native said seriously. "If anyone wrongs you, pay him back a hundredfold. We say that, and you're doing it."

"Yes. I'm doing it. How about that?" Hasso loved *How about that?* Along with *Isn't that interesting?*, it was one of the few things you could say that were almost guaranteed not to get you in trouble.

And I'm already in enough trouble, thank you very much.

***

He ended up in more trouble when they got to Muresh. His name pursued him through his dreams. He knew what that meant: Aderno and Velona were after him again. He tried to wake himself up, but couldn't do it. And here in the west of Bucovin, magic worked better than it did farther east.

So Aderno caught up with him in the corridors of sleep. "What did you do?" the Lenello wizard demanded.

"I pay you back for trying to kill me, that's what," Hasso said savagely. He found he liked Rautat's proverb. "You try to kill me three times now. You think I kiss you after that?" He told Aderno where the wizard could kiss him.

"And you pay us back by working magic for the savages?" Aderno said. "You don't know how filthy that is."

Lying in these dream quarrels wasn't easy—Hasso remembered that. So he didn't say anything at all. He just laughed his ass off. Let Aderno make whatever he wanted out of that. And if he thought Hasso'd routed Bottero's army with spells, he would only have a harder time figuring out what was really going on.

"Why should I worry?" Aderno said. "If we don't get you, the Grenye are bound to. They don't trust renegades, you know."

"They don't try to murder me," Hasso answered. "That's you."

"Yes, and we'd do it again in a heartbeat," Velona said, appearing beside Aderno out of thin air—or, more likely, out of thin dreamstuff. "You deserve it. Anyone who goes over to the savages deserves it. And everyone who goes over to the Grenye will get it. The goddess has told me so."

"Telling things is easy. Backing up what you say is a lot harder." How many promises did Hitler make? How many did he keep? "Is the goddess really big enough to swallow all of Bucovin?"

"Of course she is." Velona had no doubts—when did she ever? "This land will be ours—all of it. So even if you showed the barbarians the trick of your thunder weapon, it won't matter, because the goddess is on our side."

God wills it! the Crusaders shouted. And sometimes He did, and sometimes He didn't, and after a while no more Crusaders were left in the Middle East. Velona was smarter than Aderno, though. She'd figured out what the booms were, and he hadn't.

"We should have killed you the last time," she went on. "We'll just have to try again now."

"This is what I get for loving you?" Hasso asked, though all the while he knew the answer was yes.

"No one who beds Grenye women can truly love the goddess in me," Velona said. "And if you don't care about the goddess, then you don't care about me, either. Now the goddess cares about you, Hasso Pemsel." She was still beautiful—beautiful and terrible and terrifying. "I warned you long ago that there was more danger to loving me than the chance of a broken heart. Now you begin to see, and now you begin to pay!"

She gestured to Aderno. Hasso didn't think she would have let him see that if she could have helped it. But the other side evidently had trouble lying in the dreamscape, too. That was something of a relief. And Hasso sorcerously braced himself as well as he could.

The blow wasn't so strong as the one a few nights earlier. His being farther east likely had something to do with that. He woke with a shriek, yes, but by now he was almost used to doing that. He didn't heave his guts out or foul himself, so he reckoned the encounter a success.

Rautat was less delighted. "Do you have to make so much noise?" he asked crossly. "You sound like you're dying, and you scare me to death."

"Sorry," Hasso said. "What do you want me to do when a wizard's after me?"

"Go after him instead. Make him wake up screaming instead. You can do that shit, right? So do it."

"I wish I could," Hasso said, but the Bucovinan underofficer wasn't listening to him any more. He swore under his breath. He had no idea how to track Aderno through the Lenello wizard's dreams, or what to do if he caught him. Having the ability and having the knowledge were two different things. Expecting Rautat to understand that was … hopeless.

Not a sword. A shield. Hasso was a mediocre chess player, but he'd learned enough to know defending was easier than putting together a strong attack. If the other guy needed to work hard to beat you, maybe he'd get sick of trying and go away. Maybe.

"What do you people do against sendings of bad dreams?" he inquired.

"Why ask me?" Rautat said. "Whatever we do, it isn't real magic." The common Grenye mixture of fear and bitterness edged his voice. Coming up against magic that *did* work must have been as horrible a shock for the natives here as the Spaniards' gunpowder was to the Indians.

"Just curious," Hasso said. Whatever the Grenye did wasn't real magic for them. For him, with the right spell cast by the right kind of mind, it might be. Their notions would give him a place to start, anyhow. And he knew he couldn't screw every night till he got to Falticeni. He didn't *want* to screw in Muresh. It would remind him of all the rapes here during the sack.

With the air of a man humoring an eccentric—a lunatic?—Rautat answered, "Well, we use nettle and yarrow and prayer."

Hasso discovered that he was smiling. What did Shakespeare say? *Out of this nettle, danger, we pluck this flower, safety*—that was it. Maybe old Will knew more than he let on. He often seemed to.

"Can you get me some of each?" Hasso asked. He knew nettles when he saw them. Yarrow, to him, was only a name.

"I'll send someone out to get you the plants, yes." Rautat gave him a crooked smile. "You'll have to find our own prayer, though. I don't know where that grows around here."

After what the Lenelli did to Muresh, Hasso guessed all the prayer in these parts had been torn up by the roots. He laughed anyway, to show Rautat he got the joke. And, a couple of hours later, a gray-haired Bucovinan woman brought in a nettle and another plant—Hasso supposed it was yarrow. The woman eyed him. "Do you speak our language?" she asked.

He nodded. "Yes—not too well, though."

"Were you in Muresh when the Lenelli ravished it?"

"Yes," Hasso said again.

She nodded, too, as if he'd proved some point. And he must have, because she said, "No wonder you have bad dreams." She knew what the yarrow and nettle were for, then. Well, who likelier to believe an old wives' tale than an old wife?

"I take any oath you want—I fought clean here." Hasso was amazed by how glad he was to be telling the truth. He couldn't have said the same thing about what he'd done in Russia. Well, how many Russians had clean hands in Germany?

And, truthteller or not, he failed to impress the Bucovinan woman. "Even so," she said, and walked away without waiting for an answer. What had happened to her when Bottero's army came through Muresh? What had happened to the people she loved? Hasso didn't have the nerve to ask.

Yarrow had fine, tiny leaves and a spicy scent. As the woman had, Hasso handled the nettle by the root to keep from getting stung. He held the yarrow in the other hand and chanted in German. He was sure the natives would rather he'd used Bucovinan. But he had no idea whether magic here paid any attention to the natives' language. He knew damn well he could cast a spell in German that worked: he'd done it before. So he tried it again.

And what would happen when Aderno and Velona tried to afflict him again? *That's why you're casting the spell, jerk—to find out what'll happen.* With luck, Aderno wouldn't be able to get through at all. *I'm sorry, sir. You seem to have reached a disconnected brain.* Hasso snorted. Yeah, his brain seemed disconnected, all right, even to him.

The only way to discover what would happen was to fall asleep. Hasso approached the night with all the enthusiasm of a soldier about to have a wound tended by a drunken, stupid medic. When it came to wizardry, that was about what he was, and he knew it. The only reason he looked like a doctor in a clean white coat to the Bucovinans was that they were even worse off than he was.

He lay down. After a while, he slept. Next thing he knew, it was morning. He approved. Of course, he had no idea whether Aderno had tried a spell of his own during the night. But no news seemed good news.

He wasn't the only one who thought so. "You didn't scream. Your magic must have worked," Rautat said. "It's a lot more restful when you don't scream, you know?"

"For me, too," Hasso said, and the underofficer chuckled, for all the world as if he were kidding. Nobody'd ever tried to blow Rautat's head off from the inside out. The Bucovinan didn't know how lucky he was. If he stayed lucky, he would never find out, either.

Hasso did feel a pang at riding away from the remaining pots of gunpowder: they ended up stowing them in the castle on the east bank of the Oltet, which, like Muresh, had been—somewhat—repaired. There was bound to be more explosive in Falticeni. The Bucovinans knew how to make the stuff now, and they wouldn't have stopped because he'd ridden west.

He did wonder whether Zgomot would have the chopper waiting. If the ruler decided he'd learned enough from the dangerous blond … Hasso shrugged. He just had to hope that wasn't so. Bottero's men wanted to kill him. If Zgomot's did, too… He'd damn well die in that case, and he didn't know what he could do about it.

"Catapults," he said out of the blue. He said it in Lenello, but the Bucovinan name was almost the same; the natives had taken the word as well as the thing. It was what Drepteaza called a bastard word, with long and short vowels.

"What about them?" Rautat asked.

"We need light ones on wheeled carts," Hasso said. "Then they can throw pots of gunpowder at the Lenelli."

"Oh, yeah?" A slow grin spread over Rautat's face. "I *like* that, Lavtrig give me boils on my ass if I don't. What other sneaky ideas have you got?"

"That would be telling," Hasso answered. Rautat laughed. So did Hasso, but he wasn't kidding. What kept him alive was being the goose that laid golden eggs. As long as he could keep laying them, and as long as none of them turned out to be gilded lead, he figured he was all right. If he screwed up, Lord Zgomot would start sharpening that chopper.

So don't screw up, he thought. Good advice—but hard to live up to.

***

Coming back to Falticeni wasn't exactly coming home. Hasso had no home in this world, and wondered whether he ever would. But he knew lots of people in the palace. Zgomot was interesting to talk to. And Drepteaza—was Drepteaza. Hasso sighed. He would be glad to see her. One of these days before too long, he would probably need to get drunk, too.

Hell, he'd done that on account of Velona, too. But it was different with her. He'd got smashed because she screwed Bottero. Drepteaza wasn't screwing anybody, not as far as Hasso knew. That was the problem.

How the natives stared when he rode through the crowded, muddy, smelly streets with his Bucovinan escort! Nobody had any idea who he was—the Bucovinans figured him for a Lenello. Without photography and printing, nobody except kings could get famous enough for everyone to recognize them. And kings put their portraits on coins, which struck Hasso as cheating.

"Look at that big blond prick," a Bucovinan said, pointing at him.

"Who are you calling a prick, you asshole?" Hasso replied in Bucovinan. The native gaped. His buddies gave him the horselaugh. Rautat slapped Hasso on the back. They rode on.

"So he did it?" one of the gate guards said to Rautat when they got to the palace.

"He sure did." The underofficer sounded proud of Hasso. He probably was. If he hadn't found the *Wehrmacht* officer in the pit and decided not to finish him off, he wouldn't have got soft duty at the palace. He was enough of a *Feldwebel* to know when—and why—he was well off.

"Good," the gate guard said. "About time we had some magic on our side."

It wasn't magic. Lord Zgomot understood that. So did Drepteaza. So did the Bucovinans who worked with gunpowder. As for the rest—well, what if they thought it was? That was probably good for morale.

Grooms came out to take charge of the travelers' horses. Hasso stretched and grunted. He stumped around bowlegged, like an arthritic chimpanzee. That got a laugh from Rautat and the rest of the Bucovinans. Then he said, "I want a bath."

"Me, too," Rautat said. Gunoiul and Peretsh and Dumnez and the others who'd ridden with them nodded.

"Boy, when he says things like that, you'd hardly think he was a Lenello," the gate guard said, as if Hasso weren't there or didn't speak Bucovinan. The German didn't bash the native in the head, however much he wanted to. The man had already shown he didn't know what the hell he was talking about.

But most of the Grenye in Falticeni were bound to think the same things about Hasso—the ones who'd heard of him, anyway. How many had? No way for him to know.

He wondered if he could figure out how to make a printing press. In the long run, ideas were as important as weapons. Ideas *were* weapons. But that was in the long run. Lots of other things to worry about first.

That bath, for instance. Hasso let Rautat lead the way. He was glad to get out of his grubby clothes, and even gladder to soak in the warm water with the root the Bucovinans used in place of soap. If only he had some cigarettes …

"If you were a Lenello, you'd still stink," Rautat said.

"If I were a Lenello—" Hasso dropped it right there. If he were a Lenello, he would have deserted when he got to the west. If he were a Lenello, he probably would have got away with it, too. "But I'm not." He was sick of saying that. If only the Bucovinans would listen to him for a change!

Or maybe Rautat *was* listening. "I said, 'If you were,'" he reminded Hasso. "You don't stink. You enjoy being clean, just like a human being does."

Back in Drammen, Hasso hadn't especially missed baths. When you got into the field, when you stayed in the line for weeks at a time, you learned to do without getting clean. You stopped worrying about it. It was nice to have the chance to scrub the dirt off, though. Hasso grabbed it without hesitation.

He didn't even have to get back into his dirty duds. Servants laid out some others that fit him, no doubt borrowed from one renegade or another. "Not bad," he said. "Not bad at all."

"Not even a little bit," Rautat agreed. He had on clean clothes, too. "Now I could do with chopped pork and garlic over millet. That'd fill up the hole in my belly—and some mead to wash it down, too."

"Sounds pretty good," Hasso said. Rautat leered at him. He even understood why. The underofficer's meal was what the Lenelli would sneer at as native food. Hasso didn't care, even if he wasn't wild about garlic. Once you spent some time campaigning, you ate anything that didn't eat you first. Either that or you starved. He did add, "I think beer goes better."

"Suit yourself," Rautat said magnanimously. "Let's go get outside some."

"Sounds like a plan."

Food brightened the way Hasso looked at the world. It always did. Some of the meals he remembered mostly fondly were, by any objective standard, pretty horrible. Half a kilo of part-burnt, part-raw horsemeat wouldn't put the Ritz out of business any time soon. But when you'd had nothing but snow and a mouthful of kasha for three days before you stumbled over the carcass, it seemed like the best supper you'd ever had.

The Bucovinan meal wasn't half bad, even if it wasn't what Hasso would have ordered given a choice. He'd just emptied his mug of beer when an attendant came up to him and said, "Lord Zgomot wants to see you now that you're done eating."

"He tells you to wait till I finish?" Hasso asked. The man nodded. Hasso shook his head in amazement. A ruler who thought of things like that! What was this world coming to? The *Wehrmacht* officer got to his feet. He towered over the native, as he towered over all the natives here. "I am at his service, of course."

∗∗∗

"Congratulations, Hasso Pemsel," Zgomot said.

Hasso bowed. "Thank you, Lord." As usual, he found the throne room cold and drafty and badly lit. Zgomot's throne looked like a dining-room chair smothered in gold leaf.

"You kept your promise. Your weapon did everything you claimed it would." The Lord of Bucovin raised an eyebrow. "Do you have any notion of how unusual that is, Hasso Pemsel?"

How many people—renegades and Bucovinans alike—would have promised him and other Grenye rulers that they could drive back the Lenelli? How many of those snake-oil salesmen would have been talking through their hats? Just about all of them, or the big blonds wouldn't have pushed forward as far as they had.

"What I say I can do, Lord, I can do," Hasso answered stolidly.

"So it would seem," Zgomot allowed. "If you knew how many of the others said the same thing, though…" His mouth tightened, likely at some unhappy memory. Then he brightened—as much as he ever did, anyhow. "And you did something else marvelous, too."

"What's that?" Hasso asked.

"You came back," Zgomot said. "We trusted you. We had not a lot of choice, maybe, when you were showing us something so new and strange, but we did it, and you did not betray us." He might have been a priest solemnly proclaiming a miracle.

Shame flooded through Hasso. He hoped the throne room was too dim to let the Lord of Bucovin see him blush. Yeah, he'd come back, but only because the

Lenelli didn't want him any more. He wondered whether Bottero was wishing he'd given his soldiers different orders. And he wondered whether Velona wished she hadn't lost her temper with him.

Maybe Bottero did wish he'd welcomed back the man from another world. Hasso couldn't make himself believe Velona felt any different about him. Velona didn't do things because they were expedient. She did them because she felt like doing them. She loved as she pleased—and she hated as she pleased, too.

"Here I am, all right," Hasso said. Let the Lord of Bucovin make anything he pleased of that.

"Yes." Zgomot actually smiled a smile that didn't look cynical. That didn't happen every day—nor every week, either. "And now that you are here again, what other things can you show us that will drive the Lenelli wild?"

"Well…" Hesitantly, in a mixture of Lenello and Bucovinan, Hasso explained what he hoped to do with catapults and flying pots of gunpowder.

"Interesting," Zgomot said—which, from him, was better than wild enthusiasm from a lot of people Hasso knew. "But a catapult only shoots so far. It only shoots so fast. How do you keep the Lenello knights from charging up and murdering the crew while they put a new pot in the throwing arm and cut the fuse just so?"

Hasso bowed low. "Those are the right things to worry about, Lord." He wasn't trying to butter Zgomot up, either. The Lord of Bucovin had a good eye for problems. Spending his whole reign trying to hold off people with more tricks up their sleeve than he had doubtless contributed to that. Hasso went on, "Very steady pikemen with long pikes can hold off knights. Good archers can do the same thing. If you have knights of your own, they can keep the Lenelli from getting too close in the first place."

"How sure are these ploys?" Zgomot asked.

"It's war, Lord." Hasso spread his hands. "Nothing is sure in war. You already show that to King Bottero, yes?" He mimed falling into a pit. "And you already show that to me."

"We have to do such things," Zgomot said. "When we face the big blond bastards straight up, we lose. We don't have enough big horses to raise swarms of knights the way they do. We will one of these days, but not yet. How long would your long pikes have to be?"

"About ten cubits," Hasso answered. That was five meters, more or less. "Several rows of spearheads stick out in front of the first row of soldiers. If the pikemen stay steady and don't run, knights can't get through. A hedgehog, we call that." The proper term was a Swiss hedgehog, but Zgomot didn't know anything about the Swiss.

The Lord of Bucovin thought hard now. "These men would need training. They would need practice. What would happen if a wizard beset them?"

Again, he saw the problems very clearly. "They would need training, yes," Hasso said. "As for a wizard … A wizard is more likely to go after the catapults and the gunpowder, I think."

"I think so, too," Zgomot said. "But we could use a hedgehog against the Lenelli even without catapults and gunpowder, could we not?"

"No doubt about it, Lord." And no doubt that Zgomot was one plenty sharp cookie indeed. Hasso added, "Archers would need better bows to fight knights. They would need training, too." He knew of English longbows, but he didn't know much about them.

"So this is not something we can do right away?" Zgomot said.

"No," Hasso admitted. "War is a trade like any other. You have to learn how if you want to do it well."

The Lord of Bucovin sighed. "I suppose so. If we get beaten before we can learn, though…" He sighed again. "That only means we should have started sooner, I suppose." He was right, however little good being right might do him.

***

Hasso was eyeing the dragon's tooth in the corridor on the way to the throne room when Drepteaza came up. She stopped when she saw him. "So," she said. "You came back after all, Hasso Pemsel."

"People keep telling me so," Hasso said. "Here I am, so I suppose I have to believe them." He gave her something more than a nod but less than a bow. "I am glad to see you."

"And I'm glad to see you—here," Drepteaza said, which wasn't the same thing at all. "Lord Zgomot was worried about you."

"Yes, I know." Hasso frowned. Something in her voice wasn't quite right. "Were you worried, too?"

"Not as much as Lord Zgomot was," she answered.

Whatever was bothering her, it wasn't aimed at him. "Why are you angry at the Lord of Bucovin?" Hasso asked.

Drepteaza gave him a sidelong glance. "You ought to know."

"Me? What have I got to do with it?" Hasso had thought he was off the hook. Maybe he was wrong.

"I told you—Lord Zgomot feared you would run off, run back to the Lenelli." It all made perfect sense to the priestess.

Not to Hasso. "What does that have to do with you?" he asked.

"You really don't know? You really don't understand?" Drepteaza sounded as if she couldn't believe her ears.

In some exasperation, Hasso shook his head. "If I understood, would I be asking?"

"Well, you never can tell." Drepteaza had to tilt her head back to look up at him. He always wondered if she was looking up his nose. With the air of someone giving a dull person the benefit of the doubt, she said, "If you had run off to the Lenelli, Lord Zgomot would have blamed me."

"You? What could you do about me?" Hasso reached to scratch his head—and banged his knuckles on the ceiling. Dammit, he didn't fit in castles built for

Grenye. "You stay here in Falticeni."

"Yes, and that's part of the problem, too," Drepteaza said. "Lord Zgomot worried you might go back to the blonds because I wouldn't go to bed with you. He was angry at me because I didn't."

"Oh," Hasso said. Yeah, Lord Zgomot was a sharp cookie, all right. Hasso didn't like seeming so transparent, especially to a man he still thought of as more than half a barbarian. Like it or not, he evidently was. He tried to put the best face on it he could: "You see? You don't have anything to worry about. Neither does he." But only because King Bottero's men had orders to kill one Hasso Pemsel on sight. If they didn't … *If they didn't, I'd be back in Drammen now.* Luckily, the Bucovinans didn't know anything about that. Hasso's little sleep spell accomplished so much, anyhow.

"I would screw you to keep you from going back to Bottero and Velona. If that is what it takes, I will do it," Drepteaza said. Hasso's jaw dropped. He knew the Bucovinans were blunt, but he hadn't thought they were *that* blunt. When he didn't say anything, Drepteaza went on, "If you want me to like you while I'm doing it, though, I think you would be asking too much."

"Oh," Hasso said again. Not even *How about that?* or *Isn't that interesting?* seemed safe here.

"You may not care, of course. Some men only care about the screwing itself, not whether anything lies behind it. Some women, too, no doubt, but I think fewer," Drepteaza said. "I got the idea you weren't one of those, or you would have been happy enough with Leneshul or Gishte. But maybe I was wrong."

You can have me. I'll make nice, even if I really want to spit in your eye. Drepteaza was right. Plenty of men would have been happy enough with that bargain, or vain enough to be sure they were such wonderful lovers, she would melt with delight as soon as they got it in.

Had he been offered a woman like Gishte or Leneshul on terms like that, chances were he would have taken her. What she thought of him afterwards wouldn't have mattered to him. With Drepteaza, it did. That was what made her different from the others.

Or maybe I'm just a damn fool. Shit, I wouldn't be surprised.

"If you're ever interested, likely you can find a way to let me know," he said.

She looked at him for a long time. It seemed like a long time, anyway. "Thank you," she said quietly. "I am in your debt, and—under the circumstances—I have no easy way to pay you back." She walked off without waiting for an answer.

"Under the circumstances. *Ja.*" Hasso said it in German, so she wouldn't have understood it even if she heard it. But he didn't think she did. She seemed determined to get away from him as fast as she could.

Under the circumstances … He'd barely found out what Velona's name was before she gave him the time of his life. Drepteaza didn't work like that—not with him, anyway. These people weren't Catholics. There wasn't anything here about priestesses having to be virgins. But…

He'd had his chance, and he'd blown it. He probably was a fool. He sure felt like one right this minute. Well, if he felt like one in the morning he could tell Drepteaza he'd changed his mind, and how about it, cutie?

In the meantime, he went down to the buttery and asked for the biggest beaker of beer in the place. He'd seen this coming, but maybe not so soon. The tapman didn't even blink. He just handed Hasso a drinking horn with enough beer in it to drown a rhino. Hasso had to work to drain it, but drain it he did. Then he thrust it back at the Bucovinan. "Fill it up again," he said. The beer made his brains buzz, but he remembered to use the imperative.

"Whatever you've got, you've got it bad," the tapman said.

"I don't know *what* you're talking about," Hasso said with exaggerated dignity. The native took that for a joke, and laughed. So did Hasso, right up until he started to cry.

XXIII

Hasso had had his share of rocky mornings since splashing down into the marsh by the causeway. This one was a rock like Gibraltar. He staggered down to the buttery for a little porridge and some beer. With luck, no one would talk to him, and he would have the chance to forget how badly he'd hurt himself.

As soon as he saw Scanno, he feared luck wouldn't be with him. As soon as Scanno saw him, he knew all his fears would be realized. "You look like something the cat threw up," the renegade remarked.

His loud, cheerful voice reverberated between Hasso's ears. Anything loud and cheerful inclined Hasso toward suicide, or possibly homicide. "I've been better," he said—quietly.

Scanno couldn't take a hint. "Tied one on, yesterday, didn't you?" he boomed. He wasn't quite so loud as King Bottero would have been, but not from lack of effort.

"How did you guess?" The less Hasso said, the less he gave Scanno to grab on to, the better the chance the other man would shut up and go away. He could dream, couldn't he?

But Scanno wasn't going anywhere. "You're a hero," he said. "What do you need to go out and get plowed for? I mean plowed bad, not plowed happy—you hurt yourself, pal."

"No kidding," Hasso said, and then, "You ought to know. You get drunk all the time yourself."

"Yeah, sure." Scanno didn't waste time telling him he was talking through his hat. "But I like getting drunk and sloppy. You mostly don't. So what did you go and do it for yesterday?"

"None of your business," Hasso said sweetly.

"Gotta be a broad," Scanno said, which was much too perceptive for that early in the morning—and for how bad Hasso felt. "So which broad is it, and how come she won't give you a tumble?"

"Shut up and piss off," Hasso said, more sweetly still. Scanno laughed. Hasso started to get to his feet. He would have relished a fight just then, which went a long way toward saying how hung over he was.

"Take it easy. If I pull out my sword, you're dead," Scanno said.

"If you pull out your sword, I shove it up your ass," Hasso told him.

Scanno might have been a renegade, but he was a Lenello, with a Lenello's prickly pride. Telling him not to do something only made him want to do it more. "You asked for it," he said, and started to draw.

Hasso's hand clamped down on his wrist. Scanno swore and tried to break free. He was a better swordsman than Hasso ever would be. As a wrestler, though, he might as well have been a child. Hasso threw him to the rammed-earth floor of the buttery.

"I'll kill you for that!" Scanno shouted.

As his hand flashed to the hilt of his sword again, Hasso kicked him in the wrist. He didn't know whether he broke it or not. He didn't much care, either, though he wouldn't have been surprised. Scanno howled and clutched at himself. If he was going to do any swordfighting, he would have to do it lefthanded.

"Don't mess with me." Hasso stood over him, breathing hard. "Don't even think about messing with me. You mess with me, I make you sorry you were ever born. Then I set a spell on you and make you wish you were dead."

Scanno plainly weighed knocking his feet out from under him. Hasso would have stomped his hand if he tried. The German's eagerness to do just that must have shown on his face, because Scanno tried no such thing. He kept his defiance to words: "That puke of an Aderno couldn't magic me, and you can't, either."

"Ha!" Hasso laughed harshly. "I tear off your stupid dragon-bone amulet, and *then* I cast my spell."

His mouth was running a good ten meters ahead of his brain. He had no idea what he would say till it popped out. But when he heard himself, his jaw dropped. He forgot all about Scanno. The renegade could have upended him and pounded him to powder. Hasso might not even have noticed.

"Fuck me," he said in German. "Oh, son of a bitch. *Fuck* me."

"What are those funny noises?" Scanno asked, still cradling his injured wrist with his other arm.

"Never mind." Hasso stepped away from him. If Scanno wanted to get up, the *Wehrmacht* officer had stopped caring. He grabbed his mug of beer off the table, emptied it at a gulp, and hurried out of the buttery.

Scanno stared after him. "I think he's gone out of his tree," he said. None of the staring Bucovinans in there argued with him.

***

Hasso knew the way to Lavtrig's chapel. It boasted more fancy decoration than the one in Castle Drammen dedicated to the goddess. That only made him surer he'd got it right before: the less a deity actually did, the more ornament he or she needed to disguise that laziness.

Drepteaza was lighting a silver lamp in front of a gilded statue of the chief Bucovinan god when Hasso walked in. (He thought the statue was gilded, anyhow; it might have been solid gold.) What burned in the lamp smelled of perfume and, under that, hot lard. The priestess glanced up in surprise. "Good morning, Hasso. What is it?" After a moment, she added, "By the look on your face, it must be something important."

"You might say so. Yes, you just might." Hasso nodded emphatically. "We need to talk—right now."

Her mouth tightened. "Are you sure? Or will it only cause more trouble and pain than it eases?"

"It will cause trouble and pain, all right—for the Lenelli," Hasso answered.

"Then I will listen," Drepteaza said at once. "Can we talk here, or do you need to go someplace where no one else can listen?"

He looked around. A couple of other Bucovinan priests, of rank lower than hers, were puttering around in there. "It doesn't matter. They can hear. I think I know why magic doesn't work so well around Falticeni. I think I can make it so Lenello magic doesn't bite on Grenye most of the time. Not always, I suspect, but most of the time."

Her eyes widened. The way she looked at him ... It might almost have been the way a lover eyed her beloved. Almost, but not quite. Hasso made himself not think about that. It didn't matter, not for this. "Well, you've got me interested," Drepteaza said. "Tell me more."

"I do that," Hasso said. "In this palace, you have the tooth of a dragon."

"Yes. It is a treasure. And so?"

"Under the walls here, you have more bones of this dragon, right?"

"Of course we do. We are proud that we managed to kill it. We are lucky that we killed it, too. If we hadn't, it could have wrecked Falticeni worse than the Lenelli might."

"Ja." All Hasso had seen of the late, unlamented dragon was that one fang, but it was plenty to convince him. "You know that magic does not bite on Scanno the renegade?"

"I have heard it, yes," Drepteaza said. "I don't know for myself that it's true, but I have no reason to doubt it."

"It's true. I see—I saw—it for myself. It drove Aderno crazy, trying to figure out why his spell wouldn't work." Hasso remembered how the wizard had experimented on a Grenye woman to find out, too. He didn't say anything about that to Drepteaza. Instead, he went on, "Scanno wears a little piece of dragon bone on a thong around his neck for an amulet."

He wondered if she would make the connection. It seemed obvious to him. But lots of things that seemed obvious to him didn't to the locals, Lenelli and Grenye alike. Sometimes, in this world, they weren't. Sometimes he just had a different way of looking at them. They didn't think as logically as he did. Barring a few clerics, the folk in medieval Germany wouldn't have, either.

By the standards of this world, Drepteaza was an educated woman. By the standards of any world, she was a bright woman. All the same, the frown that crossed her face said she didn't get it right away. And then, all at once, she did.

It was like watching the sun come out from behind clouds. "You think dragon bones block spells," she whispered.

"That's right," Hasso said. "That's just what I think. If all of Lord Zgomot's soldiers have amulets, if their horses have them, if my pots of gunpowder have them, too … If that happens, the Lenelli have to fight fair."

"Fight fair." Drepteaza went on whispering while she echoed him. "That's all we ever dreamt of, since they first came across the ocean and landed on our shores. It would be so wonderful."

"Would be?" Now Hasso echoed her.

As she nodded, the sunshine that blazed from her face faded once more. "We are missing only one thing: dragon bones enough to make the amulets we need. There aren't many dragons, and the ones there are live far to the north. They're hard to find, and even harder to kill. Men don't just hunt dragons. Dragons hunt men, too, and they win more often than we do."

"Somewhere in Bottero's realm lies skeleton of a dead dragon," Hasso said. "Scanno knows where."

Drepteaza stared at him. He watched the sun come out on her face again. "If you are right," she said, "you know what this will do to the Lenelli?"

"I hope I do," Hasso answered. "I want dragon-bone amulet, too." So far, his own little spell was holding its own against Aderno and Velona. Here in Falticeni—which also had dragon-bone amulets of a sort—he could believe it would go on holding. If he headed west again? He wasn't sure what would happen then. He wasn't anxious to find out, either.

"Does Scanno know why the dragon bone is so important?" Drepteaza asked.

"He … may." Hasso explained how he'd brawled with the renegade, and the thoughts the brawl called to mind.

"Riskier to send him back into Bottero's kingdom, then," she said. "If he can tell us where the skeleton lies, we can have people who don't know why they're doing it collect the bones and bring them back to Bucovin."

"You should be a marshal," Hasso said. If the people getting the bones didn't know what they were good for, the Lenelli could torture them or cast spells at them till everything turned blue without finding out. The *Wehrmacht* officer did hold up a warning hand. "Not sure skeleton is still there. Scanno says he's had his amulet for years now."

"Well, if it's gone, we'll think of something else, that's all," Drepteaza said with a shrug. "This is the best chance we have, and we need to grab it." She dropped Hasso a curtsy. "Bucovin is in you debt. I'm sure Lord Zgomot will reward you as you deserve."

"What about you?" Hasso asked.

"It is not my place," Drepteaza said primly. "He is the Lord of Bucovin."

"Too bad. He is not too young and not too pretty," Hasso said.

He wondered if he would make her angry, but she smiled. "And I am too young and too pretty?" she asked.

"You are not *too* young. You are just right. And there is no such thing as too pretty," Hasso answered.

"You don't think so? You might be surprised," Drepteaza said. Sure as hell, Velona came up in Hasso's mind. Was it the goddess dwelling within her that sometimes made her beauty like a blow in the face? Or was it just that she was what she was?

What she was … was gone. Hasso didn't know how many times she had to try to kill him to get the message across. However many times it was, she'd finally crossed the threshold. He truly believed she didn't want him back. He didn't like it, but he believed it.

Drepteaza wasn't in that class—but who was? She was more than pretty enough. Hasso bowed, returning the curtsy. "I would like you to surprise me," he said.

"I bet you would." She wagged a finger at him. "You cooked up this whole scheme against the Lenelli for no better reason than to get me into bed with you."

"How could there be a better reason?" Hasso asked, as innocently as if he didn't mean every word of it.

"Go pour a bucket of cold water on yourself," Drepteaza said. "Then go talk to Lord Zgomot. He is the one who has to set things moving."

"And after that?"

"After that, go pour another bucket of cold water on yourself," Drepteaza answered. But she was still smiling. Hasso clung to that, as a drowning man would cling to … *to an anvil, if he's dumb enough, and odds are you qualify*, the German thought. He went off to see Lord Zgomot.

***

Zgomot was none too young and none too pretty. But he was plenty smart. "If this works," he told Hasso, "it will be the most important weapon we've ever found against the Lenelli."

"Not perfect," Hasso said. "If your army is in a pass and they magic up a landslide, amulets don't stop falling rocks. I am sure of it."

"So am I." The Lord of Bucovin's voice was dry. "We have tried all sorts of things to block their magic. I am not surprised no one thought of dragon bones till now, though. Dragons are just too hard to come by." He spoke to one of his attendants: "Fetch the blond named Scanno here."

"Yes, Lord." The man bobbed his head and hurried away.

When Scanno came in, he had his right arm in a makeshift sling. He took one look at Hasso and stopped dead. "Is this miserable bastard complaining about me, Lord? I ought to complain about him, the—" What followed was a colorful mix of Bucovinan and Lenello.

"He is not complaining of you. He says you know of a dragon's skeleton in Bottero's kingdom. Is that so?"

"I ought to break him in half. I will, too, first chance I get." Scanno didn't shift gears easily.

"That will be later. Answer my question now," Zgomot said. "Do you know where there is a dragon's skeleton in King Bottero's lands?"

Scanno shook his good fist at Hasso. "You were just lucky, you—" The Lord of Bucovin coughed sharply. That seemed to recall Scanno to himself. "Uh, yeah. I know where there is one—or where there was one, anyway, once upon a time. What about it? Why does it matter?"

"You will set down directions for reaching this place. You will do so as exactly as you know how to do. If we succeed in bringing back dragon bones, you will be rewarded as handsomely as we know how. If you lead us astray ... That would be unfortunate. For you."

"Hey, I wouldn't do that, Lord. You know me. I hate Bottero more'n you do, that blowhard pile of pig shit." Scanno's voice took on a certain whine Hasso had heard before—not here, but in Europe during the war. It was the whine of collaborators who knew they had to keep reminding their bosses that they were useful and that they really had switched sides. It was a whine Hasso hoped he would never hear in his own voice.

"You can do what I ask of you, then?" Zgomot pressed.

"Sure. Only I don't know if the bones'll still be there, y'know? I haven't had anything to do with 'em for years and years, so you can't scrag me—well, you shouldn't scrag me—if they aren't, like. It's at the butt end of nowhere, too."

"If my men believe you have led them to the right spot, no harm will come to you—by Lavtrig I swear it," Zgomot said. "There should be some evidence of that, whether the bones remain or not. Is that fair?"

"I guess." But Scanno's whine got stronger. "What's all this about, anyhow? How come you need dragon bones all of a sudden?"

Lord Zgomot looked at Hasso. Hasso looked back at the Lord of Bucovin. He didn't think Zgomot would say anything. But the native did: "What you don't know, Scanno, no one can drag out of you if misfortune comes."

"You've got some kind of fancy reason for not telling me," Scanno said, which was nothing but the truth. His red-tracked eyes swung to Hasso. "And fry my balls if it doesn't have to do with magic." He made as if to touch the amulet he wore, but dropped his hand before it got where it was going. "So you think the dragon bone really does have something to do with blocking spells, eh?"

Hasso and Zgomot looked at each other again. Scanno might have been—was—a renegade with a hollow leg, but that didn't make him a jerk. With a weary sigh, Zgomot said, "Well, you have made sure you will not leave Falticeni until the bone hunters return with their quarry. We cannot have the Lenelli pulling this out of you."

"I wasn't going anywhere, Lord." There was that whine again, this time thick enough to slice. Hasso eyed Scanno with imperfect trust. If Scanno brought word about dragon bones to King Bottero and his wizards, chances were the news would buy his way back into their good graces. And Hasso knew all about the impulse to switch sides. Fortunately, Zgomot didn't know how well he knew it. Scanno went on, "I'll let your people know where they can find the bones. My head will answer if they don't bring back a cartload of 'em, or at least find out where they were."

"That is what I want. Go talk to the scribes. Tell them where the place is. Draw them a map. Do that now, while the thought is fresh in your mind," Zgomot said.

"Whatever you want, Lord." Scanno sketched a salute and hurried off.

As soon as he was out of earshot, Hasso said, "Keep an eye on him, Lord. Keep an eye on his wife, too. Watch them the same way you watch me."

"I intend to keep an eye on him, and an eye on Nechemat as well," Zgomot answered placidly. "And you have an interesting way of putting that."

Shrugging, Hasso said, "I know you keep an eye on me. You need to. I hope I know the difference between what I like and what is. And now you really need to keep an eye on Scanno, too. He knows too much."

"Yes. And he likes to talk, too. You do not have that vice, anyhow," Zgomot said.

"In my world, I know how important keeping secrets is," Hasso said. "Now some secrets to keep here, too."

The Lord of Bucovin nodded. "Yes. I would not have thought that, but yes. And you realize you will not be leaving Falticeni, either, or not without guards, not until the bonehunters have returned."

As steadily as he could, Hasso nodded back. "No one is ever going to trust me again. That is part of what is, too. Not what I like, but what is."

"We will see what we can do about what you like." Zgomot sent Hasso away without explaining himself—he had the ruler's privilege of the last word.

***

Hasso didn't think the Bucovinans had beauty contests. If they did, the girl who came to his room that night would have finished no worse than third runner-up. Her name, she told him, was Tsiam. Seriously, she added, "Lord Zgomot says I am to do anything you want."

"Anything?" Hasso said.

"Anything." Tsiam nodded, but she couldn't keep a touch of fear from her voice. Who could guess what big blond foreigners might like?

"What would you do if it were up to you?" Hasso asked.

"Why, whatever Lord Zgomot told me to do, of course," Tsiam answered.

"Let me say it a different way. Where would you be if Lord Zgomot didn't tell you to be here?"

"With Otset. But he's starting to get tired of me. That's why Zgomot sent me to you."

Otset was the Bucovinan who'd warned King Bottero to turn back not long before the natives laid their trap and captured Hasso. Up till now, Hasso had thought he was pretty smart. But if he was, why would he get tired of a girl as pretty as Tsiam? One more try: "Do you want to be here? If you don't, you don't have to be. You can go."

"You don't want me?" Tsiam seemed—affronted?

"Not unless you want me."

She frowned. "How do we really know till we try?"

And what am I supposed to say to that? Hasso wondered. He found only one thing, and he said it: "Come on, then, and we try."

Try they did. When it was over, neither one of them would have called it a success. Tsiam said, "You were thinking about someone else, weren't you?"

"Afraid so," Hasso answered. "I'm sorry. Don't mean for it to show so much."

She shrugged. "Nothing much to do about it. Do you want me to bother coming back?"

"No. It's all right. Tell Lord Zgomot I am not angry at you—that is the truth. I thank you for your kindness. Tell Lord Zgomot I thank him for his. But this is not what I am after."

"All right. I hope you find it, whatever it is." Tsiam quickly dressed and slipped out of the room. Hasso made a fist and slammed it down onto the mattress. That didn't do him any good, either.

He was eating a glum breakfast the next morning when Drepteaza set her bowl of mush down by his. "By Lavtrig, why doesn't Tsiam suit you?" she asked. "She's much prettier than I ever will be. And after spending a couple of years learning to please Otset, she's bound to be better in bed, too."

"Then why doesn't he want her any more?" Hasso asked.

"He's had time to get bored with her. You gave her one night."

Hasso shrugged. "She isn't what I want." He paused to spoon up some more of the mush, and to wash it down with bad Bucovinan beer. None of that changed his mind, so he went on, "You are. You know that."

"Yes. I do know that. It only makes things harder for both of us." Drepteaza looked down at the rough planks of the tabletop.

"I'm sorry. Not sorry, but—you know." Again, Hasso hated stumbling through a language he didn't speak well. "Curse it, do you fall in love just where you are supposed to?"

"I haven't fallen in love at all, so I can't really answer that," Drepteaza answered. "But you, Hasso Pemsel—it seems to me that you look for the worst places to fall in love, and then go and do that."

If she'd mocked him, he would have gone up like jellied gasoline. But she didn't. She simply sounded as if she was telling him how things looked to her. And maybe she wasn't so far wrong. He doubted he would have had a happy ending with Velona even if the Bucovinans didn't capture him. Something else would have gone wrong, or she would have found somebody new. And then … No, that wouldn't have been pretty. It might have been lethal. Velona herself had warned him.

He didn't want to think about Velona. It still hurt. So did thinking about

Drepteaza, but not the same way. Stubbornly, he said, "You are not a bad place to fall in love. You are the best place I know."

"Here," she said: one quiet word that hit him the way a *Panzerfaust* blew the turret off a Soviet T-34. His face must have shown as much, for she softened it a little: "Maybe I would not be such a bad place for you if I felt for you what you feel for me. But I don't. I almost wish I did. It would make things easier for Bucovin."

"This is not about Bucovin. I do plenty for Bucovin."

"I know you've done plenty for Bucovin—more than I could," Drepteaza said quickly. "But you're right. This has nothing to do with that. This is just about us."

"No us to be about," Hasso said, which held more truth than grammar.

Drepteaza understood it anyway, and nodded to show she did. "*That* is what this is about—why there is no us," she said.

"*Us* takes two," Hasso said. "Without two, forget it. If you don't like me—"

"It's not even that," she broke in. "By now, I know you as well as anyone in Falticeni is likely to." She was bound to be right, especially with the qualification. A couple of people back in Drammen, or wherever they were these days … But that was another story, and looked as if it always would be. The priestess went on, "You are brave. You are not stupid—anything but stupid. You are not a bad man. If only—"

"If only I don't look the way I do," he broke in.

She nodded. "Yes, that might do it," she said.

"Maybe I should wear a mask. Maybe I should walk on my knees." Hasso was joking, and yet he wasn't.

Drepteaza understood that, too. "You are trying to be as difficult as you can," she said, her voice full of mock severity—or maybe it wasn't mock at all.

Hasso bowed. "At your service," he said. "Or I would be, only…"

"Yes. Only," Drepteaza said. "I *am* sorry. If I could do anything about it, I would, and that is the truth."

He thought about telling her he was such a wonderful lover he would make her forget all about the way he looked. If he were speaking German, he might have tried it. In Bucovinan, it was bound to come out wrong. He didn't even want to imagine it in Lenello. Lenello was what he was doing his best to stay away from.

Much better not to try a line like that than to botch it. So he said, "No mask and knees, eh? Maybe I make a magic to look like one of your folk instead." He remembered, too late, that Velona had done something like that. He waited for Drepteaza to throw it in his face.

She didn't—not directly, anyhow. She said, "A spell like that might not work in Falticeni. And even if you did use magic, that would remind me of what you… what you look like. I know it is not what you are. But what you look like matters, too. What a woman looks like matters to you, doesn't it?"

"Yes." He wished he could have said no, but he knew damn well he wasn't that good a liar. He could add, "A woman doesn't have to be big and blond to be pretty for me. This is the truth." He held up his right hand with first two fingers upraised, as if taking an oath back in Germany.

"I believe you," Drepteaza said; he couldn't tell if she understood the gesture. "But most men are less fussy than most women when it comes to such things. Often enough, even a Grenye will do."

"You talk about the Lenelli. I am no Lenello, no matter what I look like."

"You look like one, no matter what you are." The old impasse. *You're ugly. Go away.*

"I can't help what I am," he muttered.

"And I can't help what I feel," Drepteaza said. "I almost wish—"

"What?"

"Nothing. Let it go."

"When you start to say something like that, you should finish."

She sighed. "I suppose you're right. I almost wish I could help what I feel. It would keep you from mooning around the way you do. At least you don't paw me all the time, the way a real Lenello would. If you did, I would have to learn to throw you over my shoulder. And who could I learn that from but you? You see what a problem it would be."

He couldn't help smiling. She had a barbed wit when she felt like turning it loose. "If you want to learn to throw people, even people my size, I can teach you."

He thought she would say no, not wanting to give him any excuse to get his hands on her. But she nodded. "That might be useful. Lenelli aren't the only troublemakers around here. We have thieves and robbers of our own."

"Sometimes, if someone comes with a sword or knife, better to give what he wants," Hasso said. "Don't be stupid. You can get killed for no good reason if you are stupid."

"I understand," Drepteaza answered. "Is there ever a good reason to get killed?"

"You ask a soldier, remember. Sometimes it's worse for everyone else—and for you, too—if you run away instead." How many men, friends and enemies alike, had Hasso seen making that same unhappy choice? A lot of soldiers—most of them—died from being in the wrong place at the wrong time. But some chose their time and place, and died trying to keep the bastards on the other side from doing something nasty. And sometimes it made a difference, and sometimes it didn't. You couldn't know ahead of time. You did what you did, that was all.

"Am I big enough to throw you around if I have to?" Drepteaza asked, derailing his train of thought.

"To throw someone my size, anyway. I throw Lenelli much bigger than me. Maybe throwing me is harder, because I know what you do before you do it," Hasso answered.

"I see." She nodded. "How does someone small throw someone larger, though?"

"Size is not the trick. The trick is knowing what to do." Hasso muttered to himself. He wanted to say *leverage*, but he had no idea how, either in Bucovinan or in Lenello.

"I hope you're right. Let me go change into breeches, so I can get thrown around without embarrassing myself."

Hasso laughed in surprise. "What about the baths?"

"The baths are the baths. This is different," Drepteaza said.

"Why?"

"I don't know. I never thought about it, but it is. Doesn't your country have customs that wouldn't make any sense to an outsider? The gods know the Lenelli do."

"Maybe we do. I'm sure we do." Hasso sketched a salute. "All right. Go change, then. I meet you in the fencing practice room."

"See you there." Drepteaza got up and left the table.

As Hasso walked down the corridor, he almost ran into Dumnez. His driver said, "Hello. I'm going to be one of the people getting dragon bones. We set out tomorrow."

"No!" The *Wehrmacht* officer clapped a hand to his forehead. "You can't! You mustn't! Somebody screws up to let you."

"Why shouldn't I? I want to give the Lenelli one in the teeth, same as everybody else does," Dumnez said. "This has to do that some kind of way. It's too important not to."

"But you know about gunpowder. You shouldn't go where they might catch you." Security! Hasso was sure Lord Zgomot would see it when it got pointed out to him. He'd worried about Scanno, who could tell the Lenelli just why Bucovin wanted their dragon bones. The people who were going didn't know that, which was all to the good. But Zgomot hadn't thought about other security worries.

Dumnez looked mutinous. "They won't catch me."

"True. You don't go, so they don't catch you," Hasso said. Dumnez tried to slip past him, but Hasso grabbed his arm. For a moment, he wondered if he would need his dirty-fighting talents. Taking on somebody he outweighed by more than thirty kilos wasn't close to fair, but if Dumnez grabbed a knife.... To forestall him, Hasso added, "We talk to Lord Zgomot. If you don't listen to me, you listen to him, right?"

"He won't waste time on the likes of me," Dumnez said.

"He does—he will—for this," Hasso said. "Come on."

He had to talk his way past the stewards and chamberlains who shielded any ruler from the slings and arrows of outrageous reality. But, even though gunpowder wasn't magic, it was a magic word. It got Hasso and Dumnez through to the Lord of Bucovin in short order. Zgomot listened, pondered, and spoke: "The foreigner is right, Dumnez. You stay here. Is anyone else who knows about gunpowder going?"

"I don't think so, Lord," Dumnez replied.

"Go find out. If anybody is, pull him off," Zgomot said. "Good thing you bumped into Hasso. We don't want to take chances we don't have to." Dumnez gave the *Wehrmacht* officer a sour look, but he didn't argue with his sovereign.

And Hasso wasn't very late to the fencing room. He apologized to Drepteaza, explaining what had happened. "That wouldn't have been good," she agreed, and then got down to business. "So. You're going to throw me around, are you?"

"Yes. You know how to land soft?"

"I think so."

"All right. We go slow at first."

He showed her how to flip a man. He didn't take any undue liberties with her person when he flipped her. He was sure he bruised her, though she did land well. She was strong for her size, and well coordinated. He'd thought she would catch on fast, and he was right. It wasn't hard—grab, turn, duck, twist, heave.

"Now I come at you," he said, and he did. When she flipped him, he didn't do anything to try to stop her. He went over on his back, and got a bruise or two of his own.

"You let me do that." Her voice was accusing. "You even helped."

"Well, sure," he said as he climbed to his feet. "You have to learn." He tried not to think about the feel of her against him. "I went easy with King Bottero's master-at-arms at first, too."

"So he knows these flips?" Drepteaza said.

"Not any more. He's dead."

"Oh." That seemed to satisfy her. "Let's try it again. Faster this time?"

"A little," Hasso agreed. He went over her shoulder and thudded down. "Oof! That's good."

Drepteaza smiled. "It is! Again!"

Hasso picked up more bruises. He couldn't have cared less. "You will be sudden death on two legs," he said. Drepteaza positively beamed.

XXIV

When Hasso started working with gunpowder and catapults, Lord Zgomot changed his mind and suggested that he move away from Falticeni for a while. Hasso didn't say no. The Lord of Bucovin had two excellent reasons on his side. One was not showing everybody in a good-sized city what Bucovin was up to. The other was not unnerving everybody in a good-sized city with strange booms and blasts.

The place where Hasso ensconced himself was more than a farm and less than an estate. Maybe it was as close as the Bucovinans could come to a Lenello-style estate. It had a big, fancy house—but one with a thatched roof. Several peasant families who worked the fields and tended stock in the meadows lived in cottages not far from the big house. The house and land belonged to Zgomot himself. The place was more than thirty kilometers away from Falticeni—far enough to let Hasso and his men make as much noise as they needed to.

Rautat and Drepteaza went with him. The underofficer translated for him with carpenters and catapult makers when his Bucovinan ran dry. The priestess did some of that, too. She also taught him more of the natives' language. And she seemed intent on learning all the dirty fighting he knew how to teach.

"'Sudden death on two legs,'" she quoted. "That's what I want."

"You're on your way," Hasso said. She wasn't as strong as he was, and she didn't have his reach. But she was a long way from a weakling, and she was fast as a striking snake. She could hurt him, and she had, more than once. He'd knocked her about, too; once you started practicing anywhere close to full speed, that was bound to happen. Thumping down on thick grass in a meadow hurt less than the rammed-earth floor of the fencing room had.

The more-or-less estate didn't stink the way Falticeni did—another advantage of moving to the country. Sure, it had a dungheap and some odorous privies. But it didn't have tens of thousands of people crapping and pissing and not worrying much about how to dispose of the filth. Bucovinans bathed more than Lenelli, but their notions of sanitation were just as rudimentary as those of the blonds.

Once Hasso got the carpenters to understand what he wanted, they had no trouble mounting catapults on wheeled carts. Horses—or even donkeys—could pull them. "Field artillery," he said happily. Back in the world he'd left behind, you couldn't live without it … not very long, anyway. The *Wehrmacht* always used as much as it could. The Red Army had guns in carload lots.

Yes, the field artillery was easy. The ammo wasn't. Hasso rapidly found earthenware pots wouldn't do. He couldn't fuse them precisely enough. If a pot hit the ground before a spark hit the gunpowder, it smashed like a broken plate. That wasted far too much precious gunpowder to work.

"Have to be metal," he said. "Bronze or iron."

"Expensive!" Rautat said in dismay. He wasn't kidding, either. Part of Hasso still took an industrial economy for granted. Where everybody did everything by hand … You didn't get anywhere near so much, and what you did get cost a lot more.

But he answered, "Not as expensive as losing to the Lenelli, eh?"

"Lord Zgomot will have to say," Rautat told him. "I can't order smiths to start making these things, not by myself I can't."

"Send to him," Hasso said. "We find out. If he says no, we go back to Falticeni."

Zgomot must have said yes, because several bronzesmiths and ironsmiths came out to the estate to find out what Hasso wanted. He explained. One of the smiths tapped his forehead, as if to say this foreigner was out of his mind. Hasso let the short, wide-shouldered men watch an ordinary clay pot full of gunpowder blow up. One of them pissed himself in surprise and fear. After that, they didn't think he was crazy any more.

"Hollow balls," one of them said. "Can we make halves and solder them together? That would be a lot faster."

Hasso shook his head. "Not strong enough, I'm afraid."

"Can we rivet halves together?" another smith asked. "That should hold them till your magic works."

"It isn't magic," Hasso said wearily. "But yes, try riveting." It wouldn't be as fast as soldering, but he could see that it would be a lot faster than making hollow spheres from scratch. The bronzesmiths looked especially pleased. They could cast their hemispheres instead of beating them out. The Bucovinans knew how to make and work wrought iron, but they couldn't cast it.

Yet another smith asked, "How many do you need, and how soon do you need them?"—the basic questions of war.

As many as you can make and a hundred more besides, and I need them all yesterday. That was any field officer's automatic answer. Here, though, caution looked like a good idea. "How many do you think you can make? How fast?" he asked in return.

They had to put their heads together before they gave him an answer. Some of them were scratching their heads, too—they weren't used to thinking in terms of numbers. When they did speak up, he was pleasantly surprised. Even cutting their claims in half, he'd have enough shells to fight a battle soon enough to give the Lenelli a proper greeting.

"You really think you can do that?" he asked.

"We do. By Lavtrig, we do," answered the man who spoke for them. He had impressive dignity—and scarred, gnarled hands that were even more convincing.

All the same, Hasso pressed: "Lord Zgomot is not happy if you promise one thing and give something else."

"We will not disappoint the Lord of Bucovin," said the senior smith, whose name was Unaril.

"Go, then. Do it," Hasso said. And maybe they would, and maybe they wouldn't. If they didn't, Bucovin would fight the Lenelli the same old way, and chances were she'd take it on the chin.

But the big blond bastards would have a harder time if Zgomot's men got back with the dragon bones. As soon as that went through Hasso's mind, he wondered, *Did I just think of the Lenelli as big blond bastards?* He didn't wonder long. *Damned if I didn't.* Maybe he really had switched sides after all, even inside himself.

And wouldn't that be weird? he thought.

***

A double handful of bronze shells came to the estate. Field Marshal Manstein would have laughed his ass off as soon as he took one look at them. Hell, so would Frederick the Great, for that matter. When you measured them by the standards of an art that had had some time to grow, they were somewhere between funny and pathetic.

When you measured them against nothing at all, though, they suddenly didn't seem half bad.

He didn't load them with gunpowder right away. He had the catapult crews practice flinging them while they were empty. They went somewhere close to 400 meters. He had to hope that would be good enough. He thought it would, for one battle, anyway. The Lenelli would be looking for buried pots of gunpowder—and he intended to use those, too. Artillery would take them by surprise … unless they had better spies than he thought.

Some of the shells dented a little when they came down. A few rivets popped. A smith who'd stayed behind repaired them—and sneered at the workmanship. Hasso only grinned at him. The *Wehrmacht* officer hadn't imagined everything would go perfectly. The Bucovinans were doing things they'd never tried before. He was pleased they'd done as well as they had.

He filled a shell with gunpowder and lead balls—the Bucovinans had no trouble making those, because they used slingers as well as archers. He jammed down the stopper: a wooden plug with a hole drilled through for the length of fuse. And then he assembled everybody by the catapult to watch as the shell went downrange on the meadow he'd been bombarding.

"As soon as I light the fuse, you shoot," he told the catapult crew. "I light, I yell 'Now!' and you shoot. No waiting, not even a little. You understand?"

"What happens if we're slow?" a Bucovinan asked.

"You get a lead ball in the face, that's what. Or in the nuts." *And so do I,* Hasso thought. He wished for an 81mm mortar and a trained crew. Since wishing—surprise!—failed to produce them, he got back to business. "You ready?" The Bucovinans solemnly nodded. Hasso waved a stick of punk to heat up the coal. Then he brought it down on the fuse, which sizzled to life. "*Now!*" he shouted. He didn't throw himself flat, not because he trusted the catapult crew but because the natives didn't know enough to do the same. If something went wrong, the survivors would think he took unfair advantage.

Swoosh! The catapult arm shot forward, hurling the shell far across the meadow—but not so far as a lighter, emptier one. It was just about to hit the ground when fire touched the main charge.

Boom! Hasso whooped. If he could do it that well all the time, he'd make one hell of a gunner. Then he stopped whooping, because a catapult man yelped and grabbed his leg. Blood ran out between his fingers. One of the lead balls had flown all the way back here. Hasso hadn't dreamt that could happen.

"Lie down," he said. "Let me see it."

"Hurts," the catapult man said as he obeyed.

"I bet it does." When the German got a good look at the wound, he breathed easier. It was a gash, not a puncture—the ball must have grazed the Bucovinan going by. If he bled freely, chances were he wouldn't get lockjaw. If he did, neither Hasso nor anybody else in this world could do anything for him.

One of the other catapult men handed Hasso a rag for a bandage. It looked pretty clean. He put it on. One of these days, he would have to talk about boiling bandages. No time now, and he didn't figure it would matter here.

"Can you walk?" he asked the wounded Bucovinan.

"I … think so." The fellow got to his feet. He limped, but he managed. "Yeah, it's not too bad. Thanks, foreigner. You tied it up good."

"Sure." Hasso always would be a foreigner. That didn't mean he enjoyed getting reminded of it.

The catapult man hadn't meant any offense. "You've got a demon of a weapon there. I never figured it could bite from so far off. You weren't kidding when you said close would be worse."

"No, I wasn't kidding," Hasso agreed. Why had the other man wondered if he was? Because he'd never seen anything like this, that was why. Hasso understood as much. Well, now the native hadn't just seen it—he'd felt it. And he was a believer.

Everybody except the wounded man walked out into the meadow to see what was left of the shell. What was left was about what Hasso had expected: some sharp, twisted shards of bronze casing, and not much more.

"Lavtrig! Every time you throw one of these metal balls, you waste it." The smith who'd stayed behind at the estate sounded appalled.

"Not waste." Hasso shook his head. "We hurt the enemy with it."

"But you can't use it again," the smith said. "The metal flies once, and it's gone."

Gone for good. Metal isn't cheap, you know."

"Neither is losing a war," Hasso pointed out once more. "You want your smithy burned? You want to get killed? You want your daughter raped and killed? You want another Muresh?"

"Of course not," the Bucovinan answered. "But I don't want to go bankrupt, either. We could win the war and throw all our metal away. Then where would we be? Does Lord Zgomot really know this is how things are?"

"Yes," Hasso said, a one-word reply that made the smith blink.

"Hasso is right. We have to do this. Lord Zgomot says so, and I think he is right, too," Drepteaza said. "The other choice is giving up more land and more people to the Lenelli. Do you want that?"

"No, priestess," the smith answered. He would argue with Hasso. The German was just … a foreigner. But he wouldn't argue with Drepteaza. He assumed she knew what she was talking about because she was a priestess.

Well, Drepteaza commonly did know what she was talking about. But that was because she was Drepteaza, not because she was a priestess. Hasso understood as much. He thought Drepteaza did, too, which was a measure of her good sense. The smith, by contrast, had not a clue.

"Shall we send off another one?" Rautat asked.

"Maybe not right now," Hasso said. "First we make sure our wounded can do what they need to do."

"I'm all right," the injured catapult man said.

"It can wait. It should wait," Hasso said. "One thing at a time."

"Suits me—and not because of my leg," the catapult man said, wrinkling his nose. "Smells like demon farts around here."

"How do you know what demon farts smell like?" That wasn't Hasso, even if he had the thought. It was Drepteaza.

"Well, I don't, not really," the native soldier admitted. "But it smells like what I think demon farts ought to smell like."

"Does it smell that way to you, too, Hasso?" Drepteaza asked.

He shook his head. "It reminds me of fireworks." The key word came out in German. He had to explain what fireworks were, starting just about from scratch—the Bucovinans had no idea. "They can light up the sky with flames of different colors," he finished. "Best at night, of course."

"How do you make flames different colors?" Rautat asked. "Flames are flames, right?"

Hasso didn't know how pyrotechnic engineers did what they did. But Drepteaza said, "Haven't you seen how salt makes a flame yellower?"

"Bits of copper or copper ore can turn flames green," the smith added.

"You should know that, Rautat," Hasso said. "You were a smith."

"An ironsmith, not a coppersmith or bronzesmith," Rautat said. "That's why I went to learn Lenello tricks. Iron is the coming thing. I wanted to see what the blond bastards knew that we don't."

The coming thing. Hasso hid his smile. Rautat wasn't wrong, not for the way things were in Bucovin. And if iron had come to Germany a couple of thousand years earlier ... well, so what? Hasso damn well wasn't in Germany any more, and he never would be again. A damn good thing, too. He was better off here. There he would have got killed. Or, if he was very lucky—or maybe very unlucky—he would have ended up a Russian POW.

He supposed he was still a Bucovinan POW. But the Ivans wouldn't have hurt any V-2 engineers they caught. They needed what those fellows knew. The Bucovinans needed what Hasso knew. If good treatment was the price of getting it, they were willing to pay. The Reds were probably doing the same for their German engineers. Come to that, the Amis were bound to be acting the same way.

Love got stale or flamed out. No one knew that better than Hasso these days. Common interests, on the other hand, could last. *They'd better*, the *Wehrmacht* officer thought. If they didn't, he was dead.

***

Without the least bit of warning, flat-footed, Drepteaza tried to kick Hasso in the crotch. He sprang back out of danger—one of the rules when they trained together was that you had to be alert every second. She'd never actually got him in the balls. Bruises on his hip and thigh where he'd had to twist away instead of jumping back said she'd come close more than once.

She looked disappointed that she hadn't made him sing soprano this time. "What did I do wrong?" she asked.

"Nothing," Hasso said. "But I know you are dangerous, so I watch you all the time. When you move, I move, too."

"You're fast," she said. "I didn't think anybody that big could be that quick. I'm sure you're faster than most of the Lenelli who live in Bucovin."

She didn't say *than most of the other Lenelli*. Hasso couldn't remember when she'd last said that. It had been a while, anyhow. He shrugged. "They can do things I can't. I am never going to be anything much with a sword. They learn when they're little. I learn now. They have too much head start. But this? This I know how to do."

"You must," she said. "You—" She tried to kick him again. Again, she gave nothing away beforehand. If he hadn't suspected she might try to give him a double shot, she might have done what she aimed to do—leave him writhing in the tall grass clutching at himself.

Instead of leaping away or twisting, he grabbed her right foot and yanked it up farther than she'd intended it to go. She let out a startled squawk as she lost her balance and went over on her back.

He sprang on her and pinned her to the ground. She tried to knee him when he did—he really had trained her well—but he didn't let her do that, either. "Got you this time," he said, his face a few centimeters above hers.

She nodded. "Yes, you did. Now will you let me up? You're squashing me flat."

"Sorry." He shifted so he took more of his weight on his knees and elbows. But then he said, "I let you up in a little bit," and leaned down and kissed her.

If she'd wanted to nail him then, she could have done it. He realized as much just after his lips met hers, which was exactly too late. If she'd twisted away and screamed ... Well, nobody was anywhere close by, but someone likely would have heard her. People would have come running. And then he wouldn't have got hurt—he would have died: chances were, a millimeter at a time.

She didn't do either of those things. For a couple of seconds, she didn't do anything at all. He feared it would be a hopeless botch like the one in the garden back in Falticeni. But then she kissed him back—after a fashion. It was the most... experimental kiss he'd had since he was a kid and learning how himself.

The way she did it convinced him he'd better not push anything too hard. He drew back instead, and asked, "Well?"

Drepteaza stared up at him. "Not ... so bad," she said, sounding honestly surprised. "I didn't used to think I would ever want a big blond to touch me in any way. But with you teaching me to fight ... You had to touch me for that. And it was what it was, and after a while I didn't worry about it any more. And this, what you just did, what we just did, wasn't so bad after all."

Hasso bent toward her again. "How about this?" he asked softly.

This time, the kiss got down to business. She knew how, all right. She hadn't been sure she wanted to. Now she seemed to be. Quite a while later, when their lips parted, she murmured, "That was pretty good."

"*Ja*," Hasso said, and she smiled. So did he, no doubt like an idiot. He went on, "I want to do this for a very long time."

"You haven't known me for a *very* long time." Drepteaza was relentlessly precise. "What else have you wanted to do?"

He did his best to show her. He hadn't thought he would be her first, and he wasn't. He did hope he pleased her. He wasn't sure, because she didn't show what she felt as extravagantly as Velona. That he should think of Velona now, even for an instant ... only showed he really had it bad. Well, he did, dammit.

Afterwards, he had no idea what to say. Before he could come up with anything, Drepteaza beat him to the punch: "There. Are you happier now?"

He started to laugh. That was as blunt as usual. "Yes," he answered. "Are you?"

She frowned, thinking it over the way she so often did. If she said no, he thought he would sink down into the ground. But, thoughtful still, she nodded. "Yes, I am. I don't know whether I will be if I bear a wizard's child three seasons from now, but that is in the hands of the gods."

Could a halfbreed work magic? Hasso thought so, but he wasn't sure. He also wasn't sure a German-Grenye halfbreed would be the same as a Lenello-Grenye halfbreed. Since he couldn't do anything about that, or about whether Drepteaza would catch, he asked her, "Was it all right for you?"

If you have to ask, you won't like the answer. That was a rule as ancient as women. Drepteaza, though, was out of the ordinary. She kept so much of herself to herself.

She nodded now—slowly, but she nodded. "You were ... sweeter than I thought you would be," she said. "You really meant it."

"I said so," Hasso replied. "What I say, I mean."

"It would seem so," Drepteaza admitted. "But I told you before—I know a lot of men will say anything to get a woman to go to bed with them."

"Not in bed," Hasso said with dignity—and with precision of his own. "On the grass."

"So we are," Drepteaza said. "We ought to get dressed, too, before someone comes over to find out why we're not trying to ruin each other."

"Wait," Hasso said, and kissed her again. The kiss took on a life of its own, but not quite enough to start a second round. *I'm getting old, dammit,* the German thought. Even if he was still this side of forty, two in a row were only a memory.

She shook her head as she put on her breeches and tunic. "You are a very strange man, Hasso Pemsel."

He shrugged. He couldn't very well tell her she was wrong, not here, even if he would have been ordinary enough in the *Reich*. "I come from another world. What do you expect?"

As she had a habit of doing, she answered what he'd meant for a rhetorical question: "I expected you to act the way you look. I expected you to act like a Lenello. If I'd doubted you were one, I'd be sure you weren't now."

How did she mean that? Did she know how Lenello men made love? Did she know from experience? *Do I want to find out?* Hasso wondered, and decided he didn't.

He pulled on his own trousers. "A good thing I see—uh, saw—those kicks coming," he said. "Otherwise, we never do this now. If both those kicks get home, maybe we never do this forever."

"I just have to practice more," Drepteaza said sweetly. And how the hell did she mean *that*? Once more, Hasso decided he didn't want to find out.

***

Even if no one came out on the meadow and caught them *in flagrante*, the rest of the Bucovinans didn't need long to figure out that Hasso and Drepteaza had become lovers. Rautat spoke for them: "You make her unhappy, you big blond prick, and I'll cut you off at the knees so we're the same size. Then I'll really give you the whipping you deserve."

"I don't want to make her unhappy," Hasso protested.

"You'd better not," the underofficer growled. "She's special, and not just 'cause she's a priestess, either."

"You think I don't think so, too?" Hasso said.

Rautat snorted. "Who knows what you think? Who knows *if* you think?"

"I love you, too," Hasso said.

"Fat chance," Rautat said with another snort. "Are we just about finished here? Can we go back to Falticeni pretty soon? We've done all the fooling around we need. We have to fight pretty soon—or don't you think Bottero will come after us again as quick as he can?"

"Of course he will," Hasso answered. "You know that as well as I do."

"Well, no." Rautat shook his head. "You've met the man. You know him. I haven't. I don't. Being on the same battlefield with him doesn't count."

Hasso hadn't just met Bottero—he liked him. That had nothing to do with anything, not any more. Hasso thought Bottero's enmity was only professional, not personal like Velona's. When it came to wanting him dead, that might matter a pfennig's worth. Or it might not. He stuck to business, saying, "We can go back to Falticeni. You're right—we've done what we came here to do."

"What about the dragon bones? Have you heard anything?" Rautat asked.

"Not a word," Hasso said. "You?"

"Nothing," the underofficer answered. "I wonder which of us they'd tell. I wonder if they'd tell either one of us."

"They'd better. We need to know," Hasso said. "And the people going after the dragon bones better get out before King Bottero's army marches. If they come after, it's too late."

"Good point. They can make amulets for themselves and be safe from Lenello magic, not that that does us any good," Rautat said.

"They can't even do that," Hasso said. "They don't know what the dragon bones are for. They only know Lord Zgomot wants them."

"You're right. That's your fault. We never would have worried about stuff like that by ourselves," Rautat said.

"One more reason the Lenelli keep beating you," Hasso said. "Their security isn't very good. If yours is worse…" He rolled his eyes, but then he brightened. "The dragon bones should ward Zgomot's men whether they know why or not, come to think of it."

"Hmm. Yeah, I suppose so." The Bucovinan paused, eyeing Hasso. "You know something? You're starting to speak our language pretty well. Not like you grew up in Falticeni or anything, but pretty well. I think it's better than your Lenello by now."

"Maybe," Hasso said. "If it is, I have to thank you and Drepteaza."

Rautat leered at him. "Well, if you tried sweet-talking the priestess in Lenello, she'd make you sorry, and we both know it."

Hasso thought about that. Drepteaza angry wouldn't be an erupting volcano like Velona. She'd make him think a glacier had crushed him instead. Fire or ice? Better not to provoke either. The German said, "I know you think I'm stupid. I'm not *that* stupid. Hope not, anyhow."

"I used to think you were stupid," Rautat said. "Part of it was because you didn't talk very well, not in any language I know. I've found out different since. Stupid you're not, but you are bloody strange."

"Everybody says that. You'd be bloody strange in my world, too," Hasso answered. Landing in his world, Rautat wouldn't know the customs or speak the language. He'd end up in trouble before he could learn. How could he help it?

"I'd be strange anywhere," the underofficer said, not without pride. He wasn't wrong, either. Hasso laughed and clapped him on the back.

The German knew how to deal with Rautat. He'd handled plenty of *Feldwebels* in his *Wehrmacht* days. The language here changed. So did a few of the details. The art as a whole? No.

Dealing with Drepteaza as a lover … That he had to learn one step at a time. It wasn't simple, either. There were moments when he felt like a man trying to defuse a booby-trapped bomb. The priestess was more private and much more complicated than Velona had been. When Drepteaza was unhappy, she'd retreat into herself. She would stay polite all the time. If you weren't paying attention, you wouldn't notice anything was wrong. Then you would lose more points for not noticing.

Hasso complained only once. She laughed at him. "This is what you spent so long mooning over and chasing. Now you have it, and you find out it isn't exactly what you expected? What am I supposed to do about that? I am what I am. I can't be anything different, not for you or anyone else."

He shut up after that. She was telling the truth. And she had to put up with him, too. Well, no—in fact, she didn't. She could dump him any time she pleased.

But she didn't do that. It was as if she'd decided that, as long as they were going to be lovers, she would see just where that led. "Your world must be a funny place," she said once, as they lay side by side in a cot that wasn't really big enough for both of them.

"Why?" he asked.

"You are a fighting man. Rautat says you are one of the most dangerous fighting men he ever saw. From everything I've seen, he's right. But you are the gentlest lover any woman here would ever have known."

He grunted. Velona never accused him of every such thing. Everybody, he supposed, was different with a different partner.

"Why is that?" Drepteaza persisted.

"Partly, it's you." He pursued his own thought. Drepteaza made a small, dubious noise. "It is," Hasso insisted. "And partly, men and women in my world are closer to equals than they are here."

"Oh?" That intrigued her in a new way, as he hoped it might. "How? Why?"

Later, he wondered whether Bucovinan—and maybe even Lenello—men would have reason to swear at him. As best he could, he explained how women's rights had flowered in his world over the past hundred years.

Drepteaza reacted the way he knew she would: "That sounds wonderful! Why isn't it like that here?"

"I don't know," Hasso answered.

"You say it wasn't always like that where you come from? It used to be more the way it is here?" Drepteaza waited for him to nod, then went on, "How are things in your kingdom different now from the way they used to be?"

"Machines," Hasso said automatically. "We have machines to do the things magic can do here. But the machines do it better. They do it for everybody, not just for a few rich people. And with lots of machines, it doesn't matter so much if men are bigger than women. It doesn't matter so much if men are stronger. What you know, what you can do—that matters."

"Women are still the ones who have babies, though," Drepteaza said.

"*Ja.*" Hasso nodded. "That is one reason there are still differences. But women have babies more when they want in my world." He explained about rubbers.

"How do you make them?" Drepteaza demanded. "They would be marvelous!" The Bucovinans—and the Lenelli—used pulling out in time for contraception, when they bothered to pull out in time. They also used blowjobs and buggery, which were more fun for men than for women. Women here had lots of children. Lots of kids died here, but lots were born.

Hasso spread his hands. "No idea." He hadn't seen anything like rubber here. And had the locals had it, he didn't know how to make it thin enough for condoms. There were the ones they called skins, though.... "Sheep gut might do."

"Like a sausage casing." Drepteaza giggled and reached for him. "*Just* like a sausage casing." Even if he didn't usually manage two rounds close together, he surprised himself and did that night. Afterwards, he slept like a log.

The next morning, as they got ready to go back to Falticeni, Drepteaza kept going on about equality for women, and about condoms. She didn't seem to be able to think or talk about anything else. Hasso knew he'd changed things here with his knowledge of war. He hadn't thought what he knew about other things in his lost world might change them here, too.

Listening to Drepteaza talk, he could tell he'd been naive. She was bubbling with excitement, as if she wanted to pack a hundred years into a day. Hasso wasn't the only one listening to her, either. Rautat sidled up to him and asked, "Why is the priestess all loopy? What kind of bullshit have you been feeding her?"

"I tell her how things are in my world," Hasso answered uneasily.

"How the broads rule the roost? How nobody there ever gets knocked up, and they find babies under the cabbage leaves?" Rautat was exaggerating—but, if you listened to Drepteaza for a while, you wouldn't think he was exaggerating by much. He eyed Hasso. "If half of what she says is so, you're lucky you got out of that place. It's a demon of a lot better here."

Hasso *was* lucky he'd got out of his own world, but not for the reasons Rautat imagined. "You may be right," he said, and let it go at that.

He swung up onto his horse easily enough. He'd ridden on the Eastern Front, too. You couldn't always find a halftrack or a VW going where you needed to. If you didn't want to walk, you went on horseback.

And he was heading back towards a capital that hadn't fallen, unlike the one from which the Omphalos stone had hurled him. *A capital more like Moscow than Berlin*, he thought uncomfortably. In some ways, the Lenelli did remind him of the Germans he would never see again. In others, they made him think of the Teutonic Knights, who'd gone east against the Slavs in days gone by—and also eventually ended up losing to them. In still others, they might have been Spaniards or Anglo-Saxons bumping up against Indians.

They weren't *just* like any of those groups. However you looked at it, though, Hasso wasn't on the side he would have chosen for himself. Well, sometimes you got your sides chosen for you, that was all. The Bucovinans were people, too. Drepteaza was a very sweet person. Hasso smiled in the saddle.

The Ivans he'd fought were also people. He supposed their pagan ancestors who'd faced the Teutonic Knights were people as well. The Red Indians? No doubt about it.

He let out a startled grunt. Maybe even the Jews were people. He hadn't thought so for years—it wasn't safe or easy to think so, not in the *Reich*. But he'd known a few back in Weimar days—not well or anything, but he had. They hadn't seemed… so bad.

If they hated Germans now, hadn't Germany given them reason to? He didn't know what all had happened during the war. You didn't want to know stuff like that, not officially. But what if it was all a big fuckup? Wouldn't that be a kick in the ass?

XXV

Except for the stinks, Hasso was glad to get back to Falticeni. And Lord Zgomot seemed as glad to have him back as he was ever glad about anything—which is to say, not very. The Lord of Bucovin said, "So the gunpowder shells work the way you want them to, do they?"

"Close enough, Lord," Hasso answered.

Zgomot plucked a white hair from his beard. He twirled it between his fingers and let it fall. "*Close enough* is as much as you can expect in life most of the time, isn't it?"

"I don't argue with that, Lord," the *Wehrmacht* officer said.

"You'd better not," Zgomot told him. "You're old enough to know. So tell me, Hasso Pemsel—are you happy now that Drepteaza's finally sleeping with you?"

"Close enough, Lord," Hasso repeated, deadpan.

The Lord of Zgomot grunted. "Well, I'll forgive that from you—you had the Lenello goddess on earth in your bed for a while. That must have been something. Wearing, I'd guess, but something all the same. But tell me this: is Drepteaza happy, now that she's finally sleeping with you?"

She'd better be, or I'll make you sorry, his tone warned. Drepteaza mattered to him. Carefully, Hasso answered, "I think she is also close enough. If you don't believe me, you can ask her."

"Oh, I did," Zgomot said. "I summoned her before I called you. I think you are right, pretty much. I did want to find out how big a braggart you are, now that you finally got something you wanted for a long time."

"And?" Hasso said.

"And no doubt about it—you are no Lenello. If you were, I would have heard about every thrust, every gasp, every wiggle." Zgomot raised an eyebrow. "You lived among the blonds. You know they are vain that way."

From what Hasso had seen, the Bucovinans were blunter about screwing than the Lenelli. Lord Zgomot had a point, though: the Lenelli did invest more vanity in it. Since Hasso didn't much want to talk about it, he changed the subject, "Are the men back with the dragon bones?"

"No," the Lord of Bucovin replied, which answered what Hasso'd asked but

289

left him wanting more.

More involved another question: "Is Bottero moving yet?"

"Also no, for which I thank Lavtrig and the other gods," Zgomot said.

"Yes," Hasso said, though he believed in none of the Bucovinan gods. He wouldn't have believed in the Lenello goddess, either, if he hadn't been compelled to believe there was *something* there. "The border isn't closed, then."

"No, it is not," Zgomot agreed. Hasso nodded to himself. Since he'd gone over to the other side, the Lenelli were liable to have decided all his security worries and precautions were nothing but a load of crap. He hoped they did. That would make defending against them a hell of a lot easier. With a sigh, Zgomot went on, "But when Bottero does move, we are going to have to get through another invasion. Another year's crops ruined in the west. Another year of burning and murder and rape."

"That is what war is," Hasso said. "Only one thing worse than to go through it."

"Oh?" The Lord of Bucovin raised an eyebrow. "I would not have thought anything was worse. I do not think anything is worse."

"One thing is," Hasso insisted. "To go through a war and lose—that is worse. That is what happens—happened—to my land, in my world. That is why I am here." To try so much, to suffer so much, to go through so much death and devastation, to do that twice in less than half a lifetime and have nothing at all to show for it… was the lot of Germany. How might things have turned out worse? He couldn't begin to imagine.

"We managed not to lose last year," Zgomot said. "Then, Bottero started late in the campaigning season. He will not make the same mistake twice—say what you will about the Lenelli, but they do not make the same mistake twice in a row. That is my people's failing, I fear. Our imaginations spin more slowly than theirs."

"Not with you ruling, Lord." Hasso wasn't throwing out flattery to butter Zgomot up. The Lord of Bucovin was doing as well as he could against long odds.

"I think Bottero made a bigger mistake last year, too," he said now. Hasso made a questioning noise. Zgomot eyed him. "He let me get my hands on you. He will regret that to his dying day—and may it come soon."

"You give me too much credit," Hasso said.

"I'd better not," Lord Zgomot replied.

***

After Hasso and Velona became lovers, they moved in together and never separated till he got left for dead on the battlefield and she had to withdraw. Drepteaza didn't take up residence with him in Zgomot's castle, no matter how much he wished she would have. She moved more slowly than Velona in almost every way.

But she didn't stay away from his chamber, either. Sometimes he could talk her into coming by on a particular night. Sometimes she would knock on her own. Most of the time, she would make love with him. Once in a while, she only wanted to talk. He quickly decided getting annoyed about that was a bad idea.

One evening, when she was leaving after talking with him for a couple of hours, he gave her a crooked smile and asked, "Do I pass the test?"

Even in the lamplight, even with her olive skin, he could see her turn red. It took him by surprise; he hadn't meant to embarrass her. But she answered as frankly as usual: "As a matter of fact, you do. A woman wants to think a man wants her for something more than just this." She touched herself between the legs for a moment. "And I think you do. And I think that is good."

"I can talk with you better than with anyone else—except maybe Rautat." Hasso barked laughter. "And that is not the same."

"No, it isn't," Drepteaza agreed. "Not that Rautat is stupid—I've seen he's not. But there are times when he would rather not think."

"Yes!" Hasso nodded vigorously. Rautat made a good underofficer: he liked routine. He would have made a wonderful friend for another underofficer whose mind worked the same way. Hell, he was friends with other sergeants like that. Hasso's mind ranged further. In this world, it damn well had to. "You can go places with me where he doesn't want to—and not just in bed."

"You may end up changing us more than the Lenelli have," Drepteaza said. "For better? For worse? How can we know ahead of time? But you change us."

He thought again about the printing press. One of these days. When he had time. If he ever did. If the Bucovinans ever started printing books, that would change them even more than gunpowder did. But that lay in the future, a future that might never be born. "If I don't, the Lenelli do," he said.

"We know it," Drepteaza answered. "If you change us, maybe we stay ourselves, too. If the Lenelli change us, we lose ourselves forever. There used to be lots of little kingdoms in the western part of the land. They're gone now. Even the Grenye who still live in them don't know much about how they used to be. That could happen to us, too."

Hasso had seen those Grenye peasants. They had nothing but work and drink. Some of them had nothing but drink. As far as the Lenelli were concerned, that was fine.

The Germans would have run the Ukraine and Russia the same way if they'd won. Hasso hadn't thought much about that while he was fighting the Ivans. Now he did. His country had aimed to destroy another one—not just to beat it, but to destroy it. No wonder the Russians fought back so ferociously.

And what did Germany end up doing? Destroying itself instead. So much for all the glorious triumphs of the *Reich*.

"What were you thinking?" Drepteaza asked. "For a moment there, you looked over the mountains."

To the Bucovinans, that meant *a long way off*. Most of the time, it made an effective figure of speech. Not here. Not now. "I was thinking about my old land," Hasso answered. "Farther away than over the mountains."

"What about it?"

"I begin to understand why we lost our war. We wanted to treat our enemies the way the Lenelli treat Grenye," Hasso said. "But the Lenelli know more tricks than the Grenye. We didn't know more tricks—not enough more."

"Will you be angry if I say it does not sound as though your land was on a good path?" Drepteaza asked.

Hasso shook his head. "No. It does not sound that way to me, either, not now. But in the middle of a war, who worries about such things? You have enemies. You fight them. You try to beat them. You try to keep them from beating you. You don't think past that. To think past that is your, uh, king's job."

"If your king orders you to do something you know is wicked, should you do it?"

He frowned. "If you know it is wicked, no. But mostly, for a soldier, much simpler. You fight the other side's army. You try to beat it. What happens in the land you take—that's not your worry."

No. That wasn't the *Wehrmacht*'s worry. That was up to the SS, to the *Gestapo*, to people like that. They didn't think Hitler *could* order them to do anything wicked. If he ordered it, it had to be all right.

"Your conscience troubles you." Drepteaza didn't make it a question.

He could have denied it—by lying to her, and to himself. "Some," he said. "I did a lot of fighting, the last four years against our worst enemies. Maybe we were not always good. I know we weren't. Not them, either."

"Few people would choose war," Drepteaza said, and then qualified that by adding, "Few Bucovinans would, anyhow. I am not so sure about the Lenelli."

Hasso wasn't so sure about the Lenelli, either. They thought they had a goddess-given mission to civilize—that is, to conquer—the Grenye. The Germans had thought the same thing about their Slavic neighbors. They'd tried conquering them again and again … and now the Russian Slavs had turned things upside down. The Germans had usually had an edge, but not one big enough to make up for the numbers against them.

The British made it work in India and North America, the Spaniards farther south. So it could, if the gap between attackers and attacked was wide enough. Would it have been here? Hasso didn't know. All he knew was that he was doing his damnedest to throw a spanner into the works.

"Maybe," he said slowly, "maybe I owe somebody something."

***

When a Bucovinan messenger ran up to Lord Zgomot's palace, Hasso took no special notice. That happened all the time. He did notice when a messenger rode up to the palace. The natives didn't have that many horses. They saved the ones they did have for important business. And since he was waiting to hear about some important business …

A messenger—on foot—summoned him to Zgomot's throne room. "What is it about?" Hasso asked, his hopes rising.

"I don't know. The Lord of Bucovin didn't tell me," the palace flunky answered.

"If you go, though, he will tell you."

So there, Hasso thought. He made himself nod and smile and not give the messenger the satisfaction of knowing he'd irked him. "I go, then," he said, and he did.

When he got to the throne room, he found Lord Zgomot in animated conversation with the man who'd come in on horseback. Zgomot in animated conversation with anybody was a prodigy; the native ruler wasn't long on personality. But the Lord of Bucovin looked up and actually smiled as Hasso approached.

"Good day, Hasso Pemsel," he said. "I owe that drunken Lenello a large reward. I am slow to spend my gold and silver without need, but I gladly do it here."

"We have dragon bones?" Hasso asked.

"We have dragon bones," Zgomot agreed. He gestured toward the messenger. "I learn that they are in our lands, and they passed by Bottero's men without suspicion. The Lenelli thought we might grind them up to manure our soil. We did not discourage them from thinking this."

He sounded pleased with himself—and well he might. He sounded *very* pleased with himself, in fact. "A nice touch, Lord," Hasso said. "Your idea?"

"As a matter of fact, yes," Zgomot answered. "Things you said about keeping the Lenelli from knowing what we are up to came to mind. A story like that will also let the blonds think we are stupid barbarians who could not get bones closer to home. They think we are stupid barbarians anyway, of course."

"Yes, they do." Hasso had, too, when he was in Drammen. Now he was glad to get the chance to speak of the folk he resembled as *they.* Compared to the Lenelli, the Bucovinans *were* on the barbarous side. But, as he'd seen, that didn't make them stupid. The Lenelli just knew some tricks of the trade that they didn't. Well, no, not *just*: the Lenelli could also work magic.

Lord Zgomot pursed his lips. "Wheels inside of wheels, eh?"

"Always," Hasso said. "When do bones get to Falticeni?"

"I do not know." The Lord of Bucovin turned to the messenger. "Yurgam?"

"Ten days or so," Yurgam answered. "Once they made it over the border, they got horses instead of donkeys, but they are still pulling a heavy wagon."

Hasso shrugged. "It has to do." He would have wanted the bones here sooner, but he couldn't turn a horse-drawn wagon into an Opel truck or, better yet, a captured American Studebaker. That wouldn't have been magic; it would have been a bigger miracle than the one that brought him here. He nodded to Zgomot. "We need saws to cut bone. We need drills to put holes in pieces. We need cord or thongs to hold them in place."

"What *are* the bones for, if not manuring?" Yurgam asked.

Before Hasso could speak, Zgomot did: "I do not want to tell you, not yet. The fewer people who know, the better. The more things we learn, it seems, the more secrets we need to keep."

Hasso beamed. Sure as hell, Zgomot was starting to see what security was all about. He might be a mindblind Grenye, but he was one damn sly mindblind Grenye. There'd almost been some security hiccups about gunpowder and dragon bones. If the Lord of Bucovin had anything to do with it, there would be no more. He learned from his mistakes.

That's more than Hitler ever did, Hasso thought.

And, if the dragon-bone amulets worked, how much would being mindblind matter in a few years? Oh, some. Magic would still be able to do things to the world, if not directly to people. Wizards would still be able to ride unicorns. Hasso grinned. He could ride one himself, as he'd proved. The Grenye still wouldn't be able to.

Yeah, magic would matter some. But it wouldn't mark enormous distinctions between one folk and another, the way it did now.

Equality. This is equality. Hasso hadn't had much use for it when he saw it in action—and in inaction—during the Weimar Republic. But he'd also seen that the *Führerprinzip* had some flaws in practice. The *Führer* led, the people followed—right over a goddamn cliff. Maybe making everybody as good as everybody else worked better.

He could hope so. In fact, he had to hope so. If the Lenelli had magic and the Grenye didn't, and if that magic stayed important, he feared the big blonds would win in the end no matter what he did.

***

Someone called his name through the echoing corridors of dreams: "Hasso! Hasso Pemsel!"

He tried to shape the ward spell again, this time in his sleep. He had some luck with that, anyhow: enough to let him wake up without waking up screaming. Once awake, he went to the door of his room and told one of the guards, "Ask Drepteaza to come here, please."

The winter before, a Bucovinan guardsman would have laughed in his face at the idea of bothering her in the middle of the night. This fellow nodded and said, "All right. If she chooses not to come, though, don't blame me."

"Fair enough," Hasso said. The guard set off down the corridor.

Drepteaza was yawning and rubbing her eyes when she came back with the soldier. "What is it?" she asked blurrily, around another yawn. "Something important, I expect." *It had better be.* She didn't say that—or need to.

"Maybe. I hope you are not angry at me." He led her into the room and shut the door behind them. "The Lenello wizard and the goddess are hunting me in dreams again."

"And so? What has that got to do with me?" No, Drepteaza wasn't awake yet, or thinking very fast. Then she remembered. The dim lamplight shadowing her face only made her smile look more crooked. "Oh. A woman will hold that away from you, for a night at least. A new way to tell me you care, eh?"

"Sorry," Hasso said. "Should I get someone like Leneshul? I don't much want her, but if you want me to use her for medicine and not bother you, I can do that."

Drepteaza started to laugh. "The really funny part is, I believe you when you say you don't much want her," she said. "What kind of fool am I, though, if I give you the chance to change your mind? I may not be at my best, but I'll try."

Hasso feared he wasn't at his best, either. Maybe they matched each other, because it turned out all right, or better than all right. "You are the best medicine," he said afterwards, stroking her cheek. "They should make you into syrup and put you in bottles."

She laughed again, on a startled note. "That's the most ridiculous sweet thing—or maybe the sweetest ridiculous thing—anyone ever told me."

"It's true," Hasso said.

"Ha!" Drepteaza replied, which wasn't a laugh at all. She yawned once more. "Try not to wiggle too much. I don't feel like going back to my room."

"You wiggle more than I do," Hasso said. From where the two of them ended up when they slept together, he thought that was true. He added, "Besides, tonight I don't wiggle at all," and mimed limp exhaustion.

"A likely story," Drepteaza said, but she closed her eyes and soon fell asleep. So did Hasso, and Aderno's wizardry didn't trouble him for the rest of the night.

The wagon full of dragon bones came into Falticeni the next morning. The driver had to fight his way through the narrow, winding, crowded streets to the palace. None of the locals knew what an important cargo he had. Thanks to the way the bone-hunters were chosen, the driver didn't fully understand that himself.

One look at some of the teeth and claws in the wagon told Hasso the bones were real. "Good," he said. "Now we go to work. We cut them up small, we make them into amulets."

"What are the amulets good for?" one of the Bucovinans asked.

Instead of answering straight out, Hasso came back with a question of his own: "Is King Bottero marching yet? Does anybody know?"

The wagon driver nodded. "He's marching, all right. He wasn't that far behind us when we left his realm. One of the border guards who passed us through said it was nice of us to manure our fields—the big blond pricks would get good crops out of them." The little swarthy man aimed an obscene gesture back toward the west. Then he noticed Hasso watching him. "Uh, no offense."

"It's all right. They are a bunch of big blond pricks," Hasso said.

"Then what does that make you?" Cheeky as a park sparrow, the Bucovinan grinned at him.

"Oh, I'm a big blond prick, too," Hasso answered easily. "But I'm a big blond prick with two differences."

"Yeah? What are they?" the driver asked, a split second in front of one of his pals.

"For one thing, I'm a foreign big blond prick, not a Lenello big blond prick. And I'm a big blond prick who's on your side."

***

When Lord Zgomot heard the invasion had begun, he started assembling his own army. Bucovin was a big, sprawling kingdom or lordship or whatever the hell the right name was. The natives sensibly laid up supplies here and there on the main routes around the realm so soldiers wouldn't starve as they came in to Falticeni. But, without the telegraph, without trains, without trucks, nothing happened as fast as Hasso wished it would.

He got a surprise of his own not long after the mobilization order went out. Into the tent city that was sprouting in front of Falticeni came perhaps a thousand men who marched with long pikes held straight up and down. They marched well, too—the pikes stayed vertical, and didn't dip and foul one another.

After seeing them come in, Hasso hurried back to Lord Zgomot. "They look good," he said. "Can they fight?"

"They have all fought before," the Lord of Bucovin answered. "They have never fought like this, but they have been drilling hard. They like being called Hedgehogs, by the way—that is what they named the regiment."

"Good for them," Hasso said. "If they don't keep Lenello knights off the cata-pults, no one does." That last was always possible, even if he would have preferred not to dwell on it. He went on, "How long are they working?"

"I pulled them together before you went off to my estate to try the catapults and the gunpowder shells," Zgomot answered. "When you described them, I thought, *This is something we really can do*. It does not take anything we did not already have—it is only a new way to use tools we already knew about."

"You did it without me, too." Hasso didn't know whether to be proud or wor-ried. If the natives decided they could get along without him, would they knock him over the head and do just that?

"You were busy with other things. I thought we could manage this ourselves, and I turned out to be right," Zgomot said. "I hope they stay steady when the fighting starts, that is all."

"So do I," Hasso said. "I am going to be with the catapults. The Hedgehogs keep—will keep—the big blond pricks off my neck."

"That would be good," Lord Zgomot said, his voice dry. "You should watch them drill, to make sure we did not forget anything."

"I do that," Hasso promised.

He kept the promise, too—as he said, it was his own personal, private neck on the line. The picked regiment of Bucovinan foot soldiers knew he'd had the idea for their formation. That didn't seem to bother them; they were used to having new ideas come from foreigners. The Japanese would have been like that in the closing years of the nineteenth century. Now they could stand up to anybody in the world.

How long would it be before the Bucovinans could stand up to anybody in this world? *Win this fight first, or you won't get the chance*, Hasso thought. He fingered the dragon's-fang amulet he wore under his tunic. Aderno and Velona hadn't paid any sorcerous calls on him since he donned it. Maybe that meant they couldn't. He sure hoped so. But maybe it just meant they hadn't tried the past few days.

Win this fight first. That was always the imperative. And when he watched the

Hedgehogs go through their evolutions, he began to think the Bucovinans could. They marched very well. They formed ten rows and lowered their pikes into a bristling wall of points. If he were a horse, he wouldn't have wanted to try to charge through them. You could hurt yourself that way.

He said as much to the officer in charge of them. The native—his name was Meshterul—nodded. "We will hold. The gods-cursed Lenelli will never get through us," he vowed.

That was an important consideration. Whether the Bucovinans knew it or not, it wasn't the only consideration. "All right. They can't get through you," Hasso said. "Can they get around you?"

Meshterul frowned. "Around?" No, he didn't get it.

"Around, yes." Hasso nodded. "Who is on your flanks? If the Lenelli get to the catapults through those people, we are still screwed."

"Ah." Meshterul nodded. He sketched a salute. "You're right. I was just thinking about the Hedgehogs. But the real point is keeping the big blond pricks off the catapults, isn't it?"

"*Ja,*" Hasso said. Drepteaza and Rautat and maybe even Lord Zgomot might know what that meant, but Meshterul only gave him a blank look. Hasso kept to Bucovinan after that: "Yes. You're right—that is the point. The Hedgehogs may be very important later on. If the whole line of foot soldiers carries long pikes, how do the Lenelli break through at all?"

Meshterul's eyes sparkled. "That'll be the day, by Lavtrig!"

"Yes," Hasso said again, once more in Bucovinan. "But that day is not here yet." *You've got the Hedgehogs, and you've got a bunch of odds and sods armed with this and that, the kind of troops the Lenelli have been licking ever since they crossed the Western Ocean.*

"We'll need riders on our flanks, then," the Bucovinan officer said.

Hasso found himself nodding. Bucovinan knights mostly couldn't match their Lenello counterparts. They were better than ordinary Bucovinan infantry, though. After some thought of his own, the *Wehrmacht* officer said, "And we put mines in front of and around the catapults, too, if we fight in a position that gives us time to do it."

"I haven't seen those in action. Everybody tells me they're strong magic, though," Meshterul said.

"Not magic at all," Hasso said ... one more time. Meshterul stayed polite, but plainly didn't believe him. If something went *boom!* and blew Lenelli to hell and gone, it had to be magic, didn't it? People in this world sure as hell thought so. Even though Hasso knew better, he also knew he had to remember to take care of a couple of things: "Some of the mines will be fakes, bluffs—just turned earth with a fuse sticking out."

"What good does that do?" Meshterul asked.

"It saves gunpowder. It keeps the Lenelli guessing. And we can make fake mines faster than real ones. If the Lenelli don't know they're fakes, they might as well be real," Hasso answered.

The Bucovinan captain started to laugh. "I'm glad you're on our side, dip me in shit and fry me for a pork chop if I'm not."

Hasso wasn't nearly so sure he was glad to be on the Bucovinans' side. But he wasn't sure he *wasn't* glad, either, which marked a change in the way he looked at this world. And it wasn't just because he was sleeping with Drepteaza; he was sure of that. He'd lived here long enough now and seen enough to have gained a perspective different from the one he had when he first got here … and different from the one he brought from his own world. *Übermenschen? Untermenschen?* No, and no. People were … people, dammit.

So here he was, fighting for the little swarthy bastards, getting ready to go to war against the big blond pricks. He started to laugh, which made Meshterul give him a funny look. He didn't care. Just because people were people, that didn't mean everybody loved everybody else. Oh, no. Not even close.

***

Several days later than Hasso thought it should have, the Bucovinan army moved west from Falticeni. He used the time as well as he could. He made sure every pot of gunpowder and every metal shell the army was taking with it had a little bit of dragon bone inside or on it. Accidents could still happen: a spark, a fire. You treated gunpowder with the proper respect and made those as unlikely as you could. And now he'd magicproofed the powder, too. Or he hoped like anything he had.

He began to believe the dragon bones would do what he wanted them to do. Aderno and Velona hadn't come close to troubling him since he started wearing his dragon-fang amulet. He didn't believe they weren't trying to bother him any more. They had every reason to hurt him if they didn't kill him. If they couldn't… then the amulet was working the way he had in mind.

By now, almost everybody in Lord Zgomot's army wore an amulet. Artisans with saws and thongs had turned them out as fast as they could. Hasso knew Zgomot wore one himself: he'd given one to the Lord of Bucovin himself, and watched him put it on under his tunic. Zgomot wore a different tunic today on horseback, but the bulge was still there.

"I tried to shoot you last year," Hasso said, riding up alongside him.

"Yes, I know," Zgomot answered. "You killed one of my guards, and wounded two more."

"You don't hold it against me?" Hasso asked.

"If you *had* killed me, I would hold that against you," Zgomot said. Hasso laughed, as much in surprise as for any other reason—the Lord of Bucovin didn't make jokes, even wintry ones, very often. Zgomot went on, "As things stand, no. You were on the other side. You were doing what you could for Bottero. I might fault your taste, but not your loyalty. If you tried to shoot me now, I *would* hold that against you—and I would have good reason to, I think."

"So do I, Lord," Hasso said quickly. "I have no reason to do that."

"Well, I hope not," Lord Zgomot said. "We are giving you as much as we can. And I hope you stay happy with Drepteaza, and I hope she stays happy with you. I spent a lot of time worrying about that."

"I know, Lord," Hasso replied. Zgomot had damn near ordered her to go to bed with him for what the *Reich* would have called national-security reasons. The only problem was, Drepteaza didn't take orders like that worth a damn. Hasso thanked whatever gods happened to be in business locally that she'd eventually found reasons of her own. He said, "I am very happy. I hope Drepteaza is, too."

"She cannot be too unhappy, or she would drop you. She has a mind and a will of her own," Zgomot said, which paralleled Hasso's thoughts of a moment before only too well. The native continued, "I have tried to ask her a time or two, but she does not always tell me all of what she thinks. She does not always tell anyone all of what she thinks."

Hasso nodded; it wasn't as if he hadn't also noticed that. "She is her own person, yes. I like the person she is."

"So do I, though not, I daresay, the same way." Zgomot smiled one of his crooked, knowing smiles. "Since you came to this world, you have been lovers with two women with minds of their own. Well, not all of Velona's mind is her own, since part of it belongs to the Lenello goddess, but you know what I mean. Attracting two women of that sort is a compliment to you."

"I would like it better if one of them didn't keep trying to kill me, Lord," Hasso said.

"Indeed. I can see how that might be so. But I assure you that you would like it less if they both did. If both of those two went after a man at the same time, I do not think he would last long."

"Neither do I," Hasso said, which was the truth. When he was coming back from trying to redefect to the Lenelli, he'd had similar thoughts about Bottero and Zgomot. He couldn't make it here without one of them, not unless he aimed to go into the king business himself. And he didn't. He might like to carry whatever they gave you here instead of a *Generalfeldmarschall*'s baton, but he had not the slightest desire to wear a crown.

Yes, if Bottero and Zgomot both wanted him dead, dead he would be. If Velona and Drepteaza both wanted him dead, dead he would be, too. He suspected he would enjoy dying a lot less in that case.

Suppose Velona didn't want him dead. Suppose she wanted him back. What would he do then? If he had any brains, he would stay with Drepteaza even so. If he had any brains … Being with Velona had nothing to do with brains. You went with Velona for the same reason a test pilot climbed into a new fighter plane's cockpit—to see what kind of thrills it would give you next. And Velona's thrills were a hell of a lot more exciting than any you could get from a lousy airplane.

Hasso shook his head. It was dead. It would never come back to life. He might miss it—he *did* miss it. If he spent all his time mooning over what was lost, he would lose sight of what he had. What he had was pretty goddamn special, too.

"The goddess' rules are different from anyone else's," Zgomot said quietly.

"*Ja*," Hasso said, and then did a double take. "Are you sure you are not a wizard, Lord?" He didn't like being so transparent. It was dangerous. And if Zgomot could read him like that, couldn't Drepteaza do the same thing?

"I am only a man, Hasso Pemsel," the Lord of Bucovin answered. "But I am a man who knows something of women—as much as a man can, anyhow. And I am a man who has heard a lot about the Lenello goddess. I am jealous of you—maybe only half an hour's worth of jealous, but jealous even so."

Half an hour's worth of jealous ... That sounded about right. Would you throw away the chance for happiness for the rest of your life for half an hour? If the half-hour was with Velona, you just might. And for a while afterwards you might think you'd made a good bargain, too. If that wasn't power, what was it?

With a shiver, Hasso said, "Let's beat them, Lord." Zgomot nodded.

XXVI

Drepteaza rode with the army, too. Hasso wasn't sure she was there to help him translate or just because she couldn't bear to stay behind. He wouldn't have wanted to wait back in Falticeni, either. Better to know than to worry about every courier who came into town.

Whatever her reasons, he was glad she was there. She had the same fears as Zgomot. They boiled down to one basic question, which she asked Hasso in the tent they shared the night after they set out from the capital: "Can we really beat the big blond pricks?"

"Can we?" the German echoed. "Yes, of course we can."

She gave him an exasperated look. "Will we?"

"I don't know," he answered. The look got more exasperated. But he went on, "I am not a god, to know things ahead of time. Maybe they ambush us. Maybe their magic works in spite of amulets. Maybe ... I don't know what. All kinds of things can go wrong." His mouth twisted. "Believe me when I say that. I know what I talk about."

Could Germany have beaten Russia? Maybe, if the Yugoslavs hadn't fought, costing the *Wehrmacht* six weeks of good weather in the East. Maybe, if the second year's campaign that led to Stalingrad hadn't got fucked up from the start. Maybe Germany could have got a draw if she hadn't thrown away so many panzers in the Kursk bulge. Almost two years lay between Kursk and Berlin, but it was downhill all the way after that.

"What are our chances?" Drepteaza asked.

That was a better question. Hasso shrugged. "Better than they would be without gunpowder. Better than they would be without amulets. Better than they would be without the Hedgehogs."

"You're supposed to pat me on the back and tell me everything will be fine," Drepteaza said.

"Maybe it will. I hope so," Hasso said. "But what you hope and what you get are two different beasts. I make no promises. I can't without lying."

"What if we lose?" she persisted.

"Even if we lose, I think we scare the Lenelli out of their hair." That was what you did in Bucovinan instead of scaring somebody out of a year's growth. "I

301

think they think twice about messing with Bucovin after this fight."

"Either that or they all get together and jump on us while they still can." Drepteaza's mood swung much more than usual. "If they see dangerous Grenye, then they will make friends. And they will stay friends till we are beaten." The priestess sounded very sure of herself.

Hasso wanted to tell her she was wrong, but that wasn't so easy. The Lenelli were full of contempt for the Grenye. It sprang from their certainty that the natives couldn't *really* be dangerous. If the Grenye suddenly turned out to be opponents worth fighting, the Lenelli might go after them like hunters after wolves—or maybe more like hunters after mad dogs.

"About time they find out they make too many mistakes when it comes to Grenye," Hasso said. "My kingdom made mistakes about its neighbors. It will spend a long time paying for them."

"You see? You can make the verbs behave when you think about it," Drepteaza said. For a moment, he was annoyed she'd changed the subject. Then he was just surprised. And, after that, he decided he'd eased her mind, at least a little.

Now if only he could ease his own.

***

Bucovinans with pots of gunpowder, fuses, and spades—and others with fuses and spades but no pots of gunpowder—did their best to delay Bottero's march east. Hasso figured they would blow up a few Lenelli and make the rest thoughtful. None of them knew how to make gunpowder; he wanted to hold that secret as tight as he could as long as he could. It would leak eventually—such things always did. But eventually wasn't now, and now was what counted.

All the natives who harassed the Lenelli also wore dragon-bone amulets. If Aderno and his pals wanted to try to pick them out by magic—well, good luck. Hasso kept gaining confidence in his amulet. Even after he'd come some distance from Falticeni, Aderno and Velona weren't able to break through and give him a hard time. As far as he could tell, no Lenello magic had come down on Zgomot's army at all.

Just as much to the point, if the wizards wanted to set off the army's gunpowder at a distance, the dragon bone would make sure they had their work cut out for them.

Had Hasso been a proper wizard, and had Zgomot had other proper wizards working for him, they could have used sorcery to stay in touch—not radio, but good enough. Hasso would have known what was going on closer to the border while it was going on. As things were, he had to wait for messengers the way Caesar and Napoleon did.

The news the messengers brought wasn't good. Bottero was tearing up the countryside as he advanced, and enslaving or killing the Bucovinans who didn't flee before him. None of the news was surprising—the Lenelli had done much the same the year before. That didn't make hearing they were doing it again any more welcome.

Bottero seemed to be taking a more southerly track into Bucovin this time around. That surprised neither Hasso nor Zgomot. If the Lenelli came up the path of devastation they'd made the autumn before, they would have a harder time foraging off the countryside, and would need to bring more supplies with them. Better—from the invaders' point of view—to let the natives feed their army.

"You can make things harder for them, Lord, if you burn the land in front of them," Hasso said.

"I know." Zgomot didn't sound thrilled about the idea, and explained why: "But if I do that, I also make things harder for my own folk. Until I fear I cannot beat the Lenelli without doing that, I would rather not start the fires."

Hasso bowed. "You are the king." He used the Lenello word, not its closest Bucovinan equivalent.

To his surprise, Lord Zgomot smiled. "Once again, Hasso Pemsel, you show that, whatever you look like, you are no Lenello. None of the big blond pricks would ever admit that a stinking little mindblind Grenye" —he too shifted to Lenello for the description— "could ever be a king."

"That only proves they do not know you, Lord," Hasso said. "Bottero is not a bad king, but you are a better one. I do not think the Lenelli have a king as good as you."

"For which I thank you. The Lenelli are strong. They can go forward with good kings or bad. Bucovin has less … less margin for error, is the way I want to put it. A weak Lord of Bucovin, or a foolish one, or even an overbold one, could cost my folk dear."

He was right. He had a tiger by the ears, and he couldn't let go. He couldn't kick the tiger in the ribs, either, not unless he wanted to enrage it and get himself torn to pieces. He had to hang on, and hope he could grow his own fangs and claws (stripes were too much to hope for). Everything the army brought with it had to give him more of that hope than he'd had before.

"Lord, you *deserve* to win," Hasso blurted.

"Maybe. I like to think so. Bottero and Velona would tell you otherwise, though," Zgomot said with a shrug. "But even if I do, so what? We do not always get what we deserve. And do you know what? A lot of us, a lot of the time, are lucky that we do not. Was it any different in the world you come from?"

Hasso didn't need long to think about that. "No, Lord," he said. "No different at all." If Germany had got what she deserved … *Well, then what?* he asked himself. The *Vaterland's* hands weren't clean. In that goddamn war, whose hands were? Maybe the scariest thought of all was that Hitler's *Reich had* got what it deserved.

***

Evening twilight. Soldiers rubbing their sore feet. Other soldiers tending to horses and donkeys and oxen. Somebody playing a clay flute. Somebody else playing the bagpipes—or possibly flaying a cat. Flatbread baking on hot griddles. Millet stew bubbling in big pots. A cook swearing at a trooper who'd stolen some sausage.

And a sentry running back into the encampment calling, "A unicorn! A unicorn!"

The Bucovinan word literally meant *nosehorn*. Since that was also the literal meaning of the German word for *rhinoceros*, the wrong image formed in Hasso's mind for a moment.

Rautat poked him in the ribs. "You're a hotshot wizard, right? You ought to be riding the bastard."

"I've done it," Hasso said. "This one probably just runs away from me."

"You ought to try," the underofficer persisted.

"Yes, you should," Drepteaza agreed. "Think how much it would mean to our warriors to see that they had a wizard, a true unicorn-riding wizard, going into battle on their side."

Infantrymen fought better when they knew a few panzers were in the neighborhood. The tanks didn't have to do anything; they just had to be there. If the foot soldiers knew armor *could* back their play, they got bolder. Hasso had never thought of himself as a panzer, but he could see that the Bucovinans had a point.

"Well, I see what I can do," he said, and then, louder, to the sentry: "Where is this unicorn?"

"Who—? Oh, it's you," the native said. "Come with me. I'll take you to him. Do you think you can mount the beast?"

"I don't know," Hasso answered. "I want to find out."

"What will you do if you *can* ride it?" the sentry persisted.

"Piss off the Lenelli," Hasso said. "Isn't that reason enough?"

"More than reason enough, you ask me." The man grinned. He pointed towards a stand of oaks a few hundred meters from the encampment. "I went out there to make sure no Lenello spies were hiding in amongst the trees, and I saw the beast instead."

Maybe it wasn't *instead*. Maybe a unicorn had brought a Lenello wizard up here to see what the Bucovinan army was up to. Maybe he was sending word to Bottero's army like a forward artillery observer back in Hasso's world. Maybe… Maybe anything, dammit. Hasso made sure his sword was loose in the scabbard as he walked out to the trees. It wouldn't do him much good against a Lenello soldier, but it might against a wizard. Those boys would depend on magic till they found out it didn't work. Hasso sure hoped they would find out it didn't, anyway.

How were you supposed to call a unicorn? *Simple. Make a noise like a virgin.* He shook his head. He really was losing it. Not only was the joke weak, it wasn't even true, not in this world.

He stepped around the trunk of a tree that had been growing there a few hundred years and … there it was. It stared at him out of big black eyes a woman would have killed for.

"Hey," he said softly—a noise more of recognition than anything else.

In the dim, fading light, that pure white coat seemed to glow even more than it would have under bright sunshine. He saw right away that the unicorn was wild; it had never borne a Lenello wizard on its back. It was unshod. No one had gilded or silvered its horn or braided its mane and tail. It had no saddle or reins.

"Hey," he said again, a little louder. He had a bit of honeycomb—a treat for his horse. He held it out to the unicorn. "Here you go. What do you think of this?"

He watched its nostrils dilate as they took the scent of the honeycomb—and, no doubt, his scent, too. Did magic have an odor? How could a unicorn tell a wizard if it didn't? Maybe the way Aderno did: by magic.

Slowly, cautiously, the unicorn approached. It took the honeycomb with as much delicacy as a cat would have taken a bit of fish. Its mouth and breath were warm and moist against Hasso's palm. After it finished, it looked at him as if wondering whether there was more. He reached out to stroke its nose. It let him do that. It felt like fine velvet under his fingers.

"Sorry," he said. "That's all I've got with me. There's more back at the camp, though, if you want to give me a lift."

It couldn't possibly have understood him … could it? It was just a beautiful animal … wasn't it? What did he know about unicorns? Not bloody much. What he knew about this one was that it knelt and gave him an inviting look.

He wasn't a terrible horseman, but he'd never ridden bareback before. He'd never ridden an animal without reins and a bit, either. The Lenello wizards didn't do that—he'd seen as much. If he tried it and it turned out not to be what the unicorn had in mind, he was in a ton of trouble. But the last invitation more definite than this one he'd had was the one Velona gave him after he shot the Grenye who were chasing her.

Yeah, and look how that turned out, his mind gibed. But you couldn't win if you didn't bet. He got on the unicorn's back and patted the side of its neck. It rose to its feet as easily as if he didn't weigh a thing.

"Wow," he said, and then, "Come on. This way." He pointed over toward the encampment, and damned if the unicorn didn't head in that direction.

The horse the Bucovinans had given him was a plodder. This … This was like riding lightning and fire. The unicorn's hooves hardly seemed to touch the ground. He knew they must have, but they didn't seem to.

When he came out of the little wood, the sentry's jaw dropped. "Lavtrig's dick!" he exclaimed. "You did it!"

"How about that?" Hasso knew he was grinning like an idiot. Well, if he hadn't earned the right, who had?

As usual, the camp was a raucous place. He could tell just when the Bucovinans spotted him, because silence rippled out and through the place. People turned and looked his way, till all he saw were thousands of staring faces, all with wide eyes, most with mouths fallen open.

He waved to the natives. "To victory!" he called. If he could have figured out how to say *In hoc signo vinces!* in Bucovinan, he would have done that.

To victory! seemed to do the trick. In a heartbeat, everybody was yelling it.

The unicorn sidestepped nervously, but calmed down when he patted it again. He didn't plan on leading a wild cavalry charge—his place was back with the artillery—but he had one hell of a mount under him.

Of course, he'd thought the very same thing with Velona, too.

When Rautat came over to congratulate him on bringing back the unicorn, the beast snorted angrily, lowered its head, and aimed its horn at the underofficer's midriff. "Hey!" Hasso said.

"I wasn't going to do anything," Rautat said. He also backed off in a hurry, which made the unicorn relax.

"Cut that out, you," Hasso told the animal. It turned its head and looked back at him as if to say, *Who's the boss here, anyway?* And it knew the answer, too—it was. Could you train a unicorn? Could you convince it that *you* were the boss? If you could, Hasso hadn't started doing it yet—and he didn't know how, anyway.

He did know he wasn't about to put up with the unicorn's doing anything like that to Drepteaza. To his surprise, it didn't even start. It stood quietly and let her come close.

"Boy, I like that!" Rautat said. "What's she got that I don't?" He snickered, coming up with his own obvious answer to that. Drepteaza bent down, picked up a pebble, and threw it at him. The unicorn let out a snuffling noise and bobbed its head, as if to say he had it coming.

"Go get some more honeycomb," Hasso told the underofficer. "I promised, and maybe that makes it put up with you." Rautat nodded and scurried away.

"Do you—do you think I could touch it?" Drepteaza asked.

"I don't know," Hasso answered. "You can try—but be ready to get out of the way in a hurry if it doesn't want you to." Without bit, reins, and stirrups, he had next to no control over the unicorn. If it decided to rear, for instance, all he could do was grab its mane and hang on for—literally—dear life.

Eyes wide and shining, Drepteaza stepped up alongside the unicorn. She reached out and set her palm on the side of its neck. "Oh," she whispered. "It's like … I don't know what it's like. But it's wonderful. It's—more finely woven than a horse, isn't it?"

"Yes." That was a better way of putting it than Hasso had found for himself.

"Thank you," she told him, and moved away. Had Velona been standing there, she would have been wild to ride the animal. Drepteaza was sure she couldn't, and didn't try.

Hasso suddenly wasn't so sure himself. He slid down from the unicorn's back. "Wait!" he called to Drepteaza. She stopped. A few quick strides brought him over to her. She let out a startled squawk when he picked her up. It was easy—she couldn't have weighed more than forty-five kilos.

"What are you doing?" she said. But she needed only a moment to realize exactly what he was doing. "No! Stop! You can't! The unicorn won't let you! The unicorn won't let me—"

And, sure enough, the unicorn looked extremely dubious when Hasso started to put Drepteaza on its back. "Cut that out!" he said again. "She's not going to hurt you. Nobody's going to hurt you." He still didn't think the unicorn could understand him, but he wasn't a hundred percent sure it couldn't.

Rautat chose that exact moment to come back with the honeycomb, which didn't hurt. Hasso set Drepteaza down for a moment and kept his promise to the unicorn. Then he picked her up again.

She had the sense not to kick and flail. She alighted on the unicorn's back as smoothly as she could, and sat very still once she got there. The animal snorted and rolled its eyes, but it didn't try to buck her off.

Hasso patted its flank. "Walk," he told it, and damned if it didn't take a couple of steps.

"It can't do that," Drepteaza said. "I'm not magic!"

"You are to me, babe," Hasso said. She gave him a look that warned she would have a lot to say to him later, but this wasn't the time or place. Pretending he didn't notice, he went on, "Maybe it just needs someone who can do magic close by. Or maybe the Lenelli are full of shit. Who knows?"

"We could never ride them," Drepteaza said. "If we caught them and tried to tame them, they starved themselves to death. But I'm really on it, aren't I?"

"You really are. And everything is good, yes?"

"Yes!" she said, but then, "Maybe you'd better get me down. I don't think I want to push my luck."

"All right." Hasso took her in his arms again. He wanted to give her a quick kiss before he set her on the ground, but he didn't. He didn't want to look like a big blond taking advantage of her in front of her people. As her feet touched the ground, she patted him on the hand, as if to tell him he'd done that right.

"I'm a Grenye," she said. "I'm a Grenye, and I've ridden a unicorn. Who could have imagined that?"

"Will it carry other people?" someone asked.

"It won't carry me, the stupid creature," Rautat said. The glare the unicorn gave him told the world he was right, honeycomb or no honeycomb.

Wondering whether the unicorn disliked Grenye men in particular, Hasso asked a cook's wife if she wanted to try it. "Sure, if the creature will let me," she said.

She giggled when he lifted her off the ground. *He* didn't giggle; she was at least fifteen kilos heavier than Drepteaza. But the unicorn made it very plain it didn't want her on its back. "Sorry," Hasso said, setting her down.

"Don't worry about it, foreign sir," she replied with more grace than a lot of noblewomen probably would have shown under the same circumstances. "*I* know I'm no priestess. The unicorn must know the same thing."

Did it? If it did, how? The cook's wife smelled of garlic. But so did Drepteaza. All Bucovinans did; they ate the stuff with everything except melons and strawberries. So what made the difference? The unicorn wasn't talking.

Lord Zgomot came over to see why people were kicking up a fuss. "A unicorn?" he said. "Well, well. I have never been lucky enough to see one close up before." He gave Hasso something that was more than a nod but less than a bow. "An advantage to having a wizard with us that I had not thought about."

"It let me on its back, Lord!" Drepteaza exclaimed. "Me!"

"Really?" Zgomot *did* bow to her. "I am jealous."

"Do you want to try, Lord?" Hasso asked. Zgomot wasn't much heftier than the cook's wife. Hasso thought he could get him onto the unicorn's back. Whether the unicorn would put up with it …

"Me?" The Lord of Bucovin sounded surprised.

"If it doesn't want you up there, it lets you know, but it doesn't hurt you. It is a polite unicorn," Hasso said.

That made several Bucovinans smile, so it probably wasn't just the word he should have used. But what the hell? It got his meaning across. And the cook's wife affirmed that she'd tried, failed, and still had all her giblets. Lord Zgomot plucked at his beard. "Well, why not?" he said. "Let us see what will happen."

The unicorn let him come up alongside it. It let him touch it, which seemed to impress him as much as it had Drepteaza. "Can you lift me up there?" he asked Hasso.

"I think so, Lord," the German answered. "You don't eat a big lunch, I hope?"

Zgomot smiled a crooked smile. "No, I was moderate." Wonderingly, he stroked the unicorn again. You had to touch a unicorn like that. If you were a man, it was like touching your first girl, only more so. "Whenever you are ready," Zgomot said.

Hasso picked him up. The unicorn laid back its ears and snorted when the Lord of Bucovin's behind touched its back, but it didn't buck or run wild or do any of the other things that could have made Zgomot's bodyguards use Hasso for a pincushion. "You are on a unicorn," Hasso told him.

"I *am* on a unicorn." Lord Zgomot sounded amazed. Well, who could blame him?

How the Bucovinans cheered! Drepteaza looked as proud of her sovereign as could be. And Hasso said, "King Bottero never does this."

"No? He is missing something, then," Zgomot said. "Will it walk for me?" He urged the unicorn forward as if it were a horse. But it wouldn't go, not even the couple of steps it had for Drepteaza. Shrugging, Zgomot slid off. "I am a Grenye, and I have been on a unicorn," he declared, as Drepteaza had. By the way *he* said it, he might have been the first man to set foot on the moon.

His subjects cheered louder than ever. Hasso looked at the unicorn. It looked back at him. If it didn't wink, he was losing his mind. Or maybe he was losing his mind if he thought it did wink. No one else seemed to notice. Was he going to start collecting omens and portents?

Why not? Everybody else in this world did. And, as far as he could see, a winking unicorn couldn't be anything but a good one.

***

A Bucovinan named Shugmeshte was almost out of his mind with glee. He was one of the gunpowdermen who'd gone forward to slow down Bottero's advancing army. "I fooled 'em!" he told Hasso and Zgomot. "Bugger me blind if I didn't fool 'em!"

"What did you do?" Hasso asked.

Shugmeshte swigged from a mug of beer. "So I dig holes in the road and run fuses to them, right? This is before the big blond bastards get there, you understand. So then I plant some real jugs in the field alongside, but real careful-like, so you can't spot 'em easy."

Hasso grinned. "I think I like the way this story is going." The Lord of Bucovin nodded. Hasso said, "Well? Tell us more."

"So the blond pricks come by," Shugmeshte said. "So they see there's trouble in the road. So they get smart—or they think they do. So they ride into the field so whatever happens in the road doesn't hurt 'em. So I light the fuses, and *bam!* They go flying! I blew up a unicorn, I did."

"I'm not sure I want to hear that," Hasso said—he was still riding the wild one himself. But he clapped Shugmeshte on the back. "You do good—you *did* good. And this says something important."

"What?" Zgomot asked.

"It says the amulets really do keep Lenello wizards from spotting gunpowder. This is good news." Hasso wondered whether Shugmeshte had blown Aderno to hell and gone. That would be *very* good news. He could hope, anyhow.

"Ah." The Lord of Bucovin nodded. "I see. Yes, what you say makes good sense. You seem to have a way of doing that."

"Thank you, Lord," Hasso said. Coming from a resolutely sensible fellow like Zgomot, that praise meant something.

Zgomot turned back to Shugmeshte. "Are you ready to do this to the Lenelli again?"

"Lavtrig, yes!" the gunpowderman exclaimed. "We can hurt them. We can scare them. We've never been able to scare them before. I like it."

"Go, then," Zgomot said. Shugmeshte saluted: clenched fist over his heart, the same gesture the Lenelli used. How long ago had the Bucovinans adopted it? Did anyone here even remember? Hasso wouldn't have bet on it. Zgomot nodded to Hasso. "We have kept security as well as we could. None of the gunpowdermen knows how to make the stuff. Not many folk besides us and the men who get them—oh, and Scanno—know our amulets are made from dragon bone."

"This is how you should do things, Lord," Hasso said. "Sooner or later, secrets get out, but you always want it to be later, not sooner."

"You *do* make sense," Zgomot told him. "One of the first things a ruler learns is that secrets always get out."

Hasso thought of the American bazooka. It was a wonderful weapon—it let a foot soldier wreck a panzer without needing to creep suicidally close. As soon as the Germans saw it, they knew they wanted something like it. They made capturing one a top priority. Once they had one, the *Panzerschreck* got into production in a few months. And it was better than the bazooka that spawned it. With a larger-caliber rocket, it had a longer range and could pierce thicker armor.

"Later is better," Hasso said again.

Once the Lenelli got their hands on some gunpowder—and they would, be-cause his fuses were imperfectly reliable—how long would they need to figure out what went into it? Not too long, odds were: none of the ingredients was especially rare. How long would they need to start making their own? That could take a while. They would need to work out the right proportions. Then they would have to figure out how to mix them without blowing themselves a mile beyond the moon. So it wouldn't be a few months. But it might be only a few years.

Cannon! Can I build a cannon? Hasso got the same answer he always did—maybe, but not right now.

And how long would the Lenelli take to realize dragon bone was thwarting their spells? Getting their hands on an amulet wouldn't be hard, but how could you sorcerously analyze something that didn't let you work magic? *Damn good question*, he thought.

Even if they did know, what could they do about it? Even if you knew what water was, could you get something to burn in it?

He wished he hadn't thought of it that way, because you could if you were sly enough and smart enough. Magnesium would burn even underwater. If you tossed a lump of metallic sodium into water, it would start burning all by itself.

So … did the Lenelli have the sorcerous equivalent of sodium? Hasso shrugged. How was he supposed to know? He was a stranger here himself.

The Lenelli—the Lenelli of Bottero's kingdom, anyhow—had Velona. If she wasn't sodium, Hasso couldn't imagine what would be. Did they know how to use her, or perhaps the goddess, to best advantage? He shrugged again. One more thing he couldn't be sure of.

We'll find out, he thought, a little—or maybe more than a little—uneasily.

***

Zgomot knew where he wanted to make his fight. Hasso hadn't been there before, so he couldn't judge the position firsthand. When he listened to Zgomot and Rautat talk about it, it sounded good. Sometimes you had to assume the other guys on your side knew what the hell they were doing.

Sometimes you got royally screwed making assumptions like that, too. Hasso had to hope this wasn't one of those times.

Knowing where his own force would stand let Zgomot chivvy Bottero in the direction he wanted him to go. Bucovinan raiding parties shoved the Lenello line of march a little farther south than it might have gone otherwise. With a little luck, the invaders wouldn't even notice they were getting shoved.

Peasants fled before the Lenelli. They clogged the roads. In the Low Countries and France, fleeing civilians had worked to the *Wehrmacht's* advantage. They slowed up the enemy. Then, years later, German civilians fled before the Ivans and made life difficult for the army. What went around came around.

At Hasso's suggestion, Zgomot tried channeling the refugees down some roads, with luck leaving others clear so his soldiers could move on them. It didn't work as well as Hasso hoped. The Bucovinan traffic cops were trying something they'd never done before, and the peasants didn't want to listen to them.

You did what you could with what you had, that was all. With a couple of machine guns and enough ammo, he could have slaughtered the Lenelli without losing a Bucovinan. With a battery of 105s, a forward observer, and a couple of radio sets, he could have slaughtered them before they got within ten kilometers of him. With experienced German *Feldgendarmerie* personnel, he could have kept the peasants from mucking up the roads so badly.

As things were, the soldiers had to push through and past the farmers and their livestock. They lost time doing it. They lost less time than they would have with no Bucovinans directing traffic, but more than Hasso liked.

"We will use more gunpowder in front of the Lenelli to slow them down, too," Zgomot said when Hasso complained. "Things will even out."

"So they will." Hasso knew he sounded surprised. He should have thought of that himself. Good thing somebody did. No, no flies on Zgomot. Who was the barbarian, anyway?

One evening, Hasso saw the smoke of Lenello campfires—or maybe of farmhouses the Lenelli were burning—rising against the bright western sky. "Soon now," he said.

"Yes." Zgomot nodded. He was never a talky man. The closer the battle came, the less he said. His whole realm rode on this, and he felt the pressure. Well, why wouldn't he, the poor son of a bitch?

Hasso said, "We put the Hedgehogs in front of the catapults, yes?" The Lord of Bucovin nodded. Hasso continued, "On their flanks, we dig trenches. That way, we worry not so much about other troops protecting them."

"Bottero's men will see the trenches," Zgomot said.

"*Ja*. So what? They see they can't get past them. They go fight somewhere else. We want them to do that, yes?"

"Yes." Zgomot nodded. "We will dig—if we have time."

More smoke fouled the horizon the next day. The day after that, the Bucovinans came to Zgomot's chosen battle site. Hasso smiled when he saw it—the Lord of Bucovin could pick 'em, all right. Well, the German had already found that out the hard way. If Zgomot couldn't pick 'em, Hasso would still be fighting for the other side. Falticeni might have fallen. If it hadn't, it would this time around for sure. And he would still be bedding Velona. Details, details…

Details here looked good. A small river anchored the Bucovinan right—the Lenelli wouldn't turn that flank. On the left, a forest made it hard for the enemy to get through. Zgomot would have to post some soldiers in there, but not many. If Bottero wanted to get past the Bucovinans, he'd have to come right at them.

And he would. Hasso knew the Lenello king well enough to be sure of that. Down in his gut, Bottero wouldn't believe a bunch of Grenye savages could stop his knights. Yes, they'd done it the autumn before, but with a trick. He'd have his wizards looking for pitfalls this time. He wouldn't get fooled the same way twice, and he wouldn't think the natives could come up with two new things in a row.

By now he would know about gunpowder, of course. Bucovinans swarmed over the field in front of where they would post their line. At Hasso's direction, they dug dummy mines and planted real ones. A lot of the real ones were nearer the trees, where soldiers could light the fuses without risking their lives ... too much. Minefields weren't made to stop enemies, though. They were made to channel them. These would aim the Lenelli right at the catapults.

That would be great—if the Hedgehogs did their job. Could they really hold off horsemen? Could they, say, hold off a deep striking column? If they couldn't, Lord Zgomot's strong position was, in a word, fucked. *If they can't, I am, in a word, dead,* Hasso thought.

He spoke to them: "You have to stand fast. No matter what, you have to. If you do, we win. Bucovin wins. If you don't, you screw us all. Have you got that?"

"Yes!" they shouted. They seemed eager enough. How eager they'd be when Lenello knights on big horses couched lances and thundered down on them, Hasso would just have to see. Even in the fight the Bucovinans lost the autumn before, he'd thought they were plenty brave. Now they had better tools to be brave with. Maybe that would turn the trick. He had to hope so.

Scouts rode out of the west, pointing over their shoulder as they came. Most of them rode donkeys, not horses; the greater part of the horses Bucovin had were under Bucovin's knights. The shouts the natives let out gradually turned into words, and the words were, "They're coming!"

The Lenelli reached the field late that afternoon. Bottero's banner fluttered, big and bright and red in the distance. Velona would be somewhere over there. Hasso spotted several unicorns. The wizards had come in force. Well, he hadn't expected anything else.

Zgomot's men stood in line of battle, ready to fight. A Lenello rode forward, waving green branches as a sign of truce. He came straight toward the center of the line—right where the charge would likely go in. He was scouting the ground, but what could you do? When he got close, he shouted, "Tomorrow, you die!" in Lenello and rode away without waiting for an answer.

XXVII

It was a long, restless night. Hasso and Zgomot feared the Lenelli might try to steal the battle under cover of darkness. The Bucovinans slept in shifts and in their armor, with weapons close at hand. Zgomot sent scouts and sentries as far forward as he could, and well out to both flanks as well.

Hasso wouldn't have wanted to try a nighttime cavalry charge. He feared an attack on foot. If Bottero thought that was the best way to cut down the value of gunpowder … well, the Lenello king might well have been right.

And, a little past midnight—so the German judged by the position of the moon—the Lenelli did try something. Bucovinan scouts gave the alarm. Horns blared in the Bucovinan camp. Soldiers who had been sleeping sprang up, clutching swords and spears. Hasso grabbed a smoldering length of punk and ran to the catapults. Lobbing shells at night was one more thing he didn't want to do. He couldn't aim, and they were much too likely to go off before they flew because the catapult men would be clumsy in the dark. He shook his head—not *they*. It wouldn't happen more than once.

But, to his surprise, the Lenelli drew back instead of striking home. Big fires blazed in and around their camp—maybe they feared Bucovinan raiders. That was a comforting thought. By the light of those fires, Hasso made out tiny figures—in reality, blonds mostly taller than he was—running back and forth and gesticulating at one another.

He wished for Zeiss binoculars. With them, he might have learned something about what was going on over there. As things were, he could only guess. Whatever the Lenelli had planned, it didn't seem to have worked.

"I wonder if they tried to use magic to lull our scouts to sleep so they could get close without our knowing," Drepteaza said when he went back to their tent. He didn't think he would sleep any more, but he hoped he was wrong.

He chewed on that. Slowly, he nodded. "Makes more sense than anything I think of," he said. "And it means our amulets work." He reached up and touched his through his tunic. "The Lenelli can't be happy about that." He imagined Bottero screaming at his wizards and the wizards yelling back. The Bucovinans couldn't have prayed for a prettier picture.

"It only means they'll hit us harder come the dawn," Drepteaza predicted.

313

"They'll think they have to pay us back."

"Pay us back?" Hasso said, puzzled.

"Of course." She sounded surprised he couldn't see what she meant. "We've insulted them. We didn't fall over when they expected us to. And when Grenye insult Lenelli, the Lenelli pay back in blood."

Hasso grunted uneasily. That had the feel of truth to it. The *Wehrmacht* felt the same way about the Red Army when the Russians didn't roll over and play dead after 22 June 1941. *How* dare *they keep fighting when they're licked?* was the thought in German minds all through that summer. The *Reich* had two years of nothing but victory behind it by then. Its soldiers expected more, as if that were theirs by right.

Well, the Lenelli had generations of victories behind them by now. They too expected more. Drepteaza was right—they were liable to turn mean if they didn't get them. The Germans sure had.

Yes, the Germans had got mean … and then they'd got desperate. If you jumped on a bear's back, all you could do was hang on tight. Sometimes that didn't help, either. Hasso wouldn't have been fighting in the ruins of Berlin if it did.

The Lenelli wouldn't have gone that far down the road yet. But they'd still be angry, affronted. They'd want their revenge, all right. Didn't Bucovin also have some revenge coming, though?

"We see who pays, uh, whom," Hasso said. Drepteaza kissed him.

***

The sun came up behind the Bucovinans. That would help their archers and slingers and hurt the bowmen of the Lenelli, who would have a harder time aiming. Were the battle different, it would have mattered more. This fight wasn't going to be about archery. It would be about knights and gunpowder.

And it would be about the Hedgehogs. They took their places in front of the catapults, a hundred men wide, ten men deep. As they marched into position, they held their spears high, and they kept on holding them high. The Lenelli would see that they had unusual weapons, but Hasso didn't want them seeing what the Hedgehogs intended to do with those weapons, not till the very last moment.

He rode out in front of the pikemen on the unicorn, just to give Bottero's men one more thing to think about. "You can do it," he told the pikemen again. "If you do it, we win. If you run, Bucovin runs with you. You will fight!"

"Yes!" they shouted. Sure as hell, they *thought* they could hold the Lenelli out. Hasso was sure of that. And it mattered. If you thought you could win, you were halfway home. Not all the way; Hasso knew that too bitterly well. But halfway was a lot better than going into a fight with your heart in your throat, sure the enemy would do something horrible to you any minute now.

Slowly, the Lenelli formed their battle line. Would they use a strike column? If they did, where would it go in? He knew where he expected it to go: toward the Hedgehogs. Whether he wanted it going there was a different story. If they held, he would blow the Lenelli to kingdom come. If they didn't … Well, shit, if they didn't he'd be too dead to worry about anything else anyway.

As he looked toward the building enemy line of battle, he didn't see a striking column, though. Maybe Bottero's men were disguising it well. Or maybe Bottero thought Hasso knew the perfect counter and so didn't dare use a deep column. Or, again, maybe the Lenello king was just against everything Hasso had ever been for.

Whatever Bottero was thinking, Hasso sure hoped the Lenelli didn't throw a striking column at his army. He had no perfect counter, and getting his line broken scared the crap out of him.

But he saw knights all the way across the Lenello front. Were more of them in one place than in another? He wished again for the Zeiss field glasses. Whatever he wished for from the world in which he was born, he didn't get it. He wondered why that didn't stop him from wishing.

Where was Velona? Somewhere in that line. Somewhere in the middle of it, odds were. If she couldn't kill him by exploding his head from the inside out, she'd be willing to try a more conventional way of getting rid of him. Willing, hell—she'd be eager. And she'd be deadly as a cobra, too.

Horns blared, there in the Lenello line. Lances swept down to point at the Bucovinans, their points sparkling in the sunshine. At the same time, Captain or Colonel or whatever the hell his rank was Meshterul shouted, "Lower!" Down swept the pikes, too. Those of the first five rows stuck out beyond the leading men, creating a fence of spearheads. The back rows of pikemen didn't drop their spears all the way to horizontal, but kept them up at increasing angles. The pikeshafts would deflect a few arrows. As the men moved forward, they would lower their spears more and more.

Hasso went from one catapult to another. Each one had a shell on the casting arm. He wouldn't do all the lighting this time, not with several catapults fighting at the same time. All he could do was fight one catapult and direct the rest. "Are we ready?" he asked. "Is everything the way it should be?"

"Ready!" the crews shouted. He hoped to God they were right. Catapults were complicated machinery for this world, and as liable to break down as panzers were back in the world he came from. Well, he'd done what he could do. Now most of it was up to the natives.

More horns blew. The Lenelli moved forward, slowly at first—they wouldn't boot their horses up to a gallop till they came within missile range of the Bucovinan line. The Bucovinan knights would have to go forward, too, or take the charge with no momentum of their own. That worried Hasso. If something went wrong, the moving wings and the stationary center could come unglued and let the Lenelli in. He didn't know what to do about it. He hadn't seen anything he *could* do about it—except worry.

There was Bottero's banner, heading straight for him. The king would ride right by his standard-bearer. His lance would be couched, and he would be ready to kill anything that got in his way. Bottero was as tough as any of the men he led, which was saying a good deal.

Before long, Hasso recognized his former sovereign. Zgomot made a better administrator. In a fight, Hasso would have bet on Bottero every goddamn time.

And there was Velona, brandishing a sword. She wore a mailshirt, but her head was bare. Her long, fair hair swept out behind her. But that wasn't what drew his eye to her. The goddess filled her; he could tell. She was beautiful and terrible and terrifying.

He glanced warily toward the sky. The day stayed bright and clear. Hasso allowed himself a sigh of relief. The worst thing the Lenello wizards could have done, as far as he could see, was to start a driving rainstorm. Dragon-bone amulets wouldn't stop that. Trying to set off mines and launch shells with wet fuses would have been a nightmare. But the wizards hadn't thought of it ... this time, anyhow.

Off to his left, on the forest flank, a mine exploded too soon, and then another one. A Bucovinan there must have come down with buck fever and lit his fuses too soon. Some of the Lenello knights' horses over there flinched inward, which threw their charge into a little confusion, but not enough, not enough.

And then a mine blew two horses off their feet fifty meters in front of the trees, and blasted another man out of the saddle. More mines went off as the foot archers moving up behind the knights came near. Some of them went down, too, and the rest, like any troops with half a gram of sense, hesitated about going forward. That was good.

But he didn't have much time to dwell on the archers. The knights were nearing him with frightening speed. They looked as if they could ride down anything on earth, the way a company of panzers would have looked to foot soldiers in his own world. If the Hedgehogs panicked and broke and ran...

They didn't. The men in the first row went to one knee, the better to receive the charge. Without Hasso's telling them what to do, the Bucovinans in charge of setting off the mines in front of the Hedgehogs lit their fuses at just about the right time. He didn't know whether to cheer or to puddle up—his students were going out into the world on their own, and they were doing well.

The world was also trying to break in on them. Velona shouted something. Hasso couldn't make out what it was, but he shouldn't even have been able to hear it from a range of several hundred meters, not through his own side's yells, those of the other Lenelli, and the rising thunder of the horses' hooves. He shouldn't have been able to, but he did. *The goddess*, he thought uneasily.

Maybe—probably—the wizards were thwarted. Whatever power Velona had was wilder and stronger than theirs. It scared the bejesus out of him, because he didn't know what its limits were or if it had any.

He didn't know, but he was about to find out. He touched a glowing length of punk to the fuse on the shell in the catapult's hurling arm. As soon as it caught, he jumped back, yelling, "Loose!"

Swoosh! Thump! The arm shot forward and thudded into place against the padded rest. Other swooshes and thumps said the rest of the catapults were shooting, too. Hasso breathed a prayer of thanksgiving to Whomever that no shell went off too soon. Blowing up a catapult crew would have been bad for morale. An air burst right above the Hedgehogs' heads would have been worse.

Boom! Boom! Those were mines, going off a little too soon. Horses reared and snorted in fear, but the Lenelli fought them down and kept on coming. They wouldn't panic the way they did the first time. Experience counted, here as anywhere else. You lived and you learned—if you lived. The Lenelli had nerve, too. Not even their worst enemies, among whom Hasso now counted himself, would have denied that for a moment.

Boom! Boom! More mines. This time, horses went down. Knights crashed to the ground or flew through the air. The charge was disordered, but it came on anyhow. German fifteen-year-olds advancing on Josef Stalin tanks with *Panzerfausts* couldn't have shown more guts.

Things happened very fast now. *Boom! Boom! Boom!* Those were the flying shells bursting on and above the Lenelli and spraying lead balls and sharp fragments of bronze and iron through them. More horses fell. More knights got blasted.

Hasso thought they would break then. His catapult crew, like all the rest, worked frantically to reload the weapon and tighten up the ropes of hair that powered it. They grunted and cursed and sweated as they yanked at windlasses. They didn't seem to have cranks. Hasso made a note to himself to do something about that before too long. He wondered if he'd remember.

Off on the wings, where the defense wasn't so tough, the Lenelli engaged the Bucovinans. If the blonds broke through on either side, they might still win no matter what happened to their center. Germany had built up motorized panzer and panzergrenadier divisions, but the rest of the *Wehrmacht*, the bulk of the *Wehrmacht*, still relied on horses and shoe leather. Hasso had modernized some of the Bucovinan army, but not all. How well would the rest perform?

For that matter, the Lenelli weren't beaten yet, even in the center. Hasso lit another fuse. "Loose!" *Swoosh! Thump!* The catapult flung it away. *Boom!* It blew up and hurt some blonds. In spite of the pounding to which they couldn't reply, they kept on coming.

He'd heard that a charging horse would stop short, and wouldn't impale itself on a picket fence of spearpoints. No doubt that was true—if the horse was left to its own inclinations. But determined riders could *make* their horses go forward against those long spears. They could, and they did.

Wounded horses shrieked like wounded women. Some of them fouled pikes as they fell. Others pushed forward into the gaps. So did dismounted Lenelli, trying to get within sword reach of the Bucovinans.

The spears held them out. Meshterul and the rest of the Hedgehogs' officers deserved the Knight's Cross with Oak Leaves and Swords. This was the first time they'd ever used their phalanx, but they performed like ten-year veterans. Every time a pike got fouled, another man stepped forward to get his point into the fight. Hasso just hoped they didn't run out of men. They were only ten deep. Next time, they'd be deeper.

Was that Bottero there, a third of a meter taller than the natives? That *was* Velona, slashing away as if possessed—and so, no doubt, she was. If even she, if even the goddess, couldn't break through... well, the Bucovinans had a chance, anyhow.

One catapult crew wrestled its unwieldy contraption around so it could shoot at the Lenelli off to the right. *Swoosh! Thump!...Boom!* One shell bursting where the blonds didn't expect it created far more fear than a whole salvo they were braced to receive.

"Good job!" Hasso yelled. "Good job!"

And then Meshterul yelled a command the natives might never have given on the battlefield before: "Forward!"

Hasso wondered if the Hedgehogs' commander had lost his mind. The pikemen had stopped the Lenello cavalry charge in its tracks. That was all they had to do. Hasso had been far from sure they could do even so much. Could they drive the blond horsemen back?

Damned if they couldn't. They thrust their long pikes at the unarmored horses, not at the knights on their backs. The wounded horses shrieked. Some reared. Some fell. Their riders had a devil of a time keeping them under control. The Bucovinans speared the Lenello knights who went down with their mounts— speared them and then trampled them underfoot as they surged ahead.

The Lenello line wavered. The knights had never met infantry like this. As Hasso knew too well from bitter experience, if you couldn't go forward, all too often you couldn't hold your ground, either. In what seemed like no time at all, there *was* no line in front of the Hedgehogs. There were only frightened knights riding away as fast as they could.

Swoosh! Thump!...Boom! More shells sped the Lenelli fleeing the center on their way. Then, at Hasso's shouted orders, all the catapult crews swung their weapons to one side or the other and started bombarding the Lenelli on the wings.

A bigger force of Hedgehogs could have rolled up the Lenelli to either side of them. By what struck Hasso as a miracle, Meshterul realized he didn't have that kind of force, and halted his men before they advanced too far and got cut off. Such intrepid, brainless heroism had cost the Saxons dear at Hastings.

Swoosh! Thump!...Boom! The catapults couldn't fling shells anywhere near so fast as a battery of 105s. They didn't have so many shells *to* fling, either. Hasso was painfully aware that they wouldn't have any more for weeks once they ran dry here. Everything rode on this battle.

Swoosh! Thump!...Boom! That was a good one. It burst just above the Lenelli on the left, and knocked down four of them. A 105 round couldn't have done much more. And it panicked the knights who were still fighting. They decided all at once that they'd had enough. Going up against Grenye savages was one thing. Facing death from out of the air? That was something else. They rode off, too.

Seeing them retreat, the knights on the right also pulled back. The Lenello archers who'd come up behind them now screened their withdrawal. Well, the archers tried. The catapults outranged them, though. Three or four shells bursting among them sent them on their way.

"You know what we just did?" Rautat said as the archers withdrew.

"We beat 'em." Hasso knew it damn well.

But Rautat was going to make his joke whether Hasso gave him a straight line or not. "We just circumcised the big blond pricks, that's what," he said, and went off in gales of laughter. All the natives who heard him broke up, too. And Hasso laughed along. Why the hell not? To a winner, everything was funny.

***

Along with the Bucovinans, Hasso tramped the field after the battle. They were looking for loot, and to finish off or capture surviving Lenelli. He was looking for faces he knew. He soon found one, too: there lay Mertois, castellan of Castle Svarag. A pike had punched through his thigh, and he must have bled to death.

"So many dead horses," Rautat said sadly. "What a waste." At least a hundred of them lay twisted right in front of the Hedgehogs' position. They'd done what their riders told them to do, and they'd paid for it. So had a lot of the men who spurred them forward. The Lenelli didn't know what they were up against till too late.

There lay King Bottero. Bucovinans had already stolen his fine sword, his helm with the gold circlet, his gilded mailshirt. Despite the byrnie, he'd taken a lot of wounds. He didn't have a son. The succession in Drammen was liable to get messy. That was good news for Bucovin, too.

And there lay Velona, her golden hair all sodden with blood. None of the Bucovinans had taken the sword from her hand. They knew who she was, and they knew what she was, and they didn't want anything to do with her.

They weren't so dumb.

Even Rautat hung back a couple of steps as Hasso knelt beside her. "So that's what she looks like up close," the underofficer said. "If you like great big blondes, I guess she's pretty."

Hasso hardly heard him. He eased the sword from his one-time beloved's grip, then reached out to touch her hand. When he did, he frowned. She should have been cooler than that if she were dead. His index and middle fingers found that spot on her wrist by the thumb side of the tendons. Her pulse was slow, but it was there. "Jesus!" he muttered: another deity missing in action here.

"What?" Rautat said.

"She's not dead," Hasso said. "She's just knocked out."

Rautat started to draw his belt knife to remedy that. Then he jammed it back into the sheath. "I don't dare," he said, "not against the goddess." He took off on the dead run.

Hasso would have stopped him if he had tried to kill Velona. He wondered why, when she'd come so close to killing him. He also wondered what the hell he was going to do with her—to her?—when she came to. He didn't fear the goddess the way Rautat did, which probably meant he didn't understand the situation as well as the native did.

Cautiously feeling, he found a knot on the side of her head. He nodded to himself. Going into battle without a helmet was great for heartening your friends and frightening your foes. When it came to actually fighting ... not so good. He probed a little harder. If she had a fractured skull, she might not wake up—which might prove a relief for everybody but her.

She grimaced and tried to twist away from him. She wasn't deeply out, then. That was a good sign, or maybe a bad one, depending on how you looked at things. Then her eyes opened. For a moment, she had no idea who he was, who she was herself, or what the hell was going on. Hasso sympathized. He'd been down that road himself the autumn before. A concussion was not your friend.

She blinked, and blinked again. Her mouth set. Reason was coming back. Those blue, blue eyes found his. "You!" she said, her voice a hoarse croak.

"Afraid so." Lenello came rustily from his lips. He wasn't used to hearing it without a rough Bucovinan accent any more, either. "Want some water?"

"Please."

He had a jug on his belt. He took it off and held it to her lips. She drank and drank. "Better?" he asked when she'd almost emptied it.

"A little, maybe." She needed two tries to sit up. When she looked around and saw Bucovinans roaming the field and Lenelli and their chargers down and dead in windrows, she looked first humanly astonished and then more than humanly outraged. "What did you do to us? What did we do to you to deserve ... this?"

"Well, trying to kill me makes a pretty good start." Hasso worked hard to remember the past tenses that had given him so much trouble; he needed them here. "I loved you, and you tried to cook my brains for me."

He watched her gaze sharpen. If she could have slain him right there, she would have done it. But she couldn't even start; it was like watching an archer try to shoot in a driving rainstorm. "My wits are all scrambled," she muttered.

"I believe it," Hasso said. "You are going to have headaches like you don't believe. Takes days, maybe weeks, to get over." He tapped the side of his own head. "I know."

"What did you do?" Velona repeated. "The flying thunder ... That forest of spears ..." She shuddered, then winced, plainly wishing she hadn't. "And none of our magic worked. We've had to deal with renegades, but this ...! How the goddess must hate you!"

"I take my chances," Hasso said, which shocked her. Well, too bad. It *was* too bad, in too many ways, but he couldn't do anything about any of them now. He continued, "I tell you something else, too. You need to remember it. All Lenelli need to remember it."

"Go on," she said. "I'm listening. Right now, I don't have much choice."

"Simple. Easy. Four words—Grenye are people, too." In Bucovinan, it would have been one word. "People," Hasso said again. "Strong enough to stand against Lenelli. Isn't that a big part of what makes people?"

Velona's chin came up. "Little black-haired mindblind savages." Cutting through a couple of hundred years' worth of Lenello arrogance wouldn't be easy or quick.

Hasso was about to remind her that King Zgomot's so-called savages had whipped the living snot out of her kingdom twice running. Before he could, someone behind him said, "I didn't know she would be so beautiful."

He whirled. There stood Drepteaza and, several paces behind her and looking scared, Rautat. Hasso felt almost as if she'd caught him being unfaithful with Velona. He glanced at the goddess on earth. She looked like hell: haggard, battered, bruised, and filthy, her hair all matted with blood. All the same, the essence remained, and Drepteaza saw down to it.

Velona was looking from one of them to the other, too. And she also knew what she saw. "Who is this … person?" she asked Hasso, and if the last word of the question held a certain mocking edge, what could he do about it? It was the word he'd used himself.

"I am Drepteaza, priestess of Lavtrig in Falticeni." She spoke for herself, in her own excellent Lenello. "And…" She stepped forward and took Hasso's hand in hers.

"Yes. And." He squeezed hers.

Velona's eyes flashed. "Disgusting," she said.

"As a matter of fact, no," Hasso told her. This time, Drepteaza squeezed him. But he had to speak to Velona again: "You warn me not to love you. How do you blame me if I love someone else?"

Velona stared at him. So did Drepteaza. Had he said anything to *her* about love? He didn't think so. His timing was less than ideal. He'd have to fix that later. Now… Now Velona spoke to him as if he were an idiot—and she doubtless thought he was. As if spelling out what he should have known already, she said, "I meant a Lenello, not a Grenye."

"Too bad," Hasso said. "Grenye *are* people, too." He underscored that by switching to Bucovinan to ask Drepteaza, "What do we do with her?"

"I don't know," the priestess answered in the same language. No, Velona didn't speak it—Hasso hadn't thought she would stoop to learning. Drepteaza went on, "We could do two things, I suppose. We could kill her or let her go."

"Not keep her prisoner, the way you do—uh, did—with me?" Hasso asked.

"If she were only Velona, I would say yes, we could do that," Drepteaza said. "With the goddess in her…" She shook her head. "I don't know how much power she can pull through that connection. I don't want to find out. It could be worse than keeping all your gunpowder prisoner in one place."

Hasso grunted and nodded. He'd always thought Velona was so much female dynamite. Here was his own thought come back to him transmuted. "How much bad luck goes with killing her?" he wondered aloud.

"I don't know the answer to that, either," Drepteaza said. "Even with an amulet that works, I'm not sure I want to find out. Do you?"

"She would kill me in a heartbeat." Hasso's eyes kept sliding to Velona. Beat-up as she was, she still looked damn good to him. Drepteaza had to know it, too. He would likely end up paying for that later. He sighed. "I haven't got the heart to do it, regardless of bad luck."

"I told you you were a fool. But then, if you love me, you already know that." Drepteaza turned to Rautat, who was hovering in the background. "Go fetch Lord Zgomot. This should be his choice."

"Yes, priestess." The underofficer seemed relieved to have an excuse to beat it.

"What are you barking and mooing about?" Velona asked Hasso: so much for her opinion of Bucovinan.

"Whether to kill you or not," he answered.

Her nostrils flared. It wasn't fear. It was more the reaction a cat would have if it heard the mice were planning to bell it. "The curse of the goddess would fall on the guilty," she warned.

"We know," Drepteaza said.

"That didn't worry the three guys chasing you when I first came to this world." Hasso used two Lenello past tenses in one sentence. He impressed himself, if not Velona.

She looked at him as if a donkey had just lifted its tail and left him lying in the roadway. "When you did, I thought you would be a blessing for my folk, not a curse."

"He is a blessing for this world," Drepteaza said quietly.

"Not if he helps Grenye." Velona had the courage—and the blindness—of her convictions.

"We are not your beasts of burden." Drepteaza's voice had an edge to it. Hasso could have told her she was wasting her breath. Odds were she already knew. A thousand-kilo bomb wouldn't change Velona's mind.

"Well, well," Lord Zgomot said—courteously, in Lenello. "I did not expect this."

Velona eyed him with a certain caution if not respect—he'd caused the Lenelli a lot of trouble over the years. "Neither did I," she said bitterly.

"What do we do with her, Lord?" Hasso asked, also in Lenello. Drepteaza filled in the alternatives—in Bucovinan. If Velona didn't like it, too bad—that was her attitude. Hasso didn't see how he could blame her.

Zgomot seldom looked happy. Maybe he had right after his army's smashing victory. Contemplating what to do with Velona gave him a good excuse for his chronic dyspepsia. "She hurts us if we keep her, if we kill her, or if we let her go," he said, which summed things up pretty well. "Best to let her go … I think. At least she won't hurt us in the realm if we do that—not right away, anyhow."

"King Bottero will thank you," Velona said in unwontedly quiet tones.

"No, he won't," Zgomot replied. "He's dead."

"Dead? Bottero?" The full magnitude of the disaster Velona's kingdom had suffered seemed to sink in for the first time. *Goddess.* Her lips shaped the word without a sound. But she got no help from the goddess then. Was she too badly hurt to sustain such aid? Did all the amulets around her block it? Hasso had no idea.

"I will give you one of the horses we captured," the Lord of Bucovin told her. "You may ride away on it. If you are wise, you will not set foot in my lands again."

"I doubt I am wise, if that is wisdom," she said. "But I thank you for the gift all the same." By the way she spoke, it was no less than her due.

Hasso wondered if she could even stand, let along ride, but she was one tough cookie. When the horse came, the groom who brought it promptly took a powder. "Do you want help getting up into the saddle?" Hasso asked.

"Not from you," she said coldly. "You beat me. You beat my kingdom. You beat my folk. You have not stolen my pride." She swayed, but she mounted without help from Hasso or from anyone else. And he was convinced nothing but that enormous—maybe monstrous—pride kept her on the horse as she rode west at a slow walk.

"Whew!" Hasso's shoulders slumped, as they might have had the Bucovinans lost.

"You ... loved her? You loved ... that?" Drepteaza asked.

"Yeah, well, you already knew I was stupid."

"There are degrees to everything."

"You must be right. You usually are." Hasso bent down and kissed her, right there on the battlefield. You probably weren't supposed to do things like that. But when he came up for air, he saw Lord Zgomot smiling at them. Zgomot pulled his face straight in a hurry, but not quite fast enough.

Drepteaza saw the Lord of Bucovin smiling, too. She sent him a severe look, then turned up the voltage when she aimed it at Hasso. "You are impossible," she said.

"*Jawohl!*" He stiffened to attention and clicked his heels, which nobody from this world did. His arm shot out in a salute nobody from this world used. "At your service, fair lady!"

"Impossible," Drepteaza repeated, but without the iron that had been in her voice before. She turned to Zgomot. "What are we going to do with him, Lord?"

"Well, as for me, I aim to keep him as long as I possibly can," Zgomot answered. "What you do with him is up to you, of course, but he does not seem to want to go away in spite of, ah, everything."

In spite of Velona, he meant. Was he right? As things worked out, yes. *Would he be right if Velona wanted me back?* Hasso wondered. *Damned if I know.* Never a dull moment with her—no, not even close—but one day, sure as hell, she'd detonate and blow you to bits. Drepteaza was quieter but safer, definitely better for the long haul.

And he had something he needed to say straight to her, not just let her hear in passing: "I *do* love you, you know."

She nodded. "Yes, I do. Nice of you to tell me, though." As his ears heated, she went on, "And if you loved her, too, I have to wonder about your taste."

"Maybe not." Lord Zgomot threw the drowning Hasso a line. "Men don't judge women the same way women judge men."

"A pretty face, a nice shape, a tight snatch ... I know," Drepteaza said, and Hasso's ears got hotter yet. She went on, "Plenty for a good-time girl, but for *love*? You ought to look for more there."

This time, Hasso spoke for himself: "Well, I did. I found you, yes?"

"Who knows what you were looking for when you found me?" she said.

"A pretty face, a nice shape ... The other I don't know about, but I wouldn't be surprised," Zgomot said. Yes, Bucovinans could be very blunt. Drepteaza squeaked. Hasso might have if she didn't beat him to the punch.

Since she did, he added, "And more."

"Impossible," Drepteaza repeated. He nodded, not without pride of his own. She made a face at him and said, "If I can forgive you for being big and blond, I *must* love you."

"Good," Hasso said, and kissed her again. He found Zgomot smiling once more when he broke the clinch. If *Bless you, my children* wasn't written all over the Lord of Bucovin's canny face...

If it wasn't, then maybe Hasso was seeing sheer relief. All across the field, Zgomot's men were slitting the throats of Lenelli or leading them off into captivity. Some would make useful laborers. Others would know things the Bucovinans didn't, and that Hasso didn't, either. Bucovin was still behind its neighbors most ways. Now Zgomot's realm had more of a chance to catch up, and now the Bucovinans knew a few things the Lenelli didn't, too.

I did that. For better or worse, I did, Hasso thought. Now he'd seen from both sides what happened when technically superior enemies who thought themselves the lords of creation came at you. It was great fun when the panzers rolled forward or the assault column of knights struck home. Being on the receiving end was a different story—yeah, just a little.

No wonder the Russians fought back so hard. No wonder they hated the German invaders so much. Hasso hadn't got it then. Even the Red Army's counterattacks hadn't made him understand—he'd only understood that there were way too many Ivans. If the other guy aimed to take *your* land and wipe *you* out or enslave *you* forever ... Nothing like putting the shoe on the other foot.

It would have happened here. It would have, but it hadn't, and he had a lot to do with that. Maybe Velona was right after all when she said the goddess brought him here for a reason. It just wasn't the reason she thought. He kissed Drepteaza one more time. *Good-bye, Velona.*